A Fatal Winter

ALSO BY G. M. MALLIET

Wicked Autumn

Death at the Alma Mater

Death and the Lit Chick

Death of a Cozy Writer

A Fatal Winter

A MAX TUDOR NOVEL

G. M. MALLIET

MINOTAUR BOOKS

A THOMAS DUNNE BOOK

NEW YORK

A THOMAS DUNNE BOOK FOR MINOTAUR BOOKS.
An imprint of St. Martin's Publishing Group.

A FATAL WINTER. Copyright © 2012 by G. M. Malliet. All rights reserved. Printed in the United States of America. For information, address St. Martin's Press, 175 Fifth Avenue, New York, N.Y. 10010.

www.thomasdunnebooks.com
www.minotaurbooks.com

Endpapers map design by Rhys Davies

ISBN 978-0-312-64797-1 (hardcover)
ISBN 978-1-250-01825-0 (e-book)

First Edition: October 2012

10 9 8 7 6 5 4 3 2 1

In memory of Dave F, Dave L, and Ranger Mike
~December 2011

TABLE OF CONTENTS

ACKNOWLEDGMENTS

With all my love to my private cheering section. Some of you are no longer with us, but you walk beside me every day. This book is proof.

I am especially grateful for the generosity of these authors, who so warmly welcomed me to the writing community: Donna Andrews, Rhys Bowen, Deborah Crombie, Peter Lovesey, Margaret Maron, Louise Penny, Julia Spencer-Fleming, Marcia Talley, and Charles and Caroline Todd.

Special thanks to the superstars of publishing: Vicky Bijur, Kat Brzozowski, Karyn Marcus, Marcia Markland, Andy Martin, and Sarah Melnyk. You make it all possible.

And to Bob. You, too. Always.

CAST OF CHARACTERS AT CHEDROW CASTLE

OSCAR, LORD FOOTRUSTLE

LETICIA, LADY BAYNARD

RANDOLPH, VISCOUNT NATHERSBY

LESTER BAYNARD and his wife FELBERTA ("FESTER") BAYNARD NÉE OLIVER

LADY JOCASTA JONES NÉE FOOTRUSTLE (by Oscar's first wife Beatrice Briar)

SIMON JONES—Jocasta's husband

LAMORNA WHITEHALL—adopted by father Leo Whitehall (deceased) and mother Lady Lea Whitehall (deceased)

GWYNYTH, LADY FOOTRUSTLE NÉE LAVENER—mother of the Twyns

THE TWYNS—ALEC, VISCOUNT EDENSTARTEL and LADY AMANDA— Jocasta's stepsiblings

CILLA PETRIE—assistant to Randolph, Viscount Nathersby

MILO and **DORIS VLADIMIROV**—a married couple employed as the butler and the cook at Chedrow Castle

MR. WINTERMUTE—the family solicitor

Footrustle Family Tree

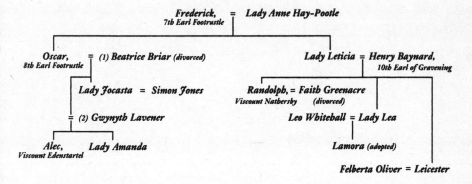

Frederick, = Lady Anne Hay-Pootle
7th Earl Footrustle

Oscar, = (1) Beatrice Briar (divorced)
8th Earl Footrustle

Lady Jocasta = Simon Jones

= (2) Gwynyth Lavener

Alec,   Lady Amanda
Viscount Edenstartel

Lady Leticia = Henry Baynard,
10th Earl of Gravening

Randolph, = Faith Greenacre
Viscount Nathersby   (divorced)

Leo Whitehall = Lady Lea

Lamora (adopted)

Felberta Oliver = Leicester

Marley was dead: to begin with. There is no doubt whatever about that.
~Charles Dickens, A Christmas Carol

AUTHOR'S NOTE

The rules for properly addressing members of the British peerage are so complex it is a wonder any of them can remember who they are without consulting *Debrett's*. Wherever possible I have used the least cumbersome forms of address for my characters (for example, "Randolph" rather than "Viscount Nathersby") and I have included a family tree to help the reader trace the relationships in this tale.

Obviously, the Footrustle family is fictional, as is their home, Chedrow Castle.

PART I

PROLOGUE

DECEMBER 26

Good King Wenceslas looked out
On the feast of Stephen

Oscar, Lord Footrustle, was in his castle, spying from the squint in his private chamber overlooking the Great Hall. The little window was concealed in the wall decorations, and in this manner had lords and masters through the centuries kept an eye, literally, on the goings-on at Chedrow Castle—retreating to the solar, as the room was called, to peer stealthily at the Great Hall antics through small openings in the thick walls. There was a larger squint overlooking the castle grounds and the fields beyond, and the Eighth Earl Footrustle now shuffled over to again take up a somewhat hunched position, for the squints were created in an age when men tended to be half a foot shorter.

He wrapped his woolen robe tighter against his aging body, a body still lean from years of shooting and fishing and on occasion riding to hounds—in general, a life spent killing things, for which he made no apology. That was the way of life, and of death. It was the shooting season now, and he missed the camaraderie. He used often to shoot with friends—eight guns, twelve beaters, three pickers-up. But he didn't like being out in the cold any longer, in more ways than one.

He had a shock of thick white hair, which he smoothed now

behind his ears, but his once-tan skin was now damaged and spotted from the outdoor life.

He'd been handsome once, and bore the remains of that handsomeness still. Any vanity he'd had on this score had been tempered by his prolonged encounter with his second, much younger wife. He accepted now that he was old.

But on a slow night—and they were all slow lately—he could pretend he was one of his ancestors, girded in leather and fur, and on the watch for invasion by land, or for betrayal from within. On the south-facing wall of the solar was a window that looked over the sea, a window enlarged and made modern in later, safer centuries—no attempt at invasion from that direction could ever go unnoticed, either.

But tonight's spying was hardly satisfactory, could indeed hardly be called spying, for the scene he looked out on was bleak and barren, a cold frost blanketing the ground under a bright moon.

It was the night after Christmas, and not a creature was stirring.

What the scene was missing was people. There was a certain amount of wildlife, but Oscar was a man more captivated by humanity, its foibles and failures, and having few people around to inspire and divert didn't suit him. After a long career in London, he missed the hurly-burly, and was coming to realize the idea of retirement was much more captivating, and more fun to brag about to those less fortunate, than the reality of being retired, with time hanging heavy each day. He was too isolated out here, that was the problem. Yesterday, he and his sister Leticia had celebrated the holiday together, just the two of them. Well, along with that half-witted Lamorna—he supposed that made three. There were the servants, of course, as he still thought of them, but that hardly counted for company. Indeed, it would be standing at the top of a slippery slope to start inviting the servants in for family occasions.

Should he move back to the city, he wondered (not for the first time)? Or should he—wouldn't it be easier . . . yes. He could invite his family to visit. Even to come and live with him awhile. It's not as if they had anything keeping them at home. It would even be rather nice to see the twins—briefly. What were they now, thirteen years old? Fourteen?

He made a wheezing sound, a noise like a door swinging open and shut on rusty hinges. It might have been a laugh.

Of course they'd *all* come running, he thought. The lot of them. They all think they're going to inherit from me, so all they have to do is sit and wait. Hah! Lazy, leeching band of so-and-so's. I'm only seventy-five. I'll live to bury them yet.

Just then, in the distance, was a movement—a flash of bright blue against the white and gray world. It was Jake Sloop, the farmer who lived nearby. What was he doing? Stopping and bending, gathering. Gathering wood, Oscar supposed. He sold firewood in Monkslip-super-Mare sometimes, not always legally, and he often stopped by the castle to see if he could sell some to Doris, the cook. The words to the old Christmas song came into Oscar's mind: ". . . a poor man came in sight, gath'ring winter fuel." The radio and telly this time of year were relentless in their playing of such songs; he felt he'd been forced to memorize the words to all of them.

Oscar hadn't ever known what it was to do manual work—his wealth had been inherited, and his vaster wealth came from thinking—from the blinding flashes of insight that had turned inherited wealth into a far-flung empire. The sight of old man Sloop made him think, long and hard, and in the end he decided it was time to get in touch with his loving family.

He wanted next year's festivities to be different.

And they would be.

ELEVEN MONTHS LATER: NOVEMBER 27

Deck the halls with boughs of holly . . .

"Poinsettias are not poisonous," said Suzanna. "It's an old wives' tale." For old wives like you, she added mutinously, if silently.

"They are so too poisonous. They're *highly* poisonous to cats," retorted Elka Garth, owner, sole proprietor, and chief cook and dishwasher of the Cavalier Tea Room and Garden. She had been reading up on the care of poinsettias on the Web, where she had come across the warning.

"Then keep the fucking cat out of the church," said Suzanna.

Elka reeled back in a somewhat stagey posture of horror. She was used to Suzanna. All the Nether Monkslip villagers were.

"Really, Suzanna!" she said, just to keep in form. "You might remember where you are."

Suzanna, caught up in the fizz of the moment, had actually forgotten she was standing in the narthex of St. Edwold's, where she and Elka had repaired to continue what had escalated from casual discussion to simmering warfare. They had gone there to talk away from the ears of the church handyman Maurice, who was again painting over the persistently recurring water stain on the church wall.

"Sorry," she said, automatically.

Elka, seizing the momentary advantage, pressed on: "Luther lives here. He's the official St. Edwold's mouser. But we can't afford to have another debacle like last year. Don't you remember the nativity scene, when one of the lambs burst out crying when one of the angels pulled its ears, and Mary dropped the baby Jesus, which fortunately had not been a *real* baby, of course. Actually, she didn't so much *drop* it as it came unwound from its swaddling clothes and sort of rolled naked down the chancel steps. The children didn't quite know what to do and several more of them burst into tears. They thought they'd be held accountable, you see, for all of its going tits-up so quickly. It doesn't do to have children younger than five up there. If they haven't taken their naps that day, well—what can you expect? It would be like sending me on stage before I'd had my coffee in the morning."

Suzanna had just stared at her throughout this recital. "Jesus," she said at last.

"Precisely," said Elka. "I mean, not precisely, it was a baby doll, but you do see why we can't have anything go wrong this—"

Suzanna cut her off. "Yes. Say no more. Please."

She sighed heavily, her buxom figure straining the fabric of a bright red woolen dress that wrapped and tied at her waist. She wore tan knee-high boots of a buttery leather and an antique brooch of holly leaves and berries, and she'd recently had her thick blond hair swept into an updo at the Cut and Dried Salon. She knew she looked smashing.

Although why I bother in this one-donkey town, she thought, where the only male of any viable interest is the vicar, who is *not* taking the bait, is beyond me.

"Mice," she said now, enunciating slowly in her husky voice, "have rights, too. Did you ever think of that? We'd be doing them a favor—entire families of helpless mice. Fathers and mothers, struggling to raise tiny newborns, under constant threat from Luther. What's one life weighed against so many?" Suzanna loved cats, and would never see any animal harmed, but Elka, she suddenly realized, was driving her quite, quite mad. Even if hell prevailed, she would never allow herself again to be paired with Elka Garth on the church flower rota. Never, never, ne—

Suzanna's thoughts hung suspended in midair, for just then, the Reverend (and extremely dishy) Max Tudor came into view, walking down the High. Blundered into the situation, as he would later recall it.

Elka turned toward him, relief making her plain round face shine. Suzanna tucked a stray wisp of hair back into her French twist and began smoothing the fabric of her skirt over her hips. Both women approvingly watched his approach. He had a loping gait, and the long stride and easy movement of the athlete.

For his part, Max was thinking of his sermon for the next day, which was Advent Sunday. He was preoccupied by metaphors for this time of waiting, an occasion that too often had nothing to do with patience and calm, but with frantic rushing about and shopping and overindulgence. Simultaneously, he was giving some advance thought to his Christmas Day sermon. Always so important to get right, he told himself. In actuality, Christmas was his favorite holiday and working on the sermon a particular pleasure. What was most to be avoided, as always, was providing a sense of dreary, never-ending monotony with a sermon that would have parishioners wondering, with Tom Stoppard, "Where is God?"

Max was so preoccupied, in fact, that initially he did not recognize what was at stake in the women's discussion.

"Hello, Father!" said Elka, shouting her greeting and not-so-gently elbowing Suzanna aside as he approached. "Poinsettias are poisonous to cats, aren't they?"

Max, startled by the question, fell unwittingly into the trap.

"I believe I've read somewhere they can be toxic."

Elka whipped her head round to look at Suzanna, the *Told you!* plain if unspoken.

"But only mildly," he said, opening the church door. "It's the holly berry that can be extremely toxic."

As his eyes adjusted to the darkness, his gaze wandered to either side of the altar, where copious sprays of both offending items were beautifully arrayed, reflecting hours of effort by both women.

"Oh," he said.

Suzanna, who had also supplied the holly berries, driving all the way to Monkslip-super-Mare to collect the donation from the flower shop, looked crestfallen. As if to underline the point, Luther chose that moment to sprint in front of the altar in pursuit of some unseen and possibly imaginary quarry.

"I'm sure something can be arranged," Max said, with a bright but feckless optimism that, given his knowledge of his contentious parishioners, bordered on insanity. Still, he was hoping the generally amenable Elka would volunteer a home for Luther. Or even that Suzanna would, given the circumstances.

"Allergic," said both women in unison.

"Awena?" he said hopefully. Awena, the village's so-called New-Agey Neopagan, was known to have a soft spot for animals.

The women shook their heads in unison.

"I happen to know she's in London," said Suzanna. "Shopping for decorations for her holiday party." Thank God. She could just picture Awena trotting along right about now, swinging her little basket (probably full of eye of newt or whatever a neopagan would haul about with her), and Max's eyes lighting up at the sight.

"Well, of course," Suzanna continued, "she's calling it a *holiday* party to be inclusive, but she told me she was doing her solstice shopping. The party's being held on the winter solstice, did you realize? That's a big festival for someone of Awena's . . . persuasion."

"Yes, and there will be a full moon and a total lunar eclipse that night besides," said Max, smiling his oblivious smile. "That's rather rare, I understand. Sounds to me like the perfect time for a birthday celebration. Especially *this* birthday celebration."

"Right," muttered Suzanna. "All we're missing now is a star in the east."

If she had hoped for a stronger or more disapproving reaction from Father Max, as the villagers called him, she was disappointed. She was not alone in noticing the vicar's fondness for Awena. To be fair, it was a fondness shared by most of the villagers, of whatever religious persuasion.

The trouble with Awena was that everyone *liked* Awena so. Suzanna herself liked Awena, which made her recent dislike all the more puzzling and irritating. Suzanna acknowledged to herself that all this made no sense at all. But it was the Reverend Max Tudor's evident awareness of Awena, all the while Suzanna was practically throwing herself into his arms, that was feeding this aversion. What Suzanna didn't need right now was competition. Max Tudor was a tough enough nut to crack as it was.

"Anyway," she said. "She won't be here for a while. Maybe you can get your Mrs. Hooser to feed him, at least until Awena gets back."

Max bridled at the notion of Mrs. Hooser, the woman who "did" for him with an incompetence bordering on domestic sabotage, being in any way "his."

"Thea . . ." he began.

"Thea is the gentlest dog that ever lived." It was Elka's turn to press home the advantage. "She'll get along fine with Luther. She'll welcome the company, more like as not."

"I don't know . . ." said Max. "I have to be in London myself, the early part of December, for a symposium of sorts."

"Mrs. Hooser can cope," said Suzanna brightly.

Both Max and Elka turned to look at her. *Really? Since when?*

But in the face of the women's predicament, and allowing his helpful, peacemaker tendencies again to get the better of him, Max nodded and said, "Okay. Fine. I'll take Luther in. What harm can it do?"

DECEMBER 3

'Tis the season to be jolly . . .

Jocasta and Simon Jones were flying coach, a rare economy in a lifetime of wild, even frenzied, spending. So as not to be recognized, Jocasta was wearing a wig. Or perhaps, thought a cynical Simon, *hoping* to be recognized as one so famous a wig was required for her to get from point A to point B in public, unmolested by a ravening media.

But flying coach was a novel experience for Jocasta. And her entry into this new world was not going well.

The choices, as their flight attendant Wendy had chirped over the PA system, were between two boxed lunches. Jocasta, at fifty a worshiper at the altar of youth and vitality, chose the "Healthy Option."

She unwrapped the box when it had been deposited on her tray table and peered inside. There nestled a small tin of albacore, a small plastic tub of applesauce, and a large bag containing approximately ten crisps, along with plasticware wrapped hygienically and impenetrably in plastic. There was also a large, round, nubby object that might have been a biscuit or a cow pat.

Jocasta pushed the button on her armrest for the attendant. Two seconds later, she pushed it again. On, off. On, off.

"Seven *dollars* and fifty *cents* for a box of *tuna* and *applesauce*?" she cried, when Wendy had rushed to her side, expecting no less than a passenger in the final stages of cardiac arrest. "Are you quite mad?"

The flight attendant grinned her determined, battle-stations grin. It was the wide grin she saved for the type of passenger she would refuse to assist with their oxygen mask and flotation device should the need arise, hewing close to her own survival-of-the-fittest philosophy. Sod the lot of them, anyway.

But the airline had only yesterday caught major media flack for its unfriendly service and everyone was on short notice to start being nicer to passengers. Just my rotten luck to draw this witch today, Wendy thought, grinning yet more broadly.

"What's so funny?" demanded Jocasta suspiciously.

"I'm afraid we have no control over the food choices the airline offers." She was thinking how you used to be able to tell the Brits from the Yanks, and it wasn't just the accents—you could tell by the shoes and clothing. And the haircuts. This one was British but she'd been in the States a long time. The haircut—or was it a wig?—was expensive, and subtly American in style. The clothes? Designer stuff, but last year's. It was the clothing that made it hard to tell anymore. We're all starting to dress alike.

Wendy leaned in confidingly, a past mistress of the art of talking down the obstreperous passenger. She whispered, "It's chronic, isn't it? We have to eat that muck, too—even the pilots!—and we all complain about it, believe you me, dear."

Jocasta merely scowled and demanded her money back. She had already eaten the "Healthy Option" crisps and fully intended to eat the rest of the box's contents. But the flight attendant was too quick for her.

"Certainly, madam," she said, seizing the box and turning away, never to reappear until the plane landed at Heathrow. "I'll credit your charge card."

"I simply can't believe this," Jocasta fumed to Simon. "I suppose these seats don't convert into a bed, either? No free champagne? No gourmet meal, just that box of crap? No Canadian Ice Wine to go with the pudding?"

Her chin quivered with outrage. Jocasta, her husband noticed, was again getting a bit fleshy around the neck, despite the ministrations of a renowned Hollywood doctor who "did" necks as a specialty, much as a garage might specialize in mufflers or brake pad replacement. You could have hidden marbles in the folds of her neck before she had the first of many surgeries. Now she had that death's-head look, so common in Hollywood, of skin stretched too tautly to fool anyone into believing they were looking at the full bloom of youth.

Simon had come to regret his role, however well remunerated in the past, as a propper-up of a fading actress's ego—an ego otherwise sustained only by her bottomless belief in her own attractiveness. Jocasta was an actress of a particular stamp: the damsel of horror or science-fiction films, permanently typecast as the moronic but nubile maiden who explores the castle alone with only the aid of a flickering stub of a candle, and later as the moronic but spry matron who is generally the first victim of the headless corpse/marauding microbe. But the longer her career went on, the shorter seemed to be Jocasta's time on screen. Roles calling for nuance and subtle shading generally going to actresses roughly of her generation like Emma Thompson and Meryl Streep, Jocasta soldiered on, increasingly baffled by her agent's inability to keep her image before a fickle public. The pinnacle of her career was now considered to be her portrayal of Jula Bates in *I See Crazy People*, which had developed a (very) small cult following, after which it had all gone downhill. Roles having disappeared entirely, Jocasta had formally announced her retirement, in the hope of generating a clamor for her return. The announcement had been greeted with a stony silence—even the Hollywood trade papers had ignored the press release spat out into the tray beneath their fax machines.

That Simon was fourteen years his wife's junior was starting to bother him—in the early days he could not have begun to predict how much it would. He supposed it was because despite the difference in their ages, he was much the more mature of the two, the stabilizing force. But to this day he could not watch *Sunset Boulevard* without flinching, particularly at the opening scene in which William Holden's body floats lifelessly in Gloria Swanson's pool.

". . . watery grave."

He tuned back in to Jocasta's broadcast on words eerily tracking his own thoughts. Surely, he reasoned, one prerequisite for reading another's thoughts is empathy? Jocasta's empathy tank always seemed to him to be running on empty.

"What's that, dear?" he said easily, well-practiced in soothing and taming the wildebeest.

"I said," she repeated irritably, "I said it's a miracle they don't send us to a watery grave, if this is their idea of running an airline."

At least, thought Simon, she *might* have been irritated. The Botox injections, a lucrative sideline of the neck specialist's, made her appear to be in a perpetual state of pouty "What*ev*" adolescence. This alternated with a frozen scowl, which at least went with her querulous personality.

Not sure he followed the connection between food service and plane maintenance, he nodded, checking his watch, a fifth-anniversary present from Jocasta worth the equivalent of the original mortgage on his parents' old house back in Omaha, Nebraska. He and Jocasta would land in half an hour to find a limo waiting to transport them to Monkslip-super-Mare and then on to Chedrow Castle, where, so Simon had gathered, Jocasta had invited them and someone, presumably the old man, had grudgingly acquiesced in allowing them to come. Everything about the setup struck him as wrong, beginning with the fact Jocasta had had to finagle an invitation. Beginning with the fact he'd not been taken to meet her father or aunt and all the rest of them before now.

Whenever he'd asked her about it, she'd replied, "They're totally dysfunctional. All of them," as if that answered it. "One of them, I've always thought, is actually insane." And then she'd change the subject.

Now she had gotten out her cosmetics bag and was busy painting little black wings at the corner of each eye, Cleopatra style, leaning back and turning her head from side to side to take in the full effect in her compact mirror. The inner lids of her eyes she had already lined in a pale electric blue. The effect was to force one to stare into her eyes—an effect that should have inspired trust. But Simon was reminded of nothing so much as snake eyes. Snake eyes edged in blue.

Don we now our gay apparel . . .

Lamorna was getting dressed: Lamorna Whitehall, grand-niece—by adoption—of Oscar, Lord Footrustle, and granddaughter—by adoption—of Leticia, Lady Baynard.

That "by adoption" tag was so automatic Lamorna barely noticed it anymore, or so she told herself. "My granddaughter, by adoption, of course," Lady Baynard would say dismissively, by way of introduction, when she could be bothered to introduce her at all. When she couldn't *avoid* introducing her, more like. Even Lady Baynard realized that to leave Lamorna standing there like a stick of furniture while guests politely, inquiringly turned their heads in her direction only made Lady B look rude, if not blind or barking.

Funny, thought Lamorna, how she seldom even thought of her grandmother—by adoption—as Grandmother, or even as Leticia. Or even as the Dowager, which suited her down to the ground. It was Lady Baynard—certainly to her face, it was always Lady Baynard.

And Lady B, but only when the old misery's back was turned.

Lamorna, adjusting her crocheted white collar to lie flat against her shapeless dark dress, straightened the large wooden cross hanging from a cord around her neck. The cross, which she always wore, added little to her ensemble, but it did tend to act as a barricade to anyone not of her religion. She assessed herself impartially, even fearlessly, in the age-spotted mirror over her dressing table, squaring up to peer at herself through the thick lenses required to correct her 20/250 vision. She was no beauty, that she knew, but she had been told she had a "noble nose." How she cherished that compliment, made by the only mother she'd ever known. (Adoptive mother? Eyewash! Lea had been all the world. *All* the world.) In response to Lamorna's anxious teenage inquiry, after a particularly brutal term among the hellions at school, Lea Whitehall had looked long and hard at her beloved, plain-as-rice-pudding child and said, "I've always thought you had a noble nose. A fine example of a Roman nose, in fact." In other hearts less anxious for approval, less in need of shoring up than Lamorna's, this blatant flattery would have been seen for what it was. That the nose in question had a cold at the moment—a cold she'd caught from Leticia, the old monster—only added rosy insult to injury, but Lamorna still saw the protuberance as her saving grace.

Her father had seen her only as a disappointment—that much she knew without being told. Not that that stopped him from dropping broad hints about her looks, her style of dress, her hair, her lack of makeup. On and on. To have lost both of them in the airplane crash was the cruelest twist—with her father at the controls, of course, killing her mother with his carelessness, although they said it had been an accident. Had it been only her father who died . . . now *that* would have been Divine Justice.

Her heart raced with thoughts of doom and retribution, which thoughts were interrupted by the tinkling of the bell installed by her bed. It connected directly to Lady B's room where it connected to a bellpull ending in a large maroon tassel. How Lamorna had come to loathe the sound. Thus must Pavlov's dogs have come to regard the bell that sometimes meant food, sometimes meant hunger. Or was that the rats and the pellets? Lamorna couldn't remember—she'd never been much good at school, its reward system having eluded her entirely.

She considered the option of dawdling rather than hopping to attention in response, but after thirty seconds the whole idea of making her grandmother wait made her nervous. Lady Baynard would not be pleased. Everything went more smoothly if she, Lamorna, responded promptly. It was undoubtedly something minor, it always was. The old ogress probably just wanted a fresh handkerchief.

Troll the ancient Yuletide carol . . .

Gwynyth, Lady Footrustle, was at her vanity table in the nearby Watch Tower bedroom, wielding a mascara brush with practiced ease, and singing softly, a bit off-key, and getting the words slightly wrong:

God rest ye marry gentlemen
Let nothing you dismay.

The tune had been playing as she shopped recently in Fantasian, the carol a piquant counterpoint to the rampant materialism on display (for who could really afford this stuff besides Gywn and her Sloaney cronies? Scarves by Hermès and Tag Heuer watches and Gucci bags to hold it all). Although in point of fact Gwynyth, having maxed out several of her credit cards, and with the bank getting quite shirty recently about her overdraft, could only just afford the cocktail dress and matching evening bag she finally settled on. She couldn't be photographed by *Tatler* over and over again in the same old party rags, could she?

Using a tweezers she picked up a snippet of false eyelash, applied glue to its base, and attached it to the corner of one eye. She sat back to observe the effect, lifting her chin and turning her head to the side. Halfway, she decided, to perfection.

As she continued her task, she thought: So, according to the song, having married, like, way above a gentleman, an actual freaking earl, and having rested, I should let nothing me dismay, right? Well. Well, well. Having married Oscar, Lord Footrustle, borne his children (nothing restful about that), and then having been dumped . . . well. Thank *God* for the children. Without them, the sodding divorce judge would have been even less generous in giving me the measly monthly allowance I was suddenly expected to live on.

The blue eyes had been completely fringed now, offering a smoky, sultry illusion of unplumbed depths; the lip gloss applied; the powder dusted to set the foundation with a few strokes of a Kabuki brush. Thinking of the twins, which she did as seldom as possible, Gwynyth crossed the room to the armoire, pausing before a full-length mirror to examine her artistry from a distance. She smoothed the silk nightgown taut against her concave stomach and observed with a critical eye. She still had, she thought, even after years of personal training, a tiny pooch where she had carried the Elephant Children (as she thought of them) for years and years and years, until finally they had emerged, both of them cabbage-heads weighing like a *ton* each. Fortunately, the nanny engaged for their care had whisked them out of sight like something that, left out, might begin to spoil. Too right, that idea, and too late—no question the pair of them were spoiled rotten. School games and uniforms, field hockey and polo and rowing—why, her own comprehensive in Luton had barely had room for a little corner by the gymnasium for the drug dealers to hang about. Oscar had at least been generous in paying for the twins' removal by Dragon Lady, as he had been in paying for the posh, la-di-da schooling. She recognized that without that generosity, she'd have been stuck caring for the twins herself. *Gack.* Just the thought of the three of them stuck in some walk-up council flat, herself slinging beans on toast for their supper, a cigarette dangling from one side of her mouth and her wearing an old wrapper like her mother used to do—the thought actually made her ill. Like *that* was ever going to happen once she was Lady Footrustle, but still . . . Oscar had insisted on paying for the twins' education directly, as part of the settlement, as if to suggest Gwynyth might spend the tuition money on makeup and wardrobe if left to her own devices. Insulting, that's what it was, but that hanging judge who handled the settlement had agreed. Bloody men stick together, her mother had been right about that if nothing else.

People thought she had frog-marched old Oscar down the aisle (actually, up the steps to the civil ceremony at Old Marylebone Town Hall) but people would think what they liked, and never mind the truth. She guessed her mother had been right about that, too.

There was a knock at the door that could only be the twins wanting *some*thing. The Watch Tower, attached to the castle and let as a holiday cottage in season, ranged over three floors with a steep set of stairs in between each. The twins had the two small bedrooms on the ground, she the double bedroom and separate lavatory on the first floor. The second floor held the sitting room where the twins seemed to spend half their time engrossed in some idiotic computer game or another. The place was painted inside in frenetic yellows and bright blues, jarringly at odds with the outer stone appearance, an attempt to deny the dark hues of winter and hurry along the closer sun of July.

She tied a robe around her waist and shouted at them to come in. With a mumbled "hello" Alec slouched through the door, grabbed some electronic gadget he'd left behind, and slouched back out. Amanda waited wordlessly by the doorjamb. Fine manners they were taught at their posh schools.

Being on the cusp of teenage-hood, they seemed to think, gave them special privileges. Little did they know that the next few years would be the worst of their lives, if history was any guide. But right now, they were by anyone's standards beautiful, clear-skinned, with the flaxen hair they'd inherited from her, and with their father's aristocratic features.

Gwynyth supposed she should be grateful for the invitation that had brought them all here, but somehow all she could do was look that particular gift horse in the mouth, wondering what the aristocratic old coot was up to now. Oscar didn't seem particularly overjoyed to see any of them, although he was trying to show an interest in the children, which made a nice change from the usual.

She needed to make sure Oscar didn't forget altogether he had children *besides* that awful actress person—Jocasta Jones, as she now was. Jocasta, who had flown to England posthaste in response to her own summons, her husband the lap dog at her side.

It was essential Jocasta not get any ideas that being Oscar's firstborn gave her any special privileges. Oscar's son—his one and only son, Alec—*he* was what mattered, in the competition for the Footrustle heritage.

See the blazing Yule before us . . .

Randolph, formally Viscount Nathersby, or simply Nathersby when plying his trade ("It's a Nathersby, of course. Cost the earth, but the man is worth it."), and Cilla Petrie, his stylist-slash-assistant, huddled in warm comfort by the fireplace, sipping a pre-dinner sherry as they waited for the rest of the castle dwellers to assemble. What was now called the drawing room, slotted into an area above one end of the Great Hall, was reached by a fifteenth-century spiral stone staircase and dated from the times, roughly the late Middle Ages, when families began to think privacy was a better idea than living, eating, and sleeping among the help. Certainly, it was a more fragrant idea. As in Lord Footrustle's nearby bedroom, one wall contained a squint through which the family could keep an eye on the merrymakers below.

It so happened that Gwynyth, now slipping into her Louboutins in the Tower Room, was the topic of their conversation.

"I give it until Boxing Day," Randolph was saying. He paused to smooth back his thick dark hair, which tended to fall rakishly over one eye. "Oscar won't be able to abide 'Gwyn and the Twyns' much beyond that. The noble experiment will end with a whimper rather than a bang, you'll see."

"I wonder why he thought otherwise," said Cilla. "Surely he just encouraged Gwynyth's ambitions by having her come here, trailing the children. Do you think he was hoping for a reconciliation—something Dickensian like that? After all, he's not getting younger."

"God knows what my uncle thought." Randolph stood back to examine the oil painting near the mantelpiece, a rare seascape by Manet, envying the way the artist had so perfectly captured the light. "He was never given to confiding in me."

"As beautiful as Gwynyth is, she's ripe for a makeover," said Cilla. "I'm itching to get my hands on her."

"Will a makeover fill her head with anything besides the rubbish stuffed in there now?"

Cilla grinned. "She has such delicate features. And that skin! The hair needs some lowlights and some hair product, that's all." She tossed back her own glossy coils of dark brown hair, rich with product, as if to demonstrate what was possible if one put one's mind to it. Cilla was an excellent stylist.

Randolph grunted, not really listening. He'd read somewhere Manet had failed the examination to join the Navy—twice. Luckily for posterity he'd rejected the life his father had tried to foist on him.

"The three of them look so much alike—Gwynyth and the twins," Cilla was saying. "Scandinavian blood, at a guess. That type washes out on film, though."

"Too bad she doesn't take herself and her whey-faced brood over there for a long visit," said Randolph, with sudden irritation. "Why is she here anyway?"

"Well, it *is* Christmas," said Cilla. "And she's rather stuck with the twins being out of school. I'd be willing to bet she played on Oscar's finer feelings."

"He has no finer feelings, that I'm aware."

"She might ring the changes on the 'poor fatherless tykes' theme. More Dickens. I'm sure she's mainly here to campaign for a bigger settlement. And Oscar may have felt it wiser to put up with them all for a few days than to have her petitioning the courts on the grounds the children are being neglected by their father."

"Interesting you should say that." Randolph drew closer, warming his hands by the fire. "It is certainly what I suspected—that he was strong-armed into this, rather than that he issued an invitation willingly as she claims. He'd rather avoid unpleasantness—unless he's causing the unpleasantness, of course. In which case, he loves to stand by watching the train wreck."

There was a pause while Cilla thoughtfully sipped her drink, hiding her expression. She said, "It will be interesting to see your cousin Jocasta. From what you said the other day, I'm wondering if she's improved at all."

"Her acting, you mean?" said Randolph slyly.

"God, no. There was never any scope for that, was there? I've sat through several of her films, I'm sorry to say. I meant, oh, as a person. You know."

"Even less scope for improvement there. Jocasta is what Jocasta is and always has been. Oops! Bad pun there—'Has been.'"

Cilla laughed lightly.

Just then there was a rustle on the steps outside, no more than the whisper of a footfall, no louder than the sound made by a mouse wearing house slippers. The massive door into the drawing room stood open, and one had to be careful what one said. It might drift out the door, spiraling down the stairs and into waiting, eager ears.

Strike the harp and join the chorus . . .

Lamorna had been drawn by the voices. She stood on the landing outside the drawing room, hidden behind the open door, one ear pressed against the jamb to hear what could be heard. It was not one of her more successful spying missions. Apart from the reference to Gwynyth's Dickensian ambitions, the first indicator that Cilla was paying close attention to the maneuverings and jockeyings for position in the castle, there was little of interest to overhear. Nothing she hadn't heard before. Now that Gwynyth and Oscar were divorced, everyone felt free to say whatever they liked about Gwynyth.

It was cold on the landing, the fingers of even such a massive fire not stretching to where Lamorna stood, and she opted for comfort, deciding there was no more to be learned by standing there freezing. Inside, all would be rich comfort and beauty: The windows overlooking the gardens had been widened during a restoration by a former earl as the centuries of need for defense gave way to decades of relative peace. Peering round the door, she could see that snow had collected in a lacy openwork effect on the windowpanes. She might have thought it a match for the pattern of the crochet around her neck if she'd been given to poetic flights of fancy.

She went into the room, feigning great surprise at finding anyone inside. She fooled neither of them; in fact, they both wondered why she bothered with the pretense, but that was Lamorna's way. The sneaky, crablike approach was her default mode, her way through a life where hypervigilance was its own reward. Or perhaps, spying simply gave her something to do with her time beyond fetching and carrying for Lady Baynard.

The arrival of the family had been a boon for Lamorna in this regard—so many more conversations to keep track of, and to write down in her diary. That was the one good thing about having so many visitors—something to write about at last! Something to break the monotony. But that was really all she could label as a bonus. Mainly, she just wished they'd leave.

Randolph, sprawled across a sofa, was saying something about Paris, in that drawling, upper-class way he had. Lamorna had read (in reading aloud to Lady Baynard from one of the tabloid newspapers she so enjoyed) that Kate Middleton had started receiving elocution lessons from the moment her engagement to the prince was announced, presumably so she could sound more like Randolph. What a mistake. Randolph sounded like a donkey with adenoids. What was he saying now? Something about Lady Baynard.

"My mother," and here he clasped his hands behind his head to add to the illusion of languor, although Lamorna could see he was rather het up. "My mother is complaining of ill health and may not be joining us, I'm afraid. Perhaps—she wasn't sure."

"When," asked Lamorna, "has she not complained? She harps on about her health day and night. Well, to me, she does," she added resentfully. "I don't know why you're spared."

"We're not," said Cilla mildly.

"Come in, Alec and Amanda, for heaven's sake," Randolph called out.

The twins entered, as furtively as Lamorna had done. She, in a case of calling the kettle black, suspected they often did this—listened outside of doors. Especially Alec. Alec was always up to something.

"What?" he demanded now, suspiciously.

"You always sound like I'm about to ask you to wear a dress or something, Alec," said Randolph in his indolent way. "Why do you always do that?"

"I do not."

"Yes, you do. I was going to ask you to go and ask your father if he'd be joining us for dinner."

Ignoring him (for although Alec didn't dare go up against Randolph—not quite yet—he was determined to show his independence in small and annoying ways), Alec turned to find someone to torment. He didn't have to look far. Lamorna was always there.

"*Dear*est Cousin," he said, in much the same voice as Randolph's—languid, impeccably well-bred, condescending. The sort of Etonian voice only money combined with an ancient pedigree can buy. "We know how hard your life is. Do *you* have to harp on about it so?"

His twin joined in. She usually did.

"Yes," said Amanda, with studied patience. "If you're so unhappy, why don't you leave?" But she wasn't really waiting for a reply. A split end marring the perfection of her silken hair had caught her eye.

Because, thought Lamorna mulishly. Because I don't look like you. Because everything isn't just handed to me.

"I mean, no one's making you stay, really, are they? You could get a job."

That was rich. This spoiled young heiress, at the tender age of fourteen, handing out career advice. But for once, Lamorna held her tongue, nodded, pretended to agree.

"I hadn't really thought of it." She rustled around in a basket she'd retrieved from behind one of the sofas, and pulled out her knitting. She'd been making new sweaters as Christmas presents for the twins, but wisely she'd kept this surprise to herself. Old habits died hard—she used to love knitting little booties and things for them when they were small. She clicked her needles, unaware that her efforts always ended up in the rubbish bin by Boxing Day.

"Perhaps after Christmas I'll see what's available."

Follow me in merry measure . . .

"And as for your mother—well!" Felberta was saying. "It's the Leticia station, twenty-four/seven. Bringing you all the news from the center of the fucking universe—Leticia, Lady Baynard herself. Plus a Weekend Update on the state of her fragile—but not fragile enough—health."

"Felberta!" her husband admonished.

"But isn't it the truth?"

"This is not a family given over to speaking truths, if you must know. And really, that's most unwise. The walls have ears around here."

Lester and his wife, Felberta, had decided to take advantage of the cocktail hour at Chedrow Castle by having a little look round. They had been at the castle since the end of November, so anxious to take Oscar up on his invitation before it was withdrawn they'd practically hopped the next plane out from Australia. An invitation so capriciously and unexpectedly issued could just as easily be withdrawn, as Lester said to his wife.

"This is an opportunity that won't come along often. She's getting older, my mother. They both are."

"Opportunity for what, exactly?" Felberta asked, although she could have guessed. She had been attracted to her husband in the first place because he always had an eye out for what her own mother had called "the main chance," and what she herself preferred to think of as advancement.

"To look around, to size up what's here. Randolph's going to try to grab everything, of course. But I want to know what there is to grab. And then I'll have a word with Mother about making sure he doesn't get it all. Do you have the camera?"

She nodded, holding out the mobile phone with its camera feature.

"Good. Then follow me. That painting in the corridor upstairs might well be a minor Reynolds. And that Rembrandt! I wonder where Oscar got it from."

While I tell of Yuletide treasure . . .

Leticia, Lady Baynard, wrapped against the cold, was walking toward the hothouse on the castle grounds, where she planned to do triage on some plants she thought were becoming pot-bound. In truth, she loved working with plants and the soil so much she sometimes found excuses to move one plant here, another there, and thus experiment with the different feeds and light she thought her darlings might like.

There are some things the National Trust can't touch, she thought. The loss of the front garden, paved over to create a large parking area for the avid history-seeking public—the great unwashed—had been a cruel blow, from which she had never quite recovered.

At the unwanted memory of the National Trust and its place in her life, Leticia felt her heart constrict. How far the mighty had fallen!—or words to that effect. Tourists in tattered jeans and trainers gawping at the priceless treasures accumulated by Footrustles over centuries, with hardly a one of the gawpers knowing the true value of a *thing*. Still, compared with what had happened to her husband's family's estate, she supposed the Footrustles—her family of birth, after all—had been lucky. As for the Baynards—well. Their stately home put on the market and sold like a common two-up, two-down to some American actress and her family. The *real* family packed off. Gone. It was the reason she herself was here now at Chedrow.

To make matters worse the actress, finding the upkeep all a bit too expensive—Leticia could have told her a thing or two about *that*—soon moved out. The place was sold again and turned into an asylum, of all things. A posh and pricey asylum, but still. Leticia couldn't—wouldn't want to—even visit. Drug and alcohol *rehab* they called it. In her day, the wealthy dipsos simply got on with it—they generally were sent abroad by their families, Africa or somewhere where no one had to deal with them. Well, presumably the people of *A*frica had to deal with them but the families were spared the disgrace. Now it was rehab, with half of them writing their memoirs about the experience. Honestly. To what had the world come?

She decided after all to join the unwanted guests for a drink before dinner. What choice did she have? She lived in an asylum now, she thought, but this one was named Chedrow Castle.

❄ ❄ ❄

A short time later Lady Baynard sat with her knitting, surrounded by family. The togetherness was giving her heartburn. She looked about her with a barely concealed contempt, like the Queen watching a performance by the Duchess of York as captured by hidden video camera and wondering where, oh, where in her long reign things had begun to go so dreadfully wrong.

There was Randolph, her eldest. A photographer. What sort of profession was that? Yes, yes, of course, everyone mentioned Antony Armstrong-Jones, First Earl of Snowdon. But he wasn't *born* into a title, was he? He was created Earl of Snowden and then given a life peerage. It's simply not the same thing. He was born (and here she gave a little shudder of distaste) a *commoner*. But a British princess couldn't have a child by a *commoner* and they'd had to fix that up, tout de suite.

So photography was all right for someone like Snowden as a little hobby—kept him busy, one supposes, but not out of trouble, if the rumors were true.

And then there was Lester, her second son—second in more ways than one. She sighed, a long exhalation of disappointment. Lester's dealings always struck her as that little bit dodgy, a bit hole in corner *and* under the table, although she understood nothing about finance and could not have said why she felt that way. As for that wife of his—merciful heaven. An Australian—of all things to have married, an Australian.

Here she paused for a good snuffle into her handkerchief. No, it simply didn't bear thinking about.

And as for Lamorna—the least said the better. Not a trace of Lea's graceful bearing, which one would think might have been inculcated somehow by example, even if her looks could not be passed on. Lea, who rode to hounds like a proper lady—for her to come home with this foundling, this, this . . . *crea*ture who looks like Rasputin and who furthermore shows every sign of incipient religious mania—well.

Breeding *tells*, and Leticia couldn't ever *quite* forgive her daughter for adopting this mutt from nowhere and then dying, leaving them stuck with this—this whatever it was. (*Sniff.*) Breeding *tells*.

But here they all were, and worse! The blonde and her two urchins—Oscar's Folly, in the flesh. And that daughter of Oscar's, and her husband, from America. The husband is much too young for her—that's what comes of becoming an *act*ress and surrounding oneself with all *man*ner of people. Sneaking a glance over to the Joneses, who had managed to drape themselves all over one corner of the room, she saw that Simon's role as courtier to the Great Queen of Hollywood might be growing a bit thin, judging by his set expression—worn to a veneer from the days when the pair of them were, and very briefly, tabloid darlings.

Lady Baynard had rudely ignored the hand Simon proffered to help her into her chair, ignored it without explanation, such as a sudden outbreak within the castle walls of the Ebola virus. She thought it best to do nothing to encourage any ideas they might have for extending their stay, any of them.

What a medley they made. Well, one thing is certain, there is trouble brewing. But that's only to be expected. To bring them all together under one roof, after so many years! I warned Oscar, the stubborn old goat. But would he listen? Has he ever listened?

She sat bolt upright, a disdainful smirk on her lips. A small sherry had appeared like magic at her right hand. So Leticia had sat at many a hunt ball, swatting away suitors. She was still youthful in appearance, with only her liver-spotted hands and the loosened skin at her neck to hint at her age. Back in the day, Oscar and Leticia, twins like Alec and Amanda, had been the main attraction at these balls, their combination of youthful vitality, titles, and wealth being irresistible. If Leticia missed those days of glory she never let it be known. There was something to be said for the power that accumulated with age, after all.

Now they were all wondering aloud what to give Oscar for Christmas—if they should pool their money to "buy him something nice." Why, she thought, not throw their purses off the parapets and into the sea?

Only Lamorna, in that idiot savant way she sometimes had, said, "He won't buy *me* anything. He never has. Why should I— why should any of us—bother with him?"

"We're enjoying his hospitality, that's why." This was Lester. To Leticia's certain knowledge, Lester had never given Oscar a present in his life. Too late now, she thought, to begin priming that pump. It would never occur to Oscar to reciprocate.

Leticia said, aware of spreading pearls of wisdom before swine, and in the talking-to-peasantry voice she adopted for these occasions: "I shouldn't bother if I were you. Oscar was always tightfisted. He stinted little on his own pleasures, mind, but he wasn't one to share his 'treasure.' He was like that even as a little boy. He gave me a rock for Christmas once."

Lester, laughing, said, "You must have been just children at the time."

"We were both in our twenties. You do see what I mean? He has always been miserly. Save your money."

And abandon all hope of great expectations while you're at it. For *I've* seen Oscar's will.

DECEMBER 12—EVENING

Fast away the old year passes . . .

"You're certain you didn't just leave the food out a little longer than you should have?" Milo Vladimirov asked his wife.

It was the sixth time Milo had asked her that in six days, and this time Doris exploded. "I'd no sooner do that than leave you to follow the circus."

For she was the cook at Chedrow Castle, and six days before, Lord Footrustle had fallen ill of something that seemed suspiciously like food poisoning. Not just a bit of tummy—it was a serious enough episode that he had been laid up for three days, from the night of December 6. He was only now just beginning to recover, and able to drink a bit of chicken broth for his supper.

"He fell ill from just about the time this family of his started collecting here," Doris said, reiterating the theory she had begun to champion with increasing intensity, the more the stress of these new arrivals began to tell. She looked about her, as if the answers to all her questions about that coincidence could be found written on the walls. It was a room where light bounced off the copper gleaming from every surface—dozens of pots and pans hung suspended from hooks and racks, as shiny as if fresh from the box. An AGA cooker had pride of place against one wall; nearby were racks of spices and aromatic fresh herbs gathered by their stems to dry.

"Just *three days* after the last of them got here from Heathrow—Jocasta and her husband Simon. No sooner were they all under this roof together than the trouble started."

Lord Footrustle had refused medical treatment—he was of that generation that believed in toughing things out and letting nature take its course. He was a big believer in homeopathic cures over the usual medicines, too. In this, he had been proved right—he was a strong old bird, for all his complaining, and no mistake. But because he would allow no doctor to be called there was no proving it wasn't ptomaine or something that originated with her cooking, and that was an insult Doris could hardly live with.

"For the last time," she said, "we all ate what he had for dinner. The identical meal. It was nothing I cooked, whatever ailed him. Or is it his granola they think I poisoned?"

"It might just have been a flu bug, too."

"That's what I said at the time. But I don't like the timing of it." She gathered her rosy face into a little purse of worry. "Do you?"

"No," said Milo, quietly and deliberately, as was his way. A good butler kept his emotions under control at all times. And he didn't want Doris upset any more than she was.

Aloud she said, "He has all that homeopathic stuff up there. So conscious of his health he is. Just like his sister."

"Those are often the first to go," said Milo. "The health conscious."

She nodded glumly. "Still, there's nothing easier than for someone to tamper with his pills and potions. None of *us* would touch it, that's certain."

"Not likely," he said, although whom she meant by "us" wasn't clear. He wouldn't put much past Lamorna Whitehall.

"You know . . ." Doris began and stopped, losing her nerve for the moment, for neither she nor her husband had ever said this aloud. "You know how we always talk about buying a small bed-and-breakfast somewhere? Wouldn't it be a wonder if Lord Footrustle or Lady Baynard left us money in their wills? Just enough for a down payment?"

Milo admonished her with a shake of his head for saying it.

"Really, Dorrie, we shouldn't—"

"And why not, I'd like to know?" she demanded. "It is no more than the rest of them are thinking, believe you me."

"That's as may well be," he said. "We have to be better bred than they are."

The irony of this statement was lost on both of them for a moment. Then Milo grinned.

"Besides . . ." he began.

"Besides?"

But he shrugged. It was a noncommittal shrug, to all appearances. But Doris, who knew him well, looked at him shrewdly.

"You know something, don't you?" she said.

"Common sense, only. Lord Footrustle must have a will. So must she. In fact we know they both have wills, because of the solicitor's visit last year—remember? What he said? Almost a year ago now. As one was not asked to witness, one must suppose . . ."

"That one is mentioned," she finished for him. Milo's English was impeccable, even if heavily accented, as befitted a butler of a famous house and family. She sometimes liked to tease him over it. "Of course you are mentioned. We are. Wouldn't it be lovely to know . . ."

31

"Yes," he said, abruptly cutting off the conversation. "She'll be wanting her tea." It need not be explained who "she" was. "She" was always Leticia.

Doris put the kettle on. "Do you really think it was just the flu?" she asked again hopefully. That was so much better than the alternate theory: a poisoner on the loose. That idea was almost as hard to live with as a careless mistake made in her kitchen.

"I am certain that was it," Milo said, in his measured English. "Do not trouble yourself about it any longer, Doris."

But he wished he were as certain as he sounded.

We should have called in the doctor, if not the police.

DECEMBER 13—MORNING

Hail the new, ye lads and lasses . . .

Milo, knowledge of butler etiquette and years of stiff-upper-lip training forgotten, stood on the threshold of Lord Footrustle's room. He could not take in what he was seeing in the half-light. The curtains were drawn, not quite shut. But there appeared to be a stain that covered the bedclothes. A dark stain. Red.

And the smell of blood, which he knew too well, was in the air.

Suddenly the aroma of fried eggs, fresh-baked scones, and freshly brewed coffee wafting up from the tray he carried made him feel quite ill. In fact he dropped the tray with a clatter of crockery, and ran.

He had lived through too much in his country. On the one hand, it had inured him to panic. On the other, it had conditioned him to run, not stand around, at the first sign of trouble. And this was the worst sort of trouble.

He ran for the kitchen, for the company of his wife, who was in her way as sensible an old soul as he. He knew she would calm him. She had to be the first to hear this news, before the family, before everyone. She had to help him make sense of the senseless, as she had done since the day they had first met.

Throwing open the door with a crash that startled the potato and the peeler straight out of her hands, he came over to where she sat at the kitchen table, shouting the news:

"It's Lord Footrustle! He's *dead*!"

She understood his words, and was saddened but not too shocked. Old Man Footrustle was getting on in years, and old people died. At least no one could say now it was from her cooking.

But she didn't understand the panic. How could she?

"I think," said Milo, "I think he's been *murdered*."

PART II

CHAPTER I

Ticket to Ride

DECEMBER 13—MORNING

Max Tudor, returning to Nether Monkslip from a routine mission on a bitterly cold but beautiful December day, was not to know he would be pulled into the investigation of strange events at nearby Chedrow Castle—an investigation that would haunt many of his future nights.

At the little self-service kiosk at Waterloo station, Max's biggest concern was what to eat to fortify himself for his hours-long journey. He hesitated over a slice of marzipan cake tightly wrapped in cling film. It made him think of the Battenberg sold by Sainsbury's, a sponge cake with not so much icing as a thick slab of sweetened concrete which had not completely set. That cake had been one of his guilty pleasures ever since he was a child. This imposter of a cake had the concrete yellow icing but not the pink-and-yellow-checkered pattern to its layers. Reluctantly, Max passed it by.

He scanned the display of food for something marginally more nutritious, but this particular outpost of British Rail offered the kind of sandwich that left you wondering if an ambulance could bully its way through the crowded London streets in time to save you.

He was returning from a symposium in London, where he'd

delivered a short, well-received talk on the need to preserve Britain's churches. English Heritage had recently launched an initiative to save such Grade I and Grade II listed structures and somehow Max's name had come up as someone having experience in these matters. Roofing and timber and masonry repairs to churches in Great Britain were endless and ongoing, and the skilled workmen needed to make the repairs dwindling in number. Worse, in some cases, the lead and copper from roofs were being stolen, so the venerable old edifices were being demolished piece by piece.

As the vicar of a small church steeped in antiquity and unparalleled beauty, Max felt he would be negligent not to exploit every avenue to funds to pay for its upkeep. If becoming some sort of expert within the inner circle of preservationists would help, so be it.

Although the symposium had gone well, he soon found himself longing to return to his isolated little village with its little frictions. Well, he thought (here hastily pushing aside the memory of a recent murder in the village) *mostly* little frictions.

For London seemed to be slowly turning into a madhouse. Almost, it seemed, in honor of his first foray into the city in months MI5 had raised the terror alert level to severe. Which meant not a lot these days in the face of ongoing threats from more than one group in more than one part of the world. A general acceptance of the fact the world had forever changed on 9/11 seemed the best that could be hoped for from a public worn cynical and wearied by a stream of heightened precautions. Besides, a recommendation for extra alertness seemed de trop when Max by nature was seldom not alert, watching, waiting—for what he could not have said.

He had stayed at a London hotel booked for him by the diocese with an eye on the bottom line—very bottom—as if left to his own devices Max might stop at Claridge's and order jeroboams of champagne sent up to his suite. The place chosen for him did not even pretend to have once been a star in the galaxy of the hospitality industry; no deposed barons of even very minor baronetcies were to be found taking tea in the lobby. The place had always been shabby about the edges and now was unapologetically shabby through and through. He had been greeted by the receptionist, a gum-chewing girl of surly disposition obviously forced to work beneath her level of unrecognized genius. It may have been a job she held for the school break, although she had the look of an actress between jobs, all sparkly mascara and languorous, studied movements. There had been a certain accretion of interest in her eyes as she took in the handsome features of her new guest. The gum chewing stopped abruptly, only to be resumed as she cogitated the question he put to her. No, she didn't think they had a room with a view. She'd check. She began flapping her long painted nails about on a keyboard and came up with the expected answer: All the rooms with views were full up.

At least, he reflected, the hotel had a plain, old-fashioned lift with deeply padded sides—none of these modern horrors made of glass, apparently conceived as a trial for people who are afraid of heights. The last time he'd had reason to stay in London, the hotel lift had been made of stainless steel with water cascading artistically down the sides—it was like being hoisted aloft in a high-tech colander.

Max, on seeing his forlorn, seedy London hotel room, longed momentarily in an all-too-human way for something gilt-edged and dripping with crystal chandeliers. But in particular he longed for the cozy if fussy and old-fashioned study of his vicarage, which he told himself now was at least rich in character.

Instead he was in an ancient London hotel whose lack of amenities in no way inhibited the management from charging an exorbitant amount for a dollhouse-sized room with no view. It was an amount that should have lent itself to luxury terry cloth robes and shower caps folded into little boxes and shampoos from the official Shampooers to Her Majesty, and yet Max was grateful to have been provided a postage stamp-sized bar of soap made from, apparently, tar and ground pepper. The room boasted a bed with a single thin mattress that might have been stuffed with straw, and a radio so old it had probably first been used by someone listening to

King Edward VIII's abdication speech. It had dials as big as scones and speakers covered in a dusty open-weave fabric like burlap. The hot water in the bathroom was as close to nonexistent as made no difference, and the breakfast the next morning made him long for the homey, calorie-laden canteen offerings of his housekeeper Mrs. Hooser, a sure sign that something in his universe had gone badly awry.

He'd had a further bad experience in London that made him eager to return to the shelter of his village. He'd seen—he could swear he'd seen—a man in the street who had been involved in the death of his MI5 colleague, Paul. At any rate, it was a man of roughly the same physical type, wearing the same weird blue sunglasses with white frames, that Max had seen hovering near the crime scene that day. He couldn't be certain—indeed, couldn't be certain the man he'd seen the day of Paul's death was involved in the killing. But Max had been sure enough that he'd spun around in the push and shove of pedestrians to follow the man, thinking as he hustled after him that his clerical collar offered the perfect cover for tailing a suspect. He followed him for many blocks, thinking how well he'd retained his training from those old days. And then, somewhere a few streets away from Pall Mall, he lost him. He looked frantically left, right, and even overhead. And then he'd pounded his fist against a wall, scraping his knuckles in his rage.

He called the sighting in directly to his old boss at MI5, dialing his private line, and ended up having dinner with George Greenhouse that evening. It was a bittersweet occasion—Max had always held the man in esteem, but he knew how disappointed George had been by Max's decision to leave the life behind for the priesthood.

He learned a few things at that dinner in Covent Garden. One was that MI5 had decided someone besides Paul and Max had been injured by the car explosion that killed Paul. For the man with those strange glasses Max had described to investigators had been recorded on one of the ubiquitous London security cameras shortly after the explosion, and he was holding his arm as if injured.

"But he didn't go to any hospital in London despite his injuries and that's further evidence it's him," George told Max. Whether he was supposed to share this information was doubtful, but then George hadn't gotten where he was by being a company man. Nerveless, famous for his bravery, he also had more integrity than practically anyone Max had ever met.

Midway through the main course George had stunned him by saying, "She's remarried, you know. Sheila. She got married again recently."

Sheila—Paul's wife. Max had barely known her, hadn't seen her since the funeral, which she'd attended, against all advice, clutching their young son, hers and Paul's—grimly holding the blue-swaddled bundle to her. She'd stumbled through the service looking as numb as Max had felt.

Max was brokenhearted by the news of her remarriage but struggled to hide it from George. What had he expected, though? That Sheila would go into some form of purdah forever? Life had gone on. But something about this permanent move on Sheila's part made him realize how much he himself had stayed in the past of that terrible day.

He wondered—idle, stupid thought—why he hadn't been invited to the wedding. And realized that in some completely mad, irrational way, this bothered him, even though he barely had known Sheila, and his presence at her marriage would have been downright odd. Then he hoped—to heaven—that it wasn't because she blamed him, Max. For Max blamed himself, and a world of invitations wouldn't change that. Paul wouldn't have been the one killed that day if he hadn't switched places on the job with Max.

Paul's death had changed Max's course in life completely, for it was not long afterward that he began training for the priesthood. It wasn't as if he believed—not really *believed*—that his life that day in London had been spared by Divine Providence. He refused to see Paul as some placeholder for himself, simply unluckier than he. They had exchanged schedules, he and Paul, as they often had done in the past, in the chaos of a crisis elsewhere, not seeing the danger in front of them. That the blast had happened that day, at that moment, was almost a coincidence. The next day would have worked as well, for the purposes of the thugs with whom they were dealing.

And yet, his escape had forced Max to slow down, to stop, and to think. It had led directly to the 180-degree change he had made in his life.

Yet . . . and yet, in the furthest corner of his mind, wasn't there a voice, a small voice that might start to jabber if he granted it freedom, a voice that said he'd left his old life behind not because of some high-flown need to serve his fellow man, but because otherwise he might die young, in the same senseless way his comrade Paul had died. This voice had a name, and it answered to either Coward or Reason, depending on the given day.

So now Paul's wife had remarried. On the rebound, or so Max would always think. Remarried to a man he would try hard to like, recognizing his instinctive dislike had little to do with Sean's—his name was Sean—with his shortcomings. It was that Sean was there only because Paul had gone.

Later that night as Max removed his clerical collar he thought of a different collar—a collar with a stain on it, a pinprick of red against the white linen. He'd never been able to throw away that shirt, stained on that day by a small drop of Paul's blood. It sat now, undisturbed and wrapped in plastic, on the top shelf of his closet at the vicarage.

So it was with a sense of relief that he began the first leg of his journey back to Nether Monkslip. He would take the Great Western from Waterloo, change trains, and eventually catch the short spur on the Swanton and Staincross Minster Steam Railway connecting to his village. He would not be traveling first class on the initial stages of his journey, of course. But on the seven-mile home stretch to Nether Monkslip he would ride a gloriously restored train, where all the seats were first class. This refurbished train, at one time for the village squire's private use, had been donated to the village in the squire's will with a fund to keep it in good repair.

It only went as far as Staincross Minster where more modern connections could be made to the wider world. The train was seldom crowded even though it was small and the service infrequent—there were easier ways for the general populace to travel to Staincross Minster without going via such an obscure place as his village. So difficult was it to get to and from Nether Monkslip, in fact, it was difficult to say quite what the village was doing there. Apart from the presence of the river, significant in terms of early commercial transport, how and why the village had evolved was lost in the mists of time.

Since few people knew of Nether Monkslip's existence (which was how the villagers liked it) the little mahogany-paneled conveyance suited the villagers' purposes exactly. It had a tea trolley (dining cars being nearly a thing of the past) but service was intermittent, and the ride was too short to warrant much more than intermittent.

Nothing was as it once had been, Max reflected sadly. Hotels, trains. And George had looked to be getting on in years, the movements of the old warrior now stiff, fraught with effort. Arthritis, probably . . .

As Max stood in this brooding manner waiting to board at Waterloo, he failed to notice the woman who had actually stopped dead in her tracks to stare at him. Her expression seemed to say: *There must be a God if he's got vicars like you.*

CHAPTER 2

Upper Crust

The waiting area at Waterloo had been, for some reason, full of young parents with their caffeinated children; he might have been in Disney World. Now contentedly settled in for the longest stretch of his journey, all was blessed silence except for the soothingly mechanical noises of a train in motion, and he watched mesmerized as the winter-barren landscape rolled past. Max loved above all the wail of a train whistle—a mournful sound that still somehow lifted the heart with hope and anticipation. Anticipation of what, he could not say. Adventure, perhaps, of which he had not been in short supply, before and during his tenure as parish priest.

Robert Louis Stevenson had written something about the heart being full of the stillness of the country, and that was what Max felt on a train. Even short delays en route didn't bother him. So long as he had something to read or something to gaze at out the window, he was renewed in spirit by the enforced stillness, even though his mind might be racing.

They reached Staincross Minster where the last part of his journey by steam engine would begin. There a group of four Japanese tourists walked by, two couples, part of the chaotic scrum of passengers sheltered by the wooden canopy. God only knew what they were doing in this part of the world. Nether Monkslip was a hidden treasure of South West England, although more and more intrepid tourists seemed to find their way there. If these tourists were headed to Nether Monkslip (and there was little point in being on this obscure train route otherwise) then they were in luck: The Horseshoe could just accommodate two couples in its cramped, ancient rooms, provided the couples didn't take up much space. Max inadvertently tripped up one of the men in the

44

group as he was getting on and with the exquisite politeness of the Japanese, the man apologized, presumably for walking where Max's foot should not have been. They exchanged little bows and "so sorry's" and forgiving smiles, and the man rejoined his group, now spilling down the corridor and into one of the antique compartments.

Max walked on to the next compartment, which happened for the moment to be empty. He was soon followed by an elderly woman struggling with a string bag and an old-fashioned Gladstone large enough to secrete half the contents of the British Library. Max, jumping to offer his aid, discovered it was heavy enough to have actually been used for this purpose, and wondered how on earth the old lady had managed to drag it this far. It was becoming harder each day to find a porter. But once free of her burden she carried herself erectly if stiffly, with the caution of one whose old bones were becoming fragile.

"Thank you so much," she brayed in an upper-class accent from behind the netting of her rakishly tilted black hat, which matched the rest of what Max was sure she would call her travel costume. The hat was in fact recently back in style because of the fondness of royalty for these creations, particularly at weddings—a hat with a dotted veil, attached to her head by an ebony hatpin. He'd seen a hat much like it on the head of one of the royals as he'd perused the magazine racks at the station's newsagent stand. This lady had just managed to avoid the Mad Hatter look the royal family went in for on formal occasions.

She had a frilly woolen scarf knotted under her chin against the chill of the under-heated compartment. Her jacket with matching skirt was a smart affair—smart for sixty years previous—of tailored wool, cut close to the waist, flared at the hips, and slightly fraying at the cuffs. She carried a lambswool coat slung over one of her fine leather-gloved wrists.

She was a woman tightly corseted and bound, whose visage brought unavoidably to mind the term "battle-axe." Perhaps the corseting had something to do with her look of chronic dyspepsia.

But she brightened visibly at the sight of Max, standing up a bit taller. She adjusted her round glasses for a closer inspection, and her blue-eyed glance as it alighted on him seemed to say, *What luck, a vicar!*

"How wonderful," she said aloud, settling in a seat opposite his, with a nod in the direction of his collar, "to share my journey with a clergyman. It seems rather providential."

Max, seeing the look, smiled politely, said "Hullo," and seized his day-old newspaper with a show of rabid interest, as if it contained news of no less import than the Second Coming. He rustled it open to an inside page—a page which happened to hold the table tennis news. The rest of the paper seemed to be taken up with intelligence regarding the upcoming royal nuptials—the engagement had been announced mid-November. The new couple apparently were busily preparing for a shared life of ship launchings, hand wavings, sporting events, and tree plantings interspersed with wild nights at members-only nightclubs. An old friend of Max's from SO14—the Royalty Protection Group of the London Metropolitan Police—had told him watching over the royals was like watching a rugby scrum with carriages.

But Max well knew the signs his companion was giving off, and although the journey in miles was short the old train would creep along like a geriatric tortoise. The woman didn't take the message telegraphed by his own body language, of course.

A young man came down the corridor and peered in the etched glass of the carriage window, a man with large earrings visible, and a tattoo or two that wasn't, Max imagined. He wore a leatherette jacket; the thinning hair slicked back on his head and the compensatory thick mustache gave him the look of a walrus with an addiction to television shopping. He had wires running from his ears into his music player. Max could see that the earplugs were a gumdrop design. Clever the toys young people had these days, he thought, and wondered exactly when he'd begun to think of himself as outside that group.

The woman gave the young man a glare and he moved briskly along, having changed his mind about entering the carriage.

There are certain topics that inevitably arise when a clergyman is forced into close confinement with a member of the curious public for longer than ten minutes. The tale of the multiplication of the loaves and fishes was one. The tangible existence of a hell for sinners in the afterlife was another. But most popular of all was the question of the place of household pets in God's grand design, invariably accompanied by tributes to a particular pet's beatific nature. So, expecting the woman to ask if her cat Fortesque Tiggy-Boots might be waiting to one day reunite with his mistress in heaven, Max was surprised when she said, "I imagine it's *quite* difficult being in your line of work, in this day and age." With a delicate cough, she raised a handkerchief to her nose. "So sorry. I seem to have come down with a *dread*fully bad cold."

"I don't know that my line of work was ever easy," said Max agreeably. "Certainly, there's never a shortage of work for me to do."

"Ooooh!" she said. She had a distinctly upper-class voice, full of trills and fruity exclamations and odd emphases on certain words. "I *quite* see what you mean. Most amusing. Sin always simply *multiplies* around one, does it not?"

"Actually, I had poverty in mind," said Max.

Again, the "Ooooh! Quite." Max, reminded of Eddie Izzard imitating a puzzled Queen Elizabeth confronted by a plumber, half expected the obviously wealthy woman to say, "Poverty? What on earth is *that*?"

Instead she said, "But where on *earth* are my manners? I should have introduced myself. I am Lady Baynard. And you would be Father . . . ?"

"Father Tudor," he replied. "Max Tudor. I am the vicar at St. Edwold's in Nether Monkslip. At your service, Lady Baynard."

"Yes, of course. As you can see, I've been doing some Christmas shopping," she informed him, in the least festive, least Christmassy tones imaginable. "In Staincross Minster. Fast Freddie's

Market has the best prices for fruit this time of year. And I had to pick up some things for my plants, you know, and visit the chemist's. And you? You've been in London, perhaps?"

It was not so much a question as a lucky guess—an opening, nosy sortie. Max suspected she felt it was her right to know where he'd been—in her universe, the local vicar was as much a subordinate as a lady's maid. One was in charge of her public communications with God, the other in charge of making sure her travel costume was kept in good repair. Both persons greased the wheels of her upper-class existence.

"Yes, just for a couple of days," he replied. He summarized his participation in the symposium as briefly as he could, not expecting anyone not immediately involved to care about his roof. Still, she listened with polite interest, only occasionally stopping to snuffle genteelly into her lace handkerchief.

"So sorry," she said again. "It's this frightful cold that's been going round . . ." Again she coughed delicately, then blew her nose with a resounding and indelicate honk. She breathed deeply, and the flesh could be seen oozing to the top of her heavily corseted body. It must have been damnably uncomfortable in there. "I can't wait until it's time to think of plantings for the garden, come the spring. To start moving things out of the hothouse."

Max, hoping the old dear was not contagious, nodded, smiled, and looked with deliberation at his sizzling-with-unread-news paper. Her cold could only get worse, as the heating in the compartment was uncertain: While his feet—indeed, the entire left side of his body—froze, his right forearm and elbow, near the vent that ran along one side of the compartment, felt as if they might ignite. He couldn't decide whether or not to remove his overcoat and in the end decided to leave it on.

He took a pen out of his pocket for the crossword and folded the broadsheet pages back with a sharp *snap*, again as if they contained a matter of some urgency awaiting his immediate attention. But he had abandoned all hope some minutes before.

"I've bought some of my son's favorite chocolates," she told him. "Randolph. Randolph, Viscount Nathersby. You may have heard of him? The photographer?"

"It sounds familiar to me, yes. What is the name of his business?"

She looked horrified. "It doesn't have a *name*. He's not in *trade*, you know." Max gathered that would be considered tacky, this whole working-for-a-living thing. "Well, not *precisely* in trade," she amended, clearly deciding it necessary to clarify this difficult point for him. "It's just that word gets round. Recommendations. A friend of a friend, you know the sort of thing."

"Not in trade, then," said Max, solemn and straight-faced.

"Oh, my dear man, *no*. No, indeed! The very idea. He was a Pootle-Fitzbutton on his great-grandmother's side, you know."

"Quite." He was not quite sure what was "quite" about it but it was a good all-purpose word and he couldn't think of what else to say. He wanted to sound agreeable without precisely agreeing with her, since he wasn't listening closely.

The train was going over the nine-arch viaduct, which meant they were about halfway to Nether Monkslip. Just then a series of musical notes erupted in the close carriage—the ring of a mobile phone. Max automatically reached for his jacket pocket but almost instantly knew it wasn't his ring.

With a flustered hoot of apology, Lady Baynard groped around in her capacious bag, finally locating and silencing the device.

Max thought, Does everyone have a mobile these days? He had recognized the tune, only because it was the ubiquitous "Speak Now." He thought it a clever song to use for a ringtone, but was astonished someone of Lady Baynard's generation would choose it.

She caught his look of faint surprise and said, exasperated, "One of the twins programmed it for me and I don't know how to change it to something more suitable."

And what would that be? Max wondered. "Rule, Britannia!"?

"Those twins have too much time on their hands. I knew that

no good would come of their visit to the castle. Of *all* their coming." She harrumphed and snuffled a bit more into the handkerchief, then with a swipe at her nose, carried on: "Visit indeed. More like a siege. The situation is positively *brew*ing. I have had the most *fright*ful sense of foreboding for weeks now. Someone is going to—oh, I don't know. Be hurt! First my brother is taken ill—he's never ill. And then . . ."

She talked for some time and he listened with but half an ear. The news he'd had from George about Paul's wife still distracted him, and memories of Paul swirled in his mind like ghosts.

". . . the twins. I tell you, no good can come of it."

He'd missed much of what she'd been saying.

"Twins? And how old are they?" he asked politely, in truth more interested in deflecting the topic of Lady Baynard's foreboding, which topic he felt might be a lengthy one with many alleys and byways and shuddery detours.

"Fourteen. They're my brother's children. You know how they're into *every*thing at that age. And these two behave as if they were raised in a barn. I blame the mother. I don't believe in mixed marriages, never have. No good can come of it. The girl was a *commoner*, you see. A rackety upbringing, a father in trade! I think she said her mother was a shop clerk. I wonder sometimes if even that is true. It doesn't bear thinking about. Gwynyth wanted to be a grand lady, of course, but ladies are born, not made."

Max struggled to conceal his wonder that someone at Lady Baynard's evident stage of life—he placed her roughly in her seventies—could be the aunt to children of fourteen. She didn't appear interested in enlightening him on this subject, instead saying, "Some days, I am just happy both of them are alive and breathing. On others, I have simply given up hope of their making a productive contribution to society. *She* may be all right, I suppose. Amanda. I'm not certain about *him*."

"Early days, isn't it?" said Max mildly. "Fourteen is so young. They just don't know how young it is." The train was lurching back and forth now, as if the driver were listening to samba music. Max returned his gaze to his newspaper, but still without much hope she would take the hint. People, particularly people of Lady Baynard's generation and background, tended to gravitate toward members of the clergy, regardless of the setting or circumstance, seeking advice much in the way people, on hearing one is a doctor, will launch into a vivid description of their recent bilious attack or their gallbladder surgery. Frequently, Max found himself called upon for similar ad hoc consultations. Presumably, anything having to do with mortality fell under his purview equally with that of Dr. Winship, the village doctor.

But this time he was to be spared, after all. Lady Baynard merely said, "Early days? Why, when I was their age I was practically running a household in my mother's stead. I was married soon after that—none of this business of putting my career first and delaying starting a family and so on. What nonsense! This is a coddled generation, Father. Too coddled. Coddled to the point of *use*lessness." There was a bit more of this and then, with a final "Harrumph!" she began scrabbling in her Gladstone bag. As she did, some of her shopping fell out, and Max spent the next few moments collecting the apples and assorted other goods that rolled under the seats and to the far edges of the carriage. Somehow in the confusion and fluster one apple ended up in Max's pocket, a fact he didn't realize until he was back at the vicarage.

Finally, she subsided into a fluffy white mass of knitting, and began furiously to ply large wooden needles. It looked like she was making a downy pup tent. Max returned to his reading and the rest of the trip passed in relative and amiable silence.

CHAPTER 3

At the Maharajah

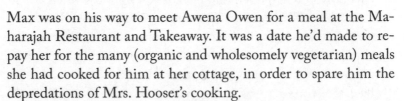

Max was on his way to meet Awena Owen for a meal at the Maharajah Restaurant and Takeaway. It was a date he'd made to repay her for the many (organic and wholesomely vegetarian) meals she had cooked for him at her cottage, in order to spare him the depredations of Mrs. Hooser's cooking.

Awena had again invited Max for dinner, shortly after his return from London. He'd asked her to meet him at the restaurant instead. Overall, he preferred taking a meal at the Maharajah partly because of the Cavalier's gossip machine, which was even louder than its new espresso machine. Most villagers were willing to overlook the sometimes glacial service in favor of being at the center of the village's social networking site.

"My treat, for a change," he'd told Awena. "I insist."

He had not long before put down the phone from speaking with his mother, who had called from Le Havre. She was on the *Queen Mary II*, continuing the almost completely peripatetic existence she'd led during her widowhood. She would be spending Christmas in the Caribbean.

She sounded the same, lovely and otherworldly, but changed since his father died—more outgoing, more adventurous. Max didn't like putting it this way, but she seemed to have come into her own with his father's passing. Max regretted how little he saw of her but realized there was little point to guilt—her active social life made her hard to reach anymore. On the phone, she mentioned as she often did how relieved she was to know he had a nice, safe job at last—she had understood vaguely that before he was involved in "police work" but not that he had been MI5.

After saying his good-byes he'd taken care of some accumulated paperwork, caught up with various e-mails, and then taken

Thea for a long walk. She'd been cooped up with Luther during much of the time Max had been in London and he felt it was the least he could do to make it up to her. Dogs are generally eager to please but he sensed Thea might be close to a prolonged pout. As Max had sat down at his desk, the dog asleep beside him, an unholy yowl had emerged from the cushion at his back: Luther shot out from behind like toothpaste out of a tube and executed a stuck landing on Thea's back. As the dog began racing around the room, Luther reared up on his haunches, clawing the air for balance in a bronco-like effort as ill-conceived and doomed as some of the early Scottish border excursions into England. Fortunately, Thea, who rather tended to expect the best of everyone, remained more baffled than offended by these attacks.

He walked with her until they came to a rest at the top of Hawk Crest, in the copse the villagers called Nunswood. This was Thea's favorite leisurely walk, full of exciting detours. They stood near the menhirs, all that remained of an ancient culture where human sacrifice may have played a role in appeasing whatever gods existed then. At least, that was what the innkeepers liked to tell the tourists, who listened, wide-eyed and gullible, like children being told a ghost story at bedtime.

Beneath the Crest ran the River Puddmill, which rambled by the cottages and ended in a splashy marriage with the English Channel at a scenic falling off not far from where he stood. Today the sea was visible, and in the far distance he could see the dark outline of the towers of Chedrow Castle. Max was reminded of his recent travel companion, now tucked safely away in her stronghold. Man and dog stood in companionable silence, enjoying the changing landscape, the castle appearing and disappearing in the mist like something out of a Grimm Brothers' tale. The scent of snow, slightly chemical but clean as fresh linen, was in the air— the tang of winter was like a tonic, invigorating but also infusing Max with a dreamy nostalgia. It was his favorite time of year.

Thea's too, apparently. With her long black-and-tan tresses ruffled by the wind, her eyes searching the horizon, head lifted high and backlit against the dying light, Thea reminded him as she often did of some film star posed for a movie still. Today it was Scarlett O'Hara, challenging God and nature, and vowing never to be hungry again.

Max ran a hand over the knobby silken smoothness of Thea's head. She was one of the most good-hearted of dogs in a kingdom full of good-hearted dogs. He had adopted her when he first came to the village, but soon realized the process was in fact mutual. Irrationally or not, he felt that Thea had chosen him.

"OK, girl, it's dinnertime. I get it. Let's go."

He returned home to feed both animals (which he had learned to do in separate rooms, Luther soon adding "food bandit" to his CV) then he took a quick shower. As he was buttoning a clean shirt he was reminded of his recent conversation with George Greenhouse. For the first time since he'd moved into the vicarage, he thought to look for Paul's shirt in the top of his closet.

And he couldn't find it where he knew he had left it. He had moved house several times in the years since the tragedy but he knew he wouldn't ever throw out that shirt.

He went to find Mrs. Hooser. As usual, much like the cartoon character Pig-Pen, she could easily be located by the cloud of dirt and dust and racket she created wherever she happened to be. This time, he followed the trail of hoovering noises interspersed with the crash of falling objects to his study.

"Mrs. Hooser, have you seen the shirt that was tucked on the top shelf of my closet?"

She knew right away what he meant. "It needed tossing out, dinnit?" she replied, proud of her proactive approach to housekeeping. "But I figured I'd get some good use of it first. I used it a few days ago to polish the silver."

"To polish . . . the . . ." he began, then said, sharply: "Show me, please."

She led him into the kitchen. There, under the sink, a fire hazard in the making, was what was left of Paul's shirt. It had been cut into bits, and some of those bits were dark with tarnished silver.

Max was aghast. For the first time in their relationship, which consisted of many calamitous mishaps, much broken crockery, and gallons of spilt milk, Max was angry, actually trembling with rage. He struggled to control himself, to conceal his anger—how could the woman be expected to know? Still, the collar was intact, the double layers of material too thick to be of use for her polishing job. But still . . .

"Mrs. Hooser." He drew a deep breath, then tried again. "Did you not wonder why it was on the top shelf of my closet, wrapped in plastic, and not stuffed into a drawer? Or on a hanger? Why—?"

But he broke off. What was the use? Gently, he took the garment from her.

"I thought it were to be throwed away. I—"

Somehow he couldn't bear to listen. He said, "I'm putting what's left of this shirt in a plastic bag and I'm putting it back on the shelf in my closet. It is never to be touched again, Mrs. Hooser. Never for any reason. Do you understand?" Seeing her confusion, he added gently, "It's very important that this shirt not be touched again. Do you understand?"

She nodded, still puzzled, but the message seemed to get through. He was "her" vicar and she'd do whatever he said, no matter how barmy it seemed to her.

He left early for his meeting with Awena, in part wanting to take a stroll around the serene village and use the time to collect himself. The memory of that shirt, horrid memento of his worst day, stayed with him. He knew he should get rid of it but also knew he never could.

To calm his mind, he breathed deeply of the winter air, fragrant with the mixed scents of leaden clouds and bread baking at the Cavalier Tea Room and Garden. A misty winter light spread across the village, puddling at the feet of passersby, making them appear to float toward him.

In its perfection, Max often thought there was something

magical about Nether Monkslip; it soothed his spirit just to walk around the familiar streets and lanes, past the well-known shops, now alight against the encroaching dark.

The other evening Max had walked by the Village Hall and heard familiar voices raised in song:

> *And did those feet in ancient time*
> *Walk upon England's mountain green?*

He had hummed along to the old hymn, pleased at this sign the village and particularly the Women's Institute had returned to some normalcy after what was delicately referred to as the "recent unpleasantness." It had been the first time he'd felt the enchantment of the village reasserting itself.

The recent demise of a villager by violent means had left a void in the spite and gossip categories and Max, knowing that nature abhors a vacuum, had feared someone would rise up to seize the throne so recently vacated. But so far no one had. While the unsavory episode had left the villagers in a state of shock for some time, there was no arguing that the village, despite the usual carefully nourished grievances and mild skirmishes, was now a friendlier place.

Max stepped briefly into his jewel-like church, St. Edwold's, which he imagined was what stepping into a large Fabergé egg would be like for a tiny harvest mouse in a children's tale. The sacred space beneath the vaulted ceiling and carved bosses shone with artistry and antiquity; it seemed to say men needled by doubt could be, if not won over to God's ways, at least seduced by the beauty of what mankind could create, swayed by the dedication of the stonemasons and craftsmen who had lived many centuries before.

He stood in the nave looking to his left, at the image that had appeared there on the wall. Mrs. Hooser's small son Tom had been the first to notice the face of a long-haired man, eyes closed, strongly resembling the face on the Shroud of Turin. The image was emerging through the whitewash again and he'd have to get Maurice on it yet again. He didn't need a load of miracle tourists and day-trippers pouring in to view what was surely no more than some weird by-product of the perpetually leaking roof.

Now as he walked away from the church, the sound of its ringing bells counted out the hours of the village, as they had always done, even though now a recording was substituted for all but special occasions. He felt that something had been lost in the quality of the sound, but who, after all, would elect to have his own personal Quasimodo swinging from the bell tower?

Nether Monkslip's economic and social life, like that of most villages in England, orbited around the sun of the shops of the High Street. Shopping for the day's supplies of food, drink, and home and kitchen accoutrements was largely a matter of popping in and out of the various establishments, although most villagers did their monthly "big" shopping in Staincross Minster or Monkslip-super-Mare. Over the centuries, various lanes and alleys and by-ways had sprouted off the High, footpaths and grooves in the grass hardening by use and tradition into appendages of the main route through the village. Since Nether Monkslip had remained remarkably free from pillage, raid, and plunder, it had not evolved like many English villages in a cluster around a large building for defense or even around a common green. Water, too, had been available in abundance, in the form of the River Puddmill. All of these factors affected how the village had grown. It seemed haphazard, even slapdash, but the logic was there once one knew where to look for it. The one universal "rule" was that the church had long occupied a central position, physically and psychically, in the lives of the villagers, as had the pubs—Nether Monkslip was anchored by the Hidden Fox on one end and the Horseshoe on the other.

There was no flower shop—in Nether Monkslip nearly everyone grew and arranged their own flowers, and shared any excess with neighbors. Similarly, many cottages had a vegetable patch, and nothing that could be shared ever went to waste.

Also central to village life was the post office, which had survived a wave of government closures even while hundreds throughout Britain had succumbed. Along with the church, this was where villagers met to deal in the coin of news and speculation. The red telephone kiosk, itself a throwback to an earlier time, sat like a beacon outside, and at night was lighted to cast a reassuring glow over passersby.

The village store which contained the post office even offered organic wine, milk, and cheeses, although faced with stiff competition from *La Maison Bleue*, which sold *real* cheese, according to proprietress Mme. Cuthbert. Max's steps took him past the shop now, with its white ceramic pig with red collar which served as a doorstop. The pig was usually accompanied by Sadie, a fine-looking (and real) bichon frise. The store was operated by Mme. Lucie Cuthbert, wife of local historian and aspiring author Frank Cuthbert. Mme. Cuthbert viewed her husband's scribbling in his off-duty time with an amused Gallic detachment, as did most of the villagers, seeing it as a harmless hobby along the lines of stamp collecting or brass rubbing.

Looking in the shop window as he passed, Max saw Mme. Cuthbert was branching out into selling imported French oddments like dish towels, stationery, and artisan soaps and toiletries. Max knew she also sold many of her oils and soaps via Awena Owen's shop, Goddessspell. Mme. Cuthbert was from the Channel Islands and was a frequent traveler to France, where she went to stock up on supplies. Tonight she was organizing a wine tasting, according to a sign in the window of her shop. Seeing Max, she stepped outside to greet him.

"A blizzard is on the way," she informed him. She pronounced it with the accent on the first syllable: *blee*-zar. "I wonder how many will brave it tonight for a wine tasting." She shrugged. "If this were France, I would have no worries."

"A blizzard?" said Max. "How extraordinary. We rarely get much snow in this part of the world."

"I know," she said, an indefinably Gallic look of satisfied gloom on her face. Just then there came the sound of breaking glass from within as Frank knocked over one of the little tables Madame had so charmingly dressed for the tasting with red checkered tablecloths. He appeared at the door of the shop wearing his usual beret, now looking like a sheepish member of the French Resistance. Mme. Cuthbert's air of doom deepened. She was clearly holding her fire until Max had passed, which he hastily did now.

Tara, the yoga instructor who rented space at Awena's Goddessspell, came sprinting by on her daily run, copper-red ponytail swinging out behind her like a metronome. The chill in the air barely impeded her progress as she shot past, aiming a friendly wave in his direction. At the same moment, Mrs. Hooser's daughter Tildy Ann ran across the High, clearly on her way to lessons at Mlle. Chevalier's in a bouncing pink tutu and ballet slippers. Her younger brother, unusually, was not with her: She rarely let Tom out of her sight. Tildy Ann's ballet lessons were being paid for on a barter system—Mrs. Hooser swept out the studio on occasion, an open area more amenable to her havoc-wreaking housekeeping methods than was the crowded little vicarage.

He turned off the High into River Lane, near the starting point of the yearly duck race, where the river slowly churned and eddied its way to the pastel pink and blue houses of Monkslip-super-Mare on the English Channel. Still early to meet Awena, he slowed his pace to walk by the river, frozen now at its edges. Eventually he doubled back toward the Maharajah, where he was politely shown a table to await her arrival.

Awena always made rather an entrance—part of the fascination of knowing her, Max thought, was that one never knew what blazingly jewel-like creation she'd show up wearing.

The restaurant was a favorite of hers—she and the owner Mr. Vijay were friends. Awena had spent some time in his country on a spiritual sojourn and had a rudimentary grasp of the language. His English, however, was precise and idiomatic: "It remains to be seen," was his frequent, cheerful reply to any queries about the state of his health, his business, or the world.

"*Namaste,*" she said as she entered, pressing her palms together and giving him a slight bow of respect, which he returned. Only Awena, thought Max, could do this sort of thing with unself-conscious grace. She then waved to him, sitting at a corner table by the fire, where a pile of heavy logs was being blackened by colorful flames.

He was not disappointed in her costume. She came billowing over, draperies flying. She wore a long emerald-velvet cloak over a gown of burgundy satin; the hood of the cloak glittered with semiprecious stones. She removed and carefully draped the cloak over a nearby chair. He saw that her thick dark hair, remarkable for the plume of white at her forehead, was caught up in some sort of jeweled clasp at the back of her neck. She might have been headed for a night at the opera, although this was pretty much Awena's usual attire. She had told him once she thought of adornment as a way of showing gratitude and pleasure for the gift of her life.

Above the portrait neckline of her dress her face shone, handsome and serene in profile, warm and animated as she turned from attending to her outer wrap.

Max thought she looked rather like a queen awakened in a fairy tale, an image reinforced by the stately way she always carried herself.

"How are you?" she asked, sitting across from him. She folded her hands on the table. "And how are you and Luther getting along?"

"Luther is getting along fine," Max told her. "I don't think he cares how I'm getting along."

"Luther," she said solemnly, "is a very old soul."

"Humph," said Max. "Well, the old soul has an odd habit of trying to climb the phone cord, especially when I'm talking on the phone. It is a very good thing he has nine lives. I think he's on his eighth right now. It's Thea I'm worried about."

"Luther has always put the 'cat' in 'catastrophe.' Thea will be fine; she's an even older soul. If dogs could talk, I think Thea would be saying, 'The greatest prayer is patience.'"

"Do you? I think she'd also be asking when Luther is due to leave."

"May I offer you the white table wine if you're having a curry?" said a lilting voice at his side. "It's a new arrival recommended to us by *La Maison Bleue*." Mr. Vijay's wife having died some years before, his daughter Prema had moved to the village to help him with the restaurant. It was she who stood there, reed slim and attractive, to take their drinks order. She and Awena shared some discussion of the night's vegetarian specials. Awena always asked how things in the restaurant were prepared so she could try to duplicate the dishes at home.

Once Prema had taken their drinks order, Awena turned back to him and said: "You collect strays, Max. Mrs. Hooser, Thea, now the cat. You're hopeless—thank heaven."

"Never hopeless. As soon as Luther leaves, all hope will return."

The arch look from her fine eyes said as clearly as words: *It remains to be seen.*

"One more life for Luther, remember?" he said. "And I promise it will be a long one once he can be returned to the church. I think he's really just bored."

She smiled and looked around. The restaurant had been converted from one of the old houses on River Lane and resembled an old pub run by a former memsahib of colonial India, with statues, prints, and hangings in every bright or pale color of the rainbow. In summer, each table would hold small vases of flowers from the garden in back of the restaurant. In this season, Mr. Vijay had artfully arranged twigs and branches in a winter arrangement.

Prema returned with their wine and they ordered fried pakoras to share. Awena chose a main course of grilled eggplant and tomato, Max the chicken tikka masala.

They chatted awhile, first talking about Mr. Whippet, an elderly parishioner who recently had defied the odds to rally, yet again, when doctors had placed him at death's door, giving him mere days to live.

"I brought some groceries round to his house the other day," Awena told him. "Made sure he had his medications and so on."

And paid for it all from out of her own pocket, Max knew. "There are some church funds, not many . . ." he began.

"Funds that are needed for a dozen other uses. It's all right, Max. It's a small amount—now it's winter, it's mainly food in tins or jars from my larder—crops I grew from seed. The cost to me is negligible and I'm happy to do it. Elka chips in with bread from the bakery; Lucie Cuthbert sends over cheese from the shop. Mr. Whippet may never have dined so well in all his life. And we all take turns driving him to his appointments. Lily, Suzanna—everyone."

"You're all undoubtedly the reason he keeps rallying."

"He's a dear man," said Awena. "He reminds me very much of my father. He likes to talk about the old days in the village, and I enjoy listening."

"Still, what you're doing is a great kindness. Providing the company as much as the sustenance."

"We're just 'doing unto others,' a precept unsurpassed as a pithy ethical framework. I hope someone would do as much for me if I become ill."

"Karma," he said.

"Count on it."

CHAPTER 4

I See You

Max and Awena sat on happily in the soft glow of the small red silk-fringed lamp on their table. The milky, veined whiteness of Awena's skin shone above the neckline of her dress. Max watched as she turned her head at the approach of Prema, carrying their first course, with a light, graceful lift of her chin; the green gemstones of her earrings swung against the column of her neck, which gleamed like marble in the firelight.

At that moment Miss Pitchford, who with the postmistress functioned as the village's breaking-news organization, happened to be walking by the restaurant. She stopped to peer in the window. Snow had settled decoratively in each corner of its windowpanes and Max and Awena, rapt in conversation, didn't notice they were being observed. Miss Pitchford, face alight with her new information, carried on walking home with a renewed vigor. Gossip added years to her life.

Meanwhile Max and Awena had gotten the plates and silverware sorted, and had helped themselves to the fried vegetable delicacies and mint yogurt sauce. Then Awena said, "You are coming to my party, aren't you?"

"December twenty-first, right? I don't think I'd miss it. Half the village plans to be there."

"I hope so," she said. "I've laid in enough food for two villages."

"Any special significance to the date?" he asked, with feigned innocence. He paid close attention to the patterns of the moon, noting with satisfaction the passing of time and seasons as the planets turned and the stars marked their passage. Max had taken to noticing moon phases and star movements even more since coming to Nether Monkslip, since there was so little interference from artificial light. The stars often shone like diamonds on a bed of black velvet.

But this year there had been special notice paid by astronomers and newspapers to the solstice, because of an unusual confluence of events.

"It's the winter solstice, as you probably know," she said. "I'm celebrating the Yule—the shortest day of the year, symbolizing the sun's rebirth, and the return of new life to the earth. But I'm billing it as a holiday party, which it is. There's no reason you or anyone else can't be there to celebrate."

"I didn't think there was a reason. If there were I'd simply incorporate your ceremony into mine, in the great tradition of assimilating pagan worship into something the Church could tolerate. Think: Christmas trees."

"*Neo*pagan, if you please." She crossed one leg over the other and the small ornaments on her beaded anklet made a faint clicking sound.

"Sorry. Neopagan. This winter solstice is a bit unusual, did you know? There will be a full moon that night. *And* a total lunar eclipse. All quite uncommon . . . *and* we just had a blue moon in November."

She nodded. "The moon will turn red. Bloodred, or at least pink. I hope the weather cooperates so we can see it."

"I wonder what early humans thought, seeing these events, and having no rational explanation. It must have been terrifying with only a Sky Wizard or whatever they had to consult."

She laughed. "'Sky Wizard.' Please. They were observant people—searching for meaning in the changing seasons, because their lives depended on it. Whereas all we need to do to know the weather is turn on the telly."

"Well, not with one hundred percent accuracy."

"True. I wouldn't be at all surprised if what we call the pagans of northern Europe didn't have a better grip on the predicting situation."

She went on, her voice as melodious as falling water. "Every religion stresses the importance of nature, in its own way. I hold with an integrated view that encompasses everything living—and from what I have seen of you, so do you, Max. Most religions regard the inventions of man—science—as part of religion, part of the universe's design for us. No one wants to go back to living in dark caves, but few stop to wonder if it isn't a beneficent force that led Edison to invent electricity."

"Discover it, actually. And Faraday, among others, set the stage for the lightbulb. But I do get your point. It's what man is doing with all his inventions—like strip mining—that worries me. Correction: frightens me."

"The Druids—environmental awareness pioneers, every last one, working from home in Anglesey—would not have stood for it."

"No question," he agreed. Awena seldom referred to her past, except to say she was from Wales, and had had a hardscrabble upbringing on the wild but beautiful west coast of Anglesey.

She paused to take a sip of her wine.

"I think the old Druids were the real thing, but their beliefs have been lost to us. Partly because they don't seem to have been awfully interested in converting or eradicating other people. They were healers and seers who wanted to protect the sacred homes of the spirits—the plants, the trees, the running waters, the hills. I believe absolutely they had the gift of prophecy, too, and could read the signs of nature to reveal our true business on this planet—but that's a voice drowned out by the noise and bustle of our modern age."

"Given where you're from, perhaps you have an affinity for the old beliefs."

"I will say that where I'm from has revised my outlook on holiday gift-giving traditions. As a teenager, like most teenagers, I coveted 'stuff.' All the things you see in magazines. Then I stood watching as my father headed out one freezing morning in his little fishing boat. I think that was the end of my wanting. Just keeping us in the basics was killing him."

She dabbed a napkin at her lips, which were as usual innocent of makeup and as softly pink as rose petals. The remembrance appeared to have made her blush; personal disclosure was uncommon for the self-contained Awena. "Anyway, there's a lot of nonsense spouted about the Druids—whose religion, by the way, was recently recognized *as* a religion in Britain under charity law, did you know?"

He nodded. "I saw something about it in the paper a couple of months ago."

"The fact is, they were eradicated so ruthlessly—fear, you know—that we don't know many specifics. What passes for Druidism now—who can say if it remotely resembles the original? Their shrines were destroyed; their vast knowledge was lost. But they worshiped the spirit, and the knowledge to be discovered in nature—that much is clear. I've often thought they were not so very different from the old contemplatives, the monks of Nether Monkslip. If only the Abbey Ruins here in the village could speak—I think they share the same energy as is found up on Hawk Crest, in the center of the circle of menhirs there."

Max nodded. In the stillness of Hawk Crest, he had felt the energy she described, but it was an eerie feeling and he had kept it to himself. A vicar couldn't run about spouting that sort of thing, but he knew the Crest had a special energy of its own.

"And who knows?" Awena, fully engaged now, airily waved her empty fork. "Maybe one day a cave in Anglesey will give up its hidden secrets. Anyway, there is more than one path and there always has been."

Max was recalled by her words to a much earlier time when he had traveled to Maui, years before he had even thought of entering the priesthood. Maui in some ways resembled Awena's Anglesey, with its waves deafening during a storm, and its unspoilt beaches. He suddenly recalled, sitting in Mr. Vijay's colorful little restaurant, in a village he had never known existed, talking to a woman he could not now imagine never having met, how mesmerized he had been by the spill of light tumbling down a hillside. He remembered thinking at the time he could see why the ancient Hawaiians worshipped more than one god. A single god could not account for the glorious variety of nature to be found in the islands.

"But I doubt very much," she was saying, "that the ancients held the current view of heaven as some sort of exclusive men's club for white males only."

Max said, "There is no point of view less Christian."

"Pre-protestant England adored the Virgin Mary," said Awena. "Literally. That was all stamped out. Fear was behind that campaign, too, of course."

They were in the middle of their main course when Max, in answer to her question of what he'd been doing lately, said, "Well, I have today been among the great and the good."

"Oh? How is that?"

He put down his fork and took a sip of wine. "I came in on the train from Staincross Minster with Lady Baynard of Chedrow Castle."

"Ah. Interesting. I was just at the castle a few months ago. A bit of a situation brewing there, if you ask me."

Lady Baynard had used almost the same words. Max said so, and Awena replied, "I wonder what Oscar—that's Lord Footrustle, to you and me—I wonder what he's up to."

"How did you come to be there at the castle?" Max asked her.

"I was on the train to Staincross Minster—as I say, it was a few months ago. Late summer, or perhaps early fall. I remember the bees were a complete plague. I was going in to town to do some shopping. And there she was, the most remarkable creature. Like something out of Queen Victoria's court, swaddled in this old-fashioned jacket and skirt, and piercing one with that blue-eyed stare. But she seemed to know who I was and we got to talking about herbal remedies and things."

Max smiled behind the wineglass he'd raised to his lips. Everyone for miles around knew who Awena was, and she was much in demand. People often wanted her to consult on their home or gardening projects, to lend her knowledge of feng shui and blessings

for the home and the medicinal uses of herbs. She was likewise famous for her shop Goddessspell, the place of one-stop-shopping
for every item designed to soothe or enchant.

"She had a cold when I saw her," said Max.

"Yes, I gather it's always something with Lady Baynard.
Frightful hypochondriac, if you ask me. She seems to 'enjoy poor
health,' as the saying goes. And doesn't she love to natter on about
pedigrees and so forth? But I was able to recommend a few herbal
remedies—she said her stomach had been upset recently—and she
seemed excited by the possibility of growing her own fresh ingredients. She invited me out to the castle to advise her on what to plant
and where, for the spring. As I had some free time, I drove over the
following week."

"Where you found a situation brewing."

"Only because of the planned addition of these new members
of the family. I gather there was always a bit of a situation with
Lamorna there, and poor Lamorna had been around for years."
She caught herself up. "It's always 'poor Lamorna,' which is rather
a slight, isn't it?"

"Lamorna? Lady Baynard didn't mention her."

"I'm not surprised. I *am* surprised her grandmother remem-
bers Lamorna exists most days. Unless she wants her to do a job
of unpleasant work. I gather Lamorna is rather stuck over there at
the castle—financial reasons. Or she let herself get stuck."

He took a bite of his meal, which was accented by a wonder-
fully light, spicy sauce of tomato and (so Awena informed him)
coriander. "So tell me—what's brewing?"

"Well, I'll have to go back twenty-five or more years to Lamorna's childhood to put you in the picture. Lamorna is the Footrustles' official poor relation—I gather every family has one. This
is the common gossip: Her father, who loved beautiful things, de-
tested poor Lamorna. All babies may be beautiful but they grow in
all sorts of unexpected ways, into all sorts of unexpected things."

"Beautiful name, though."

Awena nodded. "It's haunting, isn't it? She was named after the beauty spot in Cornwall where her parents met, so the story goes. Anyway, her grandmother pretended for a while to love her, sensing somehow that this was a basic requirement for grand-motherhood, but this fooled no one, especially Lamorna. The saving grace was her mother, Lea. She had delayed having children only to find when she wanted to she couldn't have them. Lamorna, adopted, was her most precious child and in Lea's eyes, uniquely beautiful. As I say, her mother really seems to have loved her but she died along with her father when Lamorna was just a girl."

"So she came into the care of her grandmother. Leticia, Lady Baynard."

"If you could call it that," said Awena. "The days of the personal maid having vanished, Lady Baynard seems to have latched on to Lamorna for the purpose."

"Wasn't she sent away to school? That would be the norm for children at that level of society."

"She was, if only briefly. It exposed her to things and people outside the castle, which might have been a good thing, but I gather she was teased a lot. Anyway, public school was said to have been a disaster and she ended up attending a local day school in Monkslip-super-Mare."

Awena's words were spoken with measured kindness, as were most of her opinions, but it was clear Lamorna was the original ugly duckling who had never made it to the beautiful swan stage.

"So the grandmother—Lady Baynard—rejected the girl? Rather like an animal rejecting its young?"

Awena nodded. "Something like that. After a few failed attempts to mold Lamorna into what she wanted in the way of a grandchild."

She lay down her fork and said ruminatively, "This happened well before my time, but this was the scuttlebutt as it went round the village: Leticia rode the girl day and night to try to get her to pay more attention to her appearance—to make her what she thought of as marriageable. When Leticia's attempts to get Lamorna to stick to a slimming regime and to 'do something' about her hair and makeup failed—backfired, even—she finally gave it up as a lost cause. From that point on she seemed to start looking for ways to make Lamorna useful—to herself."

Max thought suddenly of a mother-and-daughter team he'd sat next to at Waterloo, bickering over their meal, engaged in a battle of wills that neither could win. He shook his head.

"Her own granddaughter," he said. "What a shame."

"I gather that was part of the problem, where Leticia was concerned. Lamorna wasn't her granddaughter *by blood*. She was adopted as a baby from . . . was it Serbia? No, Russia—that was it. Anyway, you know what these old families can be like. 'Blood will out,' and all that rot. Leo, the father, seems to have felt cheated, as if he'd paid for and planted a packet of honeysuckle seeds but weeds had appeared instead. You can't demand your money back, can you? The poor tyke. You see, there were also emotional and developmental problems. There sometimes were with the children from some of the orphanages over there. Anyway, she seems finally to have withdrawn into herself, and never reemerged on the other side of adolescence. None of this endeared Lamorna to everyone in her new family."

"Adopted," said Max. "Unfortunately, I've seen this type of reaction before. Tragic when it happens. A child is always a joyful thing, no matter how it arrives. So, you went to the castle, and . . . ?"

"I confess," said Awena, "I went as much out of curiosity as anything. The castle is famous and the one time I'd tried to visit, most of the grounds were closed off. So I went. Randolph—that's Lady Baynard's son—met me at the door, gave me a quick tour, and then took me out to meet his mother in the garden."

They lingered a long time over dessert, savoring the company and the bottle of wine. One of the things Max had loved about Italy, where he'd spent a riotous gap year, was the way conversations expanded to fill the available time. Luncheons inched into late afternoon, afternoons painted in his memory in muted primary colors—reds and yellows and greens. Dinners ended when no one was left able to drive and were instead invited to spend the night. There was a possibility the cycle would repeat itself endlessly, with guests never leaving, and no one caring if they did. Talking with Awena was like that.

She looked carefully at him after a long but comfortable silence, out of those extraordinary eyes of a pale, translucent purplish-blue that mesmerized all who saw her. "Are you happy here, Max?" she asked him. "In Nether Monkslip?"

"Yes," he said. "I find that I am. Ridiculously so. What is it the vicar says in the movie they made of *Sense and Sensibility*? Something about a small parish and keeping chickens?"

She smiled, nodded. "And giving very short sermons. Hugh Grant was wonderful in that film."

She didn't mention that she thought Max bore a striking resemblance to the devilishly handsome actor, but she did think so.

Max returned her smile. "Well, I do try to keep the sermons short, but I'll have to get some chickens in. As soon as Luther leaves."

He spun his wineglass in both his hands. He was attracted to Awena, this he knew. What man would not want a woman as fine-looking as Awena? But since it was also an attraction of like minds, somehow he felt the more dangerous territory could be, well, skirted, as it were. A man in his position couldn't just tear about the way he had done in his youth. There had been opportunities and he had made the most of them. Even then, working for MI5 presented its own unique problems in this regard. Sleeping with someone outside the roster of available women in his own field was frowned upon—"counterfeiting," it was called, for the necessity of lying in these outsider relationships. There was a ruder term for it, of course; there always was. These mixed affairs were almost by definition doomed. There were a few young women among his cohorts with whom he'd had affairs of varying degrees of emotional attachment, especially in the hothouse atmosphere of working a case together. That type of situation brought with it its own problems, as it did in any profession.

There were several "outsiders" to whom he'd been authentically attracted—attracted for the long haul. Beyond that short list there were temporary attractions, and of course he had succumbed to some of them. All of his comrades had. But it was completely unfair on the women themselves. The situation was absurd, as well as occasionally dangerous: He could never confess what it was he really did for a living. And he never met anyone he could trust enough to confide in—putting aside the fact that such a confidence would have been a complete breach of the domestic spy agency's code.

He was content now with his life—and yet . . . Max only a few weeks before had found one of the acolytes reading a men's magazine in an off-duty moment. He recalled assuring the embarrassed Alfred that women were a miracle of engineering, and that the boy's pleasure in looking at them was part of nature's plan. "Just don't make the mistake of thinking the women in this magazine are real, in any sense. The publisher is selling fantasy—not hers, but yours. If you want a girl in your life, go find one to talk to. Then be sure you listen to what she has to say."

Later Max had reflected he might not be overqualified to speak on this subject. He wanted a woman in his own life, but living in Nether Monkslip, where everyone heard you sneeze before you even knew you had a cold, this was out of the question. Seeking out a life's partner somewhere outside the village—he had time for that exactly never. Content, busy, happy, and possibly wanting to avoid the whole issue, Max supposed God would take care of that in his own good time, as He did everything else.

Now, looking at Awena, he realized he was back in somewhat the same MI5-type situation he'd so recently escaped. He respected her completely—a casual affair was unthinkable, even leaving aside what it would do to her reputation. About his own reputation he didn't much give a damn, but he wasn't going to be reckless on both their behalfs.

He would have to venture outside the village for romance, he realized, if he didn't want to live alone forever.

And yet he was strangely reluctant to join that search party.

"More wine?" he asked Awena, lifting the bottle.

He walked her home that night. She invited him in for coffee and brandy but as tempting as it was, it had been a long day's journey, and they had lingered for well over two hours over dinner.

Walking back to the vicarage, he looked up and saw a white moon anointing the sky, waxing toward fullness. As he watched, it became shot through with clouds, nearly vanishing.

CHAPTER 5

Many Are Called

As Max had walked Thea earlier that day, winding down the afternoon, DCI Cotton of the Monkslip-super-Mare police had only just begun to gear up for one of the major cases of his career. He'd been at Chedrow Castle since midmorning when the call had come through about the finding of Lord Footrustle's body. He was barely on his way, Detective Sergeant Essex sitting at his side, when his mobile phone rang with a new announcement— the body of Lady Baynard had just been found, as well.

A twofer. Except in cases of a murder-suicide, which couldn't be ruled out yet, that sort of thing didn't happen often in a policeman's life.

He'd spent the day either interviewing the residents of the castle or colluding with his colleagues on the forensics team, seeing what was to be seen—a lot of blood in the case of the old man, and a peaceful if surprised-looking corpse in the case of the old woman, his sister. When the inhabitants of Chedrow had gone to look for her, she had at last been found surrounded by her pots of flowers and her bags of potting soil, in a garden hothouse not far from the main building of the castle. The butler in both cases had found the corpses.

The butler did it? Far too predictable, that solution, but always a possibility. Only in fiction did the butler *not* do it. They were the last of the put-upon employees, a dying breed, born forelock-tuggers with a grudge. One final demand for a scone buttered *just* so might have sent the poor man right over the edge.

Now, as Max and Awena were finishing their meal in Nether Monkslip, Cotton was in his office in nearby Monkslip-super-Mare, awaiting the first forensic results, and plotting his strategy. For with nobs dying all over the castle, they'd want Scotland Yard brought in. Someone from the castle was probably shouting down the wire already—most likely that Randolph, the lady's son—demanding special treatment from on high. Randolph—*excuse* me, Viscount Nathersby—didn't look the sort not to throw his weight around at the first opportunity.

Well, stuff the Yard! Cotton was not an overly ambitious man, certainly not in the self-important, destructive way of some of his colleagues. But this was an important case, one that would be talked about and written about for decades (*Who Killed Lord Foot-rustle?*), and it had fallen straight into his lap. He'd go begging to the Yard for help as a last resort only, if and when it seemed there were no other way to solve the crime.

It certainly beat the usual drug deal resulting in murder on a council estate. Cotton had just come from such a case. He couldn't say so aloud, but these manor murders were much more to his taste. Here we had this Viscount Nathersby and his assistant Cilla. And Lester and Felberta—Lester being Randolph's younger brother and a real piece of work. Lady Jocasta Jones—daughter of Lord Footrustle—and Simon, her husband. The stunning Gwyn-yth—ex-wife to Lord Footrustle. Two teenagers—children of the deceased lord, by said stunning Gwynyth. The Vladimirovs—cook and butler. And that oh-so-strange Lamorna person.

Of course, the Rat Pack, also known as the gentlepersons of the press, would be all over this in a way they never were for a common, garden-variety drug deal gone bad. One couldn't blame them, really, but they added nothing to the equation except in those rare instances when Cotton found a way to manipulate them to his, and the department's, own ends.

Okay, so, where to start? He would need to handpick a team. Surely they'd give him full latitude here, if only to stop the phone from ringing off the hook in the guv's office. He'd want Detective Sergeant Essex beside him, for certain. A woman terrier in appearance, and terrier in mentality. She would worry a suspect until he gave up whatever he held most dear, including his freedom, just to be shut of her.

He picked up his phone and punched in some numbers.

"Get everyone in here who isn't absolutely, positively needed elsewhere. Meeting on the ground floor in the morning—the usual place. At eight A.M. That's eight *sharp*, tell Moynahan."

Absurdly pleased by this one-sided exchange, Cotton rang off sharply, without a good-bye, just as they did in the action films. Why waste valuable time? The phone rang back almost immediately. It was Sergeant Essex, wanting to know what sort of AV equipment he might need. It rather spoiled the effect of immediacy and derring-do that Cotton had been striving for, but he asked her for a bulletin board and some markers, wishing it could be something more, well, *dynamic*, like bullets or blasting caps. Again, really pushing his luck this time, he rang off without saying good-bye. The phone obediently remained silent.

Then he began furiously to think, pacing the office in a graceful swooping motion, back and forth, hands clasped beneath his coattails. He might have been an ice-skater.

By the time nine o'clock rolled around that night, he at least had a positive ID on the body. Oscar, Lord Footrustle, was definitely the deceased. Cause of death, multiple stab wounds, although the initial fierce thrust of the knife was believed to have been fatal. It seemed a trivial and unnecessary step, this preliminary run-up, this identification—the man had been found in his own home—his own castle—by people who knew him well. But without that certain starting point, the case could blow up before it even got started. And he supposed stab wounds might be mistaken for something else, or used to disguise some other sort of injury, but this time, what looked like a stab wound was just that. They'd run tox scans, to be sure, but there you had it.

The woman, now, this Oscar's sister. Lady—he ruffled through his papers once again—Leticia, Lady Baynard. Née Footrustle. An autopsy and tox scan for her, too, of course, given the circumstances, although the doctor was saying natural causes. As far as they knew now, the only possible connection to the murdered man's death was some sort of fatal shock coming over her at hearing of the finding of her brother's body. Otherwise, the timing was the purest coincidence. Well, they were twins after all, thought Cotton, and shock might be exaggerated in such a close relationship. Their twinship was a bit of information contained in one of the reports—the statement of the butler—but Cotton had known that without needing to be reminded.

For of course Cotton knew the family, or knew of them. They were the landed gentry of the area, well known to Cotton since he was busy learning his alphabet at school.

He planned what to say when he would meet his team the next day. On a schematic of the castle and its grounds which he'd obtained from the brochure they handed out to tourists, he carefully drew Xs to approximate where the bodies had been found. Again he worried that they were going to conduct this investigation with a fraction of the help Cotton knew he would need, which meant a lot of long days and sleepless nights ahead. A handful of CID officers, a few more uniforms to do the heavy lifting.

Who would be a policeman?

But Cotton did have an ace up his sleeve. And that ace, a

compassionate man with the heart of a vicar and the soul of a detective, was named Father Max Tudor.

❄   ❄   ❄

Max wasn't back at the vicarage for a moment before the phone began to ring. The late hour didn't surprise him. Emergencies always seemed to happen at night, keeping company with dark nights of the soul.

"Hello, Max." The two friends, policeman and vicar, had long since done away with using formal titles in private conversation. "We've got a situation over at Chedrow Castle."

Wondering only briefly at the "we," Max said, "What an odd coincidence. I was just talking about the family with a friend, over dinner. With Awena—you know her. I shared a train compartment with Lady Baynard just this morning."

"Holy—. I'll certainly need to hear more about that."

"Whatever I can recall I'll tell you, of course. Lady Baynard gave me a brief rundown on the state of affairs at the castle—and she did indicate she was uneasy about the situation. She called it a situation brewing." Max thought. "She said she'd been shopping and had bought some chocolates for her son."

"Which one?"

"Randolph, I think it was. She has more than one son?"

"Two, in fact."

"That's interesting in itself. She seemed to have forgotten one. At least, she didn't mention him. She told me Randolph's great-grandmother was a Goofe-Wattle or something. She also said her brother had been ill—recently, I gather. I wasn't listening closely, sorry. It may come to me."

Cotton sighed. It was the tag end of a long, long day. He needed a shower, and as much sleep as he could manage before the morning. He fought back the weariness and took a sip of some coffee that had been cold for half an hour.

"You said there was a situation," Max prompted him.

"Yes. It's rather an odd situation. She's dead, Max, I'm afraid."

"Dead? You don't mean . . ." Max knew they wouldn't be having this conversation if some criminal activity weren't at the heart of it.

"No. We think it was natural causes."

"I am sorry to hear that. But—why call me? And why, more to the point, are you involved? She wasn't murdered, you say."

"No. No, not murdered. To all appearances, she died a natural if unexpected death. It's her brother who makes this a 'situation.' That would be Lord Footrustle."

"He was killed," Max said flatly.

"He was. Stabbed by someone determined to see him out of this world. Yes, her brother was murdered, apparently a short time before she herself succumbed."

"Oh, my God. The shock, I suppose."

"How was she when you saw her?" Cotton asked. "Her mood, her demeanor? Did she appear to be in good health?"

"Apart from a cold. And one doesn't normally die of a cold."

"Actually, among the elderly, it's not uncommon to die of a cold."

"Yes, of course you're right about that. As to her mood? Acerbic. Her demeanor? Commanding. Nothing, I gathered, out of the ordinary. She was used to command. We chatted a while, then she sat there knitting like Madame Defarge until the train pulled in to Nether Monkslip. I bundled her into a taxi headed toward Monkslip-super-Mare and her castle, and that was the last I saw of her."

"I see."

"When did all this happen?" Max asked him. "As I say, I just was talking with her this very morning."

Cotton said, "The rituals of the forensics team are as mystifying as those of the Masons. But they say, going greatly out on a limb, that he, Lord Footrustle, was killed around eight A.M., give or take two hours. They can never be *sure* and it depends on several *fac*tors such as heat and damp and, no doubt, whether or not the moon was in the seventh house. But that is the long and short of what we have to work with. No useful prints that don't belong there. The killer did not helpfully leave behind his or her footprints in blood, nor did the victim scrawl the killer's name in blood on his headboard. Although, something dramatic like bloody footprints was just possible. The poor old man bled quite a bit. Blood was everywhere but mainly soaked into the mattress of his bed."

Max said, "But you say she wasn't killed, too? Lady Barnard?"

"No! And there's the odd thing. Natural causes. The doc swears it. More tests to run, of course, and in the fullness of time all will be revealed. But he's certain it was just her time to go."

"Could Lord Footrustle's death have precipitated an event that caused her death? Heart attack, or something?"

"Yes. They're certainly looking into that possibility, and going on that assumption."

"Oh, man," said Max. "I really should have paid her more attention."

Cotton seized on this small opening. It was never hard to open a little crack of guilt in the Max facade. "You could help us, Max. We need feet on the ground, ears at the doors. You know the sort of thing."

"And you know that's not my department anymore. My days with MI5 were a hundred years ago. Besides, Chedrow Castle falls under the purview of Father Arthnot of Monkslip-super-Mare. There's a protocol, not unlike your own rules for rank-and-file."

"Actually, as it turns out, it *is* your department. The deceased—both of them—have asked in their wills to be buried out of St. Edwold's, according to my recent conversation with the family solicitor. And a dodgy old reprobate he is, but more on that later—you'll no doubt get to meet him.

"Anyway, Nether Monkslip has been requested by both Lord Footrustle and Lady Baynard in their wills as their final resting place, far in advance of need—back in the days of your predecessor, in fact. I gather they had a special attachment to St. Edwold's. Now I imagine it will be a double service, when we can release the bodies. So I'll tell the people at Chedrow Castle you are there as a special advisor regarding the religious services to be held in Nether Monkslip—helping them choose the hymns and favorite bits of scripture and so on. I gather Lady Baynard's granddaughter Lamorna is keen to talk with you. She is a bit . . . religious. You'll see. Anyway, that will get you in for one night, just so you can get the lie of the land. Or is it lay?—I can never remember. After that, we'll think of something, if need be. The family is terribly upset, naturally. Your presence would have a calming effect," Cotton concluded.

"You want me to snoop around," Max said flatly.

"Only in a calming way," said Cotton.

Max laughed, despite himself. Cotton on a case was relentless; there was no string he wouldn't pull, no angle he wouldn't try, no chit he wouldn't call in.

Cotton said, "Just do what you do best, Max. Listen, sympathize, ingratiate. Above all, notice things."

"I do not *ingratiate*. That sounds so . . . so calculating. Like some corrupt salesman."

"One thing you are not, Max, is calculating. You ingratiate because you are an ingratiating sort of person. I mean, you're—oh, never mind. Will you go?"

Cotton, who felt he knew his man by now, also felt sure he knew what the answer would be. So he sat through the hemmings and hawings, the "Well, I'd have to get someone in to take over the service"'s, examining his nails and scrabbling through his desk to find a nail file, the phone receiver tucked under his chin all the while. Max had reached the end of his recital of what-ifs and conditionals by the time Cotton had finished filing down the little snag on his left index fingernail.

"Good, that's sorted then," he said. "I'll tell them to expect you. And here's the phone number for the castle. There's rather an elaborate 'Open, Sesame' routine you have to go through at the gate. The butler chap will talk you through it."

"I'm really not—" began Max.

"Anyway, nothing could be more natural than that you attend

personally to advise on the arrangements," Cotton ran on. "Lamorna, as I say, has in fact asked specifically for guidance. I gather she's a poor relation of some kind."

"Yes, I know. Again, funnily enough, I learned quite a bit about her over dinner tonight. Poor thing doesn't seem to have had much of a life."

"So you will do it?" Cotton knew from Max's tone that he, Cotton, was winning now. Once Max met Lamorna he might not be so filled with sympathy, but Cotton wasn't going to tell him that.

"I'll be glad to talk to her and to all the family, certainly. I'll have to clear up a few things here—beginning with a call to Father Arthnot. But I don't want to be in the middle of your investigation. I'll simply muddy the waters for your people."

"They've all left, my people. The video team, the photographer, the police doctor." The image came into his mind of the two bodies, each encircled by its own technicians wearing their all-enveloping blue coveralls with elastic at wrists and ankles, accessorized none too fashionably with the booties and hoods designed to protect the crime scene from contamination. They stooped and swayed, poked and prodded, shuffled about and chanted to one another in the ritual of violent death they had all come to know too well.

"They've gone off to learn what they can from the scene photos and the bodies themselves," he told Max. "The areas where the bodies were found have been sealed off for the time being, of course. She was found in the hothouse, which is tucked into a corner of the garden, where I'm told she spent much of her time. He, as I've indicated, was found in his bedroom. The technical people have gone off to chortle over the blood spatter patterns in which they take such delight. But we're left with the suspects, who still are the main source of clues."

"Even with forensics and all the modern gewgaws, it comes down to the people in the end, doesn't it?" agreed Max.

Cotton nodded, as if Max were there to see him. "The police

surgeon thought we should ask for a postmortem on both bodies. Obviously, there's foul play in the case of Lord Footrustle. We need to be quite sure there wasn't something suspicious about Lady Baynard's death, as well."

"Poor woman. I'd never met him, but to have just parted from her . . . That is harsh."

"So you will help."

Now Max, unseen by Cotton, was nodding. But somehow Cotton knew this.

"Then I'll see you there," said Cotton. "Hopefully tomorrow—time is of the essence in these cases, as you are well aware. Just let me know when you're setting out." And he quickly rang off, again in a nod to all the film noir he'd ever seen in his life, and again not wishing to push his luck. Max could always change his mind, but somehow Cotton didn't think he would. A hound already set on the chase, was Max.

Thoughtfully putting down the colossal Bakelite phone at his own end, unknowingly dislodging Luther from another of his death-defying acrobatic attempts, Max wondered what his bishop would think of the way his pastoral duties were starting to overlap with high crimes and misdemeanors. Overall he felt it best to say the least possible unless asked directly what in the world he thought he was doing. He could argue he was doing God's work in trying to bring criminals to justice, but would the Bishop of Monkslip agree? On the whole, Max thought perhaps not. Softly, softly then. So long as none of his pastoral duties suffered, there was no reason for the bishop to even learn of Max's involvement in the affair.

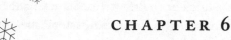

CHAPTER 6

A Man's Home

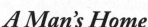

Max had a rusting old Land Rover he used mainly for home visits to farms. In the village, he could walk everywhere, often with Thea at his side. In such a small and compact area as Nether Monkslip, he seldom even used his bicycle.

He powered up the ancient but reliable engine the next day for his visit to the castle. Despite Cotton's mild protests, the business of St. Edwold's had to come first, and it took some time for him to arrange cover during his absence: Someone had to be available to administer the sacraments. His bishop was not consulted—nor need he have been, Max quickly added to the thought. If he had been, he might not have stamped his approval on the scheme insofar as the police investigation was concerned. But as it happened, the vicar at St. David's Church in Monkslip-super-Mare had declared himself glad to be relieved of the immediate need to make a condolence visit to Chedrow Castle. So much so that Max asked him, suspiciously, why that was so.

"You mean apart from the fact a knife-wielding murderer is rampaging about the castle? Do I need another reason?" Father John Arthnot was a canny, no-nonsense cleric, nearing retirement, a prospect he viewed with quiet happiness. He and his wife had three grandchildren who had arrived in rapid succession, all of them living in Bradford, and all of them in need of babysitting services.

"And the Church," John had told him, "is not what it was. It's time for the old guard like me to leave the way clear for the youthful go-getter like yourself. You've worked miracles in Nether Monkslip, I hear. Attendance is off the charts."

Max didn't want to go into the fact that the recent murder in the village, and his subsequent involvement in the investigation, had much to do with the religious revival that had gripped the village. For now, it was sufficient to know that his attendance on the castle would not be treading on the man's pastoral toes.

"Besides," John added, "the family is barking. I'm happy to hand them off to you. Never was a condolence call less needed."

"Surely not," said Max, somewhat shocked. Two people dead, and no one in need of consolation?

"You'll see," said John placidly. "It's sad, but they're probably all too busy counting the silverware and keeping an eye on one another to mourn the passing of either lord or lady."

Max set out then, but not before making half a dozen additional phone calls, some to call in his chits with other priests in the vicinity. He wasn't certain how long he would be gone, but this was a busy time of year for the church, and his duties couldn't just be abandoned at any time. He also let Mrs. Hooser know he'd be gone, to make sure the animals were fed in his absence.

He admitted to himself that part of his motivation in heeding the call from Cotton was that Lady Baynard had told him of her misgivings or forebodings. He felt that he owed it to her to find out what had happened to her brother, whose violent death so spectacularly fulfilled her premonitions of trouble to come.

The weather cooperated, but grudgingly. The South West of England boasted a temperate climate that since time immemorial had drawn visitors to its shores, and this record for scenic hospitality was only now being threatened by the caprices of global warming. The area still enjoyed what the locals called "rainfall on tap"—rain when needed, sun when not—and the deep soil of the region meant not only good planting but good grazing for much of the year. Animals also could be bred earlier than in other parts of Britain. The region generally was spared the worst of winter, but this year's had been unusually bitter, unusually cold, with snow staying on the ground longer than any of the locals could recall. The snow brought chaos with it, as many were not used to driving in wintry conditions, nor did they have the kinds of heavy automobiles designed to safely navigate snow and ice.

By this point the winter qualified as having been one of the most terrible in recent memory. From December first the country had been nearly paralyzed by icy roads and snow—elderly people, unaware and unused to the hazards, had been found frozen to death. Deliveries were halted as filling stations ran out of petrol, and people had been trapped on trains or unable to get public transport to work, further slowing the movement of goods and services.

Max steered the Land Rover, which was a bit too wide for the Lilliputian lanes leading to Monkslip-super-Mare. Despite the need for hypervigilance in this needle-threading task, it was a pleasant drive of hedgerows, stone walls, sparkling snow, and blue sky. At one point he caught a glimpse of an old barn in the distance, its roof thatched. The voices of the popular Scandinavian group Trio Mediaeval issued from the dashboard, singing thirteenth-century church music. Awena had lent him the CD.

The quiet otherwise was at a level beyond that of Nether Monkslip, as if he had slipped on noise-cancelling headphones. Mr. Whippet, the elderly parishioner Awena was watching out for, had told him the village once had been a noisy place, with the laments of animals being driven home at night, and carts rumbling down the High, and the shrieks of children at play. The village had had a school in those days, a building responsible for most of the clamor and, along with the church, for the ringing of bells. These days, the few young children were sent into Monkslip-super-Mare for their schooling. A baby mewling during church services was a welcome novelty.

Max, knowing full well that a flock of sheep would surely be around the next blind turn unless one pootled along at twenty kilometers per hour on the narrow road, resigned himself to a speed that in his pre-vicar days would have had him thrumming his fingertips against the steering wheel in barely controlled frustration. His caution was rewarded when, at the next turn, a small sheep appeared, as if from outer space, in the frame of his windscreen. It stood dead center to the road, alone and staring with startled, frozen panic at the Land Rover's approaching grille. Max stood on the brakes, fishtailing madly, and, after pulling over as far as he could to the left (which was still nearly in the middle of the road), he climbed down out of the vehicle, first trying a mild tap on the horn to move the animal, to no avail.

Clearly, not a very bright sheep. He wondered briefly if there were any smart sheep.

Cautiously he approached the creature, making eye contact. It was not fully grown, still more lamb than sheep. Didn't it need a shepherdess or something? A flock? The creature eyed him back, complacent now, since the engine that had worried it so was stopped. Max made little shoo-shoo motions with his hands, also to no avail.

Lily Iverson, who raised sheep outside the village and sold apparel made from their wool, became so attached to her creatures she had named each one. She claimed they knew and responded to their names. Knowing Lily, and her meticulous care of the animals, that was likely true. Did this sheep have a name, he wondered?

He sighed, looked about him. Privately he christened his sheep Noodlehead. They could be here all day and the next car down the road would come and flatten them both. He had never held a sheep in his life and never expected to, but holding out his arms he squared up to the animal and somehow scooped its legs together. They felt like large furry chopsticks, unwieldy in his arms. Beyond a token bleat, the creature made no protest as he lifted it, seeming to realize this mild indignity was fundamental to its wellbeing. Did sheep bite? Max had no idea. It was a soft—yes, soft as lambswool—and somewhat smelly bundle, and Max staggered up the road with it until a gap in the hedgerow revealed from whence it had come. Gently, he pointed its head through the gap and gave it a shove, a mere suggestion, which the animal seemed to understand. It disappeared, bleating, to join its mates, immediately to be greeted by a fierce blue-eyed dog who stood stock-still, clearly saying, "*There* you are. I was worried. You might have rung."

Max resumed his journey. A few cautious miles farther brought him to Monkslip-super-Mare, where he took the bypass which skirted the wanton, drunken architecture of the seaside town, with its ancient houses spilling down to the sea. He slotted the Land Rover into the traffic in the roundabout just outside the town and joined the slipstream that would carry him toward Chedrow Castle.

It was in the dying late-afternoon sunlight that he first had an up-close view of the castle. It was an image that would remain with him a long time.

He had made his approach via a long wooded drive, which seemed a veritable highway after the track from Nether Monkslip. Lined with sentinel trees on each side, the road rose at the last in a majestic sweep to the castle gates. Max imagined this road followed the same winding trail as the original, and was designed to ease descent while at the same time making a direct, plunderous assault impossible. He came eventually to a lane lined with low stone walls, which in summer would drip with vegetation, and passed through an open gate flanked by stone pillars. He could now see the castle with the latticed grille of its gateway.

The structure sat on an apron of land fanning out over the ocean far below. He could hear and smell the sea which beat at the back fringes of the compound, imagining stipples of light fighting the dark on the water's surface. The "waist" of this apron was narrow—a high stone wall joined at the middle by a gate of elaborate iron scrollwork. You could see how the land might erode over many centuries, narrowing that waistline, causing the wall to collapse, stone by stone, and finally tipping the house and all its contents into the English Channel.

It was a weighty structure of turrets and battlements, fortress-like and forbidding in aspect, even after centuries of peaceful occupation—peaceful, Max reminded himself, until the events which had brought him to this place. The collection of buildings which comprised the compound crouched now behind defenses clearly added later to the original manor house. Perhaps from its inception the place was intended as a retreat from a hostile world, even before reinforcements had been added to repel all invaders. Effectively grappled to the top of a rock, the castle was a perfect picture of stoic majesty in the face of the relentless tide of the ages.

The sky was a grainy blue, like the nighttime sky in a photo taken with a cheap camera, but the graininess came from the snow that floated lazily in the distance. This near the sea, snow crystals tended to break apart almost as soon as they formed. He could not account for the odd luminescence of this sky, which looked like the first glimmerings of the aurora borealis.

A large car park had presented itself to his right as the old Land Rover sputteringly gained the top of the hill. Max parked and walked over to the high stone wall with its wrought-iron gate. He found the buzzer and speaker on the right pillar and announced his presence, as instructed earlier by a heavily accented, impeccably polite male voice over the phone. He seemed to have anticipated Max's arrival either through the use of his good butler genes or, more likely, by peering through one of the tiny windows that dotted the front of the castle. No doubt Cotton had also given the man a heads-up on what to expect. Max was rewarded with an electronic buzz and the metallic *ka-thunk* of the gates unlatching.

Max stood looking at the castle, waiting, as instructed by the voice ("Vait zare for me, pu-leaze."), unaware that his photo was being snapped by an enterprising young reporter from the *Monkslip-super-Mare Globe and Bugle* who was staking out the castle entrance from behind one of the low stone walls. He was busy noticing there were openings between the supporting corbels, brackets helping hold up the castle's upper floors. He'd had a teacher once who was keen on old styles of architecture and some of her enthusiasm had rubbed off. But what was the name for those openings? He'd known it once. Starts with an M . . .

"The machicolations are interesting, aren't they?" said a voice at his ear. Startled, he turned to see a squat, heavy woman, so short she had to tip her head far back to look up at him. She was not very old but had the look of someone anticipating old age by many decades, as if anxious to get the aging process over with all at once.

This must be Lamorna, thought Max. The orphaned young woman Awena told me about.

Awena had told him Lamorna had been named optimistically after the romantic spot where her parents met, although there was little about Lamorna that spoke now of romance. Doughy and lumpen, her shoulders slouched inside a nappy old gray sweater that Max suspected she wore even on summer days, using its stretched and bulging pockets as a carryall. She wore glasses in old-fashioned black plastic frames that might have been issued by the health organization of a failing socialist country. These fitted her poorly, and her every sentence seemed to be punctuated by her having to push the glasses the long way back up her nose. Her eyes were very slightly crossed and too close together. The sunlight caught the highlights in the thin mustache on her upper lip, and her fringed hair sprang wildly about the black Alice band she used in an attempt to tame it. He noticed that in an additional cruel twist of fate, she wore a hearing aid.

She was saying now, "The machicolations could be purely decorative but of course they were used to drop things onto the enemy below. Stones, boiling oil, the contents of chamber pots—whatever was close to hand, presumably."

She gave an exaggerated shudder. "Horrid, they were in those days," she said. But Max thought her smile unpleasant as she envisioned such fates for the victims.

"Yes, of course," said Max. "Machicolations. I couldn't pull up the word."

"You would be Father Tudor. They said you'd be coming."

It wasn't a question. The clerical collar saved so much time in terms of identifying himself and his mission. It was like being a fireman, thought Max.

"And you are?" he asked, just in case he was wrong.

"Lamorna Whitehall." She pointed toward the castle, warming to her role. "You see the lookouts? They're everywhere, really, at ground level and above. These let the defenders observe the approach of the enemy. From the sea, the place is impregnable. It was really only this approach they had to worry about."

"But originally it was a manor house," prompted Max. "Unfortified."

"Yes. They had to get a special license from the king to castellate it and to surround it with protective walls."

"You seem to know a lot about it."

This pleased her. "We're open to the public three or four days a week in summer. Sometimes I take tours around. The family just administers the place, you know. The National Trust owns it. We live here on suffering."

Presumably she meant sufferance, but he understood that her alternate word might sum up her own feelings more precisely. Max looked up, taking it all in. It really was a fine specimen of its type of building, crenellated and dour, yet romantic. The only jarring note was provided by the tubes running up the walls, carefully painted to match the stone but tubes nonetheless, meant to conceal modern things like electrical wires. These old stone buildings had walls too thick to allow for drilling—wires and tubes had to be dropped in from the roof.

He said aloud: "It's stunning. You're lucky to live here."

"Forsooth it is," she said, oddly. But she was an odd woman. "I don't know about lucky, but the place is a beauty. You'll see soon enough. Behind the main portcullis is a small courtyard. The entry to the Great Hall is off of that."

A sepulchral but youngish man now made his appearance. Tall and broad-shouldered, he gravely introduced himself as Milo. ("Just Milo, sir. My last name is a difficult one for British peoples.") Because of the formality of his dress, Max assumed he was some sort of factotum of the castle, an official greeter/butler.

"If you could wait one moment, Father Tudor," Milo said. "I

need to close the gate at the top of the drive. I should have done it earlier but we've been in a turmoil, as you can imagine."

He set off. A clanking sound was heard as he wrestled a gate into place. Lamorna took advantage of Milo's absence to whisper, "I'm so relieved you're here," stammering out the words so softly he had to turn his head to hear.

Returning at a trot and taking Max's single bag, Milo led him under the portcullis which hung, incisor-like, over the central gateway into the main grounds. Turning to speak to Lamorna, Max saw she had beetled off without another word. He saw her round form under the enveloping gray sweater disappear beneath a stone archway into what appeared to be a garden, now dormant in its own winter gray. Presumably the hothouse where Lady Baynard had died would be somewhere in the vicinity. Lamorna had said not a word to him about her grandmother or her granduncle, or about Max's reasons for being at the castle—which was, according to Cotton, at her own request. Perhaps she was one of those who hid strong emotion behind a cool discussion of stone and machicolations and warfare. Protective walls, indeed.

He gazed about him as he walked. The buildings of the castle compound were inviting in that gloomy, portentous way beloved of history buffs. Max, who was one, found it creepily atmospheric—satisfyingly so. The corridors would probably be draughty and the rooms chilly and prone to all the ills that befall extremely old buildings, but Max thought that a fair tradeoff. If the place ran true to type, there would be a massive hall and a buttery or service room in the main part of the structure, along with living areas above; there would be a chapel, perhaps built into the curtain wall along with other buildings. The kitchen would by now have been moved into the main structure for modern convenience, but the remains of the original building might still be around. He could see a Watch Tower that dominated at one side, an anchoring building of some three stories.

Max had paused before the massive gates, calculating with reverence the man-hours required to construct them, then followed

Milo into the small forecourt, where riders would once have entered, their horses stamping their hooves, and their servants rushing to unsaddle the mounts. One could easily imagine the castle lord followed by his retinue as he strode, cape swooping out behind him, into the hall.

He followed Milo through a heavy door that groaned on protesting wrought-iron hinges and into a small antechamber. They passed through a screen on the left and emerged into what could only be the Great Hall—a large shadowy space, almost Venetian in aspect, that made one think of whispered talk of treason by dark-robed men huddled in corners, of conspiracies and the muffled clink of bags of coins changing hands. It was a room of blackened oak beams with a timber arch-brace roof, its stone walls hung with paintings and tapestries depicting stag hunts and other tableaux that would put the sensitive viewer off his meal.

The lofty ceiling, like that of a cathedral, seemed designed to intimidate and impress the visitor. There were a very few, very high windows, so as not to compromise the solidity of the heavy stone walls. A small Chartres-y stained-glass window floated high up in one wall, throwing shards of colored light on the gray stone floor and the large dining table below. The one homey touch was an enormous hearth at one end of the room with sofas and chairs ranged before it.

His guide Milo swiveled suddenly to the left and disappeared, much as Lamorna had done. Scrambling to catch up, for Max again had dawdled to sightsee in the massive hall, he saw the concluding treads of a wide spiral staircase spilling into the room. The lighting was so poor Milo seemed to have been swallowed up by shadows.

Max followed the sound of footsteps up stairs worn slippy with age and smooth as butter, cupped in the middle by centuries of wear by hundreds of pairs of feet, stairs which grew progressively narrower as they ascended. At the top he found himself in a wood-paneled corridor, darkened by time and smoke. Other corridors led misleadingly away on either side—misleadingly because

Max could see they quickly splintered off into little subcorridors and other steep flights of stairs. The whole layout was a mare's nest, like something out of "Hansel and Gretel," requiring bread crumbs to navigate one's way around.

Having rejoined Milo, he followed him down one narrow passageway that seemed chosen at random, a hallway with doors spaced unevenly along both sides. It was inadequately lit and uneven, as had been the stairs. There were no lifts, of course: The whole idea of blasting through rock to create a vertical channel was a nonstarter, and like as not to end with the entire edifice tumbling into the sea.

Milo turned to Max to say, "Watch your step" just as Max caught his foot against an uneven bit of paving and went flying, just catching his balance in time.

By twists and turns, Milo reached a door, remarkably similar to every other door they had passed, and pushed it open. His back for the entire journey had remained ramrod straight. He might have been expressing disapproval. Or nervousness.

He went in, deposited Max's bag, and proceeded to explain the location of the nearest bathroom and also the heating system, which Max gathered might require him to call on all the experts at Los Alamos to operate. Milo then gave him the time and place for dinner (unnecessarily, thought Max, for surely dinner could only be in that massive hall downstairs). But Max declined.

"I'm not really hungry, thank you. I'm meeting DCI Cotton in the morning so I think I'll have an early night."

"I'll let you know when Inspector Cotton arrives, shall I, sir? If you change your mind, Doris—my wife—can bring a tray up to you. The bellpull is over there."

Following some further instruction from Milo as to the ins and outs of the castle, Max thanked him and said, "I'm sure I'll be most comfortable."

Milo looked skeptical, so Max amended: "It should be a most interesting experience, staying in a castle," blithely unaware that this would prove to be an understatement for the ages.

❄ ❄ ❄

He stood at the door watching as the butler disappeared into a narrow service staircase near the main stairs. Back in the day it may have been a sort of bolt-hole or even a secret passageway between rooms, used for the occasional illicit rendezvous.

Max nearly hugged himself. It was all so delightfully gloomy and picturesque. An intimate castle, if there were such a thing. It bore traces of homey domesticity from the days before it became a fortified manor house, and vestiges of frippery from the days when defense of the realm was no longer the primary concern. Max felt as if he had wandered onto the set of an historical drama, or possibly a re-creation of the early life of Robin Hood. Turning back into his room, Max took a moment to assess his surroundings before unpacking (the days of the under-butler who would do this sort of thing for him being long gone). He decided to wait for morning before beginning anything like an investigation. It was late, the sun practically in free fall to the horizon.

The room had a casement window to which he was instantly drawn. His room overlooked a medieval-style knot garden with paths three feet wide, embraced by the castle's high curtain wall. In summer this would be a lovely walk; now the intricate designs, like woven threads of Celtic knot work, resembled white-on-white embroidery. Ornamental bushes were plump with snow and topped with sparkly white hats. He could glimpse a pergola showing the frozen arteries of the climbing vines that would provide a lush canopy in summer. Someone, probably Lady Baynard, had had a go at incorporating an Italianate garden into the grounds, complete with evergreen art topiary.

By placing the top of his head against the glass and pivoting it to the right, Max had a glimpse of the sea—a narrow slice of sea, but there. What an estate agent would no doubt call a dazzling sea view. He could hear the waves far below pounding against the rocks, and also could hear coming from somewhere a faint rattle of tree branches, clicking like old bones.

Nice. Very nice indeed.

Max had never aspired to great wealth—to commute from a castle, like some rock star, by seaplane and helicopter, or to have a closetful of bespoke tailoring from Savile Row. Neither did he begrudge people who possessed these luxuries, unless they were gained by exploitation. Even before the world's economies started falling like dominoes, he'd had a healthy suspicion of get-rich-quick schemes—of money earned in too vast a quantity, and too swiftly, or even at too young an age. Of rapid rises, which seemed always to be accompanied by faster, often drug-fueled, falls. He himself once had had a spacious flat along the river, not far from Thames House, and plenty of spare money if not plenty of time to spend it in. Since joining the Church, his income had slipped to precarious levels, but his needs were fewer, too. He could say he was happy to have left behind the heavy obligations of his former job, but of course his current job had more obligations. It was just that they no longer sat like a weight of metal on his soul.

Turning and peering through the somewhat murky space he saw that the room held a four-poster bed so large it must have been assembled on site, a wardrobe (likewise), and a large full-length mirror. One corner held a straight-backed chair with an embroidered footrest that seemed to depict a drowning, but Max felt on the whole that couldn't be right. An historical event involving a body of water, certainly. And someone had placed an armchair, a small bookcase, and a side table by the fire, creating a cozy spot for reading. It was faced by a small love seat upholstered in worn velvet. His eyes ranged over the books on the shelves. There were several novels of the heaving-bosom variety—the room probably was let out to visitors in season, visitors who left behind the books from which they'd extracted all the needed wit and wisdom. A King James Bible, a le Carré or two. And then—ah, yes. The perfect Christmas read:

No warmth could warm, no wintry weather chill him.
No wind that blew was bitterer than he, no falling snow

was more intent upon its purpose, no pelting rain less open to entreaty.

One almost knew this was Dickens writing of Scrooge without needing to be told. Max read a few pages of *A Christmas Carol* and stopped to wonder how much like Scrooge Lord Footrustle might have been.

And had it led to his death—a death that came for Lord Footrustle before he had time, unlike Scrooge, to repent?

With a heaving sigh of his own, he decided to shower and turn in for the night.

CHAPTER 7

A Curse on This House

A frozen mist hung over the castle as the next day dawned: The view out the windows was of cotton wool. What Max could see from his window of the water, yesterday a deep blue velvet, was in the early morning light showing its true colors: turquoise suspended in gold and silver.

He decided before breakfasting to find Lamorna Whitehall, following Milo's directions of the night before. Milo had agreed to alert her to Max's plan to visit.

"But she is early riser," Milo assured Father Max. "Reads Bible." This last ("Reads Beeble") was said with a careful, polite neutrality that seemed to be second nature to the man. Still, Max got the impression of a hidden message, even of a warning.

Cotton had said Lamorna was the one keen to see him, a "religious person," so he felt in good conscience he should speak with her first, before making his presence known to the others. That, after all, was in theory the reason for his visit—to comfort her in her loss. To comfort all of them.

Her room was at the opposite end of his own long-and-winding corridor. He was later to learn it was close to the room Lady Baynard had occupied, and he suspected its location had to do with Lamorna's role as unofficial provider of free labor.

She came to the door quickly in response to his knock and ushered him in. Then she stood about, nervously twirling the snarl of dark hair on her head. She wore the same gray sweater as the day before, but this time paired with a faded blue denim skirt. Hoping to put her at ease, he began to speak of that most neutral of topics—the weather—but she only nodded curtly in response to his theory that more snow might be on the way.

Sensing the problem—he was invading her space, after all—he asked if she'd prefer to speak with him downstairs. This nearly sent her into a panic.

"No. *No.* I wanted to speak with you in private." Her eyes slid sideways to meet his, then as quickly looked away. "Apart from the others."

So he settled into the worn armchair she indicated, and waited while she fussed with a paper handkerchief she'd drawn from one denim pocket, twisting it to shreds. The tissue did not appear to be an accessory of mourning: She was dry-eyed. He decided to skirt the topic of murder for now.

"You've been living here at the castle how long?" he asked tranquilly. "Obviously long enough to be an expert on its history."

Ignoring the blatant flattery—quite right, too, thought Max—she said, "I was just six when my parents died. I'm thirty now. I came to live here with . . . Lady Baynard."

"Your grandmother."

"Lady Baynard. That's right."

He looked about him, hoping for clues to the nature of the woman in the décor. He reasoned that her room and her mode of dress might be the only ways she could impose her personality in a place she'd been made to feel was not her real home. There were several reproduction paintings on the wall, a haphazard assortment of poor quality that suggested the room was a dumping ground for whatever could not find a place in the rest of the castle. The religious statuary, however, was clearly hers alone, representing a brand of Christianity of the most mawkish sort. This was also true of the books on her bedside table and on a row of shelves by the fireplace, which in all cases appeared to be collections of hymns or abridged tales from the Bible. Max was reminded of the simple tomes aimed at children: short and punchy, easy to memorize, and of questionable theology—the Bible according to the Apostle Barney. Illustrations were tacked on the wall that appeared to have been torn from religious magazines. Most of these were curling at the corners, and hung crookedly, but Max could discern a trend involving the heavenly host of angels, free-floating and unnaturally backlit. In one, an angel smiled coyly as it embraced a human child, carrying it aloft. Max thought personally any child would be terrified witless on such an occasion, but she seemed delighted, torn from her mundane tasks, which for some reason involved pails of milk and a pitchfork, to be lifted bodily into heaven.

A maudlin Jesus gazed at him with blue-eyed concern from the front cover of one book, looking like a parody of every tent revivalist preacher who'd ever come along to distort for profit the original message of the testaments.

Max studied Lamorna as he waited for her to start unpacking whatever burden she was carrying. There were few angles to her face to give it definition or distinction. It was mainly her nose that spoiled her chance at conventional good looks, for she had a firm, round chin and eyes of a pretty color, even if they did protrude goldfish-like from behind her glasses.

But Max knew beauty came in all guises. Mother Teresa with her betel-nut face had been such an authentic personality she became more beautiful as she became more wizened with each passing year. It was difficult to predict such a transformation happening here.

Max thought Lamorna was like a character from a nineteenth-century novel—what at one time would have been called the poor relation, the spinster of the house, reliant on the largesse of wealthier relatives. She struck him as being a throwback to the days, not long past, when an unmarried woman's choices of work outside the home—in this case, outside the castle—were limited. Someone belonging to the upper levels of society, however tangentially, might not recognize or take the few options available to her.

As if following his thoughts, she said, "Lady Baynard encouraged me to stay, you know. She would look at me out of those icy blue eyes of hers and say, 'No one would hire you. You may as well stay on.'"

"Well," said Max. "That was hardly flattering, was it?"

"I got used to it."

She further struck him as the type of individual who was compelled to tell the truth, even when telling the truth was neither wise nor kind. Odd as it might sound from a priest, Max knew that the type of person who couldn't dissimilate, who could not tell a lie if only to spare feelings—her own or another's—could be a dangerous type of personality.

"Why don't you tell me a bit about the others?" he said. "It would help me understand some of the dynamics here."

There was an intensity in her expression as she listened that suggested someone hard of hearing, or slow to understand. Max, remembering she wore a hearing aid, began to enunciate more slowly.

"I'm not sure what to tell you. I don't notice much. I stick to myself."

Well, *that* is a lie, thought Max. He would be willing to bet she noticed everything, if only because nobody noticed her watching them. There was a stillness, a quiet but alert watchfulness to her manner. He actually recognized some measure of that quality in himself. In another life, with a personality less strange and less riddled with odd religiosity, she might have made a good candidate for MI5.

He said aloud some version of what he'd been thinking. "I think, Lamorna, that in fact very little gets past you."

She sniffed and gave him that odd sideways look, but with a shade of a smile this time. Max thought she might be beginning to thaw toward him.

"Well, there's Gwynyth, for a start," she said. "Her proper name is Gwynyth, Lady Footrustle—despite the divorce she gets to keep the 'Lady,' you know. Gwyn and the Twyns, we call them. That's T-W-Y . . . oh, never mind. Anyway, they came to stay. And stay. And stay. Somehow they seem to be becoming a part of the household." Her voice was studiedly neutral but her eyes were burning with ill will. "I don't mind the twins, I practically raised them, you know. When I remember them as cute babies . . . well, it's different. But not her."

"They were invited?"

"So Gwynyth says." Lamorna might have been sucking on lemons, so pinched with disapproval was her expression. "Now, why would he invite her here—Lord Footrustle? He couldn't stand the sight of her before. But I guess he couldn't invite the children to stay without their mother dragging herself along. I don't hold with divorce and I'm certain you don't, either, Father. But in this case I saw it was necessary. She was in show business when he met her, you know. Lady Baynard was outraged and for once I could only agree."

It was as if she collected her grievances in a bowl and would paw through them, turning first one, then another, to the light. He wondered how much of her time was spent in this manner. With Lady Baynard gone, she would have too much time for that sort of thing.

"Gwynyth kept leaving the twins with us when they were little," she said now. "With *me*, that is. Whenever the last nanny quit. So she got free babysitting, too. I never got a word of thanks for it."

"I see," he said neutrally, trying and failing to imagine a worse caretaker for small children than this bitter woman.

"Then there are the Americans," said Lamorna. "Lord Footrustle's daughter Jocasta and her husband, Simon." She paused dramatically and actually tapped her index finger against the side of her nose. "From California. And you of all people must know what that place is like: Sodom and Gomorrah."

Max decided to breeze right past that one. "Surely Jocasta is British?"

"Her mother was American. And Simon is American. And Jocasta's been there so long the taint of sin is upon her now, never to be washed away. But what you should know is this: I've seen them wandering about at all hours. Up to *no good* at three A.M."

"What were they doing?" asked Max.

"They were looking *very suspicious*," said Lamorna. With a significant nod, she parted her lips in a wintry smile.

"Quite likely they're jet-lagged," said Max. "I well remember how upsetting long-distance travel is to the eat-and-sleep cycles. At three A.M. here they would be expecting their dinner back home. Or their stomachs would be expecting it."

While he thought this was likely true, he made a mental note to have Cotton ask about these nocturnal wanderings. They—or one of them—might have seen something the rest of the house had not.

"You don't find their behavior suspicious?" Lamorna demanded. Clearly he had lost points with her for being such a thick nincompoop. "Given what's happened? Given that just days after their arrival—three days, in fact—Lord Footrustle was poisoned?"

Cotton had told Max what little he knew of this episode.

"I'm not sure that's significant," said Max aloud. "The timing of their arrival." In fact, he thought it as likely the poisoner—if poisoner there were—waited until the entire family had gathered so as to throw the net of suspicion as wide as possible.

"It is significant," she pronounced. "There was no love lost between Jocasta and her father. To become an actress! It's as if she chose the one profession most likely to upset him."

That Lord Footrustle had himself later married a woman in show business seemed to have escaped her for the moment.

"I gather you were here when he married Gwynyth. How did Jocasta take that?"

He expected a rebuke for asking such a nosy question. In fact, he couldn't have said why he asked it, but it seemed to release a flood of pent-up emotion.

"Hah!" she said. "How did she take it? *I'll* tell you how she took it. She didn't like it any better than I did, but my dislike was based on moral reasons, as you shall hear: The pair of them weren't married two minutes before those twins came along. Not two minutes! If you ask me Alec and Amanda escaped the curse of illegitimacy by a hairsbreadth! Never doubt"—and here she raised a finger heavenward—"never doubt Lord Footrustle was shanghaied into that marriage. Gwynyth is nothing but a brazen hussy." *Sniff.* "No better than she should be."

She was reminding him an awful lot of her grandmother by this point. He wondered if there were a gene marker for blatant snobbery. At least Lady Baynard seemed to have missed the religious nutter gene. But here Max pulled himself up short, for he'd been forgetting Lamorna was adopted.

"But as to how they all came to be here," she said. "I'm afraid they don't share that kind of thing with me. As I told you, I'm here on suffering."

The truth of that was becoming undeniable. She was a member of the family, in fact, but also an outsider. This could be useful to the police—she might see an angle the others might miss. That this angle might be skewed and distorted, however, he didn't doubt for a moment.

"Tell me about your grandmother. How did you get on?"

"Lady Baynard? She came back to the castle when her husband died." He noticed she'd ignored the second half of his question.

"Lord Baynard."

"Yes." She seemed strangely reluctant to pursue this topic. She began worrying a button on her sweater. The thread holding it had begun to shred.

"Wouldn't," he said, "wouldn't it be more usual for a widow of her station in life to have remained living at her husband's ancestral home?" He reached for the old-fashioned word. "In a dower house, perhaps?"

"Usual," she mused. "Yes. Except that her husband was a rotter." The *really* old-fashioned word surprised him so, he struggled not to laugh. "He *gambled*," she went on. "They had to sell his ancestral pile to some American actress and her husband—and *he* was some sort of singer."

Well, the disgrace of it all. She said this the way others might mention a drug dealer and her consort.

"It was her own fault, of course, for choosing him," said Lamorna now.

"What do you plan to do?"

"I plan to do what I've always done," she said, a look of faint surprise on her face. "I'll stay on, look after things, lead the occasional group through on tour."

"Will Viscount Nathersby . . . erm . . . *will* he need help, do you think?"

"Randolph? He won't want to live here, and he never has. Why wouldn't he want me to stay on and help? Besides, it's Alec who inherits the title from Lord Footrustle. It's not really Randolph's business."

Max thought he was beginning to see the situation from her side. There would be free room and board as there always was, but without the fetch-and-carry that her grandmother had subjected her to, and the contempt her granduncle had subjected her to. It was a motive for murder, certainly, and a powerful one. People had killed before to ensure their own safety and security, keeping a roof over their heads.

"He may have other plans," said Max carefully. "You should ask him, ask them both, once things are a bit . . . quieter."

At the thought of leaving, or being cast out, fear stretched across Lamorna's face, pulling the skin tight around her eyes.

She suddenly burst out, "Lady B was a manipulative liar. She told people stories about how much they would inherit from her, thinking it would make them be nice to her. But I—I didn't care.

I have no use for money." Then she diluted the impact of this righteous statement by adding, "Besides, her husband ran through so much of it before he died."

"I see," said Max. "Randolph has a brother, as I understand it. Lester. And Lester has a wife."

This immediately brought down her scorn.

"The Australians," she said. "I hadn't seen either of them in years. You can be sure they're interested only in money. Lester 'does something in finance,' or so I was told. Again, why would Lord Footrustle do this? Bring all these people here? Strangers, really. Upsetting everything."

"It may have been simple loneliness," said Max. "The castle is isolated, and I don't know how many social outlets he had left. Don't you think it may have been a desire for companionship?"

"No, I don't. He had me and Lady Baynard for company. He never could stand any of the rest of them, so far as I could tell. That's not surprising, is it?" She began to speak with a nervous and erratic intensity. "Heathen!" she cried. "That's what they are. It's what they all are."

"He was getting older, Lord Footrustle," said Max. "It makes a difference, and they *are* his family."

Too late, he saw the trap he'd sauntered into.

"And I'm *not*?" she snapped.

"Of course you are," he said quickly, placatingly. "Yes, of course. Every bit as much as they are."

She didn't look convinced because he wasn't convinced himself. Everything he knew of her situation—and he trusted Awena's version in particular—painted her as an unwanted outcast. Family by law but not by love.

"It couldn't have been easy for you," he said. "After your parents died."

"A motherless orphan. That was me," she said. "Like *Jane Eyre*—that show on the telly last year. Handouts, hand-me-downs." She adjusted her glasses, pinching the frames on both sides to push them to the bridge of her nose, where they promptly slid down again. Sisyphus glasses.

No mention of being fatherless as well. Max reflected that Lamorna's view of herself—labels like "orphan" and "hand-me-downs," however accurate, said much of what he needed to know of her personality. Self-pity was easier than trying to change her fate, and was a trap Bronte would never have allowed her heroine to fall into.

"I used to hear them talking, Lord Footrustle and Lady Baynard," Lamorna said now.

Max wondered, not for the first time, at this insistence on using their formal names.

"I wasn't eavesdropping," she said, with an emphasis that suggested that was precisely what she had been doing. "But I heard them. 'If there's money involved you'll find them perfectly polite, even sober.' Lord Footrustle said that."

Max nodded encouragingly. The recent deaths seemed to have loosened her tongue—he doubted very much she'd have felt as free to share with him her views even a week before. Anything that could add to his store of knowledge of what had happened in the days and weeks leading up to the murder would be helpful.

"He said that, you see, because Lady Baynard was worried about spiteful goings-on with all of them here. Fights and quarrels, you see."

Max did see.

"Was she worried about any one of them in particular?"

Did he imagine it, or was she was tempted to mention a particular name? After a pause she just shrugged and said, "She was worried about all of them."

"That's very helpful," said Max, smiling. *No, it wasn't.* "Anything like that you can think of to tell me, please do so. Right away."

"It's all just frightfully inconvenient," pouted Lamorna, sounding more than ever like her grandmother. "We had all these strangers in the house—that was bad enough—and now we have dozens more, snooping and prying and asking questions."

"Yes, that is the worst of an unpleasant incident such as this."

"What happens now?" she asked worriedly.

"The DCI from Monkslip-super-Mare will want to talk with everyone, sometimes more than once. You must be patient. You do want to find out what happened to your grandmother, and to your granduncle, don't you?"

"Not really." Clearly realizing how cold that sounded, she adopted a look of simpering piety, in imitation of one of the angels adorning her walls, and added the platitude, "It won't bring them back, will it?"

She was hapless, thought Max, listening to Lamorna. Without hap, whatever that meant. Without happiness, presumably.

Now she pressed the edge of one fist against her mouth in a sudden paroxysm of worry.

"They're all jealous of each other, you know. It reminds me of Jacob and Esau, the envy. That's a venial sin, isn't it? But it seems so much worse." Then she added, "Please stay until this is sorted. I don't feel safe around the others."

"I can't promise you it will be sorted," he said. "I can promise to learn what I can, to try to set things right. And you couldn't be safer with a house full of policemen."

That earned him a baleful glance. "They'll only make things worse, you know. They couldn't possibly begin to understand."

One glance at her, at the stubborn set of her mouth, convinced him that mere logic would likely confuse her. Much better to approach any subject obliquely.

"It's a judgment on this castle, I tell you!" she said now. Which Max found more than slightly absurd. This castle had been the scene of so much mayhem, betrayal—surely, yes, even murder—over the years, that if God had not reduced it to rubble long before now, then God never was going to take an active interest in the goings-on at Chedrow Castle.

As she droned on in this vein, literally quoting chapter and verse, Max, smiling amiably, wondered if he could make his escape unnoticed by plunging out the window into the bare flower beds below. He thought Lamorna would have been a fitting companion for Savonarola with his apocalyptic messages and his "Bonfire of the Vanities" burnings. Dealing with the intense yet boring fanatic was another hazard of his profession, like the fawning attentions of elderly ladies.

He felt a barrier had come up between them now, so he said, in his most soothing voice, "I absolutely promise you no harm will come to you." And because he felt she was keeping something from him, hiding it in all these cries to heaven, he added, "So long as you tell me whatever it is you know that is worrying you so."

"As I have said," she intoned with heavy emphasis, "there is a curse on this house. It will fall like the Tower of Babel."

"There's actually some debate about that. Whether it actually fell," Max began, and caught himself up. The last thing he wanted was to enter into that sort of conversation with someone like Lamorna. She was such a poster child for the twisted result of clinging to a joyless, punitive religion, a religion that sapped all the joy from life and led, in its final stages, to the extremism that poisoned the well of sane discourse.

"After all, what goes around comes around," she said now. A smile of deep, anticipatory satisfaction settled on her lips. Max felt he had heard as much of the collected philosophical wisdom of Lamorna Whitehall as he could take in one sitting. With the repeated assurance that she need not worry and should feel free to come to him with any information or concerns, Max took his leave of her.

He thought perhaps the castle staff could give him a more detached account.

CHAPTER 8

In the Kitchen

He could smell coffee and hear laughter coming from the kitchen as he walked down the dark-paneled passage leading from the Great Hall. It was an incongruous sound for a house in mourning. He recognized one voice: Milo's deep boom was unmistakable. The other voice was a woman's.

The door was ajar, and the woman, seeing Max, stood up from the wooden kitchen table and introduced herself as Mrs. Vladimirov ("Call me Doris."). Max could understand why her husband stuck to the simpler Milo. She was a sturdy British woman with a wide smile and open expression. At the moment, her hands were covered to the elbows in flour.

"Isn't this a fine mess," she said. Max assumed she didn't mean the flour. "A murder investigation at Chedrow Castle. My parents can talk of nothing else. No one will be talking of anything else for years to come."

Despite the scowl caused by her stated exasperation with the situation, Max thought she had a kind face. Certainly, she viewed Max with ill-concealed friendliness and warmth, but then, most women did.

As she resumed her seat to continue her floury task she sized him up. He was a prepossessing figure but the words that came into her mind were simpler ones from her magazine reading at the hairdresser's, words like "hottie" and "dreamy," with dark gray eyes of a peculiar intensity that made Doris feel she was the one person in the world this man had been hoping to meet.

"Good morning to you, sir," Milo, sitting across from his wife, thundered in his deep bass voice, aware of and unaffected by his wife's evident interest in Max. He had had Doris at hello, as the saying went, and she him, and their trust in one another had never faltered.

"Would you care for some coffee, Father Tudor?" Milo asked him.

"I would like that very much."

"Get him some breakfast cake to go with that," directed Doris. She was punching at some dough on a cutting board like a boxer keeping an opponent against the rails. She planned to serve the castle guests a lunch that she explained was "on croot." It looked to Milo like plain old Cornish pasties and he made the mistake of saying so.

"On *croot*, on *croot*," she said. She stood to refill her own cup and to check on something in the oven, thumping about the kitchen as she did so. "I would know what a Cornish pasty is, now, wouldn't I?"

Soon Max was holding a warming cup of coffee in both hands. Milo sat down next to him, having served him a pastry made with blueberries, nuts, and oatmeal. Max had been fed similar confections by Mrs. Hooser that he would not have offered to a horse. This was sublimely crunchy but moist—made with buttermilk, Doris told him, when he complimented her on it. The kitchen was the epitome of a cozy place that invited one to settle in for long sessions of talk and the exchange of confidences. It had a small fireplace, size being relative—smaller than the fireplace in the Great Hall, yet large enough to roast a good-sized specimen of livestock. The murmur of the sea against the rocks could be heard from a window opened to release some of the cooking heat of the room. The soothing hum served as a counterpoint to the crackle of the hearth.

"I have just been talking with Lamorna Whitehead," Max told them.

Doris, who had resumed pummeling her dough, looked up briefly from her task. *Poor you*, said her expression, but she merely waited for him to continue.

"How well do you both get along with her?" Max asked. "With Lamorna?" There was little point in asking *if* they got along with her.

Milo said, "As well as can be expected. She does not have any—what do you call it? The skull?"

"The brain?"

"That's right. Any brain. She is full of doom and does not have the brain of a boiled egg."

Doris nodded. Delivered of that somewhat gastronomic opinion, Milo crossed his arms and waited for the next question.

But Doris added, "Mind, she's got her reasons. The life they lead her, it's not a fit life for a mule. Surely not a good situation for a young woman. But she puts up with it. Hasn't the gumption to leave, or to get some training, or to strike out on her own. Or even to spruce herself up—lose that horse blanket she always wears, for one thing—and go looking for a bloke. Puts up with all manner of rudeness just for room and board in a draughty castle. So it's hard to feel too sorry for her, even given the cards she's been dealt."

Her manner as she spoke was down to earth. Max felt her beliefs as well as her loyalties would be unshakable, founded as they were on common sense mixed with a splash of sympathy.

"Her parents left Lamorna some little money," said Milo. "Of course, there wasn't a lot to leave. Or so we hear. It is not our business, is it? But it stands to reason. So we don't know why she stays."

Doris turned her dough over and gave it a good thwack.

Milo said, "She is the type of person full of rules."

"Dogmatic," said Max.

"No, more catlike, I think. She creeps about—well, we have seen her . . ."

"She sneaks around the place," Doris finished for him. "Especially now, with all of them here. Trying to find out what they're all up to. She is not happy about that situation, you can be sure."

"I gather Lady Baynard felt the same way," said Max. "Or did you gain the impression she had in any way instigated this family get-together over the holidays?"

Doris Vladimirov threw back her head laughing. The dough took a hit to the solar plexus. "Of *course* Lady B didn't agree to having them all come here. She'd rather be shot, I'd have said. She did what Lord Footrustle wanted, in the end, whenever she couldn't talk him out of whatever it was. She was very old-fashioned in that and other respects, was Lady Baynard. In most respects."

"The male ruled."

"He was *Lord Footrustle*. And that was that. Unless, as I say, she couldn't first talk him out of whatever it was, using whatever means. She had her little bag of tricks, did Lady B."

Milo nodded in agreement.

"He's one peculiar old duck, always was, Lord Footrustle." She paused to fork in some cake and to take a sip of coffee. "A-course, I don't call him that to his face. A duck. Didn't call him, I mean. Didn't . . ." Suddenly caught up by the memory of what had happened, she blanched, all the color draining from her hectic complexion. Putting down her cup, she took a moment to dab at one eye with a corner of her apron. Milo stood and gave her an encouraging thump between her shoulder blades, as though she were choking. Finally she heaved a mighty sigh and said, "Still, no cause to kill the man in that horrible way. Mostly what was wrong with him, he was lonesome. It made him crotchety."

She tried for another sip of her coffee but her hand trembled too much.

"And Lady Baynard," Max asked gently. "How did you get along with her? Was she, erm, crotchety sometimes, too?"

Distractedly, Doris made a production of dusting flour off her fingertips with a linen dish towel that commemorated one of the royal weddings. Her mouth set in a firm line that plainly said, *If you can't say something nice, say nothing at all*. Max waited. Then, after a moment's internal struggle: "She was horrid. *Horrid*." The dam breached, Doris poured forth some further opinions which were apparently of long standing. "It seemed to me all she cared about was her garden and her flowers. It was as if she thought we were all living in some daft production of *Upstairs, Downstairs* or *Downton*

Abbey. As if there'd never been a war—first or second—and all the changes that came with it." Anticipating his question, she said, "I put up with it because it was a job, and she saw to it we were paid well, I'll say that for her. There isn't much call for a cook in this type of setup these days, and I never trained as a restaurant-type chef. Never wanted that kind of high-pressure environment. So this job was what was here and what was available, in the back of beyond, as we are."

Max glanced at her husband. His grave manner seemed to overlay an impish intelligence that missed nothing but held its own counsel. There might just have been a spark of humor glancing off the eyes, which otherwise looked iced over, and while his stiff comportment seemed to convey disapproval, Max felt somehow that Milo was thoroughly enjoying all the palaver. It must have made a break from his usual routine.

"Were there often visitors to the castle? Apart from the family, I mean."

"Oh, yes. Lady Baynard had the nobs down from London sometimes. She really put on the dog when it was someone she thought was important. She didn't truck with mixing with the 'lower orders of people'—her words. Like the rest of us was bacteria. We had to ship folk in so she could have someone good enough to dine with. That it cost me no end of extra work was beside the point."

Suddenly her hands, square as the spade one might use to turn over a garden plot, cut the air with a decisive slice. "Enough of that," she said. "What must you think of me, Father."

"Not at all," said Max. Actually, more of the same was what was needed. He would never arrive at the truth of the matter if everyone went around speaking no ill of the dead. It was their ills that led directly to murder, in nearly every case with which he was familiar.

He decided to give Doris the abridged version of this truth, ending with, "I really need to know what you know about the family. Your perspective is invaluable, since you are on the outside looking in. For example, I gather Randolph, Viscount Nathersby, was Lady Baynard's eldest son."

"Yes. Then there was Lea, her daughter. She came after Randolph. She died in a plane crash with her husband Leo. That's how we come to have Lamorna living here."

She sprinkled more flour over her dough; flipping it over, she sprinkled flour on the other side and began kneading. The ropy veins in her strong hands stood out against the freckled skin.

"Then there's Lady B's youngest, Lester. His given name is Leicester but I gather no one in Australia could spell that. His wife is Felberta, but we call her Fester. Lester and Fester. Hang about them for a day and you'll see why. Any rumor or bad news or bit of snarkiness seems to start with one or both of them."

Max took a guess. "There was a rumor when Lord Footrustle fell ill, wasn't there?"

"They think I don't know," Doris fairly exploded. She stopped to push a strand of hair away from one eye, leaving a streak of flour across her forehead. "They're saying Lord Footrustle took ill because of my cooking. And don't I know where that idea got started. What a pother that created with all them police. There's nothing wrong with my cooking; I'm ever so careful about ptomaine and such." She pronounced the "P" in ptomaine, a spitting sound. "For all I have to trek some of the food from where it's stored in the Old Kitchen, now we've all these extra mouths to feed." She picked up a brochure that sat on the table, held it at arm's length, and with exaggerated pomposity, read aloud:

"'The Old Kitchen of the castle is popular with tourists, giving insight into domestic life of the Middle Ages.' Don't it just. They don't bloody have to cook in this museum, do they? Or they wouldn't find it all so bleedin' thrilling. Still, there's no time for anything to spoil. The very idea—"

"Now, now," said her husband, standing again to retrieve the coffeepot. The impeccably tailored if well-worn clothes could not conceal the toughened body beneath. Max had the sense Milo was a survivor. Of what, Max could not have said. But the broad shoulders tapering to a narrow waist spoke of someone used either to hard work or weights training. Somehow he didn't think the castle ran to a weight room, although one never knew in these days of the five-star accommodation.

"It is for best we ignore this," said Milo Vladimirov in his impeccable if gappy English. He tended to use several words while searching for the right one even if he did leave out the occasional article. Max thought it was his way of buying time while his brain was busy translating.

Doris said, "What was odd was this: People thought Lord Footrustle, the 'sickly' one, always worried about his health, would go before Leticia—if they thought about it at all, of course. Men do tend to go first. And he'd had a couple of little scares. But that's why he was so particular about his health, all them potions he had."

Her hand had begun to shake again and she set down her cup with a clatter. Her cheeks flooded with color. It was like watching a video of a sunrise play out in fast-forward motion.

"It's been that big a shock! In all my days I never thought to see the like," she said.

Max reached over to mop at her saucer where the coffee had breached the lip of the cup, then sat back in the creaking rush-seat chair to listen. He was quite certain she wasn't done yet—might never be done. She might compulsively talk of the goings-on at Chedrow Castle for the rest of her days.

"How kind you are," she said, lifting the cup with a somewhat steadier hand.

Max looked about and noticed a display of house bells ranged across one wall. Each would ring with a different pitch so the staff would know who was in what room wanting something. As Doris had said, it was all frightfully *Downton Abbey*.

Doris turned to follow his gaze.

"They're not much used except the ones connected to Lord Footrustle's room and Lady Baynard's. We've only got two hands apiece, Milo and me. Even they recognized the fact."

"Did his bell ring on the morning that he died?"

"No."

Max didn't suppose it had. Cotton had told him the old gentleman had been surprised in his sleep, in all likelihood had never awoken from sleep. A sneaky crime, the calling card left by a coward.

"But I'm not always here in the kitchen, you know," she continued.

"Ah. You have rooms elsewhere in the castle?"

"That we do. In what we call the West Wing."

Milo said, "I did not discover body until later in morning because he sleeps in late—he *slept* in late—and I had been instructed not to wake him until ten. He was a night owl who stayed up late but also woke up late, unlike most gentlemen his age," said Milo.

"He was like a vampire, actually," said Doris.

"Really, Doris," said her husband.

"Lord Footrustle never came down early," Doris said.

"He liked to stay in bed and read, and take his time getting dressed," confirmed her husband.

"You have outside help?" Max asked them. "Well, you must. The place is enormous."

Doris said, "We have a girl from the village to help with the prep for dinner, and two more to act as daily help. 'Act' being the operative word most days. Those two go home well before the sun sets, no doubt worn out from their efforts, which seem to consist of sipping tea in between jabbing feather dusters at the tops of the picture frames."

"The police will have to interview them, of course," said Max.

"They'll have their work cut out for them to try and get some sense out of Lotty. Dotty Lotty we call her. Interviewing the other two will be like talking to a bowl of goldfish. Good luck to that Inspector Cotton. He's rather a nervy fellow, isn't he?"

Max smiled. Cotton was a perpetual motion machine. If they could harness that energy nations could put an end to wars over oil.

Milo added, in the interest of thoroughness, apparently, "Iris sometimes also comes in with her mother to do for the castle. Doris can't manage it all, of course, and neither can I, although I turn my hand to whatever is needed, including some of the gardening."

"You act as a chauffeur sometimes, I would imagine?"

"Not very often. There simply is not time, even in off-season."

"How did Lady Baynard get around? Did she drive?"

Milo seemed to find this a ludicrous suggestion. People like Lady B did not drive themselves anywhere.

"I put her into taxi that came to take her to station. This was December thirteenth. The family have car but they let the chauffeur go long ago as full-time persons were not needed. I fill in as chauffeur on the special occasion but it is not practical for me to drive car and keep in good repair along with everything else I do."

It was the first hint Max had heard of complaint, and it may not even have been that. He noticed the trellis of permanent worry lines that crisscrossed the man's forehead.

"How did she seem that morning?" Max asked him.

"The same person she always was. Grumpy. Maybe little worse because she had cold."

Doris stood to attend to a dish simmering on the stove. From there she stomped her sure-footed way around the kitchen from pot to plate and back again, not a motion wasted. At one point she balanced several plates on one arm, as easily as if they'd been glued on.

Max turned to Milo and asked him how he came to be here.

"I met Doris and we married," he said simply, adding, "I wanted to live in the outer skirts of the city."

"You have been happy here?" Max asked. "I gather from what your wife has said Lord Footrustle and Lady Baynard were not always easy employers."

"Too right!" Doris exclaimed, in the midst of one of her room crossings.

Milo visibly expanded at being the center of attention—the

repository of insider knowledge regarding the doings of what he thought of as the Upper Crusts. What didn't he know about what these nobs got up to? His career working on a cruise line had removed any trace of innocence he may have had on that score. The problem was *how* he came by that knowledge, which was a matter of, well, not spying exactly. One could say, of simply being in the right place with ears unstoppered.

"Their cheques always cleared the bank," he said now. "It is all one can ask of an employer in these economic times. I have no complaints."

"Huh!" This from Doris. A glance from her husband silenced her.

"I do not think retirement suited Lord Footrustle. He was dynamic person always. I think he grew—how you say?—downtrodden in retirement."

"Depressed," corrected Max automatically. "Or despondent."

Max was a bit skeptical about anything the butler might tell him. He had the sense the man knew things—what was the saying? No man is a hero to his valet?—but how accurate would be his interpretation of what he saw and "knew"? The trouble with eyewitnesses generally was a tendency to embellish. He thought the butler might have that tendency in spades, but the embellishment would be so subtly done it would be hard to see the truth behind it.

"As for Lady B, she was, as I tell you, the same as always. But I think she worried that new arrivals might upset pushcart."

"Apple cart," said Max and Doris simultaneously.

"You are talking of Lord Footrustle's estate?"

"Yes," said Milo. He seemed happily willing to offer what information he had to buy a few more minutes in the public eye, as it were. Perhaps life with Doris was like that. "He had changed his will not a year before. But who knows if that change was to Lady Baynard's benefit—or to the benefit of any or all of them?"

"I suppose we'll soon know," said Max.

Doris had stopped dead in her tracks and stood worrying the tea towel. Lowering her voice, she said, "I've had a bad feeling since they all came here."

The phrase "déjà vu all over again" flashed through Max's mind. Leticia—Lady Baynard—on the train, and now this.

"A *feel*ing," she went on. "O' course, an old place like this is full of atmospherics. Old murders and betrayals unavenged, and such."

"And such. Quite," said Max, smiling, hoping this was not the prelude to some long tale of headless maidens and drowned sailors or even of speckled bands and silent dogs.

"Atmospherics," she repeated with relish. "There's been that all right."

"Do you think you could be more specific, Mrs. Vladimirov?" Max asked. And the floodgates again opened.

"Well," she began. *"Well."* She smoothed her apron several times over her lap, tugging and pulling at imaginary wrinkles in the floral-patterned fabric. It was a pretty compendium of butterflies and flowers that Max was nearly certain did not all bloom at the same time except in the apron manufacturer's imagination. "You want to talk about people creeping about?" This phrase was aimed at her husband. Max averred that he did want to talk about precisely that. "The whole family is greedy but you ask me Lester and Fester have the most to worry about in that department, he being the younger son. The pair of them have been on a scavenger hunt since they got here. Weighing up the value of this 'n' that. It's not right. The folk at the National Trust would be bothered if they knew, and I've half a mind to tell them to look inside the suitcases before the pair of them leave here. This castle has been home for generations to lords and ladies, and my family has been in service to them since the year aught. To treat the place as a jumble sale—well."

She seemed to include herself in this pride in the family tree. Of course, Max supposed it was even possible she was descended from those who had served here at the castle in its early days. From someone exercising his droit du seigneur.

"As to Jocasta and Simon: Let me give you a for-example. Let's say character A is good-looking, but B has more of a personality. Put them together you'd have a whole person. Don't you find that true of so many married couples? I don't think she'd last a minute without him. Weak, Jocasta. Always has been since I've known her. Borderline."

Now Doris was removing a baking pan fragrant with cinnamon rolls from the oven and placing it on a trivet to cool. Then she went to fetch milk and butter from the refrigerator. She moved in short, sturdy steps, a little tugboat plowing through choppy waves.

"Problem is, y'see," she went on, closing the refrigerator door with her hip, "he'd been generous with them always and they'd come to rely on it. Lord Footrustle, that is. Then he met Gwynyth and the twins came along. Some of the family had their noses out of joint for a while, you can bet. And it did change things. He never went back to supporting them all the way he once had. Gwynyth spoiled it for them, you might say. Opened his eyes, like.

"Mind, I'm no fan of their being here, either. Millie—that's one of the girls besides Lotty what comes from Monkslip-super-Mare to help do for us—Millie says they leave the bathroom in the Tower looking like somebody washed a pig in there."

"She is not used to children," said Milo.

"Who said it was the twins?" demanded Doris.

"Was Jocasta particularly affected by Lord Footrustle's remarriage?" Max asked.

This was so important a point she stopped midstride and turned to face him. "I should say so. Thing is, he wanted a son, Lord Footrustle, and his first wife could have no more children after Jocasta. When he took up with Gwynyth and produced Alec, and Amanda, in short order—well. It was all like something out of Henry VIII. Jocasta hides it—she's an actress—but there's no denying she felt pushed aside."

"Lord Footrustle was very old-fashioned, you see," put in Milo. "There was the title to think about."

But for Doris that ship had sailed, and she was on to another topic. "I will tell you something else for free. There have been ghosts here since I was a girl, and my mother before me, and going back who knows how far. Because there have been horrible murders in the past. Don't doubt for a moment the ghosts here, Father Max. There was that business of the wife of the third earl up to something or other in the garden. She was seen by her husband through one of the squints in the solar being flirtatious and worse with one of her husband's knights. Or perhaps it was one of the gardeners. The whole thing, it was like a story out of a Harlequin romance."

"Or out of *Lady Chatterley*," said Max.

"But he killed her. The husband, you see. He had her killed. It was easy to organize such goings-on back then. And now she seeks her revenge. I wonder what they make of this mess," concluded Doris gloomily. "The ghosts."

Milo seemed to feel a change of subject was in order. "You may want to walk this morning, in the garden. The forecoast later is for snow." Max started to correct him and then decided forecoast was much the better word, considering how near they were to the sea.

"However, what Doris says is true," Milo added. "I don't believe in ghosts but I believe in atmosphere. And there has been a—a *crackle* in the air since they all came here." Again he spoke in his measured, precise way, each thought carefully examined before release. "You will be wanting to meet the others, and now would be good time. They will just be coming down wanting their breakfast. We serve buffet in Great Hall every morning."

"We do since they started arriving by the hundreds," put in Doris. "I can't serve sit-down meals three times a day, not with the lot of them here."

"Well," said Max, standing, "I thank you for your time. That is an excellent suggestion: I'll go and see who's there."

But Doris was not yet finished. "The trouble's just starting," she called to Max's retreating figure. "You mark my words, Father."

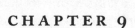

CHAPTER 9

A Small Repast

In the Great Hall, dust motes drifted in the weak sunlight streaming though the high stained-glass window. The light didn't seem to penetrate much below the arches of the ceiling, leaving the room below in murky shadow.

The room's corners were marked by four white marble statues on pedestals, all Greco-Roman in theme, and depicting the four seasons. A heavy medieval-era table ran down the center of the room that could easily seat thirty. It was dotted at intervals with massive candelabra, unlighted now but dripping picturesquely with wax. The table overall looked suitable for a twelfth-century monastery, but ranged before it were comfortably padded dining chairs rather than wooden benches. Max was for some reason surprised to notice an elaborately decorated Christmas tree tucked near the cozy seating group arranged before the massive stone fireplace. A few presents wrapped in glitter and gold were scattered underneath the tree, which itself bore gaudy bows of deep purple on its branches. The presents had the impractical, matchy-matchy look of something there only for show, like a tree in the window of Harrods. He was tempted to pick up a box and rattle it to see if his guess was right—that it would be empty.

On one wall hung family portraits, a large one flanked by two smaller. The large portrait of a man whose mustaches deserved a painting all to themselves was inscribed with a motto. Max stood closer and translated it as meaning "Move faster." He thought it was either that or something along the lines of "Don't just stand there, do something." Good advice.

The family's coat of arms (stags and sea lions rampant) hung on the screen below the Minstrels' Gallery, and on the adjoining wall were more paintings of ancestors. One of these, of a woman in a bejeweled headdress and outer coat of the sixteenth century, had been drawn by someone with a tenuous grasp of the laws of perspective, but possibly possessed of a sense of humor—the artist caught the surely unintended look of fatuous self-importance in the tilted angle of the chin, the raised eyebrows, the reproving clamp of the narrow lips. All in all, it looked to Max like the portrait of a woman who would not hesitate to have a servant flogged over a minor infraction of the household rules.

"One of our ancestors," said a voice at his elbow. "I call her the Dragon Lady, although she had a name, which I somehow always forget."

Max turned to acknowledge the speaker with a smile, then squinted at the brass label affixed to the bottom of the picture's ornate wooden frame.

"Lady Lavinia Delamarva Footrustle," he read aloud.

"That's right. And of course over there is Leticia, Lady Baynard. Now sadly deceased."

Max now saw that a painting of Lady Baynard hung over the mantelpiece. It looked like it might even be a Hockney—certainly it was in his style, at once cartoonish and realistic, capturing the essence of a personality in practiced brushstrokes. It pictured Leticia as a young woman. Her hair was a thick mass of auburn sworls and curlicues and she glared from the canvas with a determined gaze, her firm jaw set in a pugnacious line. Max had not felt she would be a woman to cross and the painting confirmed his impressions of the living woman.

"And you are . . . ?" he asked politely.

"I am Felberta Oliver Baynard. Lester's wife."

She was a round woman in a sweater, lettuce green in color and unfortunately of a lacy knit that resembled the yuppier sort of lettuce. Max thought perhaps arugula. It had stray, fringey bits of yarn around the hem and sleeves, and those might have been curly endive.

She had masses of curly brown hair, parted in the center, which stood out about her head in a solid wedge. The hair made her look as if she were wearing an Egyptian headdress, or were peering out from the center of a pyramid. This, with her long face and nose and large, bright eyes, gave her somewhat the appearance of a standard poodle.

A red-eyed crustacean appeared to be clawing its way up her blouse. She saw him trying not to stare at it.

"I designed it myself," she said with some pride. "The sweater *and* the jewelry."

There was a large painting on the wall directly behind her, this time a landscape—all stormy sea and foamy white water and billowing black clouds. Max walked closer and stared up. It was—could it be? Not a Winslow Homer, surely.

She came up to stand beside him.

"Oh, yes," she said dismissively. *Oh, that old thing.* "We've had that ages."

He noted the "we" and said nothing, but remembered the role of the National Trust in all their lives.

A doom-laden voice from behind them seemed to echo his thoughts.

"The house owns that painting," the voice said. "Not you." It could only be Lamorna.

He turned and saw her surveying the breakfast offerings, which to Max's eye were more than generous, and were being added to even then by Milo, who had hefted in various chafing dishes and platters from the kitchen. Back in Nether Monkslip, Mrs. Hooser liked to present Max with similar large breakfasts, including those English standbys of black pudding, baked beans, and fried bread, over his repeated protests that no man not training for a triathlon could eat so much. Here at least he could exercise freedom of choice.

But Lamorna pressed her lips together in unconscious imitation of Lady Lavinia Delamarva Footrustle. Her vinegary expression suggested that things were not managed thus in the old days.

"We used to have sit-down service for breakfast," she told him, catching Max's eye on her. "But we are tightening our belts now."

"Not by the look of things, you aren't." This from a young, high male voice. "You look like you've put on half a stone in the run-up to Christmas."

A boy and girl of a startling beauty, obviously twins, had come slouching in, using the louche, sloping stride of the runway. They were very slender: turn them sideways and they'd disappear. Both were fair in a white-blond, Nordic, *Children of the Corn* way, children who with their pale blue eyes could bend adults to their wills.

Max's train of thought carried him to *Children of the Stones* with its villagers known as "the happy ones." He had watched a recording of that old series from the seventies with Mattie, his girlfriend at the time, the pair of them screeching with laughter at the cheesy clothing and stage sets, shouting warnings at the ill-fated actors of the too-evident danger, which tended to be telegraphed by a rise in the noise level of the ubiquitous chanting in the background. Mattie, as fair as these children, had long since disappeared into Majorca, where he'd heard she'd found happiness living in a house along the coast with her Spanish husband and their two cherubic children.

This blond pair seemed anxious to avoid rather than to control the adults. Knowing the sort of conversation adults tended to aim at young people, almost always on the topic of how they liked school, Max could hardly blame them. The boy and girl grabbed napkins from the buffet and stuffed them with whatever food was portable, then tied the napkins into a hobo's valise and bustled off together. Called to account for their rudeness by Lamorna, they merely mumbled good-byes, but the boy added their intention of enjoying the sun while it lasted out in the garden.

Felberta started in on what Max imagined was a recurring theme as soon as the door into the courtyard was closed behind them.

"What brats they are. Completely unsupervised." Felberta had a tendency to bob her head as she talked, a head that with its massive hair appeared too big even for the generous proportions of her body. "*Such* an ill-considered liaison, Oscar with Gwynyth. And twins—the downside of fertility treatments, if you ask me. Breeding tells—my mother-in-law was right about that. The Middleton misalliance reduced her to sobs. 'Her family is in *trade*,' Leticia would say. She called their business Party Poopers, refusing to get the name right. It was quite funny actually. Such a dreadful snob, Leticia was."

Max had chosen a plate and was ladling a portion of scrambled eggs, bacon, and mushrooms onto it. Lamorna, the early riser, had already come back for seconds of the reviled offerings. She stood piling food on a plate in a way that would have won the delighted admiration of Mrs. Hooser. So absorbed was she in her task he was surprised when she proved to be hanging on Felberta's every word and composing a response.

"I think you're horrid," she burst out suddenly, turning. A slice of bread flew off her plate and hit the floor, landing butter side down in the long tradition of fallen buttered bread. "Kate Middleton at least will have a palace full of advisors and etiquette coaches at her fingertips. Gwynyth was thrown in with a lot of folk who sneered at her—not so much for the *way* she earned her living but for the fact she was forced to earn a living at all. She was surrounded by people who had inherited wealth and sat on their arses, and on their horses, all day making fun of her. If you ask me, she was taken advantage of from the start, and she more than deserves a fairer shake than she was given."

This outburst was greeted by Felberta with something like stunned disbelief, at both its boldness and at the uncharacteristic use of the word "arses." It was also met by a small twinkle of appreciation, this from Milo, who had appeared on yet another mission to replenish supplies. It was clear neither of them had seen the case pro-Gwynyth in quite those terms before.

It was also clear that the removal of Oscar and, in particular, Leticia had gone a long way toward loosening Lamorna's tongue.

As was his way, Max countered anger with mildness. In a voice that was almost a croon, he said, "Your defense of those absent does you proud, Lamorna."

Her shoulders, which had hunched nearly to her ears with tension during her outburst, dropped into a more relaxed posture. Max always found it remarkable—the most effective weapon against anger—praise—was the most easily forgotten, especially in the heat of the moment.

But he had underestimated the depth of the well that held Lamorna's grievances. She stood abruptly and swept out of the room in a manner meant to suggest she had said all she had to say on that particular topic. But she paused dramatically at the door and swung round to deliver one parting shot.

"I tell you it's a Judgment. A Judgment on this house." A typical Lamorna remark, washed in the blood and alive with retribution. In an eerie echo of what Doris had said earlier—had Lamorna been listening at doors again?—Lamorna added, "The trouble's just starting."

And with this Book of Revelation verdict on the situation, she rumbled off, her hips like panniers beneath the blanket of her gray sweater.

"Crikey," breathed Felberta, giving Lamorna's back a look that could freeze a waterfall, as Max's grandmother used to say.

"She was a missionary at one time," Felberta said to Max, in the same tone she might use to say, "She was a prostitute." "She even begged for money on the *street* at one point. Lived as and where she could in various godforsaken parts of the world, and relied on churches to help her wherever she went. Is it any wonder Leticia was horrified by her? In the end, it seems to have been decided it was better to keep her living here, close to home, rather than have her roaming about trying to convert people."

Max murmured that there was a long tradition of that sort of thing in the early church—nothing new there. It was how the apostles had spread the word, relying on the kindness of strangers.

He didn't find Felberta receptive to this theory so he took his plate to a place at the table and sat down. But Felberta wasn't finished with her background on Lamorna. She sat down next to him.

"I remember she was a cute child but then she began to grow," Felberta recalled, almost wistfully. "Chubby knees, so adorable on a baby, were simply fat deposits on a ten-year-old. The onset of adolescence, of course, was catastrophic. It became clear that Lamorna was going to curve out in the wrong places, and curve in at others. Her complexion turned bad. About the time she began to sport a mustache and unibrow, Lady Baynard lost interest. It's a hellish time for most people, but particularly for Lamorna. This was also when she cultivated that stoop, almost like a dowager's hump. She's only thirty, for god's sake. When I first saw her again this November I thought she was middle-aged."

Max tried to deflect this outpouring with a question. "Do you and your husband have children of your own?"

"It was not to be," she said sadly. "Leticia longed for a grandchild so."

Max was thinking Lady Baynard hadn't appreciated the one she did have very much. But he kept his head down and kept busy with his scrambled eggs.

"Leticia doted on my husband," she said brightly. "Of course, she kept Lester from realizing his true potential. She could be a terrifying old trout. Just ask Lamorna."

"So I've been given to understand," said Max.

"He's ever so good with people, is Lester. He could have been something in sales, you know. But Leticia wouldn't hear of that. In the end, he had to migrate to Australia for the freedom he needed to grow."

"Hmm," said Max. The scrambled eggs really had been delicious. He was rising to get himself another serving when:

"Ah! And here comes dear, dear Jocasta," said Felberta, waving her napkin in case she might not otherwise be noticed. In the gloomy lighting of the Great Hall that wasn't entirely impossible.

"I don't suppose you've met my husband's cousin?" she went on, in a way that managed to imply he hadn't been missing much. "Jocasta Jones?"

An intensely well-preserved woman of middle years with auburn hair, dressed flamboyantly in flouncy neon blue, stuck out her hand in greeting.

"Oh, a priest!" she said breathlessly. "Just like in *The Song of Bernadette*. Wasn't Jennifer Jones—no relation, alas—wonderful in that part?"

"Actually," replied Max, who was soon to learn most of Jocasta's references were cinematic, "wrong religion."

"Jocasta and her husband Simon got here *just before* Lord Footrustle took ill," said Felberta with pointed emphasis. "Didn't you, dear?"

If Jocasta was meant to take offense Felberta's aim had missed the target. Jocasta, completely taken with Max, merely flashed her shiny, practiced smile and said, "We'd have been here sooner but we got behind some thickie in security trying to board with full-size bottles of shampoo and conditioner and a metal nail file. You wonder what planet some people have been living on. Anyway, it's jolly good to see the family digs again! And what have we here?" she asked, lifting the lid of one of the copper serving dishes. "Kippers! We can't get these back home, really—or not nearly as good. Marvelous!"

Then she seemed to remember this was too much enthusiasm, considering the events that had befallen the house.

"What a shame all this had to happen at Christmastime." She waved vaguely in the direction of the upstairs room where Lord Footrustle's body had been found.

"I don't think he deliberately got himself stabbed," pointed out Felberta. "Do you? He was a disagreeable sort, and most unkind to me and my husband, but nothing that would warrant a frenzy of stab wounds."

"Nonetheless," Jocasta swooped on. "*Nonetheless*, he was my own flesh and blood, Felberta. I would thank you to speak no ill at least until we've chosen the hymns for the service. That's why the padre is here, aren't you?"

Max was wondering how much the women knew about the crime scene. "I'm sorry if this is upsetting in any way, but did you happen to see the body following the attack?"

Jocasta's hand fluttered, as if she might fly away from the memory. "The blood, the blood!" Max was not to know it, but this was a line from a mid-career Jocasta film called *Did You Hear That?* She had played Rondella Rosemont to loud gasps of laughter and disbelief from the audience. "But did I see—him? Why, no. Of course not! No. But anyone with a shred of imagination can just *pic*ture the scene."

"Have you actually watched yourself in any of your own films, Jocasta?" Felberta asked with studied casualness. "Some of us were wondering the other night."

"Of course not," Jocasta said again. "It is best not to look back. When one is a true professional such as I, one only sees where one could have done better."

"Sometimes one would have done better to appear only on the cutting room floor," said Felberta quietly, but not quietly enough.

"What precisely do you mean?" Jocasta asked, ice dripping from each word.

Max thought it might be time to intervene.

"I can think of few professions requiring more courage," said Max. "You really have to put yourself on the line every time, don't you?"

This earned him a brave, the-show-must-go-on smile.

"Live theater, especially, is *such* a torment. But it is and remains my first love." Her lower lip trembled in a nicely gauged show of emotion. It was certainly more emotion than she had shown at the thought of her father's death, or her aunt's.

Max wanted to ask the question that had been in his mind since yesterday. He had heard of Lord Footrustle—no one could read the *Financial Times* without spotting that distinctive name in its columns—but he was not clear how he'd come by his fortune, which was said to be vast. He broached this question with the delicacy required of such monetary questions. Felberta answered readily enough:

"Uncle Oscar had inherited wealth, and then he 'did something' in electronics. Invented some gizmo and held the patent for it. Or was it telecommunications? Anyway. The patent set him up nicely. He used the money to buy a few newspapers that were going for a song, and that was the start of his Fleet Street career—the career for which he's best known. Then, well—he didn't *invent* the Internet but he was one of thirty people on the planet who didn't positively *gush* money during the dot-com bust. He didn't trust any company run by puppies, he told me. He was canny in his way, was Oscar. Excuse me—Lord Footrustle."

He had noticed that it generally was plain "Leticia" and "Oscar" as far as Felberta was concerned. Australians tended to take a more relaxed view when it came to titles.

"He was also cheap," put in Jocasta. "That helped. I prefer to put my money to use."

"Yes. You really should think about changing the family motto to 'Spend Faster.'"

"I would if it were up to me," said Jocasta. Her voice held more than a trace of bitterness. Max realized that Alec, although decades younger, would likely be the one in charge of the family fortunes. He made a mental note to get what he could out of Cotton and the solicitor he'd mentioned on that score.

"It's certainly a thought," he said neutrally, treating their conversation as playful banter, in a diplomatic voice and bearing honed to a knife edge during many hours with the more fractious of his parishioners.

"So tell me," said Jocasta, "and *please* don't take this the wrong way, but how long are you planning to stay?"

Max at first thought this was aimed at her evident nemesis Felberta but as he looked up from buttering his toast he saw she meant him.

"I honestly couldn't say," said Max vaguely. "I need a word or two with Inspector Cotton. It's rather up to him."

This was patent nonsense but it seemed to mollify her. He realized she was hoping he would extend his stay, a fancy that was confirmed when she fluttered her false eyelashes and said, "I do feel *so* much safer now you are here."

CHAPTER 10

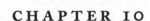

Down the Garden Path

Max decided he'd like a talk with the twins, if he could still find them. They seemed very much alone and while that may have been their choice, they surely under the circumstances were in need of reassurance or at least acknowledgement from the adult world.

The day had dawned mild, and a fitful sun had begun holding its own against the overcast sky, although clouds in a leaden horizon sagged with the weight of snow. As he opened the door to the winter air and the garden, he was remembering what Doris had said of Lady Baynard's devotion to her plants. It all reminded him of Dmitry, a man from his MI5 past he hadn't thought of in years.

Max once had been pretending to broker a deal for a sailboat with a terrorist named Dmitry. MI5 had started tracking people wanting to buy sailboats, once they'd learned how explosives were being brought into Great Britain, away from the watchful eye of customs officials. Dmitry's old sailboat had run aground in a storm and MI5 knew someone would be looking to buy and fast, with money being no object.

Many of the lies Max had told in the course of his career had led people to their deaths, people who had come to trust him. This was what Max had in the end found among the hardest of things to bear, this view of himself as the insinuating, smiling fraud.

He had tried to relay some of this to George Greenhouse at the time. He, a commonsensical sort, hardened by decades in MI5, had said, "Max, the guy was a complete scumbag. I shouldn't worry about it if I were you. The world's a better place without him."

Max had almost said, "But he was *my* scumbag"—which would never have been understood. What he meant was, he had spent months trying to find some trait in the man that made it possible for him, Max, to deal with him at all. Often his target would have children, a family, something normal that Max could cling to, but this particular man was famously a loner who trusted no one enough to form a human attachment. In the end, what good quality Max had been able to discover was the man's passion for orchids, of all things—a Nero Wolfe-like obsession with the rare, the strange, the compellingly beautiful—the jolie laide of the plant kingdom. With a focus, of course, on the most expensive plants available. The man was close to being a billionaire from his illegal trafficking, and could demand the best of everything. Max had seen Dmitry croon over these plants as they emerged from their bulbs like a mother with a newborn, this same man who devoted his days to smuggling in uranium, thorium, explosives, wiring, and other components of the dirty bombs with which he hoped to blow up central London. Or rather, which materials he was content to sell to others so they could pursue their warped ideology to its bloody conclusion. Dmitry also did a brisk business in phenol, and in sulfuric and other acids used to make explosives. The man himself never touched the stuff—it was offloaded from sailboats onto private land near Cromer, just up the coast from Great Yarmouth, often by men with no idea of the true nature of the materials they were handling. From there it would be unloaded into a small van, then transported to waiting barges headed inland into fen country.

Max, dealing with Dmitry, had only been able to smile, to laugh, to look this monster in the eye by focusing on the one area of the man's life devoted to, well, *life*. To growth and beauty and the love of creation. Max had cultivated Dmitry's trust the way Dmitry cultivated his precious orchids. Max found it unconscionably hard at the end to separate himself from the investment he'd made in finding something—anything—lovable in Dmitry.

For Dmitry was the kind of man to send back pieces of an enemy or a hostage until he got what he wanted. But how his eyes would light up as he was crooning over orchids. He would tell Max about how to raise the plants, sun exposure, etc. How they liked strong light, but not too strong. How they liked water, but not too much. How air must be allowed to flow around the roots. It all sounded to Max as if they were the "Princess and the Pea" of the plant world.

When surrounded at the end, Dmitry committed suicide with one of his imported grenades.

Max entered the garden through an archway in the inner courtyard. It was an area quiet and secluded, closed off on all sides by a high hedge or by the castle's curtain wall, which stood well over twenty feet high.

It was like finding oneself in the center of a maze, sheltered from wind and for the most part from prying eyes. When in full leaf the pleached trees would create the occasional private oasis, although in the naked gray of winter Max could view much of the area of the knot garden. He now saw there also was a rose garden and, tucked farther away, what looked to be an herb garden. All were wearing a fluffy blanket of snow.

Max noticed the bare remnants of herbaceous borders which would be in top form in June, and without which no English garden could be truly English. He threaded his way through several distinct areas which followed the principles of the formal Italian garden, as far as the soil of the coast would allow. On his way he recognized old familiars like holly and rosemary; in summer, there would be blooms, bright reminders of nature's annual triumph, ranged against the stark, cool gray walls.

Passing the walled kitchen garden, he came to an area of trees and bushes set in geometric patterns. Beneath one gnarled old specimen an octagonal bench had been built to fit around its trunk. The tree had widened in girth enough to impinge on the bench, much like a belt that has grown too tight for a man's waist. A slender, dark woman he had not yet met sat there with a sketchbook and pencil, engrossed in her work. She did not look up or seem to notice his passing but as he watched, she closed the notebook, stood, and walked away from him and toward the house, her stride long and catlike in its grace. She was dressed all in black—close-fitting slacks and a turtleneck sweater. She had still given no indication she'd seen him.

He chanced upon the hothouse where Lady Baynard had been found, hidden behind a hedge for aesthetic reasons, and now roped off in blue crime-scene tape. The door was shut and he could not get close enough to the windows to see inside without crossing under the tape. This he wouldn't do without Cotton at his side. The windows were fogged up in any event.

It was by the pond in the rose garden, frozen at its edges in a lacy, doily-like effect, that he found the twins. Amanda sat on a bench, staring sullenly into the distance.

Max watched as Alec kicked a stone lining the walk, hard, until it was dislodged from its carefully ordained place. Max suspected the lad would not have been so bold had Milo been there to see the minor vandalism.

Max heard Amanda telling her brother how bored she was. Bored? He could hardly believe his ears. But grief, he reminded himself, wears many disguises, especially at an age when emotion could run the gamut from grief to exhilaration within the space of an hour. "It's not as fun as I thought it would be," she was saying, "being in the middle of an investigation. It's not like on the telly. I want to go back to London." Alec, his eyes gleaming from under the hood of his sweatshirt, like a wild thing peering out from the undergrowth, saw Max approaching from outside her line of sight, and he loudly called out a hello to shush her.

Max introduced himself and asked how they were keeping. They grinned meekly and shrugged in unison. Max gained the impression they had loped for a while around the gardens, at a loss for entertainment that did not involve a wireless connection. The trees, the sea, the sky were seen as poor substitutes, although the girl, Amanda, was reading a book.

Max looked from one to the other. Alec had the pale, translucent skin one associated with particularly tragic, troublesome yet dashing poets of the Romantic era—a blond Lord Byron. On her it was a pallid prettiness, her eyes enhanced by early experiments with makeup.

The boy gave Max a long glance that recorded the dark hair and eyes, the collar, the good-but-worn jacket, and the trainers, a look up and down and lingering, especially on the collar. Max began to wish he'd dressed this day in mufti—the collar put many people at arm's length. The boy surprised him by saying, "How are you liking those trainers? I nearly bought some myself and then the clerk talked me up to the next price point."

Price point. How glibly the sales terms fell from his youthful but jaded lips. They talked for a while of sports, and jogging. In the lapses in their conversation, Max thought he could hear the sound of cattle lowing and sheep bleating in the far distance, perhaps the flock that included his own stray.

"I used to jog more, in my MI5 days," said Max. "I still try to keep in with it, but strangely, I have much less time since I became a priest."

"You were MI5?" Clearly, Alec was enthralled by this news. Max had intended he should be. As an ice-breaker, especially with the young, he knew it was an effective gambit. "I've always wanted to be a spy," Alec added.

"Me, too," said Amanda.

"Since when?" said Alec with the special scorn brothers seem to reserve for sisters.

"Since always," she replied.

"Be careful what you wish for," said Max.

"MI5, really?" Alec repeated, wonderingly. "What made you leave?"

Max shrugged. "I rang the bell."

"Hmm?"

"To leave the French Foreign Legion, you ring the bell—literally. This says you can stand no more and you want out. This is what I did. Figuratively speaking."

"Why?"

"Reasons of my own." It was a dismissal, but kindly done. Alec seemed to accept that they had reached a DO NOT TRESPASS sign and changed the subject.

"Got it. Top secret," he said, and wrenched his mouth into a line suggesting gravity and maturity. "But you're here officially, aren't you?"

The boy was nothing if not persistent.

"I'm no longer on a need-to-know basis with MI5."

Alec said, "Oh, come on. You're still in the loop, surely."

Max shook his head. "Not really. Once you leave that particular brotherhood, you leave." He didn't add that with his having left before his time, even voluntarily, he carried with him the taint of the outcast. One didn't simply up and leave MI5. His exit interview with George, cordial though it had been, and sympathetic as George had been, had reinforced his knowledge of that truth.

Max sat on the bench next to Amanda.

"Did you get to see your father often?" he asked. "And your aunt?"

Amanda looked up briefly from her book. She closed the pages, using her thumb as a bookmark, and he saw she was reading *The Curious Incident of the Dog in the Night-Time*. The cold had brought a little splash of color into her cheeks, and her eyes were still alight with interest in the passage she was reading, for she was still a child, of course, and able easily to slip into the parallel worlds a storyteller could create. Max was struck anew by her beauty.

It was Alec who answered, "Not really. We made him nervous, he said. She was okay—just. She bought us stuff."

"I don't suppose either of them had much of a life, stuck out here with only Muammar Gaddafi for company," said Amanda.

"You mean Lamorna?"

Amanda giggled. "The resemblance is striking, don't you think?"

It was, but Max couldn't encourage that particular form of adolescent unkindness.

"Lamorna was raised by wolves," Amanda went on.

"Fester calls her Nell," said Alec.

"Nell?" Max asked, knowing he shouldn't.

"The wild girl in the movie."

"Fester can really be mean," said Amanda.

"You're just noticing that? And look who's talking."

"Besides," said Amanda slowly, ignoring her brother. "I don't think Lamorna is all that stupid. Her views are stupid, certainly, but I think she's rather a—a *sly* person. Cunning."

Alec's eyes wandered, defeating Max's attempt to catch his attention. Was he hiding something? He gave off a suggestion either of boredom or evasiveness. If he was evading something, what was it? Max felt the boy's response to the question of how he got along with Leticia and Oscar, and that of his twin, had been prepared. No doubt they had discussed the situation between them, anticipating possible avenues the police might wish to explore.

Suddenly looking over Max's shoulder, Alec's expression changed. He said, "Here comes Lester. I can't stand that prat. Must fly."

The twins exchanged complicit glances. Max, so he gathered, was to be left to his own devices.

And effectively they vanished, their slim forms disappearing in single file behind a wide tree whose roots burrowed under the curtain wall.

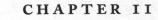

CHAPTER 11

Clear-and-Present Danger

Turning, Max saw the approaching object of this evasive action. Max had thus far managed to avoid the combined clear-and-present danger of Lester and his wife (whose true name he could not at the moment recall, so firmly had "Fester" taken hold in his mind). In any event, he thought he might get further ahead talking with Lester Baynard on his own, and was glad the rare burst of morning sunshine seemed to be bringing people out.

A slight figure with the posture of a question mark, Lester looked like a cartoon in motion, hands flapping like flippers at the ends of his arms, and his brown-and-white saddle oxfords slapping flat-footedly against the ground.

Watching Lester, Max was reminded of Father Goodwin from his time at Oxford, a priest who eschewed the pulpit for the common touch, striding back and forth before his congregation until one Sunday, entirely caught up in the thrust of his narrative, he lost his footing and actually fell off the altar. He was unhurt, but the incident finally convinced him, when no bishop could, to tone down the theatrics.

Lester walked with a swagger that sat ill on such a slight and insubstantial frame. Mick Jagger could get away with it—just. Lester, one felt, could not. He found a bench nearby and sitting down, took out a pen, bent his head with its mop of curly hair over a notebook, and began scribbling rather importantly. He wore only a lambswool V-neck sweater with the collar of a white shirt visible beneath. It was a style that would be trendy on anyone else and on Lester looked more like forgetfulness. It was far too cold for such an outfit. Even the twins had thought to wear jackets.

Surprisingly rosy-cheeked and fresh-faced, Lester looked like a child in a suit too large for him, the collar of his shirt standing out at his neck, although in reality it was probably an artifact of the shrinking that comes with age. Closer up, Lester looked to be not much younger than his brother, whom Max knew to be fifty-three. Where his wife was plump and round, Lester was spare—slope-shouldered and slope-chinned.

He appeared to be deep in thought, although it might be difficult to say for certain. His scribbling seemed disjointed rather than a sustained effort of concentration. He looked up frequently, eyes roaming blindly, randomly. During one of these self-imposed interruptions, Max approached and introduced himself.

"Of course, of course." Lester stood and offered him a hand in greeting. Then he indicated Max should sit next to him. "I can't tell you the last time we had a clergyman here. My mother especially tended to frighten them away. It's a shame as we have a perfectly usable chapel on the grounds. I'm not a believer myself, I should probably tell you that right away."

"Glad if we've cleared that up," said Max, smiling.

"My wife and I were wondering . . . well . . . how to put this?" Lester had rather large eyes, magnified to bug-eyed intensity by the glasses he wore. "We were wondering what you were doing here exactly?" He flashed what Max was sure he thought of as his winning smile and said, "No offense." Max recalled his wife's stated belief that her husband had just missed a booming career in sales, and wondered about that. There was something less than transparent about Lester Baynard, something that did not inspire immediate trust.

"None taken," said Max, answering the question, but obliquely: "Detective Cotton will want to speak with you again today."

"Fine. Whatever gets us out of this sodding place sooner I'm all for it. We all have been told to stay put but I can't wait for sodding ever."

Max waited for the usual rather reflexive apology for the vulgarity, but none came. He was used to people forgetting in the heat of the moment that they were talking with a man of God who should, presumably, be spared the worst of their language.

Of course, few realized that during his MI5 days he had often heard worse—far worse—and had even coined a few new word combinations himself.

"My wife seems to enjoy these little skirmishes with Cotton and that little sergeant he drags around with him. She was with them for ages yesterday."

"Sergeant Essex?" Max guessed.

"That's the one."

"Fes—I mean Felberta" (now even Max was doing it) "will have to meet with Cotton again, most likely. One interview creates questions that only another interview can answer."

"Is that right," said Lester flatly. More than ever, he seemed curious as to Max's role in the proceedings. If he complained formally about it, Max imagined it might create a situation for Cotton, so Max quickly said, "I was talking with the twins just now. I think they could use some attention. It was their father, after all, who was killed. They seem oddly detached from it all, when you'd think it would be the main thing on their minds."

"Oh, they'll be fine," Lester said blithely. "Used to being on their own, that pair. I don't think they knew Oscar all that well."

"That's exactly the problem, as I see it."

"Of course, it's not entirely the twins' fault they're the way they are," Lester breezed on, waving an arm for emphasis. His thin, wiry frame seemed barely able to contain his puppyish energy, which tended to explode in a series of ill-coordinated gestures. "Gwynyth, their mother, is neurotic and *completely* self-absorbed. And marriage only made her worse. She had nothing to do but think about what to wear and plan her next meal out. She had zero career aspirations or responsibilities. Unless you count the twins, which she did not. They were raised by whomever she could pay to raise them."

Max surprised him by asking, "What do you think made Gwynyth that way?"

"*Made* her that way?" Clearly, Lester was taken aback that anyone should care. "Oh, she had the usual sad story about her poverty-stricken upbringing, if that's what you mean. But some people are born to sponge—to take advantage."

"You feel she took advantage of your uncle Oscar, then."

"Tried to," Lester said complacently. "He soon caught on, though. She was seen out nightclubbing once too often, in the company of someone 'not her husband,' as they say."

Lester must have read somewhere that the way to show sincerity was to lean forward into a conversation. He did this now, radiating earnestness. Max instinctively drew back.

"Oscar used to stride about this garden in that castle-owning, king-of-all-I-survey way he had. When Gwynyth was done with him, there was no more striding about. She really finished the guy. I could feel sorry for him."

"I haven't met your brother yet. Randolph. Viscount Nathersby. This must come as a shock to him as well."

"Oh, you *are* in for a treat," said Lester, collecting his writing implements. "Well, I'm rather tired, so if you don't mind . . ."

"This is the sort of occurrence to make one age overnight," said Max, commiserating. "Losing a parent is hard to bear. I have often thought losing a mother may be hardest of all."

There was a sudden drop in temperature, a lessening of studied bonhomie. Lester, drawing in from his sincere, open pose, said, "The avaricious little shit. Ask *him*."

"Ask him what?"

Lester, while monumentally preoccupied with himself, was strangely likeable. Max wouldn't have trusted him an inch in business dealings but that wasn't the same thing as liking. He seemed incapable of self-editing—what was in his mind was soon on his lips. It was often the sign of a truthful nature, but always the sign of an impulsive, perhaps uncontrollable, one.

"For a start, ask him what he plans to do about the twins. As you say, someone has to care about them, now they've lost their father. You would think Randolph, the eldest male figure, would step up to bat there."

Again the eager, forward-leaning posture. It would have been flattering to the listener had it not come across as too practiced, too full of deliberate intent. *I am sincere*, the gesture proclaimed, too loudly. Part of his terrific sales technique, along with the blaze of concerned interest in his listener. But Max thought it was the concern of self-interest, not the concern of the concerned.

What was certain was that during Alec's minority, he would need a legal guardian to make decisions for him about the disposal of his father's estate. Max sensed there might be a jockeying for position between the two brothers, Lester and Randolph. It was not unlike the situation when Henry VIII had died, leaving Edward VI king at the age of nine. One of Edward's uncles had seized the reins. None of it had gone well, especially when Edward died, aged fifteen years, choosing (at the urging of the adults holding the real power) Lady Jane Grey as his short-lived heir.

He definitely would need to talk to that solicitor, Max decided.

Felberta came into the garden just then, looking for her husband.

"What are you doing out here without a coat?" she scolded him. She had a jacket over her arm which she handed to Lester. Her springy hair was now scraped back into a rubber band and he could see she had nice ears, flat to her head, and the sun, as it was at her back, shone through them, pink and shell-like, showing the delicate tracery of capillaries. She had a slight indentation in each lobe—Max had read somewhere that was a sign of heart disease, but could think of no way to lob that one into the conversation. Instead he said, "In the sunshine, it's not too bad."

Lamorna walked by just then, a basket on her arm and pruning shears in hand. She now wore the gray cardigan over a black woolen dress with a knitted Peter Pan collar. She apparently owned a collection of these accessories, for the collar was slightly different from that of the day before. Her costume wasn't sufficient protection against the cold of the day but Max imagined that was all part of the fun. The outfit really only needed a veil to resemble a modern-style nun's habit, right down to her sensible lace-up shoes.

Lamorna said, "I thought I'd gather some flowers for the table. I am feeling so at a loss with Lady Baynard gone."

"What would Jesus do?" said Felberta sarcastically.

"Shut up, Felberta," said Lester, nudging her, with a significant nod in Max's direction.

Max said, "He would know the truth immediately, tell it, and we could all go home. I have to help sift the truth from the lies somehow and pray for guidance."

The significance of what he was saying was not lost on Lester. Max was here to advise on more than the services for the departed. Lester didn't look pleased to have his suspicions confirmed.

"I thought that was a given," he said. " 'Seek and ye shall find.' "

"It is," said Max. "It just takes some of us longer. The truth's always there, waiting."

Lester turned to look at his wife, who was apparently not listening, but busy inhaling the scent of the fresh air. Lamorna had left them, engaged in the fruitless task of finding live blooms in the garden this time of year. It would be ages before she'd be allowed by the police into the hothouse, where she might have had better luck.

Lester, looking at her, launched into a lengthy explanation, with what he obviously believed was disarming candor, of how Lamorna had always been a problem. The point may have been to emphasize that he himself, by way of contrast, had never been the least cause for concern. Max listened to as much of this as he could and then cordially took his leave of them.

Fester and Felberta remained behind, sitting together on the garden bench.

"What do we do now?" Felberta leaned into her husband. Lester privately thought the answer to that question was, "Leave, and the sooner the better," but he doubted that suggestion would fly in the current interrogative atmosphere, however skillfully presented the suggestion.

"You heard the man," he said, smiling and patting her hand. "We wait for the truth to come out."

❄ ❄ ❄

Max saw a gate in the south-facing wall that likely led to a view of the ocean. He was just heading that way to explore when a fit-looking man in his mid-thirties went jogging past, saw him, and pulled to a stop. The man wore a balaclava which he courteously pulled down around his neck so his face was visible. He had a thatch of sandy hair, wide blue eyes, and conventional good looks. He introduced himself as Simon Jones, Jocasta's husband.

Max hid his surprise, or hoped he did. Jocasta, for all her well-maintained looks, was clearly older than her husband by at least a decade.

"A fellow jogger," said Max. "It is nice to meet a kindred spirit. I was just talking with Alec about the days when I was more faithful to my training schedule."

Simon said, "I didn't think jogging was a particularly British sport."

"Well," said Max heartily, "we practically invented running. Learned it from the Romans."

Simon, who knew when his leg was being pulled, smiled. He swept a coating of snow off a nearby bench and sat down, breathing heavily.

"I'm not feeling the benefit today," he told Max. "It's the jet lag. Completely throws you off. And it's so damn quiet here," he added. "I can't sleep for the quiet. Well, that, and the jet lag."

"This garden in winter doesn't provide ideal conditions for running, either. Where did you and your wife fly in from?"

"LAX."

"A long distance, made twice as long by today's many inconveniences of travel," said Max. "I am very sorry for the way your journey ended in such a tragedy."

"I still can't quite get over it, you know. To lose both of them the same day! And poor Oscar, killed so brutally. If I put this in a screenplay, who would believe it?"

It was the first Max had heard Oscar referred to as "poor." At least there was one person who seemed to feel the loss of the man. But he merely said, "You're a screenwriter? I didn't realize."

"I'm an aspiring one." Simon bent to adjust a shoelace that was coming untied. "After years of reading the shit my wife is offered and seeing it actually make it to the screen, I thought I'd give it a try. God knows, I could hardly do worse. And I have the advantage of being at least on the fringes of the business all these years. You meet people."

"I met your wife at breakfast," said Max. He added carefully, "She seems to be holding up well."

"There was no love lost between her and the old man, if that's what you mean. He, having jettisoned the first wife, also lost track of the product of that union—Jocasta. She left home decades ago, made it out to Hollywood eventually. That's where she and I met, of course. I was trying to get an acting career off the ground. She was—well, at one time she was promising. What's that saying about the gods destroying the promising?"

"'Whom the gods wish to destroy they first call promising.' Cyril Connolly."

"Right. That was Jocasta. Perhaps never a raging talent—well, all right, she was never any kind of talent, really—but beautiful and gutsy and willing to work. Those qualities have taken more than a few actresses further than perhaps they should have gone. Well," and here Simon slapped his knees and stood up. "I enjoyed meeting you. I'm sure there will be other occasions. If you don't mind, I need to keep at it if I'm ever going to reset the old internal clock."

❄   ❄   ❄

Max opened the gate in the wall and found it led to a cliff-top path overlooking the sea. Here he stood in a bitterly cold breeze, peering out like an old mariner, no longer buffered by the curtain wall. There was a soft green turf which spread to the cliff's edge, and beneath him a vanishing pool of deep blue disappearing into the horizon. Max stepped carefully back from the vertigo-inducing view.

The house had been built into a rocky promontory overlooking the sea, probably for the breathtaking view. But when French raids became all the worry, the manor house was reinforced accordingly.

The cliff walk was probably a later amenity, added in whatever day it came to pass that enemy invasion by sea was not uppermost in everyone's mind. A modern-day landscaper had been at work here, too. But Max's interest was in whether an outside intruder could have made it into the gardens and into the castle via this side of the castle.

He supposed a murderer could just have managed to climb up using modern equipment and then presumably rappel back down. He tried to picture such a shadowy, extremely fit figure, his imagination calling up a member of the Special Boat Service or a pirate, knife clenched in teeth. Max shook his head. Improbable, and impossible without leaving signs of such activity. Surely Cotton's people had been all over that.

Max considered what he'd learned so far and concluded it didn't add up to much. He watched the water approach only to crash repeatedly at the foot of the cliff. The climber of his imagination would have had to come off a boat and it was inconceivable any craft could get close enough to the cliff in these violent waters.

He turned and directed his steps toward the castle. It was midmorning. Cotton would be here by now.

CHAPTER 12

Max Out

Max was to be waylaid one more time, this time with maddening consequences, for Amanda was just inside the wooden door opening from the cliff walk path. He'd spent a moment inspecting that door from the outside, despite his belief no one could have made his way up the cliff, and certainly not without leaving evidence of the climb in the rock face. The door didn't even have a lock, for what it was worth, since the castle residents clearly shared with him the belief the castle was impregnable from that direction. It was kept in place with a simple slide bolt latch.

"Let me show you around," Amanda said. She was now wearing a red Peruvian-style winter hat with tassels and she'd clearly been waiting for him. "I've been reading up on the history of Chedrow Castle. Are you interested in history?" She didn't stop for an answer. "I am. I just *love* history." Big smile. "I'm going to read history at university, I've already decided. You'll want to see the Old Kitchen. It's a favorite with the day trippers."

He started to cut through the flirtatious chatter and claim his earlier appointment with DCI Cotton, but then realized he'd be missing the perfect opportunity to ask her a few questions, which was after all his reason for being here. Her brother, busy scoring points off her wherever he could, may have kept the girl from speaking freely. Certainly she was showing no signs of her former reticence now.

She began walking toward one of several tall stone towers. One was positioned to the left of the garden and near the front wall. Like the rest of the buildings near the perimeter, it was riddled with small windows and loopholes. The entire castle was perforated with these openings, like a Swiss cheese.

They passed by Milo, apparently doing double duty in the

garden, wearing fingerless gloves and a battered oilcloth coat. Max supposed that with Leticia gone his obligations would increase. They'd have to get some additional help. As they passed Milo gave a vicious tug on a weed and swore mildly: Gardening didn't seem to be his forte.

Amanda walked beside him like a model on a catwalk, a completely unnatural stride that involved tipping back from the hips, arms dangling at the sides and feet crossing one in front of the other. He wondered where he'd seen it just recently then realized that, of course, the woman he'd glimpsed in the garden with the sketchbook walked like that. And she, so glamorous and artistic-looking, would no doubt be someone a fourteen-year-old girl would want to emulate.

They skirted an herbaceous border, the gray-green plants thriving even in winter. She led him across to the tower housing the Old Kitchen.

"There's not a lot for someone your age to do around here, is there?" he asked her. "At least in warm weather, you could go to the beach."

An expression of grievance flitted over Amanda's flawless face, like storm clouds on a summer's day.

"The nearest town with anything like a nightlife is Monkslip-super-Mare, and their idea of entertainment is a pig race." Max decided not to tell her about Nether Monkslip's eagerly anticipated yearly duck race. "In the pub they're taking bets on how many inches of snowfall we'll get this year. I've been bored to sobs, but Mother says we have to stay until all this is sorted. Is that true? She's seldom the go-to person for accurate information."

Max had no idea. "I'm afraid that's probably so. The police have to solve this crime and you'll need to be available to them."

They were nearing the entrance to the tower that housed the Old Kitchen, a door of blackened wood, studded, with heavy metal hinges.

"You must miss your father," Max said. He kept his tone low; it was the unobtrusive voice he used when a parishioner was in particular distress. He might have been calling from a great distance, a mere background to the person's chaotic thoughts.

But that was a particularly lame thing to say, judging by her expression. "Do you think I must? I barely knew him. I barely can remember him now."

The studied air of disinterest was convincing, but a very thin membrane separated Max from the rest of the world. He was able to feel others' joys and sorrows, and adopt their preoccupations, forgetting himself and his own joys and sorrows in the process. This ability to relate, to cohere even to the vilest of lowlife criminal, was what had made him a valuable asset to MI5. The same ability to relate to people of all stripes also made him valuable to the Anglican Church. His sense of Amanda was that she was hiding a world of loss behind the cool façade.

They stood in the shelter of the high stone walls as she gave the round door handle a practiced twist and a downward push. The door creaked open. The sea could faintly be heard in the distance: pummeling, pounding, roaring, eternally seeking entry.

". . . ghosts in the castle."

Max, distracted by the melancholy beauty of the sound, asked her to repeat what she'd said.

"Of course they've just joined the ghosts in the castle," she said. "My aunt, and my father. They haven't really left."

"Do you seriously believe that? Believe in ghosts?" Max asked her.

She gave him the *Well, duh* look patented by teen cave dwellers at approximately the start of recorded history. He might have made the mistake of asking if she thought Justin Bieber was cute.

"There are. You don't see them, hovering just at the corner of your vision? I do. Then when I turn to look, of course, there's nothing there."

They stepped over the threshold and the temperature seemed to drop ten degrees. Kitchens in those days, he knew, were placed away from the main building because of the constant risk of fire. Max and Amanda passed through an inner door and looked about;

much of the room was roped off, undergoing renovations. The windows were set high to draw the heat and smoke up and out; an enormous fireplace with roasting hearth and bread ovens on either side ranged against one wall. Amanda pointed out the serving hatch, where servants would collect the food and carry it across the courtyard to the Great Hall.

"Imagine this job in winter," said Amanda.

"Or in a sweltering August," said Max. "Even worse."

The scullery occupied the ground floor of the next tower over, she told him. It had a drain in the floor which presumably was used to eliminate wastewater.

"But here," his guide told him, "is what is so cool. I use this as my hiding place, when I just want to read or think and get away from the rest of them."

She indicated a small doorway designed to knock the taller, modern-day visitor senseless. She motioned him through, and he saw that it opened into a spiral staircase. A panther would have had trouble climbing it, and there were no handrails.

"The general run of tourist is not allowed up here," she said. Her face became serious, closed off; he nodded in appreciation of the privileged status she had granted him. He followed as she went tripping up the treacherous, uneven steps. Round and round they went in a tight circle, hands extended to brace themselves against the walls, and finally they reached a small room two floors above the scullery.

Pushing open the door, she said, "They think it was a guard-room." He saw a round room with two-foot-thick walls: Loopholes, wide inside and narrowing to long apertures, offered defense-by-arrow of the outer walls. The openings had long since been glassed in to keep out the cold. The room was furnished, sparingly if with some charm, with a double bed, tables, and rugs, and had been fitted out with a small bathroom.

"Sometimes we let it out to guests," she said. He noted the "we" and the little throb of pride in her voice. With her father gone she seemed to have assumed ownership of a place from which she effectively had been barred by her parents' divorce. Not just a "place," he amended, but a national treasure steeped in history and beauty. Lamorna and Felberta had exhibited similar signs of possessiveness.

Max moved over to a window. He imagined he could see the tops of the trees on Hawk Crest in the far distance. His villagers would all be going about their daily lives; early risers like Lily Iverson would have been up for hours to tend to her sheep, to Dolly and Lucrezia (the black sheep) and all the rest, as mist still hovered over the hedgerows. Awena would be in her shop, dusting or organizing or keeping track of inventory on her computer.

"Do you know what's strange?" Amanda asked of his back.

"I would love to hear what is strange," he replied, turning to her.

"I think someone tried to kill my father even before they . . . they succeeded."

Of course he knew about the poisoning attempt, assumed by some to have been attempted murder. But she surprised him when she said, "I think they tried to hit him with a stone dropped from the parapets. He was walking around the garden, just as we were now, and he felt something *whoosh* right by his ear. He turned around and there was this enormous boulder in the path."

"How do you know that?"

She shrugged. "He told me, didn't he? I thought he was imagining things. Don't old people make up things to get attention sometimes? Now I wonder—now that this has happened, I wonder . . ."

"Did he have any idea who had done it?"

"No."

"Do you?"

"Not really. I mean, my mother hated him enough to do it, but she wouldn't. She just wouldn't. Except maybe . . ."

"Maybe?"

"Maybe on a split-second impulse. But it's not really in her to do that. I would know, wouldn't I?"

How often had he heard a parent of the worst sort defended by the child who depended on that parent for its own survival. For what it was worth, he filed the information away. Gwynyth, Lady Footrustle, was of course a prime suspect in her ex-husband's death.

"It was awful, when we lived here," Amanda was saying. She twirled around one finger a strand of the flaxen hair that had escaped the hat. "Fortunately, I barely remember it. I thought they were both quite mad, my parents."

Amanda had pudgy little hands like chubby starfish and she waved them now about her ears to show, presumably, how wild and crazy her upbringing had been.

"Certainly when they quarreled they sounded insane."

His conversation with Lester fresh in mind, Max asked her about her cousin.

She shrugged. "What's to say? He's *such* a prat. As for that wife of his, Fester—the one who always dresses like she's covered in algae . . . All I can say is, love really must be blind."

"I hear that it is," said Max mildly. A picture of Awena rose into his mind, but no blindness was in play there. Awena glowed from within with a beauty that was unique to her alone. It was the first time the word "love" had come into his mind in connection with her, though, and he wondered at that. He wondered very much.

". . . thing that is remarkable about Lester," Amanda was saying, "is that even when it looks like he's doing nothing, he's actually doing *nothing*. Which is a thing monumentally difficult to do, when you think about it. He seems actually to be able to empty out his mind, like a man turning out his pockets."

Max, smiling, reflected that it *was* difficult to do, if not impossible. Besides, Lester struck him as a man who was always up to something, even if something that seemed squirrelly and pointless to the naked eye.

"And his wife? Felberta?"

"Fester. She's Australian."

"Yes, all right. And what else do we know about her?"

"I don't know . . . They all like to barbeque." She tapped the fingers of one small hand against her rose-pink mouth, stifling a small yawn. He saw that she wore a skull-and-bones ring, the sort of thing popular with kids. Such an odd fashion statement but he saw it everywhere.

Was she joking about the barbeque? Max didn't think so. That probably amounted to the sum total of her knowledge and understanding of Felberta.

But: "Thick as thieves, those two," she added darkly. Her eyes shone brightly out of kohl-rimmed lids. "I think he's casing the joint, as they used to say in cop movies."

"And Simon? What do we know about him?"

"He's American. You know what they're like."

"Friendly and hardworking?"

"Noisy and pushy."

"From what little I've seen of Simon, he's neither."

She shrugged. *Think what you like, then.*

"And he's fed up with Jocasta," she said. "Join the club, I say."

She continued to give him that level gaze. This time there was a certain accretion of goodwill in her eyes.

"I'm glad you're here. I think with you here we might get it all sorted. Or at least, it won't get any worse."

Amanda was fast becoming his new best friend, he realized. She asked, "Do you have any kids?"

The lack of a wedding ring meant nothing anymore, he realized. He surprised himself a bit by saying, "Not yet. But I really would like to have children one day." In a way, the villagers had become his "children," and he was content to do as best he could to see to their care. Children of his own he rarely had time to think about. But there it was, what he had said aloud, and it was the truth. One day, he wanted a family of two or three children. He was in his forties—plenty of time biologically. But children deserved a father agile enough to—oh, to save them from drowning or some other calamity. Didn't they? He was himself mildly astonished that he remained unmarried. It wasn't through lack of trying in the past. But the person to raise children with him had not appeared in the years when he and Paul were carelessly sampling much of London's female population. Paul, who had married. Who had had a child. And who had died on his— Max's—watch.

He shook himself from the reverie and saw Amanda was looking at him curiously. He said, "No time at the present. But one day."

"I'll be available as soon as I get through my A-levels," she said. She smiled to show she was kidding—sort of—and Max let out a bark of laughter.

"Thank you. I'll keep that in mind. I suppose I should go and find out where DCI Cotton is."

"He's in the library. I gathered we're all to be positively *grilled* throughout the day. In a way, I wish they'd just leave it alone. Anyway, I must run now. If they're looking for me I'll be in the main tower. That's where we're staying while we're here."

And turning abruptly, she skipped down the stairs. Max took a final look around the room and followed, racing to keep up with her fearless descent, and wondering exactly what she meant by wishing they'd leave it alone. Surely it was in her best interests to learn the truth surrounding her father's death.

Outside, he came to stone steps with a thin veneer of black ice. He was just wondering how he was going to extend his stay at the castle. He'd have to come up with some story, some excuse to buy extra time, but that would be lying, and a step back to his MI5 days of nothing but deceit, and—

Oh—

Blast and damn it all to hell.

He was on his face in the snow, the top of the stairs was far above him, and his ankle was as sore as if someone had taken a hammer to it. Was it broken or merely sprained? He thought sprained—at least, there were no protruding bones and everything looked attached, if aching.

The castle steps at this time of year offered a kind of double whammy. Worn down to an edge over the centuries like a ski slope, and now covered with invisible ice.

Damn. He should have been more careful. His head was aching, too. He made an effort to collect his thoughts, which seemed to have scattered like marbles across a glass floor. He looked around. Amanda was long gone.

But Lamorna was beside him. Lamorna, possibly the one person one would not want around in an emergency.

"Don't move!" she shrieked, as if she'd found him planning a decathlon with the injured ankle. "I'll get help!"

Good, thought Max, gingerly turning his head, not so much immobile as wondering if God really moved in such mysterious ways as to render him sidelined from the investigation. Or was the point to force him to stay where he was and investigate at his leisure? He took the opportunity to wonder how Lamorna had appeared so fortuitously. Had she been following him and Amanda?

Lamorna's brogues came into his peripheral vision. She wore them with black socks with a subtle pattern of acorns, he noticed. The detail one could glean from ground level!

"Don't move!" she commanded again.

"I'm not moving," he told the hard, frozen ground.

"Help is on the way!"

Oh, for heaven's sake. She hadn't called an ambulance?

"Look, I'm fine." He turned over slowly and sat up with great care, as if all his bones might shatter with the effort. Wincing, he examined the offending area. "See? I'm fine. Just a sprain."

"I've sent for the nurse."

Of course, he'd forgotten that between Leticia and Oscar, both elderly, they probably kept the local nurse practically on speed dial. Max struggled to rise and the pain in his left ankle suggested he not try that just yet. In due course the nurse appeared, a supremely competent-looking soul named Emma Brown with masses of white hair ballooning about her head. She carried a little leather bag of supplies, which included an elastic bandage wrap with tabs to secure it. She first satisfied herself that Max's own diagnoses were correct. No concussion ("stunned silly for a moment, is all"), minor sprain. She cleaned and bandaged the wound on his forehead and recommended ice and elevation for the rest.

"Were you by any chance called out here for Lord Footrustle recently?" he asked her.

"Oh, yes. He had a bit of a tummy and finally let me look at him. He wouldn't have the doctor."

"What did you think was wrong?"

"Didn't I just say? A bit of tummy. Something he ate that disagreed with him."

"Could it have been food poisoning?"

She leaned back on her haunches and looked at him.

"I've known Doris all me life. No, it could not have been food poisoning. Not by accident or carelessness, anyway." She stood up. "I'll be right back."

She returned from her car with a crutch and a recommendation that he go to the hospital for an X-ray, which he knew immediately he would not do. Thanking her for her trouble, he tried walking—hopping, rather—without the crutch but decided overall he'd heal faster if for now he did as he was told.

It was time to find Cotton, while he was still able.

CHAPTER 13

Old Friends

Max reached the library by hobbling down a mercifully few short steps which began near the main staircase off the Great Hall. It was a room which must at one time have been an undercroft of sorts to the main hall. A storage area, perhaps. The original inhabitants of the house, Max imagined, would have had little time for quiet reflection over books of poetry or passionate discussions of stagecraft over tankards of mulled wine.

DCI Cotton was there along with Detective Sergeant Essex. "Where have you been?" Cotton greeted him. "In a roller derby?"

"It's just a sprain. Thanks for your concern."

Sergeant Essex, she of the choppy haircut with its multi-colored strands, smiled warmly at him.

"Glad you could join us," said Cotton, "whatever your condition."

Max collapsed into a chair, leaning the crutch against the Tudor-style dark paneling. The room, faced by bookcases built into the walls, was gently lighted by wall sconces and warmed by a log fire in the stone hearth.

"Right. So what have we got?" Max asked.

Cotton noted the "we" with a little frisson of satisfaction. Max was fully on board already.

"We haven't released the crime scene but everyone is free to roam about everywhere except Lord Footrustle's bedroom and, until we're certain what's going on, Lady Baynard's hothouse."

Cotton was examining his suit jacket as he spoke. There seemed to be an imperfection in the weave that was troubling him. Dapper and clean shaven, the promise of a dilettantish approach to crime suggested by the obvious care Cotton took with his appearance was undermined by the take-no-prisoners look that stole into his eyes when he suspected a suspect was lying.

He went on: "We've taken statements from everyone concerned—meaning, everyone in the castle—but I'll be talking with all of them again. I'd like you to sit in on these sessions, Max. I'd like to know your impressions."

"I'm happy to oblige, but as you know . . ."

"You've no official status. Well, actually you have. I've asked you to be here. If anyone objects we'll deal with it then. They're a rum bunch, I'll say that for them."

Cotton had stopped worrying his jacket to twirl a biro around the top of the desk, clearly deep in thought. He had a laptop on which he began to tap out a few notes. He was, to Max's certain knowledge, a man in perpetual, dynamic motion. Max took the moment to lift his left ankle onto a footstool. Finally Cotton sat back and said, "So, Max, you've had a little time to meet some of them. Let's have your first impressions."

Max's first and second impression had been of a household vastly on edge, but that was understandable, with a recent murder very much at their feet. Max had the feeling this edginess was of long standing, however. All this he said to Cotton and Essex, ending with, "I suppose we have to start with motive."

"Motive?" Cotton shook his head mockingly. "To hear the public, we officials never bother with motive. But here we have motive aplenty. Money—the obvious driver, since there's so much of it—isn't the entire story. There's a well of ill feeling. A sense of 'getting even' pervades this case, if I'm right. If you'd seen the body you'd agree."

"Overkill." Max nodded. "I am sorry to hear it, poor man. But Lady Baynard's death . . ."

"It was a natural death, so far as the experts can tell."

"Was it? Maybe she'd been poisoned over a long period—someone using arsenic, like all the Victorian poisoners seemed to use back in the day."

But Cotton told him that was one of the first things they tested for. "Those metallic-based poisons—frankly, no murderer worth his salt would use arsenic anymore. But overall a tox scan can take forever and never be successful unless they know the poison they're looking for. There is no such thing as an untraceable poison, just one the lab fellows haven't thought to test for."

He made another note on the laptop, then added: "I got them to call in a Home Office pathologist."

"Ah. A forensic pathologist—a specialist in the art of death by criminal means. Called in for both Leticia and Oscar, then?"

"Yes. He is likewise adamant the woman died of natural

causes. He said he'd make sure and run a few more tests beyond the standard set, but unless we're hoping for 'some nonsense like a new and undetectable poison from South America'—his words— she died because she'd reached a certain age and she had a certain condition. Nothing unnatural about it."

"The condition being?"

"She apparently died of an abdominal . . ." He paused to consult his computer screen. "An abdominal aortic aneurysm."

"Symptoms?"

"Generally, there are none. Pain is the only symptom, and I gather she never complained of abdominal or back pain. The kind of pain we're talking about would definitely have alarmed her. She seemed in the days before her death to be preoccupied only by a simple head cold. No sign of anything as dangerous as this. 'She'd have been screaming bloody murder,' is how one of the suspects put it, if she'd been in any real pain." Max thought that was probably Doris. "There is speculation Leticia's fatal symptoms emerged out of shock or remorse but . . ."

"Remorse for killing her brother, you mean?"

"Precisely. It's not completely impossible that guilt triggered a condition that was set to go off."

"And Lord Footrustle? Apart from what obviously killed him, did he have any symptoms in particular in recent months?"

"You mean the attempted poisoning, or accidental food poisoning, don't you? Well, Oscar was in poorer health, comparatively speaking, and the odds were he would go first, despite Leticia's complaints about her own condition. She was, by all reports, a bit of a hypochondriac, worse than he. Of course, what she complained of most was not what she died of. The doc says she probably had no symptoms whatsoever. That's typical of this aortic whatsis."

Max was remembering that one of his parishioners had had much the same condition. "It's some sort of silent killer, isn't it? Unless one is specially tested for it."

"A screening test is available, but it's not widely used unless they're trying to track down a specific complaint. And according to the family," Cotton added, "that must be the one potential illness she never mentioned. I understand she could have gone on for years with the symptoms she complained about—most of them imaginary: headaches and palpitations and so on."

"I see."

Cotton said, "So we're looking at an open verdict here. Meaning, the jury won't be satisfied, but they will be hamstrung by the limits set. In truth, there is nothing we could present to a jury that would lead them to find anything suspicious in Lady Baynard's death, except that a man had been murdered on the same day in close proximity. And everyone on the jury would have heard about that already." He closed his eyes, projecting himself into the room where he had so often given evidence. "You would be able to see it in their faces, this earnest desire to get at the truth, to see justice done if justice needed doing, but for now the facts we have establish a case of death by natural causes."

"How are we on time of death?"

Again, that "we." Lovely. "The police doctor who first examined him says the time of death for Lord Footrustle was eight A.M., give or take two hours. He was found by the butler, so that puts an end time to the range. But more than likely, he'd been dead at least a couple of hours by then."

He added, "Let's call them Oscar and Leticia, for the sake of convenience, rather than Lord This-and-That or Lady So-and-So. They're neither of them around to object to the informality."

Max had met the police doctor on numerous occasions. He was a man extremely competent and extremely young. Max was always tempted to ask him if they'd let him off school for the day to perform the autopsy.

"A range of several hours," said Max. "Poor man. One would like to be discovered right away, somehow, don't you think?"

Cotton and Essex both nodded solemnly. Essex had her head bent over a large illustrated tome she'd pulled from one of the shelves. She was a small, compact woman, and the heavy book entirely covered her lap.

Max said, "I've spoken with Lamorna Whitehall, the grand-daughter. She presented me with a salient motive, or at least an explanation for the atmosphere here at the castle." Max repeated what Lamorna had told him about her grandmother manipulating people with stories of what they'd inherit from her.

"That could have made one of them want to kill her—providing them a motive if she was up to silly game-playing like that," said Cotton. "Again, we're keeping our options open in case something turns up. The police doc is still running tests."

Cotton had resumed his tapping at the computer keys. Max looked at him. "Why do I have the idea you think it was murder?"

Cotton looked up from his task.

"I do think Leticia was murdered, yes. Yes, I do. It's my gut instinct, but I can't prove it. I've instructed my team to keep their minds very open on that score."

"Always wise," said Max. "Let's get back to motive for a moment. Oscar had to have made enemies in his time. Especially on Fleet Street, I understand, that is not difficult to do."

Sergeant Essex spoke up. "He may have aroused the wrath of the 'have-nots'—people not born to title and money, or people not having the Midas touch to create wealth."

Cotton nodded and smoothed his tie.

"So we're looking at enemies as suspects? Or inheritors?"

"Both," said Max. "Either, or. We can't discount either approach."

Cotton said: "We have to collect all the evidence we can for the inquest, in as orderly a fashion as we can manage. And as quickly. The real work is finding out who did this, which may take days or weeks of sifting, interviewing witnesses, and so on."

"You've ruled out an intruder?"

"We're ruling out nothing just yet, but the geography of the house as good as eliminates that possibility. We're sitting on top of a cliff that drops straight to the sea. So there's no access from that direction but we did send investigators out to make sure. The main entrance to the house is fronted, in thoroughly medieval fashion, by an insurmountable wall on all sides."

Max asked, "What about security at the castle?"

"Security." Cotton smiled. "Well, the butler locks up the castle at eleven every night, whether it needs it or not. He sets a burglar alarm that is connected to the security company. Presumably the company would contact us if it were found someone had tried to break in or set fire to the place. The police might even arrive at the castle in time to prevent the stolen items being put up for sale on eBay."

"No cameras? No motion detectors?"

"No. Instead, they seem to have had vast stores of optimism and hope that no one would attempt a serious break-in in such a remote spot. This belief carried them happily through the dawn of the twenty-first century."

"Fingerprints?"

Cotton scoffed at fingerprints. "You know as well as I do, Max. Nobody commits a crime like this without wearing gloves. They've all watched the forensics shows on television, you know."

Max moved his left foot slightly to test it for readiness. His ankle announced sharply that it was too soon for that sort of thing.

Cotton was saying now: "We'll ask that the inquest be adjourned so we can make inquiries. But the press will catch on that there's something afoot—sorry, Max, bad pun. So far, they haven't caught on but seem to be playing up the coincidence angle. This will have them speculating about Lady Baynard's death being tied to Lord Footrustle's. Well, let them speculate. We can't stop them anyway."

Cotton grabbed some pages from the desk, stood up, and began striding around as he talked.

"As I mentioned, we've had a look round the rooms and have had to allow everyone back into their assigned places," he said, flipping through pages. "There is nothing suggestive to report. Not unless you count 'several hundred little pots of makeup in Jocasta's room,' as one of the officers notes," said Cotton. "'And enough boas and scarves to launch her own costume drama.'"

"That would be PC Detton's comment," said Essex. "He's a frustrated scriptwriter. It tends to show in his reports."

"So," said Cotton. "What's the drill for today? I suppose we should start with the eldest first. Let's have Randolph in here. For the record," he said with a nod toward Essex, "that would be Randolph, Viscount Nathersby. He's actually the Eleventh Earl of Gravening, the title inherited from his father, but he'd made a name for himself as Nathersby and seems to have stuck with that for all but the most formal occasions."

Sergeant Essex waggled her head and raised her eyebrows in an almost imperceptible la-di-da manner. She hadn't had much truck with nobs before and she wasn't inclined to be impressed by them now. Max watched as the haze of contempt wafted over her eyes. She said nothing but went to find the man she had privately taken to calling Viscount His Lordship.

"Does anyone have an alibi for the time in question?" Max asked Cotton when she'd left.

"Nothing that would hold up to scrutiny. Everyone was either asleep or wandering about the castle and grounds. It's such a big place it's entirely possible that it's true. You could disappear for weeks here."

Abruptly he stopped pacing. He turned to face Max, the papers bunched roughly in his hands.

"This is an unspeakable crime," he said. "The old guy didn't stand a chance. Maybe if he'd been younger I'd feel differently. Or even if he'd been awake."

Max nodded. "I agree completely."

"Right," Cotton said. "Let's start the show."

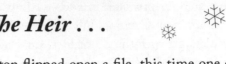

CHAPTER 14

The Heir . . .

While they waited, Cotton flipped open a file, this time one on his mobile phone, and summarized what he found there: "Randolph, Viscount Nathersby. Pretty much what you'd expect. Educated at Eton and Cambridge, where he read art history. Somehow went from there to a career as a photographer in fashion and theater—that may be one of the many jobs where having the right connections keeps you from flat-out starving. He lately has made a bit of a name for himself as a portraitist of the great and the good, but in a small way—Lord Snowdon had snapped all the truly great by the time Randolph came along. You know the sort of thing: photos of minor royalty and their dogs and horses—sometimes all three together, almost like family portraits, what?"

Here Cotton turned the phone toward Max so he could see a photo of a man in formal hunting attire astride his horse, the pair surrounded by a swirling brown sea of hunting dogs. "Married and quietly divorced," Cotton continued. "No children. His ex-wife appears to bear no grudges and lives in isolated if aristocratic splendor with a new husband somewhere in Portugal. Right. Let's get him talking a bit more about his nearest and dearest. He was a bit reticent yesterday."

And here he was, the nob himself. It was almost as if he had been awaiting the summons. Randolph, AKA Nathersby, strode into the room, trailing Sergeant Essex like a retainer.

Cotton thought: punctuality. The politeness of kings.

Randolph, tall and lanky, was somewhat folded in on himself in the way of many tall people. Cotton was struck anew by his resemblance to his uncle Oscar—he had much the same refined features as the old man. His trousers fell in a stylish woolen pud-

164

dle around his highly polished leather shoes, no doubt shoes from some Savile Row-like establishment, where the wooden casts of his feet would be preserved in perpetuity. Messrs Bullfinch and Ryestone still held the models of Cotton's own feet, but it had been years since he'd indulged in the luxury of handmade shoes. Besides, the ones he already owned, well-tended, had held up well for decades. He resisted the urge to take a peep at the polished toes, hidden beneath the desk.

Sergeant Essex took in the tall nobbish frame, the thick dark hair with its nobbish, deliberate messiness, and the confident, nobbish voice as it greeted DCI Cotton. Was it her imagination, or did he reserve for Cotton the sort of "there's a good chap" tone he'd use to ask a stable boy to saddle his horse? She thought, altogether, he did.

Max for his part was wondering why it was that upper-class men always seemed in need of a good barber.

A cravat had been tucked with care at Randolph's open shirt collar. Max wasn't sure he himself owned a cravat, or ever had. It was one of those male adornments that seemed to have gone out with period dramas like *Poldark*. He thought Randolph otherwise looked rather like van Gogh's paintings of a sinister-looking Gauguin, all dark, sharp planes to his face and a pointy beard. Especially given the excess consumption of absinthe, one knew just looking at these paintings that Vincent was not going to get along with Gauguin in the long run. It was all going to end in tears. Max thought Randolph might be rather too intentionally going for the sensitive artist look.

Cotton rose to shake the man's hand and indicated a chair across from the desk where he should sit.

"Thank you for agreeing to talk with us again, sir. I just had a few more questions."

Just then there was a bloodcurdling shriek outside the window. Given the recent events at the castle, all four people in the room jumped. Sergeant Essex threw down her notebook to crank open the window for a look.

"It's the children. Those two white-haired twins. They're only playing."

Randolph swore: "The little buggers," followed by the obligatory apology to Max for the lapse in language. Max, who still struggled to clean up the vocabulary of his MI5 days, brushed the apology aside.

"The twins seem to be bearing up all right," Max said. "The only worrying note is that their father's death doesn't seem *quite* to have sunk in."

"Yes, that may well be so," said Randolph, in a magisterial tone of voice. "Too bad their mother isn't taking more of an interest. I've tried speaking with them but you know—in their eyes I'm so ancient"—here a self-deprecating smile—"I couldn't possibly say anything useful."

Cotton sat behind the desk, first carefully hitching up his own trousers so as not to disturb the crease. Cotton loved clothes, and in another life might have done something in a sartorial way in London. On a policeman's salary he maintained an impeccable if spare wardrobe of bespoke shirts and suits that he made last for years. He eyed Randolph's hand-sewn shirt and glossy silk tie with an appreciative, envious gaze and said, "Let's talk about that situation, sir. My understanding is that Gwynyth, Lord Footrustle's former wife, came along a dozen or so years ago?"

"Fourteen. Actually, in conversation, Gwynyth would be called Lady Footrustle, even though she and Oscar were divorced," Randolph corrected him, but with a friendly smile. Sergeant Essex, dripping irony over in her corner, made an elaborate correction to her notes. "Almost no one extends her this courtesy except Lamorna, who cares deeply about this stuff, no matter how much she pretends otherwise. Gwynyth's maiden name was Lavener, if for some reason you need to know that."

"How extraordinary. I think I've heard the name," said Max musingly. "Gwynyth Lavener. Some sort of entertainer."

Randolph tossed a glance in his direction. "You may well have done—have heard of her. Yes, that was nicely put: She was *some sort* of entertainer. I gather she's been trying, rather fitfully, to restart her singing and dancing career. On the *Int*ernet." (Here an exaggerated shudder at the unspeakableness of this plan.) "Imagine if you will Leticia's pleasure at hearing that news. It was then I think Leticia, however briefly, joined forces with Gwynyth in wanting Gwynyth to get more support money from Oscar. To save us all the shame of having yet another performer swinging from a branch of the family tree."

Max decided that beneath the suave façade, the relaxed posture, and the jocular urbanity, Randolph was covering over a small case of nerves, perhaps even a mild state of shock. The recent occurrences would do that to anyone. Which was a good sign. Anyone not nervous under the circumstances would be a complete sociopath.

"You're referring to Jocasta Jones?" Cotton asked him.

"None other. Although would I go so far as to call her an enter*tain*er, like Gwynyth?" He paused, as if to give the idea due reflection. "It's a point of view, certainly. But on the whole, I rather think not. The word 'performer' suits Jocasta better."

"Are you suggesting, sir, that she may not be entirely transparent when being questioned during our investigations?"

Randolph looked shocked at the idea. "Certainly not. I'm sure she wants this situation resolved as much as we all do. The whole thing is frightful—just doesn't bear thinking about. I was merely saying that you will get a lot of fluffy, over-the-top drama mixed in with her version of events. And good luck to you sorting it all out. She seems to suffer more than ever from the personal delusion that the next phone call will be the one that restarts her career. She does this while failing to notice she never had much of a career to begin with, on the stage or in film."

"I found her to be somewhat a brassy person, yes," said Cotton mildly.

"I used to think her time in America had something to do with it," said Randolph. "I was forgetting that Jocasta has *always* been like that. She is British by birth, of course, and brassiness like that cannot be learned, no matter how many years she's been in the U.S. How long?" he answered the unspoken question. "Since she was in her late teens, so over thirty years. No, I'm afraid, that metallic sheen to her personality is an inborn trait. Jocasta has always been Jocasta."

"I found her rather interesting," put in Essex. "In bits."

Randolph swiveled in his chair. It was as if a mouse had spoken and he wished to witness such a sight. Clearly he had forgotten the sergeant's existence.

"Did you? How interesting. One never gets her in bits, though, does one? It's the full course with Jocasta, or nothing. Wait—come to think of it, 'nothing' is not on the menu, either."

"You almost sound," put in Max, "as if you don't know her that well. She is a first cousin, isn't she?"

Randolph smiled, saying, "We grew up in different households, you see. I hardly knew her as a girl—of course we were all away at school. But now I must say it's taken me no time at all to become fully aquainted. One always feels with Jocasta she might be better employed announcing the shoppers' specials at the supermarket." Randolph, when he chose to display it, had a wide, inviting smile that lit up his usual somewhat saturnine aspect and assured the listener his words were all in good fun. "She has a flamboyant acting method likened most frequently by those reaching for comparisons with Lassie fetching rescuers for little Timmy."

"She acted in Hollywood films for a number of years, as I understand it." This from Cotton.

"Yes, as I say, if we expand the definition of 'acting' to include all manner of wild gesticulations and weird grimacings. I forget how many years she has lived in Hollywood, or how she came to meet her toyboy of a husband, Simon. Jocasta isn't due to bore us with any more of her memoirs until dinnertime. I could ask her then."

Sergeant Essex was shocked but struggling not to show it. Her own cousins were numerous and varied, and misunderstandings were frequent—family reunions could be like bloodbaths with Bisto gravy instead of blood—but she'd never talk about them to outsiders the way this man was doing.

Cotton for his part was ready to move on, convinced he had extracted all the juice possible out of Randolph on the subject of Jocasta. It was undoubtedly true he didn't know his cousin very well, and had simply formed bad opinions of her that he was now repeating. It hardly amounted to evidence.

"With regard to Lamorna Whitehall, sir. Your sister's daughter was—"

Randolph interrupted. "Lea's adopted daughter. That is correct."

"What exactly happened to Lamorna's parents?" Cotton asked.

Randolph replied, "Sadly, no one knows. My brother-in-law Leo was piloting a plane that vanished over the Alaskan bush. My sister was with him. Their bodies were never found. Todd Palin with a dogsled couldn't find a downed plane in that territory. Nor could Sarah Palin, for that matter. Lamorna, who had been adopted to begin with, now officially became an orphan twice over. My mother took her in but seems to have regretted the burden. Lamorna wasn't related by blood, and blood tells."

Ouch, thought Max. Aloud he said, "Who invited them all here for Christmas?"

Randolph swiveled his head ninety degrees to take in Max, who sat unobtrusively a few yards away. "Isn't it," he asked, turning back to Cotton, "isn't it a bit unusual to have a Father Brown-style detective sitting in on all this?" He smiled at Max to take the edge off his words, but his mild irritation was plain. "It's highly irregular, isn't it?"

In truth, Cotton would have a difficult time explaining Max to any of his superiors who did not know Max, and who had not seen him in action. As with Hercule Poirot, so often at the epicenter of an investigation, one had to wonder what the little detective with the gray cells was actually *doing* there, telling Inspector Japp, or whoever it was, what to do.

But, different from both Father Brown and Poirot, Max was interested in both sin *and* crime. Which made him a potent, double-barreled investigative force. Cotton almost wanted to warn Randolph of the danger of underestimating him. He looked across the room at Max, who sat smiling beatifically, angels practically dancing on his shoulders. Cotton nearly laughed aloud.

Cotton slowly adjusted his tie, decided a white lie was in order, dusted with a bit of bluff. He said, "Father Max Tudor, because of special . . . insights and connections, has been seconded to the investigation. However, if you've an objection, here is the number for the station. Ask for Superintendent Penhallow. Sound man."

Like he'll care, thought Cotton, still smiling the smile of the reasonable and friendly public servant, eager to offer his help to a grateful taxpayer.

It worked. Randolph subsided from a boil to a simmer.

"I won't talk to him officially—the vicar—without your being present. I hope that is understood."

Cotton knew it was his parting, final shot—the man didn't seem to realize he had just agreed to that which he'd objected to in the first place: having Max in the room during the interview. Cotton was happy to oblige.

"Certainly, sir. Now, if you would answer Father Tudor's question."

"I couldn't say. Oscar—Lord Footrustle—invited me, not my mother. I assumed because he was old and wanted to make amends. My mother was less happy about having everyone come over—especially 'the Americans,' Jocasta and Simon. Oscar did admit to me the other week that he treated his first wife shamefully, and ignored a daughter he disliked mainly because he grew to dislike her mother. He was getting old, that's all. Remorse creeps up on us more the older we get—I suppose because there is more to regret with every passing year."

"Did your mother try to influence her brother? Try to stop Jocasta from being invited?" Cotton hardly knew why he asked the question, but he was finding the family dynamics so strange he wanted to learn more.

"I only know Leticia, who knew what Jocasta was like, held her fire once Jocasta and the rest of them were here—for the most part. After all, my mother reasoned, maybe it was a chicken-or-egg situation and Jocasta couldn't be held accountable for being, well, Jocasta. She might have turned out better with a more stable upbringing."

"Your mother didn't welcome having her own family near for the holidays? You, and your brother?"

Randolph smiled, shook his head, and said, "Only in a way. I asked Leticia once, 'Don't you feel the loneliness? The isolation?' 'It's the price one pays for being discriminating,' she replied. 'There are fewer and fewer people of quality around these days.' That was my mother, to the core."

There was a pattering sound as Sergeant Essex tapped her biro against her notebook, looked at Randolph, and seemed to be thinking, *This* apple didn't fall too far from the family tree.

"Yes, I know what you must be thinking," said Randolph, in that voice of calm urbanity that seemed to be his trademark. Thus would he coax the reluctant portrait sitter to loosen up, to relax, to regard the camera as his friend. "I loved her dearly but she was a dying breed, to be sure."

Interesting choice of words, thought Max.

"*And* I had the highest respect for my uncle. The loss to all of us is incalculable."

Max acknowledged the customary expressions of loss with a solemn nod. "Did you see your mother on the morning of her death?" Max asked him.

"Only in passing. She was coming down a corridor of the castle, on her way to the garden hothouse."

"Coming from her own room?"

Randolph hesitated. It was barely perceptible, but the missing beat was there. "Now you mention it, no. She was coming from Cilla's room. That's Cilla Petrie, my assistant."

"Oh? Were the two women particularly close or friendly?"

Randolph nodded, as if the unlikelihood of this was something he'd already thought of. Perhaps he had. Perhaps he couldn't bear not to be the one first to think of something.

"They weren't close," he said. "I am not certain you could say they were friendly. But they weren't hostile to each other, insofar as I'm aware."

Again the cool manner. He crossed one leg over the other, pausing to straighten the knife-edge crease of his trousers. He had the air of someone being interviewed for television. Of course, thought Max. He was used to the business of posing—of getting others to pose. Max supposed some of that technique must rub off on the coach, as it were.

"But why," asked Max mildly, "would she go to Cilla's room? Surely that was the sort of cozy informality that was foreign to your mother?"

It was clear Randolph regretted having brought up the whole topic. He said, with an air of ill grace and condescension that had Sergeant Essex itching to throw something heavy at him, "If you must know, she wanted to reassure herself that my relationship with my assistant was nothing more than that of employer to employee. She'd gotten a bee in her bonnet that I was going to taint the family bloodline by marrying a commoner."

"Were you?" asked Cotton. Max noticed that Cotton's own tone had changed, becoming noticeably more upper class, as if he were trying to out-suave Randolph by putting on a home-counties twang. "Planning to marry Ms. Petrie? We would of course treat that information as confidential, if so, unless it proves relevant to the investigation."

This earned him a well-bred sneer.

"Of course not," Randolph said. "Haven't I just explained? If I do remarry, which is not bloody likely, I shall marry someone of my own class."

Sergeant Essex wrote this sentiment down, word for word. *Lucky girl.*

❋ ❋ ❋

"I wouldn't trust that man as far as I could throw him," said Sergeant Essex to the closed door. "Too smarmy by half. 'If I do remarry, I shall marry someone of my own class.' Right. Did you believe him, sir?"

"Do I believe he had a great fondness for either of his elders and betters, now sadly lost to him?" asked Cotton. "No, as a matter of fact, I don't. I think he protests too much. But I don't think he's alone in that. There's a good chance he's our man but it's early days, early days."

Essex seized on that "our." She seized, in fact, on any sign that she was an equal partner in any investigation. Tough, smart, and capable, Essex was also easily flattered at being included or treated as an equal by the men—years on the force, which remained macho to its core, had rather worn down her starry-eyed initial expectations of a bias-free experience. She hated herself for it but she knew in some corner of her mind she was seeking their regard and approval. The hand that rocked the cradle might rule the world but the hand that wrote the evaluations determined the pay level, and for the most part that hand still had rough cuticles and dark hair growing on its knuckles.

Even though DCI Cotton in his dealings with his subordinates was scrupulously fair—blind for the most part to sex, race, or color—she was well aware that Cotton was the exception that proved the rule.

None of her thinking showed in her expression now. She nodded curtly and flipped over a page in her notebook. She sat with biro poised, her small back ramrod straight.

"What did you think?" Cotton asked Max.

"Suave. Cordial. Intelligent, to a point."

"You didn't like him, either."

"Not really. No."

"Where to next?"

"I think Lester Baynard, Randolph's younger brother, is worth a closer look," said Max.

"So do I," said Cotton. He sent Sergeant Essex on another exploratory mission.

"This may take awhile," she told them as she left. "This place is as big as the National Portrait Gallery."

"And with as many paintings," said Max.

CHAPTER 15

...And the Spare

The two men chatted as they waited for Sergeant Essex's return.

"I don't know a blind thing about the travails of the upper classes. Or the lack of travails, as it were," said Cotton. Max, a diplomat's son, had some secondhand knowledge, but couldn't claim to be an expert. He told Cotton so.

"Still, you're a better authority than I am," said Cotton. "What I get from the situation is that essentially the younger son is, well, stuffed, in terms of titles and so forth. Although I gather that the title on the Baynard side of things is a hollow honor—Randolph and Lester's father, that would be the Tenth Earl of Gravening, ran through the money needed for the upkeep of the estate. Of course the daughters of these families are valued more for the price they might fetch in marriage—their ability to catch a grand title."

Cotton removed his jacket and, with the precision of a couturier laying out a bride's dress, draped it over the back of a Queen Anne side chair. He added, "It's all so Queen Mary-ish, but not a lot has changed, has it, really?"

Max allowed that perhaps it had not. "Give me a little background on Lester before he gets here, will you?"

Cotton opened another file on his mobile. "Lester and his wife Felberta née Oliver are from Australia, where he dabbled in this and invested in that and she entertained the local notables.

Although I gather we must use the term 'notables' loosely, as well as the word 'entertained.' Neither of them seems to be widely respected. Tolerated would be a better word."

He put down the mobile and leaned back in his chair, hands behind his head.

"By the way, the original spelling of his name is Leicester, as in 'the city of.' He realized that was a bit uppity for Australia, not to mention hard to spell, so now he goes by the more matey-sounding 'Lester'."

"You say he dabbled in investments?" asked Max, putting aside the book he'd idly picked up from the stack on the table beside him. His shifted his weight, in truth finding sitting for so long more tedious than the occasional twinge coming from his ankle.

"Yes. In what, exactly, we don't know—someone over there's getting details for us but initial indications are that they're not doing well financially, Lester and his wife. She is so little loved her nickname is Fester—oh, I see you know that already. A few dodgy deals Lester was involved in went south. A dinosaur theme park, for one. He trades on his Footrustle connection to get invited places, to get introduced to the right people. You know the sort of thing." Max pursed his lips thoughtfully and nodded. "Seems to have done all right out of it, although perhaps not as all right as he'd hoped," Cotton went on. "As I say, someone official in the land down under is looking into it for us."

There was a rustle at the door, a sound as of a mild skirmish, and Lester walked his high-shouldered way into the library, arms swinging loosely at his sides. He was followed by a quietly simmering Sergeant Essex.

"How often are you going to talk to us?" Lester seemed curious to know rather than annoyed, but there was an overlay of irritation in his tone. "Your sergeant here doesn't seem to have any idea."

"We do appreciate your cooperation," said Cotton smoothly. Some of Randolph's slippery suaveness seemed to have rubbed off on the detective. "I believe you've met Father Tudor here? Yes, good. Now, one issue we didn't go into before is how you came to be at the castle for the holidays."

Lester might have been waiting for this moment. He dove into his jacket pocket.

"My uncle sent me an invitation. Here it is."

He handed Cotton a page containing a printed-out e-mail. The return address was info@ChedrowCastle.com.

It read simply, "It has been too long since I've seen you and Festus. I miss you. Please come to Chedrow for Christmas. [signed] Your uncle."

"He meant Felberta, my wife," Lester clarified.

Max considered the brief message. Oscar would have had the technical proficiency to send an e-mail—it wasn't brain surgery, after all. The real question was, why did he? Was the simple explanation the best one—he was really just an old man wanting company?

"Was it usual for him to communicate with you this way?"

Lester nodded his head. "Unheard of."

"Did he confide in you about why—what his thinking was?"

"Oscar was a secretive old bas—I mean, Oscar was secretive. However, he told me, on the QT, you know, that he had wanted us here to see what kind of people we were."

Cotton, privately wondering when was the last time he had heard anyone speak of something being on the QT, asked merely, "Did he give any indication why? What he had in mind?"

"No, he was being evasive about the whys and wherefores, but I could read between the lines all right. Oscar was getting ready to meet his maker. You don't just leave your money to a bunch of people you've rarely met, do you?"

"And I don't suppose you'd telegraph the fact that the people in question were being auditioned, in a way. Given the once-over to assess their suitability."

"Precisely," said Lester. Oozing earnestness and goodwill from every pore, Lester leaned forward to say, "He loved to spy on people, you know. Gather information. Catch them at their worst. It's how he earned his crust on Fleet Street."

"So, how do you think everyone measured up, in his eyes?"

Lester smiled another of his would-be ingratiating smiles. "Some better than others, to be sure."

Lester reminded Max of the type of politician who keeps getting returned to high office, despite the best, most determined efforts of the populace to vote him out. As with such men, there was the whiff about him of failure, but perhaps not quite enough failure for the common good.

"You got along with him well, did you, sir?" This from Sergeant Essex.

Lester clearly considered the merits in lying, and decided there was too much evidence to refute any protestations of abiding familial love.

"One got tired of being blown up all the time," he finally said. "He didn't seem to approve of anyone, and it got worse the older he got. Very judgmental, was my uncle. *And* with a touch of paranoia."

"You quarreled with him, did you, sir?"

"Not openly. I avoided him as much as possible, if you want the truth."

"It's why we're here, sir," said Cotton. "To get the truth."

Max twinkled appreciatively at the new, improved, debonair detective. It was like having Lord Peter Wimsey lead the interrogation.

"And Lady Baynard," Cotton continued. "Was she happy with Lord Footrustle's arrangements for the holidays? Would she have had any hand in the invitations going out?"

Lester let out a sudden, loud guffaw, the sort of sound made by a large zoo animal. He seemed to realize he sounded somewhat lunatic, for he quickly apologized for the outburst. "It's just that the very idea of Leticia's inviting us is impossible. It just wouldn't happen. She wouldn't actively turn us away at the door if we showed up but it would be a close thing. Well, she might make an exception in Jocasta's case but after all, Jocasta was—is—Oscar's own flesh and blood."

"There was some estrangement there, was there?" asked Cotton. "Between Jocasta and her father?"

"Yes. No one was invited to her wedding to Simon out in Las Vegas, just to give you some idea of the state of affairs. Essentially, they eloped. Simon is much too much younger than Jocasta, if you follow, a fact we only gradually became aware of and a fact I rather think she wanted to hide. Simon is totally in Jocasta's shadow. Or, if you ask me—and I take it you are asking me—he was totally in it for the money and connections, while they lasted, since it's so easy to make her believe her charm and beauty have anything to do with his interest in her. She's extremely high maintenance—if you haven't gathered that yet you will. *And* she's a bit of a hypochondriac."

"That seems to be a family trait," put in Max.

Momentarily forgetting his role as eager provider of useful information, Lester gave Max a bellicose look that didn't hold much gratitude for the observation.

"Yes, well, I didn't inherit the gene but Jocasta did. If you told her swallowing live bait prevents wrinkles or would help her to lose weight, she'd do it without hesitation."

"You got along well with your mother, did you, sir?" This from DCI Cotton, looking up from behind his desk. He'd been looking at some document or other on his laptop but now he closed the lid. "There was no sense that she favored your brother over you, anything like that?"

Lester ran his tongue slowly across his upper lip, clearly thinking hard. "Wa-a-l-l," he said a last. "No. Not really." He gave Cotton and Max a momentary glance each, then gazed with intense fascination at the faded Aubusson rug, which hardly merited such scrutiny. When Cotton pressed the issue, Lester's roving eyes, which he finally raised to meet his interrogator's, seemed clouded over.

"Not that it has any relevance to the matter at hand," he grudgingly conceded. "But the firstborn is often the favorite. It's just the way of the world." His resigned acceptance was belied by the flush the topic had brought to his face, and would have been more convincing if he had not been practically dancing with impatience in his chair.

Max privately thought the way of the world was that the youngest was often the favorite, but he said nothing. Lester, for all his occasional puppyish enthusiasm, was too conflicted a personality to be anyone's favorite.

"I've had a word with Wintermute, the family solicitor," said Cotton.

Max sensed an abrupt buildup of tension in the already tense figure.

"Oh, yes?" said Lester, with elaborate casualness. "Sound man, Wintermute."

"He says you called him yesterday morning."

"Yes." Definitely an increase in tension now.

"Your mother and uncle had only just been found dead." He let the unspoken question hang in the air.

"What of it? What if I did call Wintermute? This is neither the time nor the place to discuss it."

"It's a murder investigation," said Cotton. "I'll decide the time and the place."

"I rather think this is a private family matter," said Lester.

Cotton's patience was thinning in the face of the man's imbecilic intransigence. Gone, Max noticed, watching from the sidelines, was the sophisticated urbanity he had come to appreciate, this new aristo tool in Cotton's arsenal of weapons. One could almost see the policeman taking off the gloves. He blew past Lester's stonewalling and said coldly, "In a murder investigation, nothing is private. Wintermute found your questions premature, to say the least. Now, what did you find to talk about within hours of your mother's demise?"

Lester, head bowed, muttered something into his chest.

"I'm sorry, you'll have to repeat that."

Lester lifted his head defiantly. "I said, I wanted to know the terms of her will."

"And what were the terms?"

Sulkily: "She left everything to my brother and myself. Naturally. She even left a few quid to Lamorna. Now, there was a surprise." Lester turned in Sergeant Essex's direction. "Are you getting this down or should I speak more slowly?"

Essex bristled, already on alert for the next bit of condescension. She wouldn't have long to wait.

"That tallies with what Wintermute told me," said Cotton.

"Then why bother asking me?" said Lester.

"When did you arrive at Chedrow Castle?" Sergeant Essex asked, out of annoyance asserting herself into the conversation.

"I'll be glad to answer questions so long as they're coming from DCI Cotton," said Lester.

Big mistake, Lester, thought Max.

"The very question I was going to ask," said Cotton to the man he was privately starting to think of as "that pompous nitwit," but reverting to his dulcet, gentlemen's club tones. "How long have you and your wife been here?" As an afterthought, he added, "Sir."

"We arrived at the end of November or beginning of December. I couldn't tell you the exact date." Lester expanded his small, scrawny frame into the sofa.

"Quite an extended visit, then."

"We had a lot of catching up to do. And a flight to and from Australia is not lightly undertaken."

Cotton noticed a look of puzzled discontent on Max's face. He felt he was becoming familiar with that look. Max was the embodiment of the maxim "Look before you leap." Any doubts had to be allayed in Max's mind before he would accept what to anyone else was the obvious conclusion. It made him a brilliant priest—sympathetic and thoughtful, not prone to quick or harsh judgments. It made him an even better investigator, in Cotton's view.

"What about the terms of Lord Footrustle's will?" Max said at last.

Lester, even when seated, seemed to be in motion. Max detected the merest shuffling of his feet, as if he couldn't wait to be away, for it was clearly an unwelcome question. This energy of the highly strung he had in common with DCI Cotton, if not much more.

"You'll have to get the details from Wintermute," said Lester, now with affected patience. "I only had any business asking about my mother's will, I felt, so I couldn't help you." The postscript "even if I wanted to" was plain but left unsaid.

The door had closed behind Lester Baynard with a resounding gothic thud. Sergeant Essex, not expecting to be overheard over the sound by the two men remaining in the room, muttered, "What a load of balls."

Cotton gave her a warning look. She lifted her shoulders in silent apology. But she didn't look sorry.

"His statements would carry more weight if he struck me as someone who had ever actually pulled his own weight," she said. "A complete drain on society, that one."

Cotton, well acquainted with Essex's class consciousness, stood and began moving in a graceful swooping motion, back and forth across the room, thinking.

"So, what do we know about Lord Footrustle?" Cotton asked at last. "According to everyone we've spoken with, including Lester just now, he was a secretive man. He'd made much of his fortune in Fleet Street ventures possibly *because* he knew everyone's secrets and I guess could keep a few of his own. There's a squint in his bedroom he used to—"

"I'm sorry, sir. A what?" This from Essex.

"A squint. A little opening in a stone wall. There were two of them, in fact. One faced the outside; one overlooked the Great

Hall. He liked to spy, to keep an eye on things and people. According to the butler, he spent an inordinate amount of his time, especially once he was retired, doing just that."

"So you think he may have been killed for what he saw," said Max. "That he saw something he shouldn't have."

"I'm saying it's a possibility, and a likely one. Don't you agree?"

"Yes. I'd say it's a distinct possibility."

"I suppose we can't avoid talking with Jocasta Jones much longer," said Cotton. "And I rather think the perspective of Oscar's eldest daughter might be useful."

He went to pull up some information on his mobile and was frustrated in the attempt. He walked over to confer with Essex on some fine point of using the device.

Max, content to leave the digital future to people like Cotton who seemed to have more of an affinity, turned again to the books stacked on the table at his side while Cotton scrolled away on his little machine.

"No!" said Sergeant Essex. "Not that button. That's the del—"

"Where did it go?" said Cotton. "Where in hell did it go? It just disappeared!"

Essex sighed. It seemed she and Cotton had been round this block before. "Let me have a look, sir. I should be able to recover it."

Max, flipping through the pages of the books, many of them recent publications, felt it was hard to say who might have been responsible for their purchase. There were potted royal biographies, fleshed out with unsubstantiated scraps of scandal. There was a copy of *Royal Nursery Tales* by some royal nanny of the distant past, and a copy of *The Life and Loves of Prince Albert*. Somewhat surprisingly, he found a thin biography of the Middletons, hurriedly produced once the royal engagement had been announced, called *Life of the Party Pieces*. Max suspected that might have been a guilty pleasure of Lady Baynard's. He recalled her comments in the train about commoners and felt there might have been a morbid fascination at work, along the lines of, "First Gwynyth, now *this*." Something to chew over at dinner with her similarly minded friends.

In another stack beside a bowl of fruit there were some history books and a sprinkling of Evelyn Waugh, but nothing that otherwise caught his eye as germane to the case. Lord Footrustle or someone seemed to like paperback thrillers with historic or religious overtones, however doubtful the research on which the books had been based. The Knights Templar, so far as Max was aware, had never journeyed to Vancouver.

They—both Cotton and Essex—had quite forgotten Max was there, and he in his turn gave every appearance (quite deceptive) of having tuned out the conversation in favor of perusing the titles on the spines of the leather-bound books ranged on a shelf beside him. They forgot him, so much so that when he spoke, they both jumped and Sergeant Essex's biro went flying. Max retrieved it for her from behind a potted plant.

"Sorry," he said. He held a copy of Bram Stoker's *Dracula* in his hands, by the look of it an original edition. "I was just wondering about the business of the food poisoning, if poisoning it were. How would you go about introducing poison into Oscar's diet, if you were so inclined?"

"The whole subject is tricky," said Cotton. He leaned back in what could be mistaken for a relaxed pose, but in Cotton might be a prelude to a sprint for the door. "We don't know if we're talking about salmonella or what, and we can't say for sure when he was exposed to the poison, or even if he was. It could have taken hours or even days before he complained of illness. Toxic mushrooms are just one possibility. His age was a factor, making him more vulnerable to rapid onset. But the event was far enough in the past there was no trace of whatever it was left, since he survived the poisoning attempt—if attempt it was."

"Hmm," said Max. "But I find it suggestive, don't you? I would call it an attempt to pin the blame on the cook. Then with both Oscar and Leticia found by the butler . . . well."

They talked awhile about the attempts on Oscar's life, including the attempt Amanda had told Max about.

The three sat for some moments, taking this in. Finally, Sergeant Essex said, "Shall I go and find the next one?"

"Stay here and find that file for me," said Cotton. "I'll send one of the constables to locate Jocasta. And to organize some coffee. Be right back."

Essex watched Cotton don his jacket, shoot his immaculate cuffs, and stride out of the room, up the stairs to the Great Hall.

"I don't know how he affords it on a policeman's salary," Essex said to Max.

"Have you seen his flat?"

"Of course not! Why would I have seen his flat?"

"I just meant, there's no money wasted there, so I guess it all goes for clothing. I had to pick him up one day when his car was in the shop. You'd need to invent a new word for 'Spartan' to describe the place. It's positively Zen."

Max had just found a large, photocopied Footrustle family tree tucked into the pages of *Brideshead Revisited*. He unfolded the paper, spreading it out on his lap. It was a beautifully rendered tree, drawn in pen and ink, going back approximately four centuries, and updated within the past few decades.

Max, seeing it laid out before him, was struck by the fact of the—what was it? The lack of *cohesiveness* of this present-day family. When looked at clinically in a "cold" diagram, the nearness of the relations was evident. Why so little family feeling, then? Was there just something wrong with the Footrustles, and the Baynards? Something amounting almost to a genetic disorder?

The family tree hinted here and there at consanguinity—a dangerous intermarrying of persons too closely related. A practice that could lead to birth defects, and to illnesses both physical and mental.

It was a practice that led quite frequently to madness.

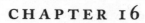

CHAPTER 16

A Star Is Born

Cotton stood, his backside to the fire, reading from a sheaf of notes.

"Jocasta and the twins Alec and Amanda inherited quite a few pounds from Oscar—nicely judged to be enough to keep them quiet, but not what they would have seen otherwise. The solicitor seems to have known what he was doing. The lion's share went to Oscar's sister: to Leticia, Lady Baynard."

He peered at Max over the top of the pages.

"I've asked the solicitor, Wintermute, to drop by sometime today," Cotton said. "I'm hoping you get a chance to talk with him."

Max's mind was elsewhere. He took a sip of the fragrant coffee, which had been delivered and poured out by Milo, and replacing his cup carefully on the saucer said, "You would think Jocasta and Randolph would have something in common, apart from being cousins. She's spent her career in front of the camera, and he behind it."

"Or it would guarantee hostilities between them. Those jobs require differing personalities. Who can say? In any event, there is no shortage of suspects, within the castle walls or without. Oscar has been called the Voldemort of Fleet Street by both friends and enemies. He was apparently ruthless in all his business dealings."

"What do you know about the knife used to kill him?"

"Only that it came from the kitchen—a long, thick blade, a sort of all-purpose butcher knife."

"All-purpose, indeed," said Max, sadly shaking his head. "Including the purpose of butchering a man."

"My team found it in the garden, in one of the topiaries—a heart-shaped topiary," Cotton told him.

"A clue, perhaps hinting at unrequited love, or a broken

heart?" wondered Max aloud. "Or a blind? Or simply the most expedient way to lose the most incriminating item? A quick nip out to the garden on the pretext of an invigorating stroll, and a quick thrust of the knife in among the tightly packed branches."

"Hmm. Something like that. The team didn't find it until late yesterday afternoon, just as they were getting ready to pack it in because of darkness."

Cotton turned back to the pages he'd been riffling through, now propelling his lean, restless frame toward a seat near Max. "So, we have Lady Jocasta Jones née Footrustle, by Oscar's first wife Beatrice Briar. Then, completing the family tree on that branch, there are the twins (and they seem almost universally to be called The Twyns) who are Alec, Viscount Edenstartel, and his sister Lady Amanda. Jocasta is of course their much older half sister."

"I met her briefly at breakfast."

"Did you now? Once met, never forgotten, I'd say. Let's get her in here."

Jocasta's entrance was very different from her cousin Randolph's. Where he had entered with loping, forceful strides, taking control of the room, Jocasta possessed the room in quite another way. Preceded by a waft of perfume strong enough to substitute as tear gas for the police force of a chic nation-state, Jocasta twirled her way into the library, petticoats swirling about her knees, her manner fluttery, winsome, and coy. Ignoring Sergeant Essex, she aimed her charm like a beacon at the two men.

She had changed her clothing since breakfast, and now wore a retro little number in silk brocade with a cinched waist and full pleated skirt that recalled Elizabeth Taylor during her Michael Wilding years. Max was to learn she changed frequently throughout the day, although there was little reason for it. Perhaps it was how she staved off boredom. As likely, it was a hangover from her acting days.

"Thank *God* you finally got around to talking with me," she said, perching on the edge of a seat. "I've been on pins and needles, waiting."

"Thank you for talking with us," said Cotton. "This must be a difficult time."

"You've no idea," she said. "It's been a nightmare—literally." And she began to tell him of the dreams and premonitions of disaster she'd had, ever since coming to the castle ("The most terrifying of scenes—outside of my own films, of course."). Max, from his chair across the room, thought he was used to this kind of premonition thing from Awena Owen, and he was certainly getting used to hearing it from the inhabitants of Chedrow Castle. Vague insights. *Feelings.* Coming from Awena, these insights were often, well, insightful, although he put that down to her remarkable empathy, intuition, and observational skills. This woman before him seemed merely nervy. A bundle of nerves, in fact.

And weren't premonitions always easiest to claim once calamity had already struck?

Max said, "I would imagine it is strange for you being back at the castle, after so many years."

Again she said, "You've no idea!" But this time she smiled, and there was subtle shading to her voice, a sauciness of tone out of place in the interview. As she breezed on, Max concluded she was trying on various roles, or perhaps reliving old stage and film triumphs.

"What can you tell us about the night before your father's body was found?"

"We—my husband and I—played cards in the drawing room. What Leticia called a withdrawing room, a term that hasn't been used since approximately the 1700s. She was like that, Leticia. Anyway, we were in the drawing room, living room, or whatever you wish to call it until quite late that night. We tried to interest some of the others in a game of bridge but found no takers, so we played gin rummy instead. After we went to bed—which was before midnight as I recall—who knows what happened? The butler found Oscar. You'll have to get the details from him."

"What a good idea. We hadn't thought of that," said Cotton. The irony was lost on Jocasta, who had found a flaw in her bloodred manicure. "Did you hear anything, see anything unusual at all?"

"I think I heard a noise outside that morning," she told her thumbnail. "An owl, perhaps." She looked up. "The jet lag has had me awake at all hours, you see."

"Try to think, please," said Cotton. "Could it have been a human voice?"

Obligingly, propping her chin in one hand and staring skyward, she appeared to give the idea every fair consideration, although as Essex remarked later she might have been wondering where she'd mislaid her mascara wand. "No," she said at last. "No, I can't really be certain."

"Was there anything that night, anything at all that struck you as out of the ordinary? A quarrel overheard, perhaps?"

Again the pose of thoughtfulness.

"No-o-o."

"We feel, you see," put in Max, "that with your special training in the subtleties of nuance and gesture, you could be a valuable witness to any undercurrents of tension or hostility in the household."

Jocasta preened visibly. "Do you really? Why, yes, it is the attention to gesture that most critics mention in connection with my work. Oh, I still get letters! Indeed, a constant outpouring, expressing the fervent wish that I reprise some of my more famous roles."

"Ah, yes. Well—" began Cotton.

"Of course, it has been some time since my last appearance in film, which does tend to whet the audience's appetite."

"I see. Now, if we could return to the subject of your father's murder." Cotton felt he was being a bit brutal by using the word but he wasn't sure there was any other way to capture her attention, as her mind seemed to spin in a continual orbit around her past triumphs.

"My father's—oh, yes. Of course," Jocasta cooed. "What was it you wished to know?" She flashed a brilliant smile at first one man, then the other. It was a smile that assumed it was melting the hearts of all who beheld it—a smile much rehearsed and perfected during endless reviewings and rewindings of her appearances, however brief, in film. Clearly flirtatiousness was her default mode. That it was a complete disconnect to the grave topic under discussion was lost on no one but Jocasta herself.

But suddenly, there was a switch in tone. It was like watching someone play with an on/off switch, thought Max.

"Family secrets," Jocasta said darkly. "Every family has them." She gave out a diabolical screech that might have been laughter. "But I shall share my secrets with you, shall I?" Max began to wonder if she was quite sane. He stole a glance at the page that held the family tree, now lying facedown on the table next to him.

"Good," said Cotton. "Now, we can't escape the fact your father was a wealthy man."

"Certainly he was."

"Were you—how shall I put this—were you and your husband in any financial difficulty?"

Again the screech. "Why would you say that?" she demanded. "I have made a vast fortune from my cinematic and stage appearances. I don't need money. And I certainly wouldn't . . . do as you suggest . . . to get my hands on it if I did. If you want to talk about who needed money, let's talk about Gwynyth Lavener, shall we?"

"Your father's ex-wife."

"That's right." Jocasta's narrow lips disappeared into a thin, sour, red line. "Gwynyth tells everyone she was a performance artist when she met Oscar. A performance artist! That's a nice word for stripper."

"Actually," said Cotton, "we were given to understand she was performing on board a cruise ship when she met your father. Singing and dancing. That sort of thing. They don't usually offer strip shows on any cruise line I've ever heard of."

"That's as may well be," said Jocasta. Her mind seemed to have calcified on this subject. "What she did *before* she met him she's not talking about, I'm sure."

"Did your father's remarriage cause a rift between him and you?" Max asked her.

She spent a moment ensuring the flounce in her petticoats was just so before she answered. "We were quite close, really. Well, early on. The years do pass so swiftly, don't they? 'Sunrise, sunset.'" To the astonishment of her audience, she hummed a few bars of the tune. "But you've got quite the wrong idea," she finally went on. "We were *close*, I tell you. As *only* family can be. So *difficult* to explain to one who isn't family."

Her voice fluted across the Aubusson at Max, who said, "I quite understand."

She blinked, her eyes like shades pulled quickly down. Max could read no more of her, get no sense of what she really felt. Perhaps Jocasta wasn't such a hopeless actress after all.

"Now, as I say, it's Gwynyth you should be talking with. You know why she's here of course."

Cotton looked at her hopefully.

"Money! The very motive I was accused of harboring just now." Sitting up straight, she seemed to be slipping into another role: Max was reminded of an old-time star like Barbara Stanwyck, on horseback, facing down an irate posse. Fire and ice, backbone of steel. Jocasta all but flicked an imaginary whip and said, "She ran through the money he settled on her six years ago so now she wanted more. They quarreled, and—"

"You heard them quarreling?" Cotton quickly interjected.

"No, as it happens, but it stands to reason that is what happened."

"If we could stick to the facts here . . ." said Cotton.

"That's what I'm doing. Suddenly she's back, and plagued by this newfound concern for her children, is she? No, Inspector, it's money for herself she's after. The twins are an excuse."

"Hmm."

"Oh, she's quite lovely, in her way, Gwynyth. I understand she made quite a splash in the City for a while." She examined one be-ringed hand, as if to say there were splashes, and then there were splashes. "That blond hair, rather weird, I always thought. That type doesn't age well. She looks like a German airline stewardess. Simon calls the twins Hänsel und Gretel."

"I think they prefer to be called flight attendants these days," Cotton said mildly.

"Whatever. Oscar got a raw deal there. Oh, she looks nice enough, but she's thick as two planks. When she turned up with twins . . . oh, my. My father was livid."

"Why?"

"Well, I gather that was part of their agreement. That there would be no children. Then she became pregnant two minutes after they exchanged vows—*or* before. He barely tolerates those kids, and I think that's why—apart from their general snottiness, that is."

"I see," said Max. "He feels he was tricked into fatherhood. That really is too bad for the children."

"Don't feel too sorry for any of them. They were *all* trying to use my father. Randolph, for example: He's traded off the family connections for decades as a photographer. He's quite a good photographer, so I'm told," she added grudgingly. "I wouldn't know. He started out specializing in photos of dogs and horses of the gentry. Then he moved up—or down, depending on how you view things—to photographing owners *with* the dogs, et cetera."

"Were you close to his brother or his sister, Lea?" asked Cotton.

"Lester? Close to Lester? Of course not. Lea was another matter."

"You were friends?"

"She worshipped me. You know, I don't know what it is about me." One hand fluttered to her throat as she took a moment to bask in the warm glow of her immense self-regard. Adjusting an outsized pinky ring, she said, "Yes, Lea adored me."

The last person Max had met with this particular kind of blind spot was now serving time behind bars for GBH—Grievous Bodily Harm. Still, her self-love only made Jocasta ridiculous, not necessarily a murderess.

"I do miss her so." Jocasta now drew one hand across her forehead in a mournful gesture.

"To lose her so young must have been difficult for everyone," said Max. "And to lose her husband, as well."

Jocasta looked at him for a moment, incredulous, but then the gracious smile (Celine Damascus, *The Seething Serpent*) inched its way into place, the red lips like curtains slowly parting to reveal the gleaming white teeth.

"No one missed him," she said. "Frightful man."

"I did hear," said Max, "he was unkind to Lamorna."

"He was unkind to *me*," said Jocasta. "In Lamorna's case his reaction was understandable. Lamorna was trouble from when she was a baby. Wouldn't sleep, wouldn't eat."

Cotton referred to his notes. "Lea adopted her from St. Petersburg, is that right?"

"That is correct."

She rose from her chair and danced across the room.

"I had a few questions about the plane crash that took the lives of her parents," said Cotton. "There was no suspicion of foul play at the time, was there?"

Jocasta had stopped in front of a gilded mirror near the fireplace. She had been told by cinematographers the right side of her face offered her best profile, and she struggled always to be back-lit from this flattering angle. The light coming into the room was cooperating, casting a halo behind her head.

"Hmm?" Jocasta, lost in blissful contemplation of her image in the mirror, had only just realized the last question was directed at her.

"I wonder, Mrs. Jones, if I could have your full attention for just a moment?" said Cotton patiently.

"Certainly."

Cotton repeated the question. Surprised, she actually tore her eyes away from the mirror and turned to face him.

"Foul play? Oh, surely not. Not that I ever heard."

"We'll have our colleagues in North America look through the old files. Just in case."

This sent her into a complete dither of protestations, and the interview looked set to end in a shambles. She dug out a hankie from somewhere within the bodice of her dress and dabbing at her eyes began to wail. "Poor, dear Lea! Will she never rest in peace?"

To distract her, Max thought to ask about one of her films, which, by a most unlikely happenstance, he had both seen and remembered. He didn't remember it for the right reasons, perhaps, but remember it he did.

Soon Jocasta, having wiped away nonexistent tears, began to gush about her career, a glossy tale of her meteoric rise to stardom.

"Of course I also starred in the sequel, *Blue Noon*. The reviewers were *most* kind."

At their blank expressions, she drew back, astonished. "Don't tell me you've not seen it?"

Cotton and Max both shook their heads, the picture of polite regret.

"Oh, the limited film distribution in the United Kingdom has been the *plague* of my career. To think of the millions who have been deprived of the chance to see me in my best roles, all because of the wanton, willful laziness of my producers."

She abandoned the mirror and sat again, crossing her legs in an obvious and provocative way in Max's direction. The legs, and fine legs they were, looked like a cancan dancer's emerging from the foamy skirts.

Sergeant Essex's mouth tightened. It wasn't right, flirting like that with a man of the cloth. Especially *this* man of the cloth. Essex reserved a special place in her heart for Max, who had given her dying grandfather a measure of peace as he passed out of this world and into the next. This woman had no idea what she was messing with. Essex turned a page in her notebook with more energy and racket than was strictly necessary and, snapping it into place with the elastic, glared across the room at the bosomy actress. Any more plastic surgery and this Jocasta Jones wouldn't be able to bat those heavy false eyelashes at Father Max.

Jocasta warbled on in answer to a question from Max about the family's history, having to be corrected on some point of fact at least twice, which improvements she completely ignored. Finally, with a shrill cry reminiscent of a vulture spying a small woodland creature, she clapped her hands together and said, "Well, if there's nothing further, I have *stacks* of scripts I've brought with me to read. Ron Howard is awaiting my decision on whether I'll appear in one of his projects, but I've been *so* busy."

And she began to swan her way out. Cotton, who could think of no further questions for the moment to detain her, thanked her. As if she'd just thought of something, she turned at the door and said, "I should ask Lamorna where she was at the time of the crime. There is something . . . rather odd . . . about that girl."

"One more question from me if you wouldn't mind," said Max.

"Yes?" That "yes" had a hollow ring that belied the expression of patient cheer she'd pasted onto her face.

"Your arrival here came just before your father fell ill, did it not?"

"Ye-e-ess? Surely you're not suggesting . . . ? I mean, really." The look of helpful merriment began to slip. "The cook needs to be more careful," she said. "I had a touch of tummy myself after we first arrived. I was up half the night with it. I shall leave you now, even though my own life is at risk now and no one seems concerned about *that*."

She swept out of the room in an eddy of churning crinoline so wide she could barely clear the door. As it was, part of her hem caught in the door's closing, and Cotton was forced to become engaged in the momentary struggle to free her.

"As you know," said Cotton once she'd safely gone, "I have rather a complicated relationship with theatrical people. So you tell me what you thought of that performance."

Max knew Cotton's mother had been a hippie rock star who dragged her son to "gigs"—an upbringing guaranteed to produce the kind of child who craves routine and order and does things like join the police force as a form of rebellion. Max thought that flamboyant history explained as well some of Cotton's energy, and the touch of dandyism in his love of clothing and costume.

"I thought it was a performance," said Max. "In part."

"But which part?"

Max shrugged. "Most of it. I'm not sure how much control she has over that. It seems to be the habit of a lifetime."

"I thought so, too," put in Essex.

"I know nothing about the profession," said Max, "but it does seem to attract the insecure, and then feed their insecurities until they grow to monstrous proportions."

"Do you think so? I rather always thought the job attracted large egos—egos large and tough enough to withstand the occasional bruising by fans and critics."

"Maybe it attracts both types, or a combination of both," said Max. "People who fluctuate between arrogance and insecurity."

"But here we're looking for someone with daring, don't you think? And brains." This from Essex. "I'm not sure she qualifies."

Max, nodding, said, "Her role-playing seemed nearly delusional to me."

Cotton said, "Or is she just such a good actor—are they all called actors now? Anyway, is she so good at her profession we're being tricked into thinking she's delusional?"

"I think you're overthinking this, Chief. I really do," said Sergeant Essex. "She's thick as two planks, is all. And so much for family values. She seemed determined to drop a few of her nearest and dearest in it, didn't she?"

Max picked up the paper with the drawing of the family tree again. He mused over it a moment and said, "Oscar and Leticia were born within minutes of each other, is that right?"

"Yes."

"Just like Alec and Amanda? With the male in each instance being the elder? If only slightly?"

"Yes. I don't see how that gets us any further ahead, do you?"

"No. It's not important. Twins, as we all know, run in families."

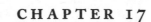

CHAPTER 17

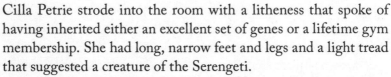

Picture This

Cilla Petrie strode into the room with a litheness that spoke of having inherited either an excellent set of genes or a lifetime gym membership. She had long, narrow feet and legs and a light tread that suggested a creature of the Serengeti.

She sat gracefully in the leather chair Cotton indicated, having scissored her way across the room like a ballerina, every movement as sure as if choreographed.

In a long dark-gray sweater—or was it a short gray dress?—over ankle-length, black leggings paired with flat patent leather shoes, Cilla looked not just artistic but frightfully artistic, a creature of the demimondaine. Cotton had noticed it was an appearance she cultivated by wearing dark clothing, usually a variant on a polo-neck sweater and very tight jeans. She was whippet thin. Her hair fell expensively about her face in long, precision-cut locks, and she wore a necklace, quite beautiful, of shiny glass and polished stone. The brown, black, and gray colors complemented her deep brown eyes and her lustrous dark hair with its glinting threads of silver.

Not conventionally beautiful, Max decided, watching her closely, but a memorable and distinctive woman. So this was Randolph's assistant—the stylist he used for his photographic portraits.

Cilla now crossed the long legs. She kept the toes of both legs pointed, a posture as unnatural as it must have been uncomfortable. The reason for the artful posture seemed to be to draw attention to the perfection of her long, narrow calves.

Duly noted, thought both Max and Cotton.

"Now, Miss Petrie, you say you are here as Randolph's assistant?" Cotton began the interview.

A rustling of paper came from the far corner as Sergeant Essex prepared a new page in her notebook. Cilla glanced over, noticing her for the first time. She gave her a tentative smile. Cilla, like most people seeing that their words will be written down, was slightly taken aback.

"Please call me Cilla. Yes. We were just passing through, actually, on our way to an assignment in Cornwall. I believe Randolph planned to return here, and I was going to travel on to London to stay with family for Christmas."

"So you weren't one of the castle's Christmas visitors."

She shook her head decisively. "The intention for me was not to spend the holidays here, as most of them were planning to do. Obviously, a family affair at the holidays is a different sort of occasion. Special. I was invited to stay, in fact, but I didn't want to intrude."

"Invited by whom?"

"By the old man, of course. Oscar. He was rather a poppet, you know. I can't bear to think about what's happened to him. What was done to him, rather."

"Had you visited before?" Max asked.

She turned toward him. Noticing the crutch for the first time her eyes widened. She asked what had happened (interestingly, none of the others had; perhaps sprains were a way of life around the castle) and she made the conventional noises of concern. Then she said:

"As to my visiting before: here and there, yes I had. The castle is a nice stopping-off point for many of the places to which Randolph and I have to travel to meet clients. They generally like to be photographed on their own turf, you know. Or astride their own horses. Randolph liked to drop in to Chedrow when he was anywhere in the vicinity and see how his mother was doing. He was rather devoted to her, you know. Two of a kind they are, if you ask me! He's been distraught since this has happened, let me tell you, although he hides it well."

"When you say 'two of a kind,' you mean what, exactly?" Max asked her.

"They're both a bit of a throwback to the Edwardian age, is all I meant. Now, I have to say, long before Oscar . . . well, before Oscar was dispatched, shall we say, there had been quite an atmosphere here at the castle. Everyone was very on edge."

"So we're hearing. Have you any notions as to why?"

"Not really, no." She uncrossed and recrossed the long legs. "I saw you chatting with the twins earlier," she said. "It must have been pre-your accident."

"Do you yourself have children?" he asked idly.

A fleeting, wistful smile.

"No," she said simply.

In his pastoral work, he had learned that people generally loved talking about their children. Sometimes complaining about them, usually bragging. It was the best icebreaker of all. But now he felt he'd rather blundered, so he asked instead, "I think you've made a bit of an impression on Amanda. There's a bit of heroine worship going on there."

"Really? I hadn't realized. I suppose she's at an impressionable age. The twins can be a bit . . . wild, I've noticed. My own parents' divorce was the defining event of my life. Ten years ago, it was—yes, I was well into adulthood—but it affects one, regardless of age. It was a total rupture of everything I'd been brought up to believe was true. People think if they wait until their children are 'grown' that it's okay to divorce. 'They're of age now, we can do what we want'—that seems to be the thinking."

Cilla delivered this information with a lack of self-pity, and in what seemed to be her usual mode of speech: the rapid-fire intensity of a Londoner for whom life depended on an ability to act quickly and not be run over by taxicabs.

"You say Oscar invited you to stay," said Cotton. "Did Leticia seem happy about that?"

She turned back to face him.

"No. No, she did not, but as I say, I declined the invitation anyway."

"Did you have much chance to talk with her? Did you gain any impressions as to what was on her mind?"

"Her health was on her mind. It's difficult being a professional sick person but Leticia managed. Particularly with her crowded social schedule."

"I thought she was a bit of a recluse?" said Max.

"She was. That didn't stop her from inviting the good and the great to come to *her* for dinner on occasion. Her table was well-known in its day for the quality and size of the spreads produced. Not to mention the reputations established or destroyed over an hours-long meal. No, Lady B didn't care for mixing with the great unwashed, but she was generally up for importing her entertainment, so long as they met her standards."

"You didn't like her." This from Max. It wasn't a question.

"No one liked her. Everyone respected her. They even wanted to *be* like her. There are people like that, you know—people who command that sort of awe. In her day, she was a force to be reckoned with. Randolph said she had dozens of suitors."

Cotton looked up from some notes he'd been scribbling and said, "Tell us, if you will, Miss Petrie, something of your relationship with your employer."

"With Randolph? He's been a good employer, is really all I can say. And the job is fabulous—I get to meet all the second- and third-tier royalty, you know. Stay in some pretty posh places. Well," she added with a laugh, "Randolph could pay me a bit more, I suppose. But if I need time off, as I did when my mother took ill, he never hesitated."

"No . . . romantic interest then," asked Max.

She gave him a chilly smile. "Oh, do spare me the clichés, will you, please?" she said. "Starry-eyed assistant hopelessly in love with older, more sophisticated boss? I'm not remotely interested in Randolph if you must know—and I suppose a police investigation elevates this to something beyond idle nosiness on the part of the police. But Randolph is simply not my type. I find him completely charming but rather cold—*please* don't repeat that, especially not to him. But not only do I have a fiancé in London, I'll be relocating with him soon. We're going to live in the U.S."

"We'll need a name and number to verify that information." Cotton made a restless, darting movement with his hands—a signal to Essex to follow up.

"Of course," said Cilla. "That's not a problem. His name is Erick Landstrone." She spelled it for Essex and rattled off a phone number and an address in Chelsea. "That's a flat we share."

She added, smiling, "I passed Jocasta on the way in here. She said you'd positively *grilled* her for *hours*."

"A slight exaggeration," said Cotton.

"I'm afraid Jocasta is a type I'm used to. Before I started working for Randolph, I actually spent some time in the trenches as a gofer at Pinewood Studios, and at the BBC. For my sins, I also did a brief stint in Hollywood. Not to put too fine a point on it, some of the actors you meet are just poison. It's all about them and their careers and their ruddy hair and their likes and dislikes, twenty-four/seven."

"And Jocasta?"

She shrugged. "Jocasta is an old-time star, fading, married to a much younger bloke who married her, it is said, to help his own career, in a move reminiscent of the dumb starlet who slept with the scriptwriter. Apparently no one thought to warn him. Jocasta's near-uselessness in terms of Hollywood connections should have been evident, but I imagine brains were not Simon's strong suit. That, or he had been literally blinded by ambition.

"Anyway, Jocasta is a throwback to the days when Hollywood created stars who rode in limousines and wore furs, rather than campaigning against gas guzzlers and those who kill animals for their fur. While these stars might adopt the occasional orphan, that hadn't reached the peak of the trend we're seeing now. Jocasta has mentioned she's thought of adopting. Can you just imagine?"

All three listeners remained diplomatically silent.

"Anyway, it is likely she picked up the habit of retiring modesty during her time in Hollywood."

Max said mildly, "I don't think Hollywood has a lock on the enormous-ego franchise. We grow our own here, many of them in London."

"You're too right there," said Cilla. "Anyway, she talks of her many fans, but I have the most difficult time imagining what a fan of Jocasta's might look like, don't you? Listening to tales of Jocasta's brief—but not brief enough—career is right up there with the history of dentistry for grimly fascinating topics."

"Now, Miss Petrie—" Cotton began.

"Cilla, please."

"You say you worked briefly in Hollywood. Did you ever meet Jocasta in the United States?"

"Yes, didn't I say? We crossed paths, very briefly," Cilla said. "And very crossly."

"Oh?"

"One doesn't tend to have happy memories of one's encounters with Jocasta. I'd nearly forgotten all about it until Randolph told me she was a cousin."

"Did you also know her husband Simon?"

"Only in the way one runs into people at parties and things. Hollywood is a company town. Sooner or later you know everyone. I always felt rather sorry for him, poor pet. It's no life for a grown man."

Max felt there was little to be gained by further examination of the marital affairs of Jocasta and Simon. In his experience, all manner of people married and stayed married for all manner of reasons. There was no telling with folk, as an American comrade of his had used to say. Looking across to Cotton—it was his interrogation, after all—Max asked Cilla for her views of Randolph's sibling.

"Lester. Oh, yes. And Fester," said Cilla. "She of the bad jewelry and the travel wear made of some indestructible fabric that could be used in an emergency to repair a propeller blade or stop a herd of runaway cattle. She is an Australian he met over there somehow. And *he* is one of the most ghastly people you'll ever meet. One wonders how his wife puts up with it, only then one realizes she's worse than he is."

My gran would have loved these people, thought Sergeant Essex. Lobbing their grenades at each other, all over the castle. Gran had loved a bit of kerfuffle.

Cotton, meanwhile, had asked Cilla about Lamorna. Cilla was saying, "Lamorna is a religious nut, not to put too fine a point on it. On leaving school, she volunteered at a Christian mission in India—I think that was it, India. Maybe it was China. But all that wasn't deprivation enough. Next she went to Africa to 'help the women,' many of whom seemed ungrateful for the help and were profoundly glad to see the back of her. This according to Randolph. It was well before my time."

"I hadn't noticed a religious streak in any of the others," said Max.

"You won't, I shouldn't think," said Cilla. "Personally, I think people are rather unfair to Lamorna. But she has no sense of humor. And that really is too bad: It could have stood her in good stead given that she comes up short in several other departments. The other day I asked if she'd like my professional help with her styling techniques. What styling techniques, you may well ask? Just trying to be kind, you understand. Besides, there is damn-all to do around here, in case you haven't noticed. But she looked at me as if I'd suggested we perform the Dance of the Seven Veils on the castle parapets for the next busload of tourists."

Cilla had begun to fidget, shifting around in her chair. Again she crossed and recrossed her slender legs.

"I say, are we going to be held here much longer?"

"That's difficult to say," replied Cotton.

"It's just that now—you see, I already have a new job with a photographer in America. I was to begin next week. Erick has been stuck back there at our flat with the job of packing all our rubbish and I'm hearing from him hourly, it seems. I can give you the photographer's coordinates if you like—I'm hoping I can tell him I'll be allowed to leave soon?"

"Soon," said Cotton briefly. "But leave the information with Sergeant Essex. I gather your planned parting from Randolph was amicable? He took the news of your leaving well?"

"Completely!" she said, seeming astonished by the question. "He'll miss me, I like to think, but a good stylist isn't that hard to find, not when you're Viscount Nathersby. As for me, it was time for a change, Erick or no Erick. I get bored doing the same type of things. The photographer I'll be working for—in New Mexico—specializes in nature photography. He promotes ecology, sustainable resources, doing good for the earth. I've never been to New Mexico—I really can't wait to see it."

She left the room soon after that, leaving behind a name and address in the U.S. and a reiterated wish to be allowed to get to her new job as soon as possible.

❄ ❄ ❄

"So. What do we make of her?" Max asked.

Cotton said, "We make of her that she is clever and ambitious."

Essex said, "And much older than she looks. She's forty-five, would you believe? Do you like her for this crime, Inspector?"

"She has the brains for it," said Cotton. "Or maybe I mean the nerve."

"And no alibi. But that's true of all of them."

They spoke awhile longer, then Cotton said: "Do you know, from all we've been told, Oscar reminds me of some Agatha Christie-ish captain of industry plotting world domination from his castle keep. Or a shadowy spymaster of yore, called in to haul Europe back from the brink."

"It would be easy to see him only in that way," said Max, "and forget he was a lonely and aging man who'd antagonized nearly everyone in his familial orbit. A figure to be pitied rather than feared. But someone feared or hated him enough to make this brutal attack on him. In a particularly cowardly way, too—while he was asleep. I wouldn't credit a wild animal with such behavior, but here you have a human behaving thus. And no doubt justifying it somehow as necessary for his or her own survival."

"The loneliness would explain the ill-thought-out marriage to Gwynyth, I suppose," said Cotton thoughtfully, as he again spun the biro on the desktop. "I mean, apart from her obvious attractiveness, and his wealth, the two of them had nothing in common, and he seems to have paid a heavy price for that bit of folly."

"The twins don't seem to be regarded as compensation, either. There is the real sadness to the story."

"It *was* a cowardly murder, wasn't it?" said Sergeant Essex, picking up the thread. "So much blood. The poor old man bled quite a bit."

"I'm afraid so, yes."

"'Yet who would have thought the old man to have had so much blood in him.'"

They both turned to her.

"You needn't look so surprised," she said. "I won a prize for Shakespeare, in school."

Max, abashed, said, "It's a powerful line. Too true in this case."

Encouraged, Essex said, "'I am in blood / Stepp'd in so far, that, should I wade no more, / Returning were as tedious as go o'er.' That's from the Scottish play, too," she informed them.

"Let's hope," said Max, "the second part isn't also true. What we don't want most of all is for the killer to 'go o'er.' To be at the beginning of some sort of rampage."

CHAPTER 18
Simon Says

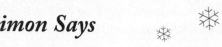

"Simon Jones next, and let's say that's the lot for today," said Cotton. "We spoke with Gwynyth extensively yesterday—as the ex-wife she merited special attention. Sad that being an ex-spouse always makes one the prime suspect, what? Still, why don't you have a word with her, Max, once we've finished with Simon?"

"All right, I will," said Max. "As to Simon, perhaps as an in-law, he'll have a slightly different perspective from the rest. What can you tell me about him?"

"He's husband number three for Jocasta." Cotton settled back in his desk chair, elbows resting on the leather arms. "The other two were divorced in a firestorm of publicity, but this union seems to be holding. In the case of the second husband, it was something to do with a secretary (him) and a personal trainer (her). Simon, her number three, is an actor—I should say former actor. She met him somewhere in her travels across the vast reaches of America when she was trying to reestablish a stage career. I call him a former actor because he seems to have stopped appearing in thespian delights only marginally more obscure than Jocasta's own. His real passion—how I have come to detest that word!— his real passion seems to be cars and car racing. His good looks kept propelling him in other directions, however. He seems to act as some sort of business manager for her in his spare time off from wishing he were behind the wheel."

"He told me he was trying his hand at writing for the screen," said Max.

There was a knock at the door and Sergeant Essex came in. Max saw behind her the man of large frame and well-tended blond hair who had been jogging in the garden. He had changed into an open-collar shirt with a pullover sweater and designer jeans.

He had the bland, tanned good looks of someone who might be employed promoting Weetabix on the telly.

Simon Jones identified himself for the record and confirmed his wife's account of the events of the night of the murder. They had played cards for most of the time after dinner. He'd come down to breakfast the next day without her, but at his usual time of about eight A.M.

"The place is overwhelming, isn't it? And I'm still getting used to all these titles and such," said Simon. "It's so—well, frankly, it's just plain un-American, this stuff. Randolph is of course not Randolph but Viscount Nathersby. The earl's eldest—and only—son Alec has the courtesy title of Viscount Edenstartel but now he'll be the earl in his late father's stead. Don't try to keep up. No one but *Debrett's* can keep all this straight. I only know because my wife is so interested."

Could this good-looking man of the world be as gee-whiz unsophisticated as he was trying to appear? Overall, Max thought not.

"You are not," said Cotton delicately, "Jocasta's first husband?"

"No, but is that at all relevant?" He wrinkled his brow with frank curiosity but seemed to take no offense. Max noted that his hands were so tightly clasped in his lap the knuckles were white. He wore a large wedding band of gold that caught the light from the lamp beside his chair.

"Not really," said Cotton, himself amiability personified. "But a lot of what we have to go on so far, until we hear more from our colleagues in America, is scandal sheet gossip. I'd rather hear a less hysterical, toned-down version of the facts."

"I appreciate that," said Simon. "Well, I'm husband number three for Jocasta. The first was someone she met at drama school." Off Cotton's look, Simon said, "Yes, I know—she actually did go to drama school. Somewhere in the States, which is how she ended up living there—he was an American so from that marriage it became possible for her to remain in the U.S. without having to overcome visa and work permit issues. Anyway, that marriage was short-lived, a matter of two years. The second husband was a producer of some very doubtful films. Such career as Jocasta has had, however, she owes to him."

"I see," said Cotton. He sat back, waiting for the man to continue. It took some moments. Simon took out a handkerchief from his pants pocket and began to mop his brow.

"This has been a complete shock," Simon finally said. "You must forgive me if I don't sound quite . . . connected to the events, or able to talk coherently about them. You see, Jocasta always felt it was Oscar who was close to extinction, to be honest with you. Leticia, so Jocasta maintains, was the picture of health, despite her complaints. The very picture of health. Until, of course, she, erm, well . . . until she died." His mind catching up to the paradox presented by his speech, he smiled bleakly. He had beautiful teeth, too white and perfect to be quite real.

"And of course," continued Simon, "Leticia had the best of everything that might help prolong her life. Randolph and Lester visited daily while they were here, and kept in touch when they weren't. Felberta tried to visit but I gather Leticia finally ordered her not to. Anyway, Randolph had a buzzer installed by Leticia's bed so Lamorna could hop to her command. I should be so lucky as to have a personal slave, although I'm not sure how far I'd trust Lamorna. There's some pent-up hostility there, I think?" He had what Max thought of as an American propensity for making a question of a statement by letting his voice rise at the end of many of his sentences. It made him sound both nonconfrontational, and uncertain.

"Had you met Leticia before?" Max asked.

"I'd met none of them."

"Surely, you kept in touch, got together on special occasions?"

"No. And that was how Jocasta wanted it. I think after so many years of estrangement, even once any bad feeling wore off, it was just simpler somehow to coast along with things remaining as they were. She'd been in the States for thirty years. It's where her life was based."

"If you'll forgive me, I am wondering how your wife knew so much about things," interjected Max. "If she was estranged for so long."

"Ah. Well, you may find it hard to credit, but she kept in close touch with Lamorna over the years."

"I see," said Max. "Interesting, that."

"I thought so, too," said Simon. "From her letters, which I glanced at occasionally, she and Jocasta had nothing in common. Lamorna doesn't inform, she pontificates. She also tries to convert people to her beliefs, which is laughable when you consider her audience."

"So I have gathered," said Max. "But she operated as sort of an unofficial spy, reporting to your wife?"

"Nothing as coherent or planned as that. But I suppose that's what it amounted to."

"If we could back up a moment," said Cotton, who, although listening closely, had been examining a cuff link with every appearance of total absorption. "You say you didn't know either of them, Leticia or Oscar, at firsthand. Not until you came here."

Simon Jones shot a rueful, blinding smile across to Cotton.

"Yes. I can only tell you that one quickly learned never to ask Leticia how she was," he said.

"Because she might tell you."

"Precisely," said Simon. "And at length. She'd tell you anyway but if you led with your chin like that you were really asking for it." Again, they were treated to a flash of that friendly smile.

"You would say Lady Baynard was what a doctor would call a hypochondriac?"

"I would say she was obsessed, certainly," Simon replied. "How much time, after all, can one devote to monitoring every single vital sign of one's body, day in and day out? Oscar had a tinge of it, and he could bore you with his herbal remedies for everything, but Leticia—well, as I say: It was an obsession that bordered on madness and probably was a form of madness."

"And yet . . ." began Cotton.

"Quite. And yet, she did die. So I suppose we need another word for what ailed her."

There was a movement from Sergeant Essex's corner. She was making little waving-from-the-elbow movements, like the Queen in a motorcade.

"Yes, Sergeant Essex?" said Cotton.

"If I may, I've a question I'd like to ask. How well did you know your wife's cousins, sir? Randolph, for example."

"Never met him. Before this, I mean, of course."

"Isn't that a bit . . . unusual?"

"As I've tried to convey, the whole family is unusual. Personally, I credit my wife's creativity—shall we call it that?—as springing from this odd background. They make fun of her, I know. I've overheard them. Hell, they barely bother to lower their voices. But I can tell you she had the potential to be great—and was *nearly* one of the greats at one time. She took some bad advice, and surrounded herself with the wrong people. She also had a tendency to overestimate, or underestimate, her true worth, so negotiations were, well, difficult and not always ending to her advantage."

"Sounds much like most union negotiations," said Cotton.

Simon grinned weakly. "All actors are a mass of insecurities. I was one, I should know. You're at the top one day, then the next day no one can quite recall who you were. That's why the salaries are so outrageous for some of these stars."

"Did Jocasta have financial problems, then?" Cotton asked.

"Well, no, I wasn't saying that exactly. She had to start living within her means, and sooner rather than later. It was a difficult concept for Jocasta to grasp. She loved the extravagant gesture— she could be very generous, to herself, and to others. That designer Christmas tree in the Great Hall was her idea. Typical."

"A bit of a shopaholic, then."

"One could say that, yes. Yes. And then . . ."

"Then?"

"Again, she made some bad career choices, relying on her own judgment and listening to no one. Her recent foray into vampire films was so ill advised her agent stopped returning her calls until the images were less vivid in the public's mind. I did try to warn her."

Max was silent, but he was thinking of the tensions in the family bubbling away for days and months, as they did in many families, harmless until a fissure, a tiny fault, was breached. His fingers drummed on the padded armrest of his chair. The room was darkening; effectively they were in a cellar, and the area was lighted artificially except for small windows high in the walls.

"I think that will be all for now," Cotton was saying, "seeing as how you only knew the 'players' here at secondhand. Unless Father Tudor has any more questions?" Max shook his head. "But we'll need you to stay on at least for a few days. That is, if you were planning on going anywhere."

Simon rose and headed for the door.

"I would say it was a pleasure to meet all of you, but that wouldn't be the truth. I need to get my wife out of here. She's not well. I think you have noticed that for yourselves."

"I understand," said Cotton. "We'll do our best. I am sure once the guilty party is caught your wife will rest easier."

❄ ❄ ❄

"I've been thinking," said Max, once the door had closed behind Simon Jones, and Cotton had sent Sergeant Essex off to interview the maids and other day help.

"Oh, yes?" said Cotton.

"About Leticia. Lady B. They all seem to have much the same view of her. No one could get past her hypochondria, or her snobbery. It seems rather to have driven them all away. I suppose it was much the same dynamic as with her brother Oscar, except his remarriage got added to the mix."

Cotton, looking at him closely, asked: "Have you remembered anything more about that day you met Leticia on the train?"

Max shook his head, frustrated. "I just can't remember more

than I've told you already." He'd been preoccupied, rehashing his dinner conversation with George in London, and wanting to be alone to collect himself and his thoughts before returning to his villagers. Aloud he said, "Because she was boring for England, for one thing." Max was uncharacteristically cross because of his ankle, which injury he saw as the result of his immersion in this dreadful situation with this appalling family. He was also thinking, guiltily: If only I had paid her more attention, asked questions, listened to what she was saying. But no, I was too invested in not being dragged into her personal dramas. And I call myself a priest of the Church of England. Whatever happened to compassion? Et cetera. Et cetera.

Cotton, recognizing the signs, again waited for the spasm of guilt to pass. He gave it a few beats, then said, "She sounds a frightful old battle-axe." And Max laughed. It was the word that had come into his own mind on that train ride with her.

"I shouldn't worry," Cotton continued. "You did the best you could and I know she never felt slighted in any way. It's doubtful she had much to tell us, really, even 'from the grave.' A vague sense of doom and all that doesn't tell us whom to nail for this murder. The feathery old dear couldn't have known how important her views would turn out to be. Nor could you."

Max, somewhat mollified by this speech, still knew he could have done better. He felt somehow he was losing the sharp edge of his MI5 days.

"You've checked out the servants thoroughly, I suppose," said Max.

"We've only just begun." He pulled up a file on his laptop this time, and said: "Milo Vladimirov, the butler and general dogsbody. From Serbia. The war ended in 1995, fifteen years ago. He's forty now, so he would have been about twenty-five. His wife is Doris, aged forty-two years. He doubles as head gardener, times being tough—supervising the locals, especially during planting season. Of course, the Trust oversees a lot of the routine maintenance of the site. If you haven't gathered already, it is a sore spot with the family that the Trust has taken over. They could afford to buy the place back now but legally it's all tied up with a big red bow."

Max told him, "Doris seems quite attached to the family, for all she doesn't seem to have cared much for Lady B, in particular."

"Her family has served here for generations, I gather," said Cotton. "I suppose she could be descended from those who served here at the castle in its early days. Or even descended, on the wrong side of the blanket, from an early earl. Perhaps she harbors some sort of seething resentment against the upper classes—is that what you're thinking?"

Max shrugged. "Doubtful. She seems too forthright to be the type to hold grudges. But it's a possibility we can't ignore."

"Point taken. Now, Milo worked on a cruise ship that docked in Southampton, which is when he met Doris, presumably while he was on some sort of shore leave," Cotton told him, summarizing aloud from his notes. "They got married quickly—a case of true love at first sight. She got him the job at the castle—her family, as I say, has longstanding ties with the family Footrustle. They took him on faith."

"And he found the bodies," said Max. "Both of them. Never the best position for anyone to be in."

"That's right. What he tells us is that he locks up at night at eleven, and he went to bed straight after, as always. He went to Oscar's room at the usual time the next day. He was sent to find Lady B once the alarm about Oscar was sounded. He first looked for her in her bedroom and then where she usually was to be found, in the garden or the hothouse."

Max frowned in thought.

"There is no telling what someone from that upended part of the world has lived through, and been exposed to," said Cotton. "Or is capable of."

"I was just thinking the same thing. Those kinds of circumstances can change a man."

"Right—too right. You can't expect to stay the same as you were before. Whatever that was to begin with. He was still a lad during the war, not yet a grown man. That has to be factored in, too."

Max nodded. "Sometimes there is no recovery from the unspeakable atrocities of war."

"You'll want to have a word with the family's consigliere," said Cotton. "I gather Lord Footrustle never made a legal move without his advice." Cotton ran his hands over his face in a washing motion. The weariness was starting to show. Even the starched pocket handkerchief looked like it was wilting. "I've spoken with this chap Wintermute on the phone, of course. He said he'd be stopping by and he can give you the details, which will be a matter of public record sooner rather than later, anyway. He's bringing us copies of Lord Footrustle's will as well as Lady Baynard's. She had a little money of her own to dispose of. I gather the butler and the cook were generously remembered—at least to their standards it will seem most generous. That will please them."

"Yes," said Max vaguely.

"What?" said Cotton. "I know that look."

"Did you notice," said Max, "that Jocasta is not tan but her husband Simon is? Does that mean they've had separate vacations?"

"Remember where they're from. That could just be the result of his addiction to tanning beds."

"It looked real to me. But no matter. Many couples are pulled apart by varying schedules. Or even likes and dislikes for the beach. I'll ask Jocasta if I get the chance tonight."

Cotton said, "If you can get a word in edgewise, you mean. Why don't you go now and have a word with Gwynyth? Wintermute may take his own sweet time getting here."

"Any background on Gwynyth, other than the biased accounts we've heard already?"

"She and Oscar met about fourteen years ago," Cotton told him. "In the 'nothing new under the sun' category, he was much older than she." He paused again to flip through his notes. "She's forty-two now—twenty-eight when they met. Nearly three and a half decades' difference between them. Apparently sparks flew, nevertheless, and twins were the result. He, Oscar, balked initially—reading between the lines, here. Quarrels, reconciliations, all the usual. Again, when the tabloids are part of your source material you have to tread carefully. But then he apparently decided to do the right thing by her, and probably didn't mind having a young and gorgeous wife to squire around, a living, breathing testament to his virility. But the marriage came unstuck when the differences in their backgrounds became too evident. Too bad for the children, of course, but they were well taken care of. Schools and clothing paid for, and so on."

"Not . . ." said Max, "not so much was Gwynyth taken care of?"

"Not to her liking. And not, to be fair, when you consider there was so very much money floating about. Oscar would hardly notice it if half went missing. She had to have had the worst possible legal advice; I would imagine she was out of her social depth, and her solicitor was in awe of Lord Footrustle. The settlement left her largely dependent on the kindness of her children for her old age, and from the looks of things, it'll be a long shot they'll care when the time comes."

There came a knock at the door. It was Milo.

"Excuse me, sir," he said. "Mr. Wintermute the solicitor has arrived."

Cotton said, "Please have him wait in the drawing room. Max, perhaps you could have a word with him first? I'll be a few more minutes here. Thank you, Milo." It was a polite dismissal. He closed the door quietly.

"I'll be having dinner with all of them tonight," Max said. He struggled to stand, tested putting weight on his left foot, and decided he'd be using the crutch awhile longer. "Wish me luck."

"The budget doesn't run to hiring a food taster," Cotton told him. "So take care."

The mobile on the desk gave a zapping sound, skidding on the polished surface. Cotton picked it up and read from a text message.

"The technicians, the doctor, the fingerprint people have had another look round and are satisfied they have what they need now—including the bodies. They have asked, however, that the family keep Oscar's room sealed and unoccupied for the time being. Would you like to see it? You can poke your head in there if you like. Just don't go inside until we've given the all-clear."

Max nodded his understanding.

"I thought the only thing of any real interest was a round table that held enough potions and tablets to subdue Caesar's army," Cotton told him. "Most of it homeopathic, some of dubious worth, some outdated prescriptions that should have been tossed long ago."

"Anything dangerous in the lot?"

"Only if taken in sufficient quantities," replied Cotton. "'Homeopathic' to some people means 'take all you want,' which is completely a false idea. Still, there's no indication anything like an overdose was the cause of death."

"Could it have been responsible for this illness earlier?"

Cotton lifted his shoulders in a *Who can say?* gesture.

Max made his way up two flights of stairs, thankful that he kept himself in shape so that he could drag himself about when he had to. He followed Cotton's directions down a short corridor to what had been Lord Footrustle's room and was now a crime scene. It turned out to be the room around the corner from Max's.

He stood at the open doorway, which was crisscrossed by crime-scene tape, and took in what he could of the scene. It was a small room, stone-walled, wood-paneled in places, dark. Cozy if you liked that kind of dark, Igor-ish, medieval look. A room furnished in a nice blend of plush Renaissance comfort and straightjacket medieval style.

"A great reckoning in a little room"—something like that—the phrase from some half-forgotten university lecture drifted through his mind. Shakespeare writing about Christopher Marlowe, who had been stabbed in the eye.

The room had been cleaned up, of course; the body taken away, and some preliminary effort had been made to restore order. The room, he knew, had two squints, and was likely historically to have been the room belonging to the lord or at least to some sort of overseer—someone whose business it was to spy on the household unobserved. Remembering the general layout of the castle, Max knew Oscar's room would overlook the sea on its south-facing side. Via one squint, Oscar would have had a view of the goings-on inside the Great Hall, and via another, a view across the garden to the surrounding lands. Max doubted he could have overheard much from up here, unless people were shouting. As perhaps, given this group, they had been.

Max craned his head to the left. A near shelf was full of tomes on ancient British history—naval in particular—and novels by somewhat old-fashioned authors like Dumas and Robert Louis Stevenson, although neither author had ever really gone out of style. A rip-roaring yarn remained a rip-roaring yarn. Still, the lack of more modern authors indicated a man who preferred the past and history, and a return to the old favorites of childhood.

Max prayed the man had taken some enjoyment from his life. Overall, it seemed he hadn't. It seemed a sad ending.

CHAPTER 19

Wintermute

The solicitor handed him a business card printed on fine, heavy stock. It carried his name (David R. Wintermute, Esq.) and addresses in London and Monkslip-super-Mare followed by his firm's name and motto: *Creating Visionary Integrity since 1797.*

Max wasn't sure he understood what Visionary Integrity might be when it was at home—could integrity be qualified? Was Visionary Integrity better than Blindfolded Integrity? Integrity in Hindsight? Definitely, he decided, better than Nearsighted Integrity. He snapped with the nail of one index finger at the edges of the card and smiled at David R. Wintermute.

His first impressions of the solicitor were decidedly mixed.

Max had seen the damage solicitors and the courts could do and was aware he did not approach the man with an open, trusting heart. Still, Wintermute struck him as the type who had, after long years in the trade, mastered the art of opaque waffling and sidestepping the questions. A shrewd man. Dry. Humorless.

He had watery bug eyes, and moist lips slack from what might have been a minor stroke. A red-tipped Matterhorn of a nose. The man drank: Max could detect the faint whiff of alcohol surrounding Wintermute like an aura. However, the solicitor was undoubtedly competent, if he worked for Lord Footrustle, and he looked alert and present, for all practical purposes. A functioning alcoholic, they called it. Max dealt with alcoholics frequently in his role as vicar, and more often with their families—those left behind by a tragic, alcohol-fueled accident of one sort or another. Max looked closely at the jowls and watery, bulldog eyes that said, "I've seen too much." Perhaps, in this case, it was, "I've drunk too much," yet Max suspected a wily intelligence peering out from behind the insalubrious, fleshy appearance.

"Thank you for talking with me," Max said.

"The pleasure is all mine. But I do hope you realize," said Wintermute, with a slight access of pomposity, "that I will be limited to some extent in what I can tell you. I've just come from talking briefly with various members of the family, quite informally you understand. There will be a proper reading of the will later after which I may be more at liberty to speak with you. And I should be easy for you to locate if need be: The new young lord will have a mountain of legal papers to sign so I will be a recurring feature of life at the castle for a while."

"Can you tell me how it went?" asked Max. "The talk with the family?"

"In general terms, yes. Randolph was stunned; Lamorna disgruntled—but she always appears disgruntled, does she not? Gwynyth was the picture of frustration, since she had not had time to work on getting her share increased, presumably." Now, *there* was a slip in the professional façade, thought Max, hoping there would be many more. "She is not frightfully good at hiding her emotions, Gwynyth."

"I understand Lester had already been on to you."

A dry smile. "Oh, yes."

Max waited, but there were to be no further disclosures. "Let's do it this way," he said. "Tell me what you feel you are free to tell me, having spoken with the family and brought them up to date on the situation."

"Well. I cannot get into precise figures, except to say the estate is significant. Oscar, Lord Footrustle, was worth fifty or sixty million pounds at one time. Still, even he had lost some of his wealth in the economic calamities of the past year or two."

Max was stunned by the figure mentioned. He had known Oscar was wealthy but these were figures designed to tempt the unscrupulous.

"How did he take that?" Max asked. "The financial losses?"

"I don't think he was happy about it, Vicar. No one has been happy with the market lately. It's been a complete bloodbath for— Oh! Do forgive the expression. Poor Oscar."

"I meant, was he upset, angry, especially depressed?"

"I couldn't say," said Wintermute, breezing on. "I will say, more's the pity the castle was handed over by one of Oscar's forebears to the National Trust. Because thanks to Oscar's efforts, there would now be more than enough funds to maintain the property. It can't simply be taken back, you know. However, his son Alec will carry on the title. He will also come into some of his father's wealth."

Some. "The last time you saw Lord Footrustle was when?" asked Max.

"Nearly a year ago. Eleven months ago, when he revised his will. Of course, I was going to see him after the new year."

Max leaned back, surprised. "Really? You had an appointment for next month? Why was that?"

"I've no idea. Perhaps he'd changed his mind. His old will was unnecessarily mean-spirited, I rather felt. A slight to his family. Charity begins at home."

"I don't suppose you could elaborate on that?"

"No."

"Were you also to see his sister, Lady Baynard?"

"I was to have dinner with her."

"But not see her in a professional capacity."

Wintermute shook his head. Max took it to mean a "no," not to mean he wouldn't discuss it further. Wintermute suddenly shot out of his chair and helped himself to the drinks tray. At his questioning look, Max in his turn shook his head. "Too early for me."

David R. Wintermute, Esq., shrugged and poured himself a good slug of the drink into a crystal glass. He toasted Max in mock salute, then said, "Oscar had a few surprises up his sleeve. Several charities were to receive large bequests, including Tiggy-Winkle's, a hedgehog rescue charity, and a donkey rescue group. That one is called Hee-Haw, as I recall. Charities that feed the poor were remembered. Those issues—the homeless, hunger—became important to him of late. He had so much to give, you see. The local cricket team was to benefit, as well. Lord Footrustle was a great cricket fan. It was one of the things we had in common. I consider his loss to be not just that of a client but a friend. And someone with first-rate knowledge of the game."

Max nodded, but absently. Cricket was up there with the sports he understood but hardly saw the reason for, knowing only that a Zen-like patience was required of its fans. Looking at Wintermute, it was hard to reconcile him with the Buddha, but he supposed there were physical similarities.

The liquor seemed to be having an effect, if the wavering focus in Wintermute's eyes were any indication. Max thought this might be a good time to ask how Jocasta fared in Oscar's will.

"Jocasta and her descendants, had there been any, were remembered in Oscar's will, along with the twins. Gwynyth faired poorly, as I've said."

Wintermute spread himself a little wider in his plush chair, ran a hand through his thinning gray hair, and said, "Do you know, I have always found inherited wealth to be corrosive and disincentivizing. And the longer I am in my line of work, the more I believe that. In amounts seemingly finely calibrated to produce the effect, I have seen it breed some of the laziest human beings on the planet. Rarely does there emerge a personality strong enough to rise above the effects of the inculcated sense of entitlement, and to put the money to good and creative use." It was an unexpected, even confessional, outburst, coming as it did from a man whose bread was buttered by the upper classes he served. "In the case of the Footrustle family," he went on, "you could see the blood rapidly thinning out by the time of the present generation."

Max said, "I wouldn't be too sure of that just yet."

"You are thinking in particular of the peculiar intelligence of Alec and Amanda," Wintermute said, again surprising Max. The mind operated clearly despite the alcoholic fog. "It's too early to say there. Gwynyth—Lady Footrustle—may have provided just the infusion of fresh blood that was needed. Non-blue blood, of course. Occasionally that's necessary, you know, to keep the upper classes from going completely potty with all the inbreeding." He tipped back his drink. Before he could head off to fetch a refill, Max asked how Lady Baynard's death affected the situation.

"To answer that I'll begin by referring you back to Lady Baynard's inheritance from her husband," said Mr. Wintermute. "There was little to inherit, I hasten to add. Old Baynard was what we used to call a blackguard, a word that sadly has fallen into disuse, along with cad and bounder. What money there was went to her in trust for life, and she had no control over its dispersal. Under the will of her late husband, it went to their children at her death. Of course, Lady Baynard was remembered handsomely by her brother."

"Her estate would go to Randolph and Lester?"

"That is correct. And there's a sum going to Lamorna, the granddaughter. Not as much as to the sons, but she was not left out."

"That is interesting."

"Hmm. Never leave grounds for a contested will. That is my motto," said Wintermute.

So much for the visionary integrity motto, thought Max. Perhaps the real motto wouldn't fit on the business card. "Have you yet met Simon, Jocasta's husband?"

"Briefly," said Wintermute. "That was all I needed. He's likely a fortune hunter, but surely there can't be all that much fortune to hunt, not if the quality of Mrs. Jones's movies is any guide to her pay scale. Still, if you ask me, he's kept her glued together all these years. If he's a fortune hunter, he's at least earned his fortune."

"What about the money Jocasta might expect to receive from Oscar, her father?" said Max. He felt that Wintermute was positively letting his hair down at this point, and he wanted to press the advantage. "You don't include that when you speak of her fortune?"

"Ah. Well. Oscar didn't much approve of her choice of career, you know. Both he and his sister seem to have held old-fashioned views on this subject and regarded a career on the stage or in film as one step up from prostitution."

Max chanced his arm. "One wonders how much inheritance Jocasta might in fact expect to, well, inherit?"

"Ah." Again with the "Ahs," thought Max. It appeared to be a topic full of hesitancies and doubts. "Not as much as Alec. Amanda also inherits less than Alec. If there had been natural issue of Jocasta's union with Simon, well . . ."

"It would have made a difference to Lord Footrustle," Max finished for him. "As you say, you had known Lord Footrustle—Oscar—a long time. Certainly you knew him when he first met Gwynyth?"

"Indeed, I did. And I did try to talk him out of it. As a friend, as a solicitor."

"How did they meet? Lord Footrustle and Gwynyth?"

Wintermute replied, "He met her on a cruise to the Baltics, one of those cruises where widowed women outnumber eligible males by a thousand to one." Max thought fleetingly of his own widowed mother, fascinating male passengers and crew as she sailed practically nonstop from one destination to another.

"So what were the chances he'd come home with a new bride—that he'd actually be married as soon as they landed?" Wintermute was saying. "She'd been a showgirl, part of a dancing and singing troupe onboard ship. Some cabaret-type extravaganza. It was a classic middle-aged crisis situation with Oscar. If he had not been on a ship he'd have bought a red sports car, too, no doubt."

"Marriage to Gwynyth changed the equation for all of them, didn't it?"

"Yes, it most certainly did, at least for a while—until the divorce, of course. She came back for more several times, and I would imagine that is why she is here now."

"I'm not sure I understand the anger I'm sensing here, among certain of the family members."

"Don't you really? You'd have to go back a few years, I suppose. Lord Footrustle paid for everyone's schooling, but they took the 'fun' courses rather than get proper qualifications. Lounging about became a permanent trait. Even Randolph's photography was the sort of choice made by a young man who knows he has great wealth at his back. Lester, on the other hand, never made any choices that stuck and seemed to regard fast dealing as the best way to get ahead. Their cousin Jocasta—well, she at least tried to parlay that feeble talent into something, I'll give her credit for that. Great expectations, yes, indeed. Then along came Gwynyth. It was what they call a real wake-up call for the younger branches of the family. It wasn't until her removal—and some of them campaigned mightily for her removal—that hopes rose again, but the twins coming along in the meantime somewhat diluted those hopes. They were his flesh and blood, after all, and baby Alec was much to be desired as a male to carry on the title."

"I gained no impression that Oscar was fond of the children," said Max.

"Fondness had nothing to do with it. A hereditary title did."

"Lord Footrustle was married before, a union which produced Jocasta. What happened to his first wife?"

"Oscar's first wife is both divorced and dead," said Wintermute. "In that order. Rather inconsiderate of her not to have spared him the trouble of divorce, so Lord Footrustle always seemed to think."

"No love lost between them, then."

"No."

"He rather lost interest in Jocasta, I gathered, when the marriage dissolved."

"Yes. And I have gathered from my very occasional reading of the more sensational press that Jocasta therefore sought attention elsewhere. Sadly, that's not an uncommon reaction, is it?"

Wintermute was by this point on his third drink. He went to reach inside his jacket pocket for his Montblanc and dropped it on the floor. The interview ended with him on his knees crawling about while Max hobbled about trying to help, scanning the floor and the far corners where the pen might have rolled.

"The thing is," said a thick, garbled voice coming from behind the sofa. "The thing is that I feel there will be an explosion, and soon. So much money, so many who feel slighted. Yes, it—aha!" Wintermute stood, holding the errant pen aloft.

"Mark my words," he said. "We haven't come to the end of the trouble yet."

❄ ❄ ❄

Max left Wintermute shortly afterward in the company of Cotton, who was attempting to get what sense he could out of the man while he was still on this side of sober. From outside the door, where Max listened unabashedly, he heard Wintermute again mention money in the neighborhood of fifty-plus million pounds.

A sum worth killing for, some might think. Max leaned back against the wall and wondered: Did Wintermute's being again called to the castle become a sort of catalyst, speeding up the plan to kill Lord Footrustle—if plan there had been? For the killer, the natural assumption would be that Wintermute was contacted to draw up a new will for Lord Footrustle. And perhaps also a will for Lady Baynard, if for some reason she had changed her mind about including Lamorna in her bequests, or about any of a dozen other things. The killer wouldn't want this complication . . . it could mean being left out. So any old, existing will was preferable to one that didn't yet exist and might be deleterious. Of course, it might also have been to the killer's benefit, but could he or she take the chance? One thing was certain, there was no way to ask anyone, and the killer couldn't risk waiting to see—waiting for the final will to be prepared and sent back for signing. Or worse, to be signed.

And all this begged the question, did the killer even know about Oscar's appointment with Wintermute for the coming new year?

Inheritance. Musing on the topic, Max was reminded of Lamorna's mention of Esau and Jacob. She had said the whole thing reminded her of that Bible story. There had been an inheritance at stake there, and a trick played on the father. Jacob, with the connivance of his mother, had tricked his father into giving Jacob the blessing reserved for the firstborn son, Esau.

Max had always felt it was an unsatisfactory story in terms of bad behavior being rewarded rather than punished—the moral logic somehow felt muddled to him, and he always had the sense that pieces of the story were missing.

In addition, Max had always found it incredible that an old man, however blind, could mistake goatskin for his son's hairy forearm.

He would have to look up the passage this evening. The day was getting away from him now. He wanted to talk with the disappointed Gwynyth, Lady Footrustle.

CHAPTER 20

I Feel Pretty

Max had hopped his way up a mercifully short flight of steps to the Tower Room of Gwynyth, Lady Footrustle, and knocked at the wooden door.

"Come on in," she called. "I'm just putting on the finishing touches before dinner."

He had a struggle with the massive door so she had had to come over to admit him. She wore a skirt that was more a suggestion of fabric than it was actual garb. It bore a print in shades of tan and buttercup yellow to match her hair, somehow highlighting her fairness, and the frailness of her fashionably thin form.

"That nice Inspector Cotton sent that dour little policewoman to tell me you'd be dropping by," she told him.

Max watched her resettle herself at her makeup table, this gossamer woman who had somehow given birth to those changeling children. Her hair, held back with combs, fell into soft curls at the nape of her neck. As he watched from a chair by the window, she sucked in her cheeks and dusted a brush dipped in pearly pink over the resulting cheekbones before painting her Cupid's bow mouth in a harmonizing shade. Now she had a little black pencil she was using to dab at her eyelids, a process Max could barely stand to watch without flinching and covering his own eyes.

"I've told the police everything already," she said. *Dab. Dab.* Blink. "So I can't imagine what new information you think can emerge now."

"I just had a few questions. Call it curiosity, if you like. Of course, you're not officially obliged to talk to me."

She pivoted around to give him a flirtatious once-over.

"I can't say I mind," she said. "It's just that I think you're wasting your time."

She sat posed like a Selfridges mannequin on the bench before the makeup table, toes pointed inwardly in a would-be sexy ingénue pose that managed only to appear infantile. He thought fleetingly of Lolita and her Humbert Humbert. It occurred to him that Gwynyth, even in her forties, had not quite achieved adulthood.

She had a face smooth as glass—a perfect complexion, with a somewhat flat aspect to her expression around the blue eyes. Like Amanda's, her skin was so thick and creamy it seemed impossible blood could be flowing and veins pulsing beneath with the force of life. That type of skin barely wrinkled with age. Max was reminded by her flawlessness of a famous rock crystal skull he had seen once in the British Museum. Supposedly Aztec, it had been examined and proclaimed a fake. Max wished it were that simple with humans to spot the counterfeit.

She looked at him in the mirror, blinking her eyes and smiling with conscious allure.

"You wanted to ask me about something?" she said. "Well, shoot."

"I gather Leticia's death was as much a surprise to everyone as was Oscar's?"

"Oh, yes. It was to *me*, anyway. It was surprising in completely different ways, of course, but it really is a double whammy to lose them both. Leticia complained of aches and pains, maybe too often. Is there a subject more *bor*ing? Mostly it seemed in line with her age. She was ancient. Seventy-five! But she was lively with it, if you follow. Given to loud, strong opinions, not all of which made perfect sense. One thing she said that I agree with was that all was not well in the Joneses' marriage, if the veiled references to starlets and harlots were any guide."

"Jocasta's show business career was a problem for Leticia, I gather," said Max.

"Oh, and mine!" Gwynyth abandoned her makeup for the moment, turned, and leaned forward in an exaggerated bid for sympathy. The wide-set eyes bored in on him with flattering attention. Max was reminded somehow of Lester. She was trying too hard. "Leticia could not seem to get it through her head that showgirl and prostitute are in no way related professions. I worked jolly hard, singing, dancing—I was rehearsing or performing *all* the time."

"That must have given you and Jocasta something in common— your similar backgrounds."

"You must be joking. Besides, Simon paid me much too much attention for Jocasta's liking, if you know what I mean."

She turned back to her mirror. The little outburst had dislodged a speck of mascara. She dipped a cotton swab in one of the little jars on her table and cleared away the smudge.

"Lamorna is free now, I gather," said Max to her reflection. "Free to leave. Do you think she will?"

Gwynyth had been leaning away from the mirror for a wide-angle view. Now came the first flash of anger, one that almost sounded like spiteful jealousy. Perhaps she had been told about Lamorna's inheritance.

"What a complete balls," said Gwynyth. It was a voice that could have been used to flash-freeze vegetables; Max was to hear the tone more than once in the coming hours. "Lamorna has always been free to come and go as she pleased. She makes it sound like someone held her captive. For Oscar's part, I know he didn't like having her here. Certainly he'd have shed no tears over her leaving."

"Like Dorothy," said Max.

"Hmm?"

"*Wizard of Oz*. She only thought she didn't know the way home. Anyway, why the anger, Gwynyth? Surely you didn't have a lot of hope things would change during this holiday?"

"Didn't I? He told me himself he was going to get that solicitor in here after the new year, and he'd make sure I was better compensated. What he meant by that exactly, I don't know. But it sure would have been more than the nothing I got." She was now busy applying some sort of metal curling device to her lashes. Max felt overall it was a task to be undertaken when she was calmer.

"At least your children are provided for. That must be a relief and a blessing."

"Yes, I suppose there's that," she said vaguely.

"The boy seems to be coping well. So does Amanda. But I wonder if the stiff upper lip thing can't be carried too far."

"Alec's always trying to prove how macho he is. When one has been simply *handed* everything in life there is more to prove, isn't there? He's got looks, now he's got money. As for Amanda, she'll be all right—don't you worry about her. She's tough as old boots."

She set one of her makeup brushes down on the tabletop and reverted to the topic uppermost in her mind.

"I want someone to at least *try* to understand this. I know what they all say about me, about why I married Oscar—for money. Trading youth for money, isn't that the expression? Even the twins think so—of their own mother! But they're all wrong. Lots of rich men were after me, but I chose Oscar."

Again she leaned toward him, as if desperate for his understanding. "I didn't know which fork to use 'til he taught me," she said. "Or what food to eat, and what wine to have with what food. You can't get in the door without the right manners, for all I became Lady Footrustle when he married me. He taught me it was lower class to say I was completely whacked, upper class to say I was utterly exhausted. Things like that—things that give you away. Give *one* away, I mean."

"Is that grounds enough for love?"

She shrugged. "I thought so."

It seemed clear to Max that while she may not have loved Oscar in the conventional romantic sense, she appreciated that he had things to teach her, things she was smart enough to learn. She still dressed more like Lady Gaga than Lady Muck, yes, but he filed that in the category of youthful exuberance. It would soon be time to outgrow some of it, however.

"So he did a Professor Higgins number on you," said Max.

"Higgins? Who's he when he's at home?"

"He's a fictional character in a play. He transformed a flower girl into someone who could pass as a lady."

"I was no bleedin' flower girl," she said, sounding remarkably like an Eliza Doolittle who has skipped a few lessons. "But I take your point. Funny thing is, he wasn't a snob, Oscar. Not really. But his sister! It was as if everyone she met would of course know the place of the Footrustles in the constellation of royal personages, and God help anyone who didn't."

She screwed up her eyes in remembrance, risking another smudge to the mascara so recently and artfully applied. Then she swiveled round in her chair, her superb ankles and knees angled to the side in a ladylike pose, and looked at Max with a doggedly earnest sincerity. Again he was momentarily reminded of Lester.

"Oscar never gave up trying to improve me, you know. He said my history books were rubbish and he encouraged me to find something better in the library—take what I wanted so long as I left the rubbish books behind."

"That would be books about the Knights Templar, would it?"

"How did you know?"

"Lucky guess," he said.

The silence hung in the brightly colored room for some seconds while they scoured each other's faces for clues. Max had a sense of a woman looking down from a mountain, seeing how far she had come, and how far she had to fall back. She would be afraid of losing her tenuous hold on the social ladder, realizing her relationship with her children was her only chance at retaining that hold.

"Look," she said finally. "I loved him in my way, at one time. But in the end there was no love lost between me and Oscar. He was ruthless in the divorce, as nasty as could be. But I didn't kill him. To tell the truth, I don't think I'd have the nerve to kill anyone. Not even in self-defense."

Max could almost see what she meant. Killing someone would muss her hair. She was far too girlie a person for such exertions.

He said, "I gather this holiday, he was making some attempt to reconnect with the twins."

"I thought so, too. Poor tykes haven't had much in the way of fatherly influence."

"You've not thought of remarrying?"

"What makes you think anyone has asked?"

It was a clear bid for flattery and he ignored it. Gwynyth's beauty would ensure she would never lack for suitors.

But despite the expressions of concern for the twins' health and morale, Max gained no impression that her children were anything more than a means to an end. It was an impression confirmed in the next sentence.

"Besides, until . . ." She waggled her fingers, trying to recall some minor detail. "Until What's-their-names are grown and gone, there won't be anyone willing to put up with them."

Now she attached a necklace of what looked to be Murano glass, blues tinged with greeny-golds. He remembered seeing the jewelry everywhere in Florence, in Lombardy, most of all of course in Venice. It was similar in style to the necklace worn by Cilla Petrie. He complimented Gwynyth on it, mentioning Tuscany, to which she replied, simply, "We spend the winters there. We have a house . . ."

Thus did the wealthy speak, in that offhand way. Not bragging. "We have a house." Didn't everyone have a house in which to escape the winter? A town house and a country house, and for the very fortunate, a whatever house in another country altogether?

And it was always a house, in upper-class speak, as in weekend house—never home. Oscar must have taught her that.

That she had not escaped this winter but had chosen to remain in England seemed suddenly to have occurred to her.

"The twins were clamoring to see their father," she said, to his unspoken question. "What could I do?" The winsome cat smile crept across her face. No doubt many men had told her it was a captivating smile, for it was. Warmth dissolved some of the iciness of before. He saw the charm, and felt it being exercised for his benefit.

"You say they were anxious to see him," he took up.

"It helped that I promised them a shopping spree if they behaved while they were here. There was money riding on it." She stopped, a pout on her shiny lips. "Well, for some people there was. At least, I don't have a motive for killing him, now, do I? The police can't pin this on me, something to be grateful for."

She caught his eye in the mirror, turned, and said, "You think I'm silly, don't you?" That was so close to what he had actually been thinking Max was momentarily at a loss for words, although "frivolous" was the word he had in mind.

"I think your priorities may have wandered a bit out of line," he said at last, gently.

She shrugged. "As the saying goes, 'Walk a mile in my shoes.'"

Gwynyth's beautiful wide eyes with their coal-black liner followed him as he left. The door closed on his broad back. She noticed he was barely using the crutch and instead seemed to be testing his weight on the injured foot.

Good heavens, she thought. What a dishy parson or whatever the hell they're called. I'll have to start going to church.

But after a moment she leaned her head in her hands, exhausted and defeated.

Whacked.

To think I went through all that, for nothing.

CHAPTER 21

At Dinner

The pale December day had rapidly given way to a silvery gloom. Fading light iced the water, and a cold wind told the story of more snow on the way.

It was approaching the time of the full moon. Max, standing at a casement window in his room, saw the castle's winter garden under a sky like a sheet of aluminum, dense and impenetrable. He thought with a sudden, sharp longing of Nether Monkslip, its fields and gardens filled with flowers in summer, when he would gorge on the colors of his newfound village.

He was turning back into the room when a sudden movement caught his eye. It was Lester, capering in the garden—there was no other word for it. First loping across the open area, limbs flailing, like a puppet guided by an indifferent puppeteer; now crouched and trying to hide behind a pergola, peeking out periodically. It was the darting movements Max had seen; a smoother operator than Lester might have gone undetected. With his slightly protuberant teeth, Lester resembled a rodent with curly black hair scuttling in the dark, a look of weak cunning on his face.

As Max watched, Lester straightened, spun unexpectedly to the left as if grabbed by unseen hands, and disappeared in a narrow walkway between the castle buildings.

What had the man been looking at? Wait—he saw it now. Two figures, both wearing coats, one male, tall and lanky, and one curvaceously female, headed for the door leading to the cliff path. The curving castle walls seemed to cup them in a wintry embrace. It was Randolph and he was with Gwynyth—there was no mistaking her fair coloring in the moonlight. As Max watched, Randolph bent toward her, intimately putting an arm around her shoulders. The sea far below made a distant swishing sound, barely audible through the windows set in the deep stone walls. He couldn't hear what was said. It was like watching one of those old silent films, the kind Jocasta with her extreme gestures always reminded him of.

The pair reached the wooden door. Randolph pushed back his hair, a pointless exercise in the wind at water's edge, but apparently an incurable habit. The moon moved from behind a cloud and Max could see his smile. That patronizing smile. Gywnyth's face was blocked from Max's view. They disappeared through the door.

Max turned from the window, a frown of concern on his handsome face. He hadn't made the association before, but why wouldn't Randolph take a romantic or sexual interest in Gwynyth?

He reflected how perfectly set up the castle was for spying on one's friends, family, or servants.

And what in creation had Lester been doing out there?

Music drifted up the stairwell to Max's room, and entered with a gush as he opened the door into the hallway. It was a stately tune he didn't recognize, full of menacing strings and twiddly flutes, and suitable for background music in a costume drama. He realized the whole situation was like that, the shadowy castle walls casting a baroque quality over everything, adding to the sense of gathering menace. Entering the corridor, he was swallowed up by the darkness, the electric sconces offering faint illumination until he neared the top of the stairs into the Great Hall.

A gong sounded, echoing and ominous as it reverberated up the staircase. He found Milo near the foot of the stairs hauling back to give it another good whack, although the first might have woken the dear departed.

In the cavernous silence of the Hall, its oak walls darkened with the glaze of centuries, an aroma of onion mixed with garlic hung in the air, and that of seafood broiling in butter. Max realized he hadn't eaten much since the morning and his stomach started to send hopeful signals of good tidings to his brain.

The room was in shadow, its small windows partially blocked by snow and casting a white gloom. This was only slightly relieved by the march of candelabra down the center of the table and by the Christmas-tree lights illuminating one far corner. He supposed Milo had felt the family needed cheering. The Great Hall had no windows at floor level, only openings high in the walls where the vivid hues of stained glass shone like gemstones. Just as no marauder could peer in, neither could anyone peer out. If you wanted to know what the weather was like, you had jolly well better go outside and see.

The dining table chairs were all massive and high-backed with large, carved wooden arms—suitable for a coronation or a royal wedding. Max tried settling back in one. It was like being strapped to a gurney. He shunted himself forward, sitting perched half on, half off the seat, thinking: Uneasy lies more than the head that wears the crown. Larger armchairs that looked like his-and-her thrones guarded each end of the central table.

There was a roaring fire, and crystal vases filled with plump, fragrant flowers. Plush chairs ranged around the sides of the room—chairs that looked as if they were never sat in. They kept company with a sideboard that he appraised at "Priceless."

Gwynyth and Cilla entered more or less together, Gwynyth

now wearing a white dress that ballooned around her hips and thighs like a failed parachute. Max gathered it was the latest fashion, since the rest of Gwynyth looked so fashionable. She smiled at Max, flushed and happy.

Cilla wore her usual somber, clingy black, nipped at the waist with a silver band. She had back-combed her hair into a trendy mare's nest, deliberately mussed and moussed to suggest recent emergence from a wind tunnel following a skirmish with wild dogs. Women's fashions would forever be a source of bafflement to Max. Max noticed for the first time she had a little butterfly tattoo on her neck.

And here came Lester and Felberta, Lester none the worse for his own outing in the garden except for a hectic flush of red across the cheekbones. Felberta wore another of her confections that seemed only to lack a salad dressing, and a necklace like a string of eyeballs. The flowery pattern of her blouse was an odd choice for the dead of winter—too youthful and fussy by half. Still, Max supposed the colors might be meant to cheer her up. Surely, someone or something needed to.

"How I shall miss Leticia and her spreadsheet-like analyses of the bloodstock lineage of this or that Great and Noble Family," she was saying as she entered.

"And Oscar! How I shall miss Oscar," said her husband. "He was so full of . . ."

"Life. Yes," said Gwynyth, looking up. Max may have imagined it, but it seemed to be a warning movement.

"Shit. He was so full of shit."

"I see you've heard about his will," said Gwynyth.

"He left us a pittance, considering what there was to go around."

"You're telling me?" But she no longer looked as perturbed as she had been. Had Randolph been making reassurances on that score?

"It makes it harder to mourn him, knowing how he really felt," said Lester.

"Speak for yourself," said Gwynyth. "He was, after all, the father of my children."

Max stole a look at her. This was certainly a new tune she was singing now.

Lamorna clumped in and sat down heavily next to him. She wore a *Why bother?* sort of frock that may have been, and probably was, from the last-chance bin at Oxfam. Over it she wore a moose-colored sweater that fell in droopy folds to a puddle at the top of her thighs.

She leaned in to him with an urgent whisper. "There is something I just remembered, passing by Lady B's room." She looked around, then lowered her voice still more. "On the day of the murder, I heard her talking loudly with Cilla in her room. *Quarreling*. It must have been just before she died."

"Quarreling about what?"

"I was too far down the hall to tell what it was about. But what I want to know is, could it have brought on her attack?" This was said with more than a little hopeful relish. Max thought this was the kind of thing Lamorna might say, to create a bit of drama out of an ordinary event, not that she had a particular desire to chuck Cilla into it. Her eyes were gaunt, from worry or lack of sleep or both.

"I doubt it, Lamorna. Apparently your grandmother was carrying this time bomb inside her that could go off at any time, for any reason."

Max noticed Lester and Felberta, who had taken seats on the opposite side of the wide table, were closely watching the conversation. Hurriedly, in case they could read lips, he changed the subject, suggesting a few hymns for the service for Oscar and Leticia.

Amanda drifted in in her ethereal way and sat to Max's left with a shy smile, her twin Alec following. Despite the usual sibling rivalries, the pair seemed nearly inseparable. Alec, after a moment's hesitation, moved to sit at the head of the table in what likely had been Oscar's chair. Max thought it an interesting choice.

Simon had arrived, and sat near Lester and Felberta. Jocasta was not with him.

It was Amanda who asked, "Where's Jocasta?"

"She's upstairs Googling herself on my computer," said Alec. "Seriously: It's pathetic. She hasn't had a fresh mention in the news in decades. The murder has put her in the spotlight for the first time in ages, but in a way that has nothing to do with her acting."

Simon put his napkin on the table and said, "I'll go find her."

Watching Simon's back as he loped acrobatically up the stairs, Lester said, "I suppose it's too much to hope she's packed up and left."

"None of us are allowed to do that, as you well know, per that dandyish inspector. Perhaps she's fallen off the ledge and into the sea, though?" offered Felberta hopefully.

"Really. That is rather unkind, don't you feel?" said Cilla. "She can't help being . . . well . . ."

"Is 'stupid' the word you're reaching for?" asked Felberta.

Lamorna, her face puckered with disapproval at the large scotch Lester held in his hand, pointedly asked Milo for her *usual* lemon squash.

The twins sat whispering past their mother as if she weren't there, shutting out the adult world in favor of their own dark little Narnia. Max could hardly blame them but found something rather . . . creepy, he decided, in their determined isolation from the others. The broken rays of the stained glass caught the threesome's pale hair and turned it into a pastel riot of color.

"This place is always freezing. I hate it. I shall live in Italy when I'm grown," Max overheard Amanda say. "Somewhere where it's always warm."

"Spoken like a true product of the current education system, a product with a shaky grasp on geography," said Alec, reverting to his "superior older brother" role.

"What do you mean?"

"Italy has snow. Much of it is covered by mountains."

Amanda gave him a mutinous look.

"You know what I meant. I want to go somewhere where we don't get this ghastly freaking weather."

Max stole a glance at the seat at the other head of the table, presumably reserved for Leticia. It was of course empty and likely would remain so, with no one willing to usurp the throne, at least not so blatantly.

"Who outranked whom?" Max idly wondered aloud. "Leticia with her Baynards or Oscar and the Footrustles?"

"Oh, don't get them started or they'll pull out the family trees and squabble all night," Alec said. "Both families are frightfully old, you know. My aunt Leticia only lost out because the lot she married into lost the family fortune and had to sell up. We at least get to live here still. That is, if we want. Which most of us don't."

"How I have longed for a real English Christmas dinner," Felberta could be heard saying. "I wonder if Doris might serve goose?"

"All this Tiny Tim rubbish." Alec stared down the long table from his throne. "First Jocasta and Simon, and now you. There never has been goose served before for Christmas. I don't see why Cook would start now."

Doris had come from the kitchen to serve, replacing Milo. The transition was so smooth it was barely noticeable. The couple was evidently used to working in tandem.

"At least we're not getting the usual requests for ghost stories," said Amanda.

Alec said to Max: "You've come to the right place. This castle *does* have ghosts. It needs an exorcist."

"A deliverance minister, you mean," said Max. He tasted the soup Doris had ladled into his bowl, a soup made of buttery potatoes flavored with ginger. It was delicious: Doris really deserved a five-star rating.

"You're not serious," said Alec.

"Of course I am. Every diocese has one. Sometimes people think their homes are haunted, so they call the Church for help."

"And do they? I mean, are they able to help?"

"Quite often," replied Max. "The question of course is whether the visit by the deliverance minister had a placebo effect. Or whether the priest was able to help some troubled soul find rest at last."

Alec stared at him for a moment and then said, "I don't believe in God."

Max quietly put down his spoon. He was reminded of the rabbi who had once said in reply to this claim, "What makes you think God cares?" Reams had been written on this subject, but in the end it came down to the rabbi's simple question, and man's hubris in questioning the existence of a power higher—and smarter—than himself.

Max was used to this sort of thing from young people like Alec. It was, after all, their job at that age to challenge the status quo. He was somehow not too surprised when Lester joined in the discussion, adding his none-too-original views, which mirrored Alec's.

Many people on first seeing a clerical collar felt the need to draw a line in the sand, offering the many, many reasons for their beliefs (or lack thereof). Lester seemed to fall into the category of "nonbeliever who doth protest too much." If Max had wanted to, he felt he could have converted the man on the spot, but people made their own peace with the divine, each in their own way.

Max smiled and said, "All religions offer a template for a moral code for mankind. Sometimes, they offer more. It is up to the individual to believe, or not, as they choose. God simply waits for us to catch up."

"I believe in karma," said Amanda. She said it with such conviction he wondered if the current events in the castle weren't uppermost in her mind.

"Hinduism is a wise religion," said Max. "As well as being an extremely ancient one."

"Not everyone would call it a religion," said Amanda. And she launched into a comparison of spiritual traditions and organized religions, with an emphasis on the theories of reincarnation. She was fourteen, he marveled, and younger only by minutes than her brother. She seemed much the more mature of the two, despite Alec's evident cleverness. As she spoke, he watched her face, its planes fine and sharp as cut glass. It was a mirror for her mother's, but rounded where her mother's was sharply defined.

Alec said, "I think reincarnation would be cool."

Max started to reply, calling Alec by his first name. "But I'm forgetting," said Max. "You are Lord Footrustle now, aren't you?"

Alec looked straight ahead to the empty seat at the opposite end of the table, the seat where Leticia should have been.

"I will never get used to that. Please call me Alec."

Max was relieved, after Alec's bold choice of sitting in Oscar's chair, to hear indications of humility and normalcy. Perhaps Alec had felt that Oscar would have wanted him to take charge.

"If you will call me Max," he replied. "I never got used to being called Father Tudor, even by someone of your generation, and even when I'm old and gray I don't think I'll care much for it." Max took a slice of bread from the silver breadbasket. "You're not thinking of renouncing the title or anything like that?"

"Are you mad? Titles are a chick magnet."

At that, his sister made a choking sound as if her soup had stopped in her throat. So much for Amanda's vaster stores of maturity. But she had been keeping a careful eye on Max, and she now said to him, "I know why you're here."

Max thought that certainly put her one step ahead of both his bishop and even himself. He turned to give her his full attention.

"You're sizing us all up," she said evenly. "You're gathering impressions as you weigh our potential as murderers."

That was so near the mark—spot on, in fact—that Max chose to elide past the moment rather than directly lie to the child.

"It was actually Lamorna who wanted me here." He glanced at Lamorna, who sat grimly staring across the table at Felberta. Lamorna's sudden windfall might have been expected to make her happy, but it seemed to be making her anxious. He didn't suppose Lamorna had had a lot of practice in thinking and acting for herself, and her situation might indeed be anxiety-provoking.

Max tuned back in just in time to hear Lester say, "I need to make friends. You know, business contacts. Maybe I should join Twitter or something." From somewhere in the room came a discreet snort. It might have come from Alec or Randolph—from any of them.

Just then a voice cried stagily from the stairs. It was a voice designed for cattle drives; for tornadoes and similar grand-scale, noisy calamities.

"I'd be careful if I were you, Lester. Just think of all the enemies you could make."

CHAPTER 22
Ready for My Close-up

Jocasta, having delivered her opening lines, waltzed slowly down the spiral stone staircase into the Hall, trailing a black chiffon scarf. She was followed by Milo and Simon, who had collected her from somewhere in the castle.

She tottered unsteadily on the style of high platform shoes with which many a more nimble woman had come to grief. Around her shoulders was a cloak with a stiff, stand-up collar, not unlike the Queen's in *Snow White*, a cloak she held close against the chill. She looked like a child playing dress-up.

Randolph rose to take her hand, kissing it in an exaggerated, courtly fashion.

"Let me help you to your seat, dear cousin," he said.

Jocasta smiled her *over the rainbow* smile, a fluttery beam of gratitude and whimsical yearning.

"What melancholy!" she cried, looking up at him adoringly. "How do you bear it here, on this lonesome coast? And such tension within, as if the very *ribs* of the house were breathing" (Ruthelle Narwith, *Knives at Midnight*). She rolled the "R" in "ribs" like an opera singer, her voice trilling to a high falsetto that pinged off the high ceiling.

"Whatever are you talking about?" Alec wondered.

"I think you'll find the line was 'roof of the house,'" said Simon.

"Hmm?" said Jocasta.

"Oh," said Alec. "She's in one of her movies again, isn't she?" He said this flatly, as if it were a normal occurrence, Max noted. Undoubtedly it was.

Jocasta, if Simon read her right, and he was certain he did, was tonight playing the part of an upper-class woman with a Roedean accent possessed by a mysterious flesh-eating microbe. Jocasta raised one eyebrow now at the interruption to her performance, an eyebrow waxed to a perfect half-moon shape. The price for such glossy perfection, as Simon recalled, had come to something like twenty-five dollars a brow.

Max studied Simon closely, while pretending to be absorbed in buttering a piece of bread. By a trick of the candlelight, Simon appeared to be wearing eyeliner. Very Hollywood, but Max decided overall he'd been blessed with the kind of thick eyelashes most women could only envy. The Valentino-ish touch was at odds with his boyish, all-American appearance.

Jocasta, beneath her cape (which she dropped on the floor for Milo to pick up), was ready to party in a sparkly gold-and-silver top, cut low and worn over a floaty, too-short gray chiffon skirt. Max recalled that she was no doubt dressing from a suitcase full of clothing brought with her for the holidays, an impression confirmed when he heard her say, "I suppose I must get into town soon to buy a mourning costume."

Max's mind filled with wonderful images at this idea, most of them Victorian and involving heavy black veiling and locks of hair wound inside mourning lockets, or braided into heart shapes. Leticia at least would have appreciated the gesture of the net veiling.

Cilla complimented Jocasta on her jewelry, and Jocasta reached up to touch one diamond earring.

"The real ones are in the safe back home," she said. "I never travel with real jewelry."

Cilla wondered if that were true, about the real earrings being safe back home. They might well reside in a pawn shop. She'd heard rumors Jocasta was on her uppers, along with Simon, of course.

Milo, with Jocasta's cape draped over one arm, said, "I wish to ask everyone if everything is satisfactory." He smiled, the candlelight throwing the planes of his face into fantastic hills and valleys. "It is my desire to assist the family however I can, especially at this time of such tragedy."

The group regarded him in strained silence; a few nodded their satisfaction. After a moment Milo left, gliding around a stray footstool in a graceful skater's motion, a footstool evidently put there for no other purpose than to waylay and topple the unsuspecting.

Alec murmured to his departing back, "He's like something out of an old black-and-white movie."

Jocasta agreed. "Lon Chaney," she said, nodding enthusiastically. "Only much better-looking. How that man could act! They called him the 'Man of a Thousand Faces.'" She sighed. "Such a pity they don't make stars like that anymore."

Milo and Doris reappeared with the main course, which was fresh-catch turbot broiled in lime and butter. This came with rice and wild mushrooms sautéed with onions and garlic, and was followed by salad.

The food was a welcome distraction and silence fell as they began to eat. Having served the table, Milo stood to one side, an erect, still figure—ever-present, yet ever invisible. He lifted his eyebrows in a characteristic gesture that seemed to hide a world of contempt, had the diners had the wit to notice it. Only Max did.

Jocasta fell ravenously upon her meal, displaying an artificially large shelf of puffy bosom. Max, reminded of a pigeon wearing an elaborate necklace, wondered privately if she weren't cold in the outfit, a question soon answered.

"It's ruddy freezing in here. How expensive could it be to install proper heating?"

"We're not in California anymore," said her husband mildly.

Max noticed that her wedding band, in contrast to her usual

overblown style, was a plain band of gold to match Simon's. Perhaps, thought Max, she had gotten the expensive baubles out of her earlier marriage or marriages; he suspected Simon's charms had not included sacks of gold he'd brought into the partnership. What he did bring was easy to guess. Max wondered if Simon rued the bargain he'd made: Jocasta looked very high-maintenance. That the irresistible sexpot ship was slowly but surely leaving the port seemed not yet to have dawned on her.

She sipped steadily from her wineglass, which her husband kept steadily filled, and stared with glassy-eyed concentration at the tapestries ranged about the stone walls.

Not knowing quite how they ought to act, the assembled company tried on a succession of masks and attitudes. Worry. Apprehension. Grief of the kind natural when a relative of any degree of nearness dies. And here and there, the merest soupçon of pity for the departed.

Underlying it all, thought Max, was a sense of excitement at the novelty.

As often, Jocasta said what no one else would.

"Well, they were very *old*, weren't they? No use crying over spilt milk."

"I hardly think murder falls into the same category as spilt milk," said Randolph sternly. "As to their ages—Oscar was a vital man, taken before his time was up. She may well have been, too, if it's the shock of his death that finished her. That's simply not right, however one looks at it."

Jocasta might not have noticed the tone, as indeed she had not. Many a movie director had experienced this same peculiar tone-deafness and could have warned Randolph not to bother trying.

"It's just like Leticia to hog the spotlight by dying right on top of my father," she said.

"Are you completely mad?" asked Randolph. "As if either of them had a say in what happened. For heaven's sake, Jocasta. And please remember we're not alone now." This last was said with a significant nod in Max's direction. Max, in fact all ears, pretended not to have heard.

Jocasta pushed back a lock of auburn hair, a typically theatrical gesture that she happened to share with her cousin Randolph, saying, "The problem with Leticia was she'd been on the brink of death for decades, to hear her tell it. It's hard, when the brink has been—what, brinked so often?—to know quite how one is supposed to *feel* when faced with the reality. No disrespect intended—it's just that we've been in dress rehearsal for this occasion for positive *eons*."

Max reflected how much like Lady Baynard she was beginning to sound. Jocasta turned her head with its mound of hair slightly away from him and Max realized for the first time she was wearing a wig: A line of sparse gray hair showed briefly along the back of her neck, beneath the dark reddish-brown, as the wig slightly slipped its moorings. Max had known the bright color must be a dye job, but not that the hair itself was false. He found something about this inexpressibly sad, and was sorry to have been let in on her secret—that her hair was thinning so much as to require a wig. He wondered if perhaps she had been ill, but overall she seemed to be in robust health.

"Oh!" she cried now in reply to some further remonstrance from Randolph. "You are horrid. It was horrid growing up here. So gloomy, so full of . . . well, gloom!"

Lamorna, meanwhile, could be overheard quoting at Cilla one of the more apocalyptic Bible verses of the sort Lamorna seemed to favor. Jocasta continued talking in her Kabuki-theater way, eyes and gestures wide. Suddenly she regarded Max with the flickering blink of eyelids that with her seemed to pass for intense concentration. He suddenly realized that although her posture was upright Jocasta was extremely drunk; she had to have been drinking for a few hours before dinner to have achieved this condition. He wouldn't have been surprised to see her slide suddenly from her chair onto the floor.

She had moved on to the topic of her early days in film, and about her star turn with Elizabeth Taylor and Richard Burton.

"*Cleopatra*? Really?" said Randolph, suspecting a fabrication. "Which part did you play? One of the crowd scenes, was it?"

"No, I was . . . I was a priestess."

"A *high* priestess?" whispered Lester to his wife, with assumed innocence. "It was the sixties, after all."

"I heard that," said Jocasta. "Anyway, I was too young for the role of high priestess. And Elizabeth had her little jealousies where Richard was concerned."

"Do tell."

But Jocasta, realizing her mistake (she would have been just out of diapers when *Cleopatra* was filmed), and sensing she had wandered too far into unrehearsed territory, subsided into a haughty and dignified silence. The conversation went from there to recent Oscar winners like *The King's Speech*, with Cilla arguing for the overall brilliance of *Benjamin Button*.

Max tried without success to capture Lamorna's attention, if only to rescue a polite and patient Cilla.

But the situation had been kindled and now was set to erupt.

CHAPTER 23

We Are Family

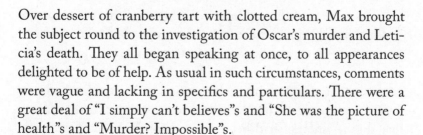

Over dessert of cranberry tart with clotted cream, Max brought the subject round to the investigation of Oscar's murder and Leticia's death. They all began speaking at once, to all appearances delighted to be of help. As usual in such circumstances, comments were vague and lacking in specifics and particulars. There were a great deal of "I simply can't believes"s and "She was the picture of health"s and "Murder? Impossible"s.

So all were in agreement with the general trend of these sentiments, which essentially covered the waterfront of the more genteel reactions to murder. Indeed the word, when uttered for the first time by the police, had sent a frisson of something approaching excitement down all their spines, for knowing something in one's heart is not the same as having that knowledge confirmed by officialdom. "Killed" leaves open the possibility, however absurd, of freak accident. "Murder" removes that possibility.

Finally they simmered down into a deep silence, thoughtfully sipping their drinks. Lester began making a slurping sound with his until he became aware of the hostile stares emanating from his family. Sheepishly he stopped, only to begin drumming his fingers against his armrest.

At length he said, "Obviously it was a roving gang of marauders."

Randolph lowered his chin and aimed at Lester a look of exaggerated patience, like a lord listening to the tale of a credulous and rather smelly peasant. "I believe the police have overruled that suggestion. Nevertheless your opinions, however preposterous they may be, are welcome. We need to explore every possibility to get to the bottom of this. So long as the police are here, we'll never be able to resume our normal lives."

"You mean you think it was one of us," said Alec.

Randolph seemed to weigh Alec's young age in his reply. The truth was harsh. But Alec wasn't the type who could be shirked off with a half-truth.

"I'm afraid so," said Randolph. "It had to have been, don't you see?"

His voice held the talking-to-infants tone that had failed to endear him to people of all ages. It was the same voice that had presaged many an unruly family dinner discussion. Tonight was to be no exception.

A memory flashed into Max's mind of a scene he had witnessed one day at the beach, in Brighton or somewhere ordinary like that. A mother had been haranguing her young daughter, giving her a public dressing-down that had gone on several minutes too long over some minor infraction. Perhaps it was that the child had not washed the sand off her feet and legs as instructed—yes, that was it. There was a mutinous look on the child's face as she went into the water to do as her mother had commanded. The mother, busy packing up the beach paraphernalia, missed seeing it. A thought had flashed unbidden into Max's mind: She'll bide her time and when she's bigger, she'll get even with you.

Lamorna's contribution to the discussion had been to repeat several times her theory of divine retribution, interspersed with little outbursts of "frightful" and "my goodness gracious." There was a ragged edge to her voice, but she was dry-eyed. They all were. Cilla, the most personally unaffected by the disaster, was if anything glowing with allure and energy.

An intensely nervous Lester insisted, "Well, it couldn't have been one of us. Someone got in from outside."

"I'm afraid the police do think that is quite impossible," said Max.

Lester rejected police thinking with an airy wave of his hand. "Nothing is impossible," he said. "And I wouldn't believe a word the authorities said, if I were you." He cited an article he'd read in one of the tabloids where a space alien's ossified remains had been found somewhere in a desert but the CIA was as usual covering it up.

Unable to stop himself, Max asked, "Why on earth would the CIA do that?"

"Simple," replied Lester complacently, expanding under the attention. "So they have time to train one of their own operatives, altering his appearance surgically so they can use him as a decoy for when the aliens return."

"But, why—?"

"Never ask a question when you know the answer is going to be too stupid for words," said Randolph.

"Are you calling my husband stupid?" Felberta turned on Randolph, protective instincts aroused.

"No, I'm calling him brain-dead. Stupid would imply he was showing signs of sentient life."

Felberta, not sure what sentient might mean, sat a moment with her mouth working, then said, "I think you're vile. Vile and grasping."

"No doubt. Better vile and grasping than to go through life believing anything one sees in print must be true just because it's in print."

"I see you're picking up the snobby banner so recently left behind by our mother," Lester fumed.

"Who *are* these people," said Amanda, a shade too loudly, in clear imitation of her aunt. "And who are *their* people?"

Cilla, as if hoping to divert the escalating argument, joined in, also in faultless imitation of Leticia's crystallized accent. "And, more importantly, who are their *people's* people?"

Alec laughed loudly. The other adults turned toward the pair in disapproval. But the moment had passed, for everyone but Felberta, who said, hoping the twins would overhear, "Those children are nothing but pawns in Gwynyth's campaign to inherit. Besides, do they look anything like Oscar to you?"

"Given that he was in his seventies and they're fourteen years old, would you really expect to be able to see a resemblance?" said Randolph.

"Oh, come off it. You know what I'm saying."

"I do," hissed Randolph. "And I'm not saying you're right or wrong. I'm saying there will be a time to start flinging allegations like that around, and that time is not now."

Felberta sniffed, fluffing the collar of her blouse and adjusting her strange, unwieldy necklace.

Lamorna now sat quietly, her eyes downcast, no doubt withdrawn into her tiny, holier-than-thou world of sentimentality steeped in dark judgment and brutal remonstrance. She might have been Bloody Mary awaiting the happy news of the execution of her cousin Lady Jane Grey.

Jocasta leaned over her plate to stare down the table with the intense focus of the inebriated. Her red lipstick had smeared, an unhappy reminder of her vampire movie career. Max heard her say, slurring her words, "I wouldn't worry about any of this if I were you, Gwynyth." The "th" in Gwynyth's name gave her particular trouble. "You weren't in her will."

"I was!" said Gwynyth. "I was so too in her will."

"And you know this, how?"

"She told me so. She said I was a major ben—bennie—what do you call it? Beneficiary."

"She told me the same thing," chipped in Lamorna.

They all looked at each other.

"Well, it sounds like she's been up to her old games," said Gwynyth, putting her fork on her plate with a clatter.

"It hardly matters now," said Jocasta. She paused to empty her wineglass. "It's time you found a job, anyway."

Gwynyth glared at her. "How dare you say that to me? When have *you* ever held a real job? Playing a bimbo vampire, please note, is not a real job."

"Bimbo?" spluttered Jocasta, every word a slurred effort. "Look who's talking."

"If the Manolo fits, wear it," murmured Randolph.

Well, *zing*! thought Max. Tension crackled like lightning through the room. He felt it as a rise in his own body temperature, a faint beading of sweat across his brow.

Jocasta kept reaching for the wine bottle in the middle of the table, stretching her body across whatever and whomever was in her way to reach it. More often than not it was Lester, who sat to her left.

"Steady on, old girl," he said, on the third or fourth reach.

"Mind your own beeswax."

"Do people still say that?" Randolph wondered, with exaggerated innocence. "Isn't that expression simply ancient?"

"Like me, you mean?" Jocasta asked, pouring the wine with elaborate drunken care, a chemist on the verge of a major discovery that would both alter mankind's perception of the universe and the layout of the periodic table. "I'm not so green as I'm cabbage-looking," she added.

"What a perfectly idiotic saying, I've always thought," said Simon, sensing a brewing conflict and determined to save Randolph, if he could, from needless immolation. "Who, apart from certain of our elected officials, actually looks like a cabbage?"

"Felberta, for one," said Jocasta. She aimed an elbow at the table and missed. Wine sloshed onto her hand.

"At least," snapped Felberta, setting down her own glass none too steadily, "at least I don't dress like I'm opening a third-rate vaudeville show."

At that, the vaulted ceiling seemed to press in on them with the weight of centuries. It wasn't the first quarrel in that room—one had ended with a dagger through the heart of one of the then-earl's vassals—but there were echoes of the past in every face and gesture.

"How *dare* you," Jocasta snarled, red lips taut as wire.

Max noted with interest that it may have been the first time he'd seen the mask drop. She was clearly not acting now.

He was a peacemaker by nature, and conflict of any size sparked an overwhelming need in him to intervene, to quell the disturbance. Max now called on all his acquired skills in calming troubled waters. After all, he reminded himself, he had faced down a variety of rancorous church committees, not to mention the notoriously cranky Nether Monkslip Book Club, whose members often came to grief in deciding on the monthly read. Dealing with this dysfunctional family, a murderous psychopath among them, should be easy by comparison.

"Ladies and gentlemen, please," he said. "May I remind you of your recent losses? Let's show some respect, if you would, for the deceased. Besides, a united front might be your best defense right now. As I'm sure you're aware, the police are watching your every move closely."

His words—particularly the latter part of his message—quieted them all, but the shift in mood effectively signaled that the dinner was over. They slowly stood and made their ways with varying degrees of stability and focus toward the stairs. Jocasta overshot the exit and made a beeline toward a door into the garden. She had to be led to the stairs, with elaborate solicitousness, by her husband.

Lester hesitated, clearly wanting a private word with Max. He began to say something and then thought better of it. He swerved off, his wife at his heels. Lamorna walked out without a word.

Soon only three were left: Max, Randolph, and Cilla. The family tension seeped like vapor out of the room. Max thought it was a wonder they didn't all drink like Jocasta.

CHAPTER 24

After Dinner

Randolph, followed by Cilla, slouched his lanky way over to the arrangement of chairs and sofas by the great stone fireplace. Nearby was the elaborate Christmas tree with its artistic flourishes of holly and mistletoe attached by purple and gold metallic bows. Randolph, looking up, followed Max's gaze and said, "Jocasta ordered it in from the local florist. A typically extravagant, impulsive gesture. She's rather like a child, I've always thought."

Max stood, waiting to be invited to join them, waiting to be noticed. The squabbling he'd witnessed during dinner had disturbed him. There were strong undercurrents there. He felt he had missed something.

But it was Cilla with her preternatural awareness who had smiled first in polite greeting, including him in. Her response reminded him of Awena, whose insight—and company—he missed already.

"Join us," she said. "We're trying to digest all that's gone on. Wine as good as this, as I am sure you will discover, helps. We can't let it go to waste."

Randolph then motioned him over. Minutes later the three sat huddled near the fire like regulars at a pub, Cilla curled up in her chair like a question mark. Before them on a low table were glasses of wine in varying stages of fullness. Accompanying the Côtes du Rhône was a cheese plate supplied by Milo. Max helped himself to an excellent bleu on a wafer-thin slice of toasted French bread.

"What must you think of us?" said Randolph. "Somehow I feel I owe you an apology, although none of them are *my* doing. You mustn't mind Alec, for a start."

"Not at all," said Max. "He's still creating himself, and one way teenagers do that is to argue with the oldies. It helps them to tease out what they actually do believe."

Randolph harrumphed. "Alec seems to regard himself as representative of his generation and is given to making blanket pronouncements about the thinking processes, likes, and dislikes of everyone within that generation. However, one has to take into account that he only represents a tiny fraction of the *privileged* segment of the population at large, so his opinions may be flawed, at best. The rest of the people his age have more mundane concerns about earning a living, getting into a good school, and so on. For Alec, it has been handed over on the proverbial plate, with garnish. For all his mother's grousing about money, he's well set up compared with most."

Max said: "Do we ever really appreciate those comparisons, especially at that age? Youth, after all, is always wasted on the young. He may just not realize yet how well set up he is for the future."

"You're very kind, Vicar," said Randolph. "And if you don't mind my saying so, a tad idealistic."

It was an adjective Max had heard applied to himself before. Every time, it made him bristle. "Idealistic" was a word he equated with gullible and rube-ish, as if he were some sort of hayseed from the provinces. He sat deep in thought, holding his glass between his hands like a chalice. His eyes with their dark gray irises gleamed in the firelight. A parade of ghosts from his former life in MI5 might have been passing before him, including the elusive man with the unusual sunglasses who haunted his dreams.

"You *must* admit," Randolph was saying, "Lamorna qualifies as a skeleton in any family's cupboard."

"'The day of their calamity is at hand,'" intoned Cilla, in Lamorna's dolorous tones. "Any passage in the Bible that involves death and destruction is Lamorna's very-most favorite. She just breezes right by the 'love one another' bits."

"I wonder . . ." said Max, thinking this might be a good time to put in a word for the hapless Lamorna. "I wonder what she will do now? I think she's rather frightened of what may happen to her."

"I suppose Leticia was a form of protection from the outside world," said Randolph. "Really, I've no idea, but I can't picture the new heir chucking her out."

"Can't you?" said Cilla. "I have the idea that's exactly what he may do, when he's a bit older and a certain amount of time has elapsed." Her voice trailed off with the smoke from the fireplace. She held up her wineglass to the flickering firelight, watching the play of red and gold. After a pause she shifted the subject. "I suppose Bambi will stay with Jocasta long enough to see what his cut is."

"Who, Simon?" asked Randolph. "Most certainly."

They spoke quite openly, Max thought, with the easy give-and-take of people who had worked in harness for many years—like Milo and Doris, in fact. It was almost as if he were not in the room.

At that moment Milo entered, this time bearing the coffee tray. At Randolph's direction, he put it down with a slight clatter on the table and left the room.

A gust of wind rattled the darkened panes which Max could now glimpse beyond the screen. Ice crystals had formed fractals on the windows and tree branches bearded with ice threw their ominous silhouettes against the sky.

Max sank back sleepily into his chair, fighting to remain alert. There had been a lot of wine at dinner, a different wine for each course, and Max felt like the snake that swallowed the mongoose. He wasn't used to rich, heavy food, especially since his tofu-laden, organic years in Nether Monkslip, and he could feel his body marveling at this new, Henry VIII-ish lifestyle.

"Whiskey?" Randolph asked.

Oh, why not? Might as well be hanged for a sheep as a lamb. "Thank you. That would be most welcome."

Randolph rose and yanked on a bellpull by the fireplace. Max began to wonder if Milo ever got a break. Perhaps with their inheritance he and Doris wouldn't stay much longer.

Milo, the perfect servant, somehow knew what was wanted, and appeared almost on the instant with a tray holding a bottle and glasses.

Randolph, having formally bid Milo a good night, unstopped the decanter. He poured Max a generous dollop of a brand of single-malt whiskey Max had not enjoyed since his days of the high life in London, and then only infrequently. The strong spirit ran smoothly down his throat.

The fire crackled as a log fell, a great report that ricocheted off the stone walls. Snow piled up at the window, and the branches outside creaked under their heavy, wet burden. Max felt he'd been at the castle since its founding, and having said so, they began to speak of its history.

"The castle is built on the ruins of an ancient monastery," Randolph told him. "Apart from the chapel, there are no traces left unless you count that eerie quality one can feel around here at times. Who could live that way?"

Max shrugged. "As a monk, you mean? Any religious vocation is hard to explain to anyone who hasn't received the call."

Randolph, taking a sip, looked at him over the top of his glass. He said, "I visited a Benedictine monastery once. In Germany. It was called Maria Laach. I don't know what they're doing out there except praying for my worthless self. It's not a life I could tolerate for five minutes but you could see its beauties around the edges, as it were."

Max thought that a very good description of the way we all get a glimpse of heaven at times. Just around its edges. He said as much.

Randolph tipped his head forward in acknowledgement.

"'Our' monks here at Chedrow went elsewhere; probably they were forced out. No one is quite certain how or why. The family took over the place, and eventually they were granted the King's 'license to crenellate,' which was a very big deal at the time. It showed the king trusted you, you see. Not everyone was allowed to upgrade to the war model since you might become a stronghold in a fight against him."

"It must be wonderful to know one's family history as well as you all must know yours. Most of us are descended from serfs, and have to guess at the gaps in our heritage."

Randolph, a lock of his hair fallen over one eye, was now fully engaged. He pushed the hair back; Max was reminded of seeing him earlier outside with Gwynyth. That seemed to be a relationship they were trying to keep quiet, perhaps one in its beginning stages. "They say Shakespeare stayed here once with his fellow players, to escape the plague," Randolph told him.

"Surely they never traveled this far west."

"They say that he did—it's a family legend that's been handed down forever. And who's to say he did not?"

Max smiled, shrugging—still doubtful. He tipped the glass to his lips and finished the last of the excellent whiskey, thinking this was the life, for Max was a man of epicurean tastes whose self-indulgence was rare, not least of all because a vicar's stipend didn't run to luxuries large or small. He put down his glass. Randolph, taking it as a request, poured again from the decanter.

"How lucky you are to live on such a property," said Max. "Even though these manor houses are a huge upkeep and a worry, I'm sure." Max felt that given his experiences with the roof of St. Edwold's he was becoming rather besotted with the maintenance of ancient structures. "But it's important that they be preserved, not torn down to make way for the new. Lamorna pointed out to me some of the architectural features. Defense against invaders seems to have driven many of the architectural decisions."

"Oh, Lamorna." Oh, *her* again. "Yes, she has taken quite an interest in the castle's history." Randolph's own interest in Lamorna quickly evaporated. "Try to picture it," Randolph went on. "There would be a large fire in the center of the Hall. That's where the servants and retainers would sleep—the concept of privacy is strictly a modern one. The mind just reels, doesn't it? The lord and lady who formerly had a *smidge* of privacy on a raised dais at one end of the Hall"—and here he paused to illustrate with a wave of one hand—"eventually had a private or family room. It was called the solar, with which you are familiar—Oscar's room, of course." He paused. "I saw you taking a peek in there earlier," he said pointedly. Max did not rise to the bait. Instead, he returned Randolph to the path of the family history, in which he seemed to take as much of an interest as Lamorna.

"The family were explorers," said Randolph, in answer to Max's questioning. "Gambling blood runs through our veins, you could say. Because it wasn't all just about the challenge and the thrill. Oh, no. There were great fortunes to be made out of the undiscovered or unsettled lands. That those lands were already in the possession of the native populations—well, that didn't enter into the thinking, not for a moment.

"One ancestor in particular, Sir Champerson, took after Sir Walter Raleigh and that lot—he lost a fortune several times when one ship or another came to grief. He didn't turn a hair. That kind of thing—well, it's in the blood. Lost his life to it, in the end, did Champerson. Drowned with his crew. Poor buggers. Imagine crossing the Atlantic in the type of ship they had—little better than a wooden tub with sails."

"Raleigh lost his life in a different way."

"Oh, yes. The famous charm that worked so well on Elizabeth failed him when it came to James. Funny thing, charm. And luck. I suppose it really does run out for some. Anyway, now the place is a tourist haunt for part of the year and people show up at all hours expecting to see the sights, or to retrieve the umbrella or whatnot they left behind over the summer. It's quite absurd, but they think somehow because a family is known to live here, that makes it different from a museum or an unoccupied National Trust stately home. As if we have nothing better to do than keep track of their rubbish all day.

"They have weddings now here at the castle during the summer months, a development my mother viewed with special horror.

Oscar didn't mind, strangely enough. He was a bit of a romantic at heart. Well, you only have to look at Gwynyth to see that is true. The May/December marriage is a particular specialty of the romantic—a veritable triumph of misty-eyed hope over experience. My poor uncle. One could really feel sorry for him at times."

Somehow Max again brought the subject around to Lamorna. He could not have said why he persisted so, except that her particular request for his presence made him hope that if he could not get to the bottom of this crime, he could at least see to her welfare.

"From what I have observed," said Max, "Oscar's relationship with Lamorna was different from her relationship with Leticia. I gather he was indifferent to Lamorna. Leticia on the other hand at least recognized her usefulness. Am I right?"

"I rather imagine he simply didn't like having her around, which is how she escaped the indentured servitude foisted on her by Leticia," said Randolph. His eyes took on the blank cast of someone remembering the past. "Lamorna came out of St. Petersburg stuffed into dirty clothes too small for her, even though she was skin and bones. The extra poundage came later, when she began making up for lost meals, I suppose."

"Now she has her freedom. I wonder if it isn't too late. I do feel her grandmother might be taken to task for that."

"I suppose someone of your beliefs would say that she is being taken to task, even as we speak." Randolph smiled, less a smile than an aristocratic wince, a flash of teeth and an expression that said life with his mother had not always fulfilled its promise of good times for all. Surely, thought Max, I saw that for myself in my very brief time with her.

"You know, a death watch beetle burrowing into the paneling would have had a warmer welcome from my mother than her own family did," said Randolph. "And in fact, that's not a bad comparison."

"So I gathered. Did your mother say what bothered her about the invitation?"

"She seemed to think they leapt on the invitation because Oscar couldn't have much longer to live."

"That's rather a cynical viewpoint?" Max shaded the end of the sentence so it was more a question than an accusation. Randolph merely answered with a lift of the eyebrow and a question in return.

"Do you think so, Vicar?" Pause. "More whiskey?"

Randolph as he spoke looked closely at Max Tudor. What he saw was a sincere-looking man, an attractive man with an open, honest face that seemed to welcome confidences. That face also held a hint of worry, even of alarm. Randolph supposed that was only natural: Murder would be far outside the man's normal experience of sermons and flower rotas and parish council meetings.

Cilla said, "She was extremely old-fashioned, Leticia. A real throwback. When was the last time, for example, you heard someone talk of 'running an affair'? It was like we were always starring in a revival of some campy production dating from between the wars."

"In what context did she use that phrase?" asked Max.

Cilla blushed. It was clear she had stepped right into it. With an apologetic glance at Randolph, she said, "She got hold of the idea that Randolph and I were an item. As I've told you, nothing could be further from the truth."

"Although I did beg her for her hand in marriage, many times," said Randolph jokingly. "The truth is, I was always romantically engaged elsewhere—fool for love that I am—and then when I looked around, Cilla had been taken. Swiped right out from under my nose. Her fiancé is a fantastic fellow, really one of the best, so I don't feel I can complain. I've only myself to blame."

Cilla greeted this with a cheeky, happy smile. "And if you don't mind," she said, "I'm going to go try to call my paragon now. I couldn't reach him earlier."

"Oh, do stay for a bit."

Randolph poured her another drink. Reluctantly, she subsided. "Just a small one, then."

As Randolph sat back in his chair, he sneezed. "So sorry," he said. "Some of us have been passing this cold back and forth for weeks."

Max was not surprised. Without the fire in the room it would have been freezing. Half of them must be down with perpetual colds living here in the damp. He had to remind himself that that wasn't what had carried Lady Baynard off in the end.

"Lady Baynard had a bad case of cold," Max said aloud. "Before she succumbed."

"Yes, I know," said Randolph. "I suppose I caught it from her. Poor old thing."

❋   ❋   ❋

Over Randolph's protests, Max took his leave of them several minutes later. Cilla watched him head upstairs. The ankle was coming along nicely; he was avoiding using the crutch, but she saw he did have to use the wooden rail that had been installed some years ago for safety. His progress was slow.

"Nice chap," said Randolph. "And a sound fellow. Too bad he's been dragged into this."

"Yes," said Cilla vaguely. "It is unfortunate, of course, but things happen as they must."

"Oscar was a grand old fellow in his way," said Randolph musingly. "She, one has to admit, was . . . rather tiresome at times. But so old—it would have happened soon anyway. We have to take that view."

"They were both seventy-five," Cilla said.

"Old, like I said."

Something hung unspoken in the air. She looked hard at him out of expertly kohl-lined eyes. Her own mother had lived to be eighty-five.

❋   ❋   ❋

Fortified by Randolph's whiskey, Max felt able to tackle the complexities of the castle's corridors and byways, and to find his room at last. Easier, as it turned out, said than done, and coffee might have been better than the whiskey for gearing up his logic and reasoning abilities.

He made his way up the stone steps, the sounds of their conversation fading behind him. The castle's corridors wound round and round him in an intricate crochet.

Max slipped into the shadowy hallway, followed by the castle ghosts, who wished him Godspeed.

CHAPTER 25

Lost Sheep

Getting to his room, even once he thought he knew the way, had involved a number of false starts throughout his stay at the castle. He would stride out confidently in one direction, unshakable in the knowledge that his room was oriented to the south, only to be met with a dead end or a small cupboard. Retracing his steps, less assured now, he would enter an empty space which seemed to serve no purpose except to offer him three or more closed doors from which to chose his next path. He soon would find himself in another corridor to nowhere that might end in an otherwise blank wall with a little window, peephole, or arrow slit. Max pictured knights in clanking armor, as in some old Robert Taylor movie, jostling their way down the narrow confines of the castle—rats in a maze, defending against all comers.

It didn't help that this night he had left the Great Hall in a thoughtful, distracted frame of mind. It was as he was finding his tortuous way back to his room that he collided with Alec coming down the servants' staircase—the same stairway Milo had disappeared into after first showing Max to his room. Alec was headed for the outside, judging by his coat and scarf.

"It's time you were asleep, Alec."

The boy smiled, that guileless, open smile that would carry a young man far through this life, melt many hearts, open many doors.

"I know. I was just out for a stroll."

Max's glance at his watch showed it was midnight.

"You'd best get back. Your mother will be worried."

This earned him a *you must be joking* look, but Alec shrugged agreeably and continued his downward progress.

Finally in his room, Max pulled the Bible from the shelf, not really intending to read it, but to hold it as a talisman against the disquiet he felt. It slipped from his hands and fell open to this passage from Matthew:

> *Ye have heard that it was said of them of old time,*
> *Thou shalt not kill; and whosoever shall kill shall be in*
> *danger of the judgment:*
> *But I say unto you, That whosoever is angry with his*
> *brother without a cause shall be in danger of the judgment:*
> *and whosoever shall say to his brother, Raca, shall be in*
> *danger of the council: but whosoever shall say, Thou fool,*
> *shall be in danger of hell fire.*

Raca. Worthless. Certainly the opinion Randolph held of his brother Lester, as some form of idiot, with the feeling being mutual. This grisly passage, as Max recalled, was the one that went on to advise the plucking out of eyes and so on.

The house had two brothers at odds, that was certain, if the narrowed eyes and jutting jaws indicated anything. Max leafed through the pages, which fell open to the start of Genesis 27:

> *And it came to pass, that when Isaac was old, and his*
> *eyes were dim, so that he could not see, he called Esau his*
> *eldest son. . . .*

The story Lamorna had mentioned. More about squabbling sons and an inheritance, and trickery over an inheritance. Max closed the pages, using one index finger as a bookmark. The hairs on the back of his neck bristled as if a skeletal hand had touched him.

"What?" he said aloud. He raised his eyes. *What is it?* He read the entire chapter slowly and then he put the book aside. He stood and walked to the east-facing window. As before, a movement caught his eye. Was it?—yes. A dark shape moving among the shadows—a black shape against a black wall. In the sea fog coating the garden, the shape floated free under a sky pocked with stars, making footless progress in the direction of the archway leading to the back regions of the garden. He'd have missed it altogether but that the shape, momentarily washed by moonlight, turned to look back toward the castle for a flash of an instant, and Max saw a countenance dimly lit—gray with dark sockets, an indentation for nose and mouth. That was all he could have sworn to have seen. An impression, merely. Then the face, the mask, turned away. It was as if nothing had ever been there.

He knew if he tried to follow the figure would be long gone, with a hundred places to hide, so he stood awhile, waiting for it to reemerge, hoping for a better glimpse of the face in the changeable blue snowlight of the half moon. It never reappeared.

No less quiet in his mind, Max undressed for bed.

Max in the long watches turned over restlessly, burrowing deeply into his high-count cotton sheets smelling of lavender and soap. The wind outside howled as he dreamt that leprechauns with tiny metal mallets were pinging away at his swollen ankle. Their pounding grew louder, more insistent. Coming fully awake, Max bolted out of bed. Someone was at the door.

He allowed a moment for his eyes to adjust to the darkness, for fear of walking into some massive, immovable piece of furniture that had stood rooted to the floor since the fifteenth century. Fortunately he had left the curtains undrawn—there was no need for privacy as there was no one who could see in from below.

And above the sound of the wind, he heard a scream. It was a scream worthy of the worst of Jocasta's movies—high-pitched, shrill, and frenzied, it seemed to go on forever, until it was silenced by a tremendous thud of something heavy coming up against something immovable.

The knocking at the door began again, a furious pounding. Through the thick wooden door he heard a muffled cry.

He recognized Lester's voice.

Cautiously, he inched open the door. And there was Lester peering back, a picture of stark panic.

"Did you hear that?" he demanded. "That scream?"

Max, already on the move, nodded. "One second." He felt his way to the light on the bedside table, then threw on a thermal jacket over his bare chest and drew running pants over his pajama bottoms. He slipped his feet sockless into his trainers and flung open the oak door, which had creaked its way half shut, and rushed into the corridor, colliding as he did so with a brown bear. His heart gave a colossal leap, but the bear was Lester, wearing the kind of fur hat with earflaps favored by Russians during their long winters, as if he'd planned a stop-off in Siberia after his visit to South West England.

"What on earth was that?" asked Lester. He carried an electric torch that seemed to need new batteries.

What in hell, more like, thought Max. Aloud he said, "I think it came from the servants' staircase." No need to say what "it" was. There was nothing about that sound that portended finding a whole and healthy person at its source.

The light directly over the main staircase was turned off, and the corridor had only feeble electric light from the faux-medieval sconces on the wall. These seemed to cast shadows more than they did light.

Max and Lester sped down the long passage as quickly as the darkness would allow, then hurtled through the stairwell's oak door, which stood open. They began an ungraceful descent, Max hampered by the ankle, and Lester by an overwrought imagination and an incapacitating case of nerves.

Max, thinking there might be a need for silence, was grateful that at least stone stairs do not creak. There was no banister or handrail. He edged his way down the steps, the dim, narrow lighting of which did not allow for headlong galloping downward. The stone steps, worn to a high and deadly gloss over centuries, could as easily catapult an agile man to the bottom as permit him a graceful if sporty descent.

Lester, behind him, had started to jabber in his ear.

"I followed Lamorna earlier, you see. To see what she was up to. And I was following her again just now. I decided to keep an eye on things tonight, because before dinner I saw her, you see? And she was skulking as only Lamorna could do. Why is she skulking about, I asked Felberta. What is she up to?"

Yap yip yap. Max shook his head, turned, and held one finger to his lips in a shushing motion.

Lester scuttled on behind Max, his bowlegged gait adding to the impression of a spider's locomotion. As awkward as Max was nimble, Lester might have been a groundhog lumbering along behind a panther. A flop of curly hair corkscrewed over his brow. He finally was saving his breath, which was jagged from panic and exertion.

Max thought he had heard something—a scuffle? A cry? But he couldn't be sure with Lester's rasping breath in his ear. Again, Max swiftly held up a hand for silence. *There.* It was a cry of astonishment, weak with shock and fear, all encapsulated in a brief inarticulate outburst, and followed by the most thunderous sound, as of a heavy weight falling a great distance. The spiral staircase magnified the sound.

The cry interrupted Lester in the middle of a reverie in which he starred, Walter Mitty-like, as the savior of the situation. He froze momentarily as Max spun into action, propelling his trim, muscular body as fast as it could go down the stairs, pain forgotten.

Lester, fearing being left alone, resumed his scuttle. "Shouldn't we wait? Call someone? Hmm? Father?"

Max, ignoring these little bleating sounds, forged ahead.

As for Lester, his heart and stomach had taken on lives of their own, distinct from the rest of his body. His heart in particular thrummed against his rib cage, demanding exit. For the first time, Lester thought of his mother's death and wondered if it had been painful. Certainly, if it had been anything like this, it had been frightening. He barely fought off the impulse to cling to the back of Max's jacket. He hung back, then recalled his fear was greater of being left alone on the stairs. He resumed his downward progress.

They found her at the base of the spiral stone stairwell. Max first saw her hand, unmoving, sticking out of a deeper shadow, a shadow improbably shaped like the Eiffel Tower.

Lester was now making the sounds of a man who has unexpectedly stepped in a pool of quicksand. His white face, lit by the torch which flickered in his trembling hand, was a picture of terror. Now he began to emit little squawks of panic, complete with a flapping of both arms.

"Do be still. There's a good man," said Max mildly.

Lester squared his rounded, scrawny shoulders as best he could. Lester, whose heart was dancing to the beat of a mariachi band, and whose stomach seemed to be playing host to a tiny Olympics gymnastics team, now managed to squeak out a tiny sound of acquiescence, an "Okay" that a mouse standing on his shoulder would have had trouble hearing. He breathed deeply and patted his chest in a desperate attempt to calm himself, eyes wide beneath the ridiculous hat.

Max widened his own eyes to let in as much light as possible as he gazed at the body. The quote flitted through his mind: "My bones are not hid from thee." He knelt before Lamorna, sat back on his haunches, and raked his fingers through his hair. She was no longer hidden by the darkness; he supposed that was why he had called up the familiar old words. Only later did he come to know the true reason. Automatically, he sent up a prayer for the soul of this woman who seemed to have gone through life unfriended and unloved.

She would have to have been kicked and shoved down the

staircase, he realized, as it was so narrow, just narrow enough for a single person to pass, and the walls, as someone flung her against them, acted as weapons in themselves.

Lamorna's face, which Max could see had sustained serious injuries, thankfully was hidden from Lester's full view by Max's body. As with most head wounds, there was a lot of bleeding. Blood covered her face. Poor soul.

Lester didn't look like he could take much more, and was only a heartbeat away from running for his life from the castle. He now emitted a sound that could best be described as a high-pitched yodel. Max spoke sharply to him and again he seemed to collect himself, but with effort. "How?" he began. "How did . . . ?" Again, his vocal cords seemed to be shutting down under the strain.

Max looked closer, but without touching the body. It looked like in addition to the head injury, the neck had been broken. Max, peering through the dim light, could see the outline of a torch. It was presumably hers: If it had belonged to her assailant it would almost certainly have been used as a weapon, and covered in blood. It was turned off.

"She was pushed," Max told him.

"How can you be so sure of that—that she was pushed? It's dark as a tomb in here. No pun intended."

"I can't be positive," said Max, "but think about it. She's lived here for years. She knows these stairs are dark, and she knows to bring a torch to go down them. Why isn't it switched on?" He stood and peered around at the stone walls.

Lester stared mulishly at the body, as if willing it to rise and quit playing possum.

"The fall knocked it into the off position," he said at last.

"Why would she fall if she had the torch switched on?" Max asked, reasonably.

"I don't know, do I?" the man nearly cried. "We just can't have any more of this, I tell you!"

"The police may be able to tell us more. I think those are signs of a scuffle, but we need better light in here to be sure. For now, it's a crime scene and we'll need to treat it as such." Max pointedly stared down at Lester's feet. "Move back, please."

"Oh, for Chrissake. Fine. *Fine!* Play the big action priest-detective if it makes you happy. I'm tired of being a suspect! I'm tired of being held in this place. The killing has to stop!" He held his stomach as if it had given him a small kick, as if politely to suggest now might *really* be a good time for him to leave. "I want to go home!"

"Not happening anytime soon," said Max. His eye had caught on something. "Is that paper?" he asked.

Lester dragged his mind back from the volcano ledge of horror and said, "Sorry. What?"

Lester stood sheltering at Max's side, his chin nearly resting on Max's shoulder as he stood on tiptoe to peer cautiously at the body.

Just then they heard, as if from a great distance, the approach of footsteps. Could hair actually stand on end, Lester wondered? His felt as if someone had sprayed his scalp with dry ice. He forced himself to turn his head round to look back up the stairs. He let out a whinny that even he seemed to realize sounded absurd, since he immediately clamped a hand over his mouth to contain the noise.

Doris Vladimirov came into view around a turn of the spiral staircase, a near-Victorian vision in a ruffled nightgown and chenille bathrobe. On her feet were what appeared to be enormous caterpillars.

She uttered a small cry of astonishment that hardly rose to the strangeness of the occasion.

"Heavens above," she said.

"It's Lamorna," said Lester.

His voice was still keyed up several octaves, minutes away from melting into gibberish. The sudden appearance of the cook may actually have stopped his heart.

"I see that," she said placidly. Bodies in the stairwell might have been a weekly occurrence. Max almost expected her to wonder aloud who was going to clean up *this* mess.

Max's gaze returned to the body. Lamorna seemed to have something clutched in her hand. A scrap of paper.

"Shine that light over here a moment, will you?"

Lester's hands were shaking so, Max finally took the torch from him.

What he could see of the note said, "Meet me at the OK at midnight." It was signed with what looked like a letter D.

He looked at Doris but said nothing. Let Cotton handle it when he got here.

CHAPTER 26

Family Conclave

Max sent Lester to rouse the household, on the theory that giving the man something to do would calm him. Given the timing of the finding of the body, he didn't think Lester could have had anything to do with Lamorna's death.

"Tell them to meet me in the Great Hall," said Max. "Ask Milo to get the fire going."

Max found some matches in the sideboard and lit the candelabra on the dining room table. Eventually they began to emerge like moles from the dark stairwell, blinking in the quavering candlelight. He did a head count as they arrived.

Max had already put in a call to Cotton after finding Lamorna. He planned to issue strict instructions to everyone not to move from the spot, then set out to wait for Cotton's arrival.

Jocasta had fluttered into the room in a bright kimono, scarves trailing (red and orange, this time), her arms waving to telegraph her distress to the cheap seats. Diamonds twinkled at her ears. What sort of woman wore scarves and diamonds to bed? Max wondered.

"Oh, my God!" she cried. "Whatever next?"

Simon was with her, tying an elegant silk men's dressing

gown around his waist. They were soon joined by Felberta in a woolen gown over her nightdress and a white cotton sleeping cap. Tufts of her unruly brown hair peeked out around the edges. She looked like an illustration for a children's tale, only lacking a candlestick for the full effect.

Milo and Doris wore matching bathrobes. "I heard someone cry out," Milo told them.

"It was the ghost," Doris said matter-of-factly.

Eventually they were all there, Randolph and Cilla, Lady Jocasta Jones and Simon, Felberta. Gwyn and the Twyns. The Vladimirovs. The company was completed by Lester, clearly relishing his role as sheepdog, nipping at a thoroughly irritated Randolph's heels. Max started to go and await Cotton and his team, but not before Jocasta erupted. She sucked in her cheeks and began to breathe in and out of her nostrils like a horse (Beulah von Blatt, *I Scream My Head Off*). "Here we are, waiting about like lambs to the slaughter!" she cried.

Lester shook his head decisively. The thick locks of his hair bounced energetically, taking on a life of their own.

"No way," he said. "You'll be just fine. I'll see to it." Lester put one arm around his wife. He was in his element now: protector and defender of women. Hadn't he been the one to discover the body?

Jocasta snorted dismissively. She looked round in something like triumph at the assembled family.

"I told you something like this would happen."

"You most certainly did *not* tell us anything of the sort," said Randolph testily. Cilla, in black satin, looked ready to chime in but perhaps, as often, felt her "otherness" as being not part of the family—and thus not free to comment on the more trying of their imbecilities.

"It's a curse upon this family." Jocasta raised both hands in classic silent-cinema fashion to illustrate her shock and revulsion.

"Oh, do shut it," said Felberta. "You're starting to sound like Lamorna."

Jocasta drew back. "I resent that," she said. "I really do."

"Yes," said Randolph. "Let the poor girl rest in peace—there's no need for character assassination now."

Jocasta in full flood was not to be stopped. "Call me psychic if you like, but I tell you I *knew* something was going to happen."

No one looked like wanting to address her supernatural abilities. In fact, from behind her, Alec rolled his eyes at his sister and clutched his throat in a parody of gagging. The rest of the group turned to Max as someone who might be the voice of reason in this particular situation.

Felberta fed her husband his lines. "You said you found Lamorna? How did you come to find her?"

"I saw her out the window, walking about," said Lester importantly. "And I just knew she was up to something. So I followed her. Then there was a scream." An afterthought: "Father Max here helped. I needed someone to hold the torch."

"Surely you could have done something to prevent this," said Gwynyth to Lester. She was in pink silk and what Max thought were called mules—fuzzy pink high heels. "You couldn't have been following her all that well."

"Me?" said Lester, an expression of confusion on his face. He flapped his hands in a gesture of helplessness. "How was I to know what she was up to? The ingratitude of this family. It's breathtaking. I've probably just saved all of your lives."

The tremor of fear running through the room was real enough, at least in Jocasta's case, but no one could be said to be in mourning for Lamorna.

It made Max angry—so angry he needed a moment to collect himself.

He turned to look out the window beyond the screen and saw that snow had now hardened into something dense and wet that coated the windowpanes with a slushy curtain.

Jocasta exhorted everyone to remain calm, in a loud voice guaranteed to spike everyone's blood pressure. She looked set to say, "The show must go on," and then, in an all-too-rare lapse into good taste, seemed to think better of it.

Max said to her, "I saw someone in the garden, very late last night after dinner. Did you?"

"Me? Of course not. Bloody freezing out there at night, isn't it? I was doing my vocal exercises, then I went to bed early. I was exhausted after that excruciating dinner."

"Anyone else?" said Max. But no one did, or no one would admit to it. The fact remained someone had seen Lamorna, someone had followed her back inside, and someone—there seemed no reason to doubt it—someone had killed her.

"If you are hiding anything, any information at all, this might be a good time to mention whatever it is. Because Lamorna knew something, and you can see where it got her."

Was it his imagination, or was there a slight shuffling or disturbance at the outer fringes of the crowd? He thought it might be coming from one of the twins, who stood behind their mother, who sat on the sofa, but when he looked directly at them, they stared back, both the picture of blue-eyed innocence.

"Lester?" he said.

"Hmm?" If Lester feared that Max might reveal his cowardly participation in that night's events, he didn't know his vicar.

"Can you be quite sure," said Max, "that you saw no one? That you couldn't see who it was Lamorna was following?"

Lester shook his head decisively, importantly—once more the go-to guy at the nerve center of the investigation.

"Too dark," he said. "I only saw her and that wasn't easy."

The return of Lester's usual cockily confident manner continued, his poise seeping back into the cracks opened by his terror. Assuming the stance of a professional now hardened to crime, he said, "She was killed instantly, I would say. Wouldn't you, Father Max?"

Max paused only a moment to wonder at the transformation before him.

"No, I wouldn't," he said. Jocasta gasped. "But I don't think she suffered unduly, except from the initial fright at finding herself being propelled down the stairs."

271

"'Being propelled?' What, she didn't fall?" asked Simon.

Max shrugged. He was sure she hadn't fallen but he didn't know what purpose might be served by airing his suspicions now. The set of his mouth and the fiery red of anger blazing across his cheekbones would have told Simon all he needed to know of Max's suspicions, but Max turned his face. Time enough for suspicions and accusations when Cotton got here.

❅ ❅ ❅

The rapid shift in an already depressed mood after the death of Lamorna continued. As Randolph said, "If someone could find it in themselves to kill that colorless little drudge, none of us is safe."

They sipped coffee, thoughtfully augmented by Milo with a bottle of brandy, and waited.

And thought.

Lester was wondering if he could parlay the situation into some new business introductions. His wife was having much the same sort of idea. After all, as cocktail party conversation, it was hard to beat being in the center of a murder investigation—twice!

Somehow Lamorna's death seemed much more at second remove than Oscar's, Gwynyth was thinking. She was such a nonentity.

Jocasta was wondering whether she shouldn't have bought those shoes she saw in London—they'd be gone when she next went to the store; it was always the way. Also whether she'd remembered to run the garbage disposal before leaving the house. There was that awful smell last time . . .

It was a peaceable silence, although one filled with uncomfortable anticipation of more grilling by the police.

It was Simon who finally said, "I can't just sit here. I'm going to go watch for them."

In the end, they decided to join him. While no one said so, they shared a desire to remain within the safety of the herd.

There was a room in the tall tower at the front of the castle, over the main portcullis, and they climbed to the top to wait and watch the police arrive. Lester grabbed the bottle of brandy and took it with him.

The air in the unheated room was chill. They joined Max, who held his arms tightly around his rib cage, wishing for gloves.

At last they heard the sounds of Cotton and his people arriving, careening up to the castle as if speed might yet save Lamorna's life. First came the uniformed constables and lower ranks, and finally Cotton himself, his car fishtailing on the snow and ice in the untended parking area.

Max signaled from the window, using the torch to gain his attention. Cotton, looking up, nodded in acknowledgement. Max went down to meet him at the main door, and to show him to the crime scene.

"'Fasten your seat belts,'" said Jocasta, watching him go. "'It's going to be a bumpy night.'"

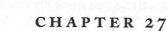

CHAPTER 27

By the Sea

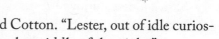

"Let me get this straight," said Cotton. "Lester, out of idle curiosity, was following Lamorna in the middle of the night."

"That's what he says."

"Are we to assume some macho adventure was at the heart of his wanderings? Was he having an affair with one of the women here?"

Max could scarcely contain his astonishment. "Who, Lester? For what it's worth, I think he is completely faithful to Fes—I mean, Felberta. He was suspicious of Lamorna, who was suspicious of someone else, and following them. It was like one giant conga line weaving its way about the castle tonight."

"Her death could just have been an accident . . ." began Cotton.

The two men stood on the ledge of the cliff looking out to

sea. Dawn would soon break. The waves, folding and refolding themselves, scraped steadily away at the rock face. One day the persistence of these waves would pay off, but not for many centuries more. The sea was rough and the words of the two men were at moments lost on the wind. But they had chosen to come out here to ensure they couldn't be overheard.

"But it wasn't," Max finished for him. "You've seen the body. It was overkill. If someone was trying to make it look like an accident they badly misjudged."

"Right. I totally agree. What happened to you when you fell was understandable, given the ice and the eccentricities of those varying treads. But she knew those stairs, knew the house, and was indoors besides. The whole thing begs the question of why she was wandering about at that time of night, anyway. I'm having forensics look over the scene with a view to signs of a struggle, and we'll have the police doctor look for self-defense wounds. He's already reported preliminarily that there are signs of those."

Cotton continued, musingly, "I always liked Lamorna for this crime, but obviously, under the circumstances, I'll have to revise that opinion."

Max nodded glumly.

"I have people checking the grounds and windows," said Cotton, "just on the off chance we're dealing with an intruder. But on the whole, we're not hopeful of finding anything."

Max shook his head. "They won't find anything."

He looked at the waves, then up to the window of what had been Oscar's room. The castle seemed to rise as a piece from the rock. Strangely confident of its impregnability by sea, its builders had focused most of the castle resources on an overland attack, with token openings for pouring oil on or shooting arrows at anyone foolish or desperate enough to attempt the rock climb.

They were on a very narrow walkway and Max, who suffered from a fear of heights, a fear he never seemed able completely to overcome, carried himself carefully as they approached the edge, and cast only glancing looks at the water far below. There was no guardrail—the public weren't allowed out here and apparently those who lived at the castle grew used to it.

"It's an inside job," said Max. "Has to be."

Cotton nodded. "And keep in mind, there is nothing to prevent complete freedom of movement within the 'compound,' for lack of a better word," he said. "The individual doors to private rooms had locks, but access to any of the main buildings from inside the castle grounds was wide open."

"We're not overlooking the obvious, are we? I don't suppose there was any way in from the outside via the main door?"

"Not without a Russian army at one's back, no. Locked, bolted from the inside—quite secure in the entirely medieval way of craftsmen who once knew a thing or two about sturdy locks and bolts. And the alarm had been set."

"And no way in from the sea." It was not a question.

"If there were, someone would have figured out a way to breach the walls centuries ago. One would have to have been an Olympic gymnast or a rock climber to even consider climbing the steep face of the cliff outside, *and* one would have to do it from a rowboat or similar, being tossed about all the while on the waves. There would be no other way, but the whole idea is ridiculous— fraught with difficulties. We'll look for telltale signs of a boat being tied up down there just to shoot down the worst flights of fancy a prosecutor might try to get past a jury. But, no, I'm afraid we're again stuck with the inmates for suspects.

"And really, when you think about it, would anyone have repeatedly broken in here to keep on murdering the inhabitants, especially after the first murder, when they knew security precautions were especially likely?"

Max, who had already followed the same train of thought, shook his head: *Of course not*.

"She was clutching that note," Max told him. "And I think she meant it as a clue for us—what else could have compelled her to keep hold of it while she was being pummeled like that? 'Meet me at the OK at midnight,' it said. 'OK' could be Old Kitchen.

Has to be, doesn't it? The note was signed 'D,' but it was scrawled, a childish hand in a hurry. It could have been a P or S or even a J."

"D for Doris?" asked Cotton.

Max shrugged. "You're the detective."

"So now *I'm* the detective," said Cotton.

Max threw up his hands. "Detect away. I'm not doing too well at it."

"I was joking, Max."

"Sorry." Frustrated, Max added, "I wish I *could* do a better job of detection. I don't see that I'm doing any good here. The bodies are simply piling up. I should probably leave. Perhaps I'm some sort of lightning rod."

"Rather an egocentric point of view, wouldn't you say? Which would be completely unlike you. I need you to stay on, continue your investigation—casually, of course, finding out what they're thinking and feeling, as much as that is possible."

"Stay imbedded." Max sighed. "All right. I badly need to know who did this now." Actually, Max was beginning to wonder if his bishop might not have a problem with all of this. He voiced the wonder aloud.

"Does he have to know?" Cotton asked.

Max smiled. It was a rueful smile. "Perhaps. Yes. But . . . Not yet. Maybe when this is over."

The man had better things to worry about, thought Max, knowing he was rationalizing—a bit.

"So long as my regular duties are covered, and no one in my care is neglected, another day or two shouldn't matter. I have to say in all honesty that for me to stay any longer than that, well . . ."

"I quite understand," said Cotton. "We'll make certain not to drop you in it. If you have to leave in a day or two, that's fine. Do what you can for us in the meanwhile, won't you?"

Max, who wanted desperately to remain with the investigation, nodded.

Cotton's mobile sounded. He looked at the display. "I have to take this," he said, and he turned away to listen.

Max, eavesdropping on Cotton's side of the conversation, was also thinking hard about the victim, about Lamorna. The clue to any crime began there. Even completely innocent victims had their stories to tell of bad luck or bad timing. And he wasn't at all sure Lamorna was completely innocent.

He was thinking that Lamorna in another life might have joined the military, given her thirst for rules and order, and of course, for retribution, for due process. All the authorized processes of revenge.

But was she not also, wondered Max, the type to think *she* should decide what that due process should be—to take the law into her own hands? Max thought, overall, that was exactly what she would do, and how she would think. So would that mean she would be foolhardy enough to confront the killer on her own? Would she? Was she quite mad? Max was sorely vexed in his mind, and suddenly found himself wishing Awena were here. What would Awena make of it? No reason he couldn't just call and ask her what she thought, of course, but then that would be dragging her straight into a police investigation, and into danger. It was unthinkable. Something chivalrous was roused in Max. Awena must be kept clear out of things.

He nearly wrung his hands in consternation. Know-it-all Lamorna. Why hadn't she come to him with her concerns? He was a man of the cloth, after all. She could have confided in him, and presumably she would have felt comfortable doing so. But then, Max had the idea she'd made up her mind about something, and she probably realized he'd try to dissuade her if he knew where her thinking was taking her.

He summarized some of his own thinking for Cotton, who had finished his call and was tucking the mobile back in his inside coat pocket.

"It makes sense to me," Cotton replied. "Lamorna, with her highly developed sense of morality and rectitude, would have felt obliged to act on what she saw, what she knew. She would have seen it as her duty. It's a shame, rather, that she never considered a career in the military. Chain of command, lots of rules to follow—she'd have been in her element."

"How very odd you should say that. It was just what I was thinking. So just the fact she knew something, or maybe thought she did, would be enough to put her life in danger," Max said thoughtfully. "Whether she planned to put that knowledge to use, the perception of her, by anyone who knew her even slightly, would be that she would feel obliged to do something with her knowledge."

"To tell someone."

"Perhaps," said Max thoughtfully. "Or to threaten to tell, if that person didn't do as she wanted."

"Or persons," said Cotton.

"Correct. Also, if we're listing the possibilities, we have to consider Oscar's murder was unconnected to Lamorna's."

"Just to tick all the boxes," said Cotton, but doubtfully.

"I agree," said Max, catching his tone. "That is reaching into the realm of utter impossibility. She wasn't randomly murdered— she couldn't have been. The most likely explanation is that she knew or saw something that got her killed. Lamorna struck me as a sly individual—nosy in the extreme. Others commented on this proclivity of hers to spy. Also, she was someone who would be an excellent observer, since no one paid the least attention to her. She could go almost where she pleased, and eavesdrop to her heart's content. The castle is well-designed for that—for eavesdroppers— in the first place."

She was the ideal observer: an inconspicuous one. Just because no one noticed Lamorna except as it was convenient for them to notice her did not make her unable to see what was going on around her quite clearly. Life with Leticia and Oscar, both demanding people in their different ways, might have created the perfect conditions for a household spy to emerge from the dun-colored personality that was Lamorna. Max could almost wonder how much was an act, and how much self-effacing camouflage had encoded itself into her DNA.

"Are you thinking blackmail?" asked Cotton. "That doesn't jive with the religious bent."

"Yes I am, or something very like it. Lamorna wouldn't blackmail for money, not for her own gain. Of that I am certain. But could she have thought blackmail for a noble cause was all right? To feed the starving orphans in Third World countries? The more I think about it, the more that suits her character exactly—to punish the sinner by extracting payment. Otherwise—and I hope I'm not guilty of too much pride here—I think she would have come to me with what she knew."

Max remembered with regret that he had not always been as patient with Lamorna as he ought. And that in part of his mind he had viewed her as a prime suspect, just given her accumulation of grievances against her adoptive family. That tendency of hers to dwell on revenge was a wide streak.

Aloud he said, "Her burning ambition, if you can call it that, was to remain where she was, fed and housed. 'Safe.' But of course she was anything but safe. She was in mortal danger." He clenched his fists and compressed his lips in anger. "The whole thing is such a waste. And preventable. If only . . ." He stopped, shook his head. "We have to catch whoever did this."

They stood in silence a moment, looking out over the water's dimpled surface, their tall modern figures outlined against the medieval stone behind them. The sky was like dark glass wiped clean as the first traces of sunrise drew a neon line across the eastern horizon. With the dawn, the turbulence of the water was replaced by sighing waves. They could see their breath on the chill air, which was crisply, numbingly cold.

They were well into the season of peace on earth, goodwill toward men. So far, so not looking good on the peace front, thought Max. He turned to Cotton and said, "Tell me there's been some sort of breakthrough by now in the researches into background."

"Well," said Cotton, "there is new information we don't quite know what to *do* with. People who understand the U.S. tax code—I hear there are only three of those in the world—these experts say there is something fishy in the Joneses' finances, a fishiness of which she may not be aware. Jocasta's husband Simon is also her business manager, you may recall. It would appear he is embezzling from Jocasta Jones, LLP—a matter of forged checks and a forged power of attorney."

"That's interesting," said Max.

"Isn't it?" said Cotton.

"But whether that has anything to do with this . . ."

"Precisely again. Who knows? Anyway, whatever everyone else has told us about their pasts and their circumstances checks out. It's the devil to check out what they *haven't* told us, but nothing overtly suspicious has turned up."

"Is there anything to suggest a prior relationship between Randolph and Gwynyth?" Max told Cotton what he'd seen before dinner.

"Interesting . . ." said Cotton. "No, nothing. I suppose a romance could have revved up since they've all been here."

"I think so, too," said Max. "In fact, that is highly likely. They've all been thrown together here for quite some time."

Cotton nodded. There was a pause, then he said, "The attack on Lamorna was so frenzied, so out of control. It worries me."

"Me as well. Never underestimate the power of a guilty and frightened conscience to make a killer act irrationally. But this was very cold-blooded, I think. Calculated. It is a tiny percentage of the population that does not know when it has behaved wrongly against a fellow human being, a fellow living creature. It is an even smaller percentage that wants to be caught and punished for it. Our killer acted, in her or his mind, quite sanely to protect their own safety and security. To not be apprehended. Overall, the risk, weighed in the balance, was worth it to the killer. After all, we have not apprehended whoever killed Lamorna. The killer has gotten away with it . . . so far."

Cotton sighed. "I have to get back in there. But let's quickly go back over when it all started."

Max again walked through all he'd told Cotton already, concluding with: "I remember Leticia's phone ringing, and her shopping rolling about the compartment. Her knitting—white wool. Her general high-handedness. How she first frightened away the young man who looked in the window, who was considering sharing the compartment with us. Her mention, most of all, of her uneasiness with the situation. I wish I'd pressed her on that now."

"She never alluded to anyone she suspected? You're sure?"

Max shook his head. "Not directly. She seemed to have issues with several of the family."

"And you say you saw a figure wandering about the garden earlier?"

"Oh, yes, but that could have been anyone. Whoever I saw could have been wearing any dark color, mind, but it looked like black. All cats are black in the dark, as the saying goes. Cilla wears nothing but black or dark gray, for what it's worth. Notice that it is dark as pitch out here at night, even with the stars. Without that torch you'd be in danger of falling straight off the cliff's edge and into the sea. I just can't be sure . . ."

His voice trailed off. Max was experiencing a strange uneasiness, a sense of vertigo, that had nothing to do with his nearness to a sheer drop-off into the water. As far as he could tell, it was connected for some reason with Lamorna's mention of Jacob and Esau. Jacob and Esau, who were twins. Twins who competed even in the womb. Oscar and Leticia were twins, he thought. Amanda and Alec were twins. But . . . so what?

He dared a peek into the water and just then, as he was puzzling his way through the clues, something slid into place in his mind, so neatly he could almost hear the *click* as it snapped into its rightful spot. His face lit up and his mind raced ahead. What did it mean?

Cotton was saying, "We've added one piece to the puzzle. Milo and Gwynyth worked on the same cruise line, and at one point were on the very same cruise to the Baltics—she as a singer, he as part of the waitstaff. But they never met, or so both claim. I suppose that is just possibly true—these ships are enormous, floating hotels. But the crew is generally kept cheek-by-jowl in the hold. And I keep thinking how alike in age they are. He's around forty. Both his wife and Gwynyth are forty-two."

"What are you suggesting?"

"I've no idea. Maybe it is a coincidence, and not an impossible one. Or they could be in cahoots."

Max fifteen years before had crossed the ocean on a private vacation, but had found himself seconded to go undercover on the trail of stolen art being used to fund an I.R.A. operation. He'd never been on a cruise before, and was surprised to learn nearly everyone on the crew did double or triple duty: the art auctioneer (who turned out to have nothing to do with the theft) turned out to be an opera singer who entertained the passengers in the Winter Garden in the afternoon; the waiter who appeared nightly at his table also did room service delivery. These people tended to crop up at all hours, working double shifts, and often wearing different attire.

He of all people was surprised to realize how disconcerting it was to have people pop out of their "assigned" roles—the roles in which he'd first encountered them.

Someone in the castle had a secret role as killer.

But who?

CHAPTER 28

At the Cavalier

It was nearly noon—well past time for elevenses. Awena decided to take a break from the Goddessspell shop for some coffee and a biscuit at the Cavalier. She and Tara having spent the morning unpacking a new shipment of medicinal plants and herbs, the shop smelled of fenugreek (for the stomach) and hawthorn (for the heart) and dandelion (for the liver). The physical work and the aroma of the herbs of course had the effect of stimulating the appetite. Leaving Tara to mind the shop, with a promise to return with one of Elka's seed cakes, Awena walked up the High to the Cavalier.

Walking into the Cavalier these days was like walking into a steam factory, for Elka, in response to a business threat from a new shop in Nether Monkslip called the Coffee Pot, which was operated with Tuscan brio by the Grimaldis, had invested in an espresso machine. Now, in addition to the clatter of cups and saucers and the clinking of spoons, to the hiss of gossip was added the hiss of a milk steamer.

Besides plain coffee, customers now could order fancy Italian drinks—cappuccinos and lattes with shots of this and that. It seemed to Elka that some of the regulars had started to compete with each other in the "knowledge of esoteric coffee drinks" department, with fancy orders for triple shots and 130-degree temperatures and the like. Elka was in fact fed up with the whole coffee scene. The espresso machine had put her in hock for years and it was nothing but aggro.

At least, she thought, the big coffee geniuses at the Coffee Pot couldn't compete with her steamed Christmas puddings. The ones she was offering this year were masterpieces—moist with fruits and brandy, made the traditional way with thirteen ingredients to represent Christ and his disciples. She'd spent the Sunday before Advent working on them—"Stir Up" Sunday—and even her son Clayton had taken a hand in stirring the mixture. She'd made several wishes as she added the traditional new coins for good luck and prosperity. As usual, the wishes all had to do with Clayton.

Awena opened the door into a fragrant, steamy rain forest of a room, infused with the enveloping heavenly aromas of coffee and vanilla and chocolate, overlaying the usual scent of pastries baked fresh that morning. And . . . was that the smell of brandy? Lovely. She was not surprised also to have found a larger-than-usual crowd sitting around the Cavalier; predictably, from what she overheard over the tinkling of the shop bell as she entered, they were immersed in talk of the murder of Oscar and the death of Leticia at the castle.

Awena, after wishing Elka a good day, asked her for a café au lait. "And I think I'll have a slice of that almond biscotti. It looks wonderful."

"And well it should," said Elka. "I was up until one this morning over that biscotti. Not as simple to make as it looks."

"I find that a high oven temperature helps," ventured Awena.

"Do you?" said Elka. "Fancy that. Let's hope you don't go and open a bakery." Smiling grimly, she put the biscotti slice on a small plate covered by a paper doily, then excused herself to answer the call of an egg timer announcing that the next batch of biscuits was ready to come out of the oven. "That's all you want?" said Elka, returning from the kitchen, drying her hands on a linen towel covered in a pattern of cornflowers. "A simple coffee with milk?"

"Ye-e-ess," said Awena, sensing a test of some sort.

"Try the macchiato," said a voice from behind her. She turned to see Miss Pitchford, retired schoolmistress, sitting at a table by a window. A shopping basket rested at her feet. "It's ambrosial." She drank deeply of her cup by way of demonstration.

"Oh, we can do better than *that*," said Elka, emptying a filter with a series of booming thumps against a rubbish bin. "I have far, *far* more complicated drinks on the menu than simple coffee and tea these days!" And she laughed—more a mad cackle than a laugh. Awena wondered if there weren't even a tinge of hysteria behind the laugh. Elka was one of the hardest-working women in the village. She got sporadic help from her son in operating her bakery business and tea shop. Now that she had effectively opened a gourmet coffee shop as well, Clayton's lack of actual help had probably become glaringly noticeable.

"For example," chimed in Suzanna Winship, who shared a large wooden table and several newspapers with Miss Pitchford. "You can have it lungo, ristretto, bollente, tiepido—whatever you want. Why settle for a simple coffee when we have all of Italia on our doorstep lately, here at La Cavalier. Or would that be Il Cavalier?"

"And chai!" added Elka. "Don't forget the chai drinks!"

"Do you . . ." And Awena hesitated, fearing this might be the very final and fatal last straw for Elka. "Would you by any chance have soy milk for my coffee? If it wouldn't be too much bother."

"Soy milk!" Elka was practically shrieking now. "Soy milk! Of course we have soy milk. How could I hold up my head in this village if I didn't have sodding soy milk—organic, of course. Almond flavored, vanilla flavored, chocolate flavored. You name it. You want soy, I've got soy. And rice milk, don't forget! Almond flavored, vanilla—"

"Just plain soy will be fine, Elka, and thank you so much for all you do for us." It seemed to Awena it might be as well to pretend this was some special favor being offered, rather than Elka trying rather frantically to hold her own against the encroachments of capitalism and the free market.

"Bring your coffee over here when it's ready," said Suzanna, as Miss Pitchford nodded and patted the seat at her side. "We've been discussing the doings up at the castle."

The village had been full of talk of the visitors when they arrived, of course. There was not so much going on in the village proper that the need to import or invent gossip didn't occasionally arise. That one of the visitors was American, married to a "famous actress" who happened to be the daughter of the deceased, quickly got round, although when that particular rumor had started it at least resembled the truth: "A formerly near-famous actress was visiting," the woman who ran the post office told everyone standing on line. "You know. She was in that movie where she was tied up and nearly pushed off a cliff. Only that dark handsome actor with the nose saved her. Now what was his name?" And so on. By the time the story reached those at the back of the line, the actress had starred in an Indiana Jones movie with (for reasons unknown) Tom Cruise.

"Rather thought you might be talking about the castle," murmured Awena, but she went to join them without hesitation.

The Cavalier, converted from the village's old communal bakehouse, now held a pleasing assemblage of mismatched wooden furniture; each wobbly table was covered by a cloth patterned with different flowers against a white or yellow background. Suzanna and Miss Pitchford were at the marigold table.

"I was just saying to Miss Pitchford here it was too bad about Lady B," said Suzanna as Awena settled herself in. "She was a nice enough old trout. Frightful snob, of course, but people of that class always are, don't you find?"

"I understood she'd been ill . . ." began Awena.

"No, she wasn't."

"It's well known Lady Baynard was a hypnochondric," put in Elka from behind the counter.

"That would be 'hypo,' Elka. Hypochondriac."

"Had you invited any of them to the party, Awena?" asked Miss Pitchford.

"I had, actually, more as a friendly gesture than expecting them actually to show up."

"She was too big a snob to mix with the hoi polloi," said Suzanna. "At least, I always thought so."

Awena, a bit surprised, merely said, "You'd met her?"

"Here and there. The doctor's sister enjoys a certain amount of prestige in these parts. Bruce saw more of her than I did, of course, although she mainly went to London to see someone in Harley Street. She would, wouldn't she? And make sure everyone knew she could afford an expensive, private doctor. But she kept to herself after the kerfuffle over the access rights or right of way or some such thing."

"Access rights?"

"You didn't come to hear of it?" Miss Pitchford, exchanging glances with Suzanna, sat back in astonishment, dropping her newspaper. It was as if Awena had disavowed all knowledge of the Great War.

"It was *the* topic at the time here at the Cavalier Tea Room and Garden, I can tell you," said Suzanna. "It was some typical country-ish thing they all get het up about. I didn't pay much attention . . . an area farmer wanted to cross the Footrustle property with his sheep or cows or some sort of livestock and the family kicked up about it—wanted him to go the long way round. It may have been his pigs that were the breaking point. Eating the acorns or whatever it is pigs do for their own amusement."

"Truffles, I think, my dear," put in Miss Pitchford vaguely. "They like truffles."

"Or maybe it was radishes," said Suzanna. "Anyway, what*ever* it is they eat."

"I think they eat pretty much anything," said Awena.

"Well, there you are," said Suzanna. "I'm sure that was entirely the problem. Anyway, there was the most frightful dustup over all of it."

"When was this?"

"Oh, a year or two ago. Yes, about that. I remember it wasn't long after I came to live in the village and I remember thinking I'd made the most dreadful mistake in coming here. Pigs and grazing rights? I mean, really."

"'How are the mighty fallen'?"

"I didn't mean that exactly." But she did mean that exactly. Suzanna, used to "being something" in the city was only slowly succumbing to the somnolent charms of Nether Monkslip—to becoming "someone," as Coco Chanel had put it.

"So, what happened?"

She shrugged and smoothed back her hair, a graceful gesture that called to mind Gina Lollobrigida or one of the other great vamps of the fifties, all insouciance and endless afternoon hours spent lolling about an Italian veranda. "It went to court and I think the farmer lost. There was *strong* feeling about that."

Miss Pitchford, her eye caught by a *Times* editorial on education, a subject dear to her heart as a retired schoolmistress, nonetheless nodded vigorously.

"So you say Lady Baynard didn't see much of your brother?" Awena asked.

"Lady Baynard—as you have gathered, it was never '*Do* call me Leticia' about that one. Anyway, Lady B was a difficult patient and she wouldn't follow Bruce's dietary advice. She was naturally thin but she didn't exercise, either, apparently, other than to potter about the castle gardens and fuss about the hothouse. Even then, she had others to do the heavy lifting. Bruce had her on medication or so he tells me but whether she took it religiously or not, who can say. Anyway, she made it plain that in her view Bruce was little better than a local horse doctor and took herself off to London, as mentioned. Good riddance, said I. Bruce could hold his own with the toffs in Harley Street any day. He simply chooses not to. 'The simple life for me'—you know how he is."

Miss Pitchford folded the paper neatly and said, "She was rude to your brother, there is no question. I well remember the occasion. But more often than not she put people's backs up simply because she had Standards, you see." The capital S was audible. "That doesn't go down well with those who cannot be troubled with having Standards." Miss Pitchford could have written the book on this subject, thought Awena. In a beautiful cursive script.

"The grazing or common rights being a case in point, I gather . . ." said Awena. "I suppose back in the day we'd all have been her serfs. Funny to think of, isn't it?"

The biscotti really was a triumph and she looked up to smile her appreciation in Elka's direction. Elka, however, was at the sink with her back turned, and was elbow deep in soapsuds.

"Yes," agreed Miss Pitchford. "Not that I can't see both sides of an issue. And she did herself no favors by the way she spoke to Farmer Braddock. A spoonful of sugar, et cetera. Especially since she knew she'd win. But that was Leticia's way."

"She allowed you to call her Leticia?" asked Suzanna. "You must have been on good terms."

Miss Pitchford blanched visibly. "Most certainly she did not—*never* would I dare call her that to her face. The very idea. I understand her niece—that dreadful actress, she played a dead Viking; I tried to watch it on the television—and her husband, the American in-law, they called her Leticia once, but their Standards are quite different to ours, aren't they? They no longer have a monarchy."

Awena knew several Americans who would debate that opinion. She corrected her gently. ("I think you must mean vampire, not Viking"). She waited patiently for Miss Pitchford to calm herself.

"Goodness gracious me," Miss Pitchford went on, patting her heart back into her thin chest. "What *can* they have been thinking?"

They were thinking that was her name and they were relatives, after all, but Awena decided there was no point in pursuing that particular avenue of discussion. There was a good bit more in the "goodness gracious" line but otherwise she felt she had learned all she could of the situation from Suzanna and from Miss Agnes Pitchford. Collecting her things about her, she was preparing to rise and depart when Miss Pitchford said, "At least we can rest assured Father Tudor won't make that mistake. *Cannot* make it."

"Oh?" said Awena, with what she hoped was a casual lilt to her voice, as she gripped her umbrella to her chest like a talisman against evil. "And why would he?"

"I saw him leaving town earlier," said Miss Pitchford, always happiest when she had a tidbit of news that clearly was news to someone else. "He said he was going to stay at the castle. Just for a day or so, he said. To advise."

"Oh."

"That divorce was his undoing, Lord Footrustle's." Miss Pitchford resumed her earlier theme, feeling all had not yet been said on this topic. "There is nothing new under the sun, is there?" She appeared to be gathering steam so Awena, still clutching her umbrella, sank back down for the duration.

"As for the rest! Of course, having invited themselves, I don't suppose it occurred to any of them to behave well whilst they were guests of the castle." She bridled, lifting her head in disdain at the thought of the goings-on of these invaders.

"I thought Lord Footrustle invited them to visit?"

"To visit, surely, but they've been there for weeks and months, some of them. Living off the fat of the land. Pigs in a poke, every one, especially that Gwynyth person."

Awena noted that it was Lady Baynard when it came to the formal niceties, but Gwynyth rather than Lady Footrustle, as she was still entitled to be called, when it came to someone Miss Pitchford plainly regarded as a common interloper. "*And* you know what they say about fish and guests smelling after three days," she added. Awena, marveling at her ability to mix her metaphors, made a mental note to ask Max on his return exactly how the family, immediate and extended, all had come to stay at the castle. And finally to find out what in the world a poke was, anyway.

She had already said her good-byes and was turning to go when Miss Pitchford said flatly, "Madness runs in that family."

Suzanna was nodding. "Bruce always thought so. You know, that's a bit of a hobbyhorse of his. Madness."

Miss Pitchford agreed. "They're all barking, to some degree or other. Daft as brushes."

"And Max is staying there," said Suzanna. "With a murderer?"

Numbly, Awena allowed the words to sink in. She was upset, she realized, that Max hadn't mentioned this plan to her.

And more upset to realize there was no reason he should have done.

"So I hear," she said.

CHAPTER 29

S.O.S.

Having spent much of the day talking with the suspects, going over old and new ground, Max returned to his room to shower and change, hoping the sluice of water would help rejuvenate his thinking.

Changing quickly into a dark wool jumper and jeans, he took out the notebook he always kept with him to capture the random thoughts that often ended up in his sermons. Using a plastic pen embossed with the Footrustle logo, a guest souvenir, he described as best he could the images that slipped through his mind in a stream-of-consciousness style. Turning to a more analytical mode, he also noted the nagging inconsistencies, but he could draw no connections there.

Frustrated, he flipped the notebook to a new page, as if the sight of a fresh, unmarred sheet of paper might clear up his thinking. Predictably, it only seemed to mirror the blankness of his mind. He kept returning to Lamorna's passing reference to Esau and Jacob until finally he looked up the passage again. At Genesis 27:41 his eyes fell upon these words:

> *And Esau hated Jacob because of the blessing wherewith his father blessed him: and Esau said in his heart, The dayes of mourning for my father are at hand; then will I slay my brother Jacob.*

Max read this and thought, Yes, that's all well and good, and I can't entirely blame Esau for his anger. Max knew by now that money and inheritance, as is so often the case, were at the bottom of the current situation at the castle as well, but beyond that, where was the connection?

He closed the book, stood, and thought with a sudden fierce longing of Awena. He badly wanted just to see her face. To be in the presence of someone who was the opposite of persons full of guile, greed, and grasping ambition.

He had well and truly had it with the Footrustles and their damnable lusting after money.

He didn't think beyond that, to what might happen between him and Awena. He just wanted urgently to see her, almost as if he feared for her safety. Yet he knew she was safe, in what must have been one of the safest places on earth. Well, despite the recent unpleasantness, Nether Monkslip was the safest of havens.

There came a knock at the door. It was probably Cotton, he thought, as he twisted the iron door handle—Cotton wanting to rehash some point of the case. Max rubbed his eyes with weariness.

And there she was. He stepped back, doing an almost comic double-take. Awena. *What in the world?*

But she looked distraught. If it were possible for Awena ever to look haggard, she did, with dark circles under the luminous, deep-violet eyes.

"You know," she said without preamble, "you really might have told me. They're worried sick back at the village." Somehow it seemed safer to present herself as a spokesperson for the villagers and their anxieties. She wasn't yet ready to admit she was at the castle after succumbing to a gnawing, mind-numbing anxiety of her own. She had to see Max, and see with her own eyes that he was safe.

He stood back from the door to let her pass. "How . . . ?" he began.

"Cotton saw me arrive," she told him. "He told me where I could find you."

"You know there's been another murder."

"He told me. Lamorna. Good heaven, that poor child."

He started to correct her, to say, *I actually meant, how did you know I desperately wanted to see you?* but settled for, "It is very good to see you."

It was a measure of Cotton's esteem for her that she was allowed here at all under the circumstances, Max knew. She could be trusted not to get in the way of the investigation, to contribute only when and if asked, and, most of all, to be discreet and keep to her own counsel.

He looked at her delightedly, disbelievingly. Awena's classically etched face mirrored the transparency of her personality, free from guile, imbued with joy. More than most people, Max thought, Awena was without barriers, her soul translucent as glass, as sheer as a seashell worn by tides and sand. He turned toward her with an embracing movement of his arms, a welcoming embrace that did not touch her, as if he feared this vision might evaporate.

Only a few miles had separated them, but she had stood in his mind like a bejeweled icon of serenity. Now holding her by the arms, he reveled in her presence. He took in the day's attire, a soft, saffron dress like a bright flame gathered with a wide satin belt. It glittered with embroidery and small, semiprecious stones of every hue.

"You shouldn't be here," said Max. "Someone very disturbed—something evil is at work here. I don't want you in harm's way." He grimaced briefly at the thought of Awena getting in the path of this horror. He thought of her as vulnerable, given to starry-eyed beliefs, and would have been astonished to know she thought the same of him. "Who saw you arrive?" he asked.

"Only the police, so far as I know. Cotton and Essex. The place is swarming, as you're aware. A veritable hive of activity."

Briskly she moved past him. She stood before the fire, warming her hands. She turned to him, those shining eyes drawing him closer. "They've cleared the roads at last, or I couldn't have made it," she told him. "I call that miraculous. Farther inland the snows have been historic."

She took a seat on the sofa before the fire and motioned him next to her.

"Tell me, now," she said. "Why poor Lamorna?"

He sat and turned to face her. "There's a reason, however mad it may seem." He noticed that she perceptibly shuddered on the word. "You know the kind of life she led here. It seems to have given her an odd . . . tendency. A 'need to know' that was probably a clinical-grade snoopiness, if you will. Knowledge being power, she went around gathering whatever dribs and drabs of information she could. Somehow this rabid curiosity got mixed up in her mind with an odd religiosity, and the idea that she could protect the status quo by holding whatever she knew over the head of the killer. She simply wanted to be allowed to live on here, protected from the outside world. Not too surprisingly, it led to her death."

Max scrubbed with the palm of one hand at the day's growth of dark beard on his face. He'd forgotten to shave, distracted.

Devastated, was the word. Another death he should have prevented and could not. If only he'd been fast enough, made the connections . . .

"She was the scapegoat," he said. "The sacrifice. Anyone could see that. I knew that. I should have—"

"'Should have'?" picked up Awena. "'Should have'? What kind of rule book are we playing by here? The Omniscient Max Tudor-Slash-Superman Regulations?"

Max, suddenly swamped by memories of Paul, of the friend and comrade whose death he could have prevented, found himself with jaws working but unable to answer her. She laid a hand on his arm, the simple compassion plain on her face, in the clarity of those remarkable eyes.

Max was so much the imperturbable one she touched him as much to be sure the Max she was used to was still there. He, now completely undone by her kindness and wanting to hide as the tears sprang from nowhere, his face contorted in a mask of pain and bleak regret, covered his eyes with one hand. Drawing her to him, he rested his head against her neck. The contact, never sexual in intent, nonetheless acted as a charge, completing a circuit, bridging them together. Max leaned against the one person he knew with certainty would both be strong enough to catch him yet never betray or judge his weakness—or even see this collapse as a weakness.

They sat together a long time, her small white hand splayed across his back, able to feel his strong heart beat, until his breathing finally began to calm. He lifted his head.

"Sor—" he began.

"If you say you're sorry I shall jump up and down and run about the room screaming. I may knock over lamps and throw things out windows. Now, when is the last time you saw Lamorna alive?"

The brisk return to common sense and the need to focus on bringing Lamorna and Oscar's killer to justice galvanized him, as Awena had known it would. There was work to be done. Max's training and his very nature came into play.

He talked for some time, and she listened. Listened to the half-formed theories. To his questions about things that had happened. And most particularly, to his question about the one thing that should have happened, but had not.

Awena had again that faraway look in her eyes, eyes that suggested a mariner scanning the horizon. It was a look that belied her lively and active participation in the world, her awareness of every moment. She hung on his words, but in the end confessed she could make no connections he had not made himself.

Finally Max said, "Tell me again about your visit to the castle that day to see Leticia."

Awena, looking confused by the request, struggled to comply. "Really, there was nothing to it," she concluded. "I was here perhaps half an hour, not more. The shallow soil and the nearby sea presented some particular challenges for growing herbs, and I advised her on that. She offered me tea which I refused, and then I left. The bees chased me out, rather. They were a complete menace that day—that summer, really. I told you this."

Max's eyes in the shadowy room grew dark, his expression distracted.

Awena leaned back, resting comfortably in the cradle of his arms. She examined his face like a buyer looking for flaws, her hands in his. After a very long while she smiled, and stood.

Awena had left, taking Max's heart with her.

Max escorted her to the car park and saw her drive safely down the road that would take her back to Monkslip-super-Mare and from there on to Nether Monkslip. She drove a car of robin's egg blue that looked like it ran on AA batteries. It had a COEXIST sticker on the back bumper, each letter represented by a symbol for a different religion. Max laughed aloud.

And Cotton watched their good-byes from an upper window, a broad smile on his face.

Max walked slowly back into the castle. A few answers to a

few more questions, a very few, and he knew he'd have the solution to the case.

But his thoughts now sprang wide, free to roam in larger, uncharted territory, considering that nearly all the matter of the universe consisted of dark energy and dark matter. Everything mankind knew or believed had to be taken on the blind faith of the heart.

No different from falling in love, Max imagined. Exactly the same.

Whether a woman who followed neopagan beliefs could be considered suitable company for an Anglican priest was very, very much open to question. To him, it didn't matter. Awena had a depth of spirituality and connectedness to things divine beyond anything he had ever encountered in his life. The official Church might not—almost certainly would not—understand.

It might end with his having to leave the priesthood, and he knew unhesitatingly that was a risk he'd accept.

He supposed he'd cross that bridge when he came to it.

CHAPTER 30

Heard in High Places

When Max awoke the next day, it was with the uneasy sense that in his dreams he had been running, charging after some creature, man or beast, so fleet of foot—or hoof—that it had already turned the next corner just as he arrived there.

Lord Footrustle's murder had clearly been at the hands of a quick, ruthless killer of unshakable nerve. A single deep thrust of the knife, no hesitation, followed up by other, dispassionate thrusts to ensure the kill. A clean killing, if any murder could be thus described. The killing of Lamorna was something else. It had an aura of ruthlessness, *and* of desperation. Clearly she was in the way. Possibly a witness. And she had been dispatched, apparently without hesitation. Their killer was without conscience, acting on instinct. "Wait and do nothing," as is often wise in a hostage situation, wasn't an option here. At least not for long, with the trail growing colder by the minute. Soon, Cotton would have to let the suspects go.

Max reminded himself that only in the abstract was evil frightening. It was the banality of evil, evil when met face-to-face, that was surprising. And that very banality reduced it to a form that could be conquered.

He elbowed a sweater over his head, tightened the bandage around his ankle until he felt he could walk without the crutch, if carefully, and headed downstairs for breakfast.

Breakfast was set out by the Vladimirovs, again in a buffet arrangement that allowed everyone to choose and settle as they wished. Max noticed the twins taking plates loaded with fruit, bread, and cheese up the stairs either to their rooms or to the drawing room. No one tried to stop them. Indeed, no one seemed to notice them at all, least of all their mother, who apparently subsisted on dry Ryvita and coffee. She smiled wanly at Max when he wished her a good morning.

Max took in the expanse of the Hall and saw Felberta sitting near the fireplace. Today she was wearing an enormous necklace that might have belonged to the chieftainess of a minor Māori tribe. He smiled at her but settled with his poached egg and baked beans at the dining room table.

Cilla came into the room. Today she was in black jean leggings that looked impossible to walk in, let alone sit in—a covering that emphasized the spidery thinness of her legs. Ugg boots had replaced the usual high heels, boots suitable for mushing on the Iditarod. A coiling tumble of dark brown hair, literally her crowning glory, fell about her shoulders.

She was looking at a message on her mobile phone and suddenly emitted a joyful bark of laughter. Max looked up, wondering to himself what had made her laugh, particularly under the circumstances. She turned the screen so Max could see a message sent by someone clearly inept at the art of text messaging. It was a message full of typos, the sender seeming like a foreigner with an incomplete and faulty grasp of the English language. It read, in part: "come form xmas. Moist welcome."

"My aunt," she said. "All thumbs."

It suddenly made him think of the mobile carried on the train by another elderly woman, Leticia. She had said the twins had programmed the phone for her, hadn't she?

Was it important? He rather thought it was.

"Did you happen to see where the twins were headed when they left here?" he asked Cilla.

She shook her head. "Try the drawing room. They like to cave-dwell in there when the oldies are otherwise occupied."

❄ ❄ ❄

Max walked up to Leticia's "withdrawing room" and peeked in. The twins were there reading, curled up like puppies on the sofa. Alec looked up at him, heavy-lidded. After nodding hello, he returned his eyes to his page.

"Could I have a word, Alec?"

His reluctance clear, Alec marked his place in his book and followed Max out to the hallway.

"I need to know what you've been doing up on the roof." Seeing Alec's face, and heading him off at the pass, Max added, "You're not in any trouble. In fact, you could be crucial to solving the case."

"Really?"

"Truly."

"But . . . how did you know?"

"I saw you coming downstairs, dressed for the weather in a coat and scarf. I wondered why you would be indoors but bundled up for the wind and snow. If you'd been headed upstairs from the garden, it would have made sense, but you weren't. Still, you had to be coming from *out*side, which could only mean you were coming from the roof. So, what exactly were you doing up there at all hours?"

In unconscious imitation of his cousin Randolph, Alec ran his fingers through his thick shock of hair to get it out of his eyes.

"It's a bit embarrassing."

"I'm sure. But I don't shock easily and I'm certain you'll live."

"It was Amanda who figured it out. She thinks she wants to write detective stories one day, you know, and she is good at noticing things."

"Go on."

"Well. To wire a castle, you have to run the wires up to the roof inside a pipe or tube that runs along the outside of the castle—have you noticed those?"

Max nodded. "I noticed them when I first arrived. For esthetic reasons the wires must be hidden as best as can be, and made to blend in somehow with the stone walls. Then they bring the power into a junction box that routes the electricity through the building. They use the roof because the stone is thinnest there, and they drill a hole through, or lift the slates."

"How did you know all that?"

"I'm a history buff and I've visited a lot of castles." And had pretended to be a stonemason during one MI5 case where he was keeping an eye on a nob with mob connections, he could have added. "But that doesn't explain what you were doing up there."

"Well, that's where it gets a bit, um . . ."

"Difficult to explain? Try me."

"You can listen in from up there, you see. We discovered it one day by accident. Well, we weren't half bored here, were we? There's nothing to do. You can also talk to someone through the pipes, depending on what room the other person's in. It's really sort of cool."

"Ah. And what can you hear?"

"I heard something that didn't make a lot of sense. It sounded like a man and woman, and they were arguing. But I couldn't tell what room it was coming from—I think it must have been the Great Hall, so it could have been any of them arguing. Even with the app it was hard to hear clearly—I had trouble with the squelch control."

"Wait a minute. What app?"

"A sound amplifier app I downloaded for my mobile." The "of course" was unspoken but his opinion of the inherent dimness of adults was evident. "'App' is short for 'application,'" Alec added helpfully, in case Max was simply too senile to comprehend this difficult point.

Max looked at him. The poem about fog coming in on little cat feet came into Max's mind, making him smile. Alec had a great career as a cat burglar ahead of him. Or a spy for Her Majesty's Government.

"I do know what an app is, thank you. So, what was it you heard?"

Alec had kept a lot to himself, having learned early that knowledge sometimes needed to be hoarded for safety's sake. Somehow it was a relief to tell Max, if it might help. Alec had had no great use for Lamorna but she didn't deserve to die like that.

"It wasn't much," he said apologetically. "Two voices, a man and woman talking—and I wondered, who was the woman? Because they were quarreling, arguing, and the couples around here don't quarrel—not with *each other*. Not since my parents divorced has there been a ruckus like that . . . and of course, my father, he's gone now." His expression closed down for a moment, then he visibly shook off the melancholy and said, "Lester and Fester are thick as thieves, always. It couldn't have been them unless they're great actors otherwise. I could hear phrases like, 'It was all your brilliant idea' and 'So what are we to do about Father Brown being in our midst?' Then, 'Quit showing off in front of him. You're overplaying your hand!'—that part was really loud. Then a door slammed and I couldn't really hear much more. I think someone turned on the telly then somewhere—or more likely was watching something on a laptop. My father discouraged the telly whenever he could."

Max was struck anew by the disparity in ages here. Oscar, Lord Footrustle, surely had been old enough to be the boy's grandfather, not his father. It was a large generation gap. Perhaps insurmountably large.

"You're sure that isn't what you were hearing all along, a movie or a television show? You're quite sure?"

"Yes," said Alec, quite assured and calm. "When whoever it was started watching the telly or whatever, there was that tinny sound, and a laugh track. With what went on before, no one was laughing, that's certain."

"Thank you for telling me, Alec. One more thing. Since you're obviously good with phones, did you program Lady Baynard's mobile for her? To play a song you knew she probably wouldn't like?"

"Who, me? Why would I bother her with a silly prank like that?"

"Did your sister?"

"Same answer. She's a girl but she puts her time to somewhat better use than that. But, ask her."

Max returned to the drawing room and did just that. Amanda was adamant she had done no such thing. And her reasoning was much the same, except she added, "My aunt knew perfectly well how to use her phone. She'd had it since the Jurassic period."

❄   ❄   ❄

Max on his way to see Cotton ran into several members of the household. The first was Felberta.

At the look of concern on Felberta's face he said, "Would you like to tell me all about it? If it's what I think it is, the police won't really care, certainly not in the middle of a murder investigation."

"It's simply not worth it, Father," she said, "if it puts Lester's life in danger." And adjusting the appalling costume jewelry around her neck, she told him.

❄   ❄   ❄

"I think you need to tell me why you were roaming around the night Lamorna was killed," Max said to Lester a few minutes later. "The other reason."

There was the expected bristling, the posing. "Does it matter?" Lester spluttered. "I saw what I saw."

"To be honest, I don't think it does matter, but for my own satisfaction I'd like my hunch verified." He had just promised Felberta to leave her name out of it.

Lester tried to face it out, but rapidly caved.

"Well, I was, if you must know . . . looking out for my best interests."

"And that would mean jewelry? Paintings? Other valuables?"

"Well, I . . ." His voice faded. He almost looked as if he might refuse to answer, but then he burst out: "I had every right. My mother had some valuable jewelry she would have wanted Felberta to have."

Max marveled at that assertion. He wondered very much whether Leticia would think first of Felberta in this connection, but he studiously guarded his expression.

"Randolph as the eldest looked set to take the lot," Lester went on. "There's so much, I didn't think he'd miss it. And he doesn't have a wife so he doesn't need it."

"Uh-huh."

"But then I saw Lamorna—definitely looking suspicious. I started following her in case . . ."

"In case she was on the same sort of mission. Really, does that sound like Lamorna to you—lusting after jewelry?"

"I guess not, really. But she was following someone, too."

"Any further thoughts on whom she was following? Did you get any indication of height, sex, size?"

"I never saw. She went over to the Old Kitchen. I waited. She came back out and I followed her back to the castle. I was returning to bed and—well, the rest you know."

Max tended to want to believe him, if only because Lester struck him as not being smart enough to lie convincingly for long. So presumably whomever Lamorna followed stayed inside the Old Kitchen, at least until Lester had given up the chase and the coast was clear. Then "whomever" came to find Lamorna.

CHAPTER 31

Be My Baby

Max actually ran into Cotton before he could get to the library. They stood to one side, conversing in hushed voices, Max being all too aware that the lack of privacy in the castle was nearly complete. He told Cotton about Alec's little hobby. Cotton blanched, then went on to say in a very low voice, "We have alibis galore, all worthless if anyone is covering for anyone else. For example, the cook and butler alibi each other, but that means nothing. They would."

Cotton's mobile buzzed. He looked at a text message.

"This just in from our U.S. colleagues." And he summarized the data in the report.

"Do you want to talk with her?" asked Cotton. "I've a feeling this may be more in your line. She might be more willing to let her hair down with you than with the 'authorities.'"

Max said, "Yes, I'll go and talk with her. Then I'll join you in the library."

He found her having coffee in the Great Hall.

"If I might have a word in private?"

They moved up into the drawing room, now vacated. Jocasta fussily sat down like an exotic bird settling on a nest, scarves fluttering.

Max said plainly, "Did Lamorna ever find out about her relationship to you? That you were her mother?"

The idea of denial played out across her face, but like Lester she had few defenses. The strain of questioning was probably wearing all of them down.

"I gave Lamorna up for adoption. Lea adopted her to keep it

303

in the family. She really loved Lamorna." This last was said with a look of utter bafflement.

"You didn't object? You never tried to see her, or to be involved in her upbringing?"

More bafflement. Max suspected also that Lea wanted to keep Jocasta away from the child, and make the child her own. That was wise, in retrospect—how confusing it would all have been for Lamorna.

He remembered that Oscar's will mentioned Jocasta and any *offspring* of Jocasta—legal or otherwise. It was standard legalese. But it meant Lamorna had shared with Jocasta in becoming quite a wealthy person on Oscar's death.

And it had long sounded as if Jocasta, and her husband, needed money to bail out her finances.

"Oscar didn't know who Lamorna really was?" Jocasta shook her head decisively. "Did Leticia?" Again, no.

"You have to remember what it was like back in the day." Jocasta was speaking softly, especially for Jocasta. "I gave up the baby to save my career from scandal. Even in those days, although ideas were changing, an illegitimate baby could be a career ender in Hollywood. So I moved to Florida for the last few months of the pregnancy, gave birth, and gave the baby up for adoption. Lea told people she was adopted from St. Petersburg and they naturally assumed Russia—there were so many adoptions coming out of there."

Max nodded. "St. Petersburg, Florida. Russia being an easy conclusion for people to jump to—'St. Petersburg' and the word 'overseas' being used, without specifying which *direction* overseas: west or east. People would take for granted she was born in Russia, and came from an orphanage there. There have been so many adoptions from Russia by wealthy, childless couples. And that bit of misdirection would leave you right out of it. She also had the dark appearance of some Russians."

Jocasta nodded.

"And you didn't know Lea had adopted her?"

"I told Lea of my predicament, but Lea, having decided to

adopt the child, kept it secret from me at first. She adopted via an intermediary. I didn't know until later, when Lea thought it was safe to tell me. She didn't realize, it was always safe. It's not like I was going to beg to get her returned to me." A pause. "Simon is the only one who knows. How did you find out?"

"The adoption records, of course. Nothing in a murder inquiry stays hidden for long. Lamorna's name was a bit of a clue—she's was conceived in Cornwall, wasn't she, but born in Florida?" Jocasta nodded, clearly growing bored with the topic of her murdered child.

"Cornwall also had romantic associations for her adoptive parents, am I right?"

Jocasta shrugged. "I think Lea said something about it. It was years ago, and she and Leo died soon afterward."

Max asked: "Did Lady Baynard never even guess who Lamorna really was?"

"I truly don't think so; it was all kept hush-hush. Would it have mattered that Lamorna was actually a blood relative? I doubt it. If anything the murkiness of her origins and the scandal surrounding them would have doubled Leticia's revulsion for her."

"So she came into Leticia's care, but let's always put quotation marks around that word 'care,' shall we? Lady Baynard seemed to regard her as little more than unpaid help, given room and board in exchange for services. The adoption was a stigma, making her an outcast. Illegitimacy was of course what really bothered Leticia. Poor Lamorna. Not much of a life, and what there was, cut short."

He was silent a moment, then asked her pointedly: "Did *she* know? Lamorna."

Silence.

"Did you get the chance to tell her before she died?"

She shot him a look of pure venom. If he'd ever suspected her of being capable of murder, that look alone would have sealed the impression.

"What good would it have done? Have ever done? I had a

career to think about. She was . . . just strange. There were complications . . . the birth . . . I was glad to have her off my hands. I had my career to think about."

❋ ❋ ❋

"It lands both Jocasta and Simon right in there," Cotton said. "Don't you agree?"

They were in the castle library. Max said, in a noncommittal voice, "Perhaps. Yes, perhaps." But his thoughts were clearly leading him in other directions, as well. His eyes were alight with detective fervor.

He shifted his weight. "However, I do see your point," he added, cautiously, and then fell into what Cotton could only describe to himself as an active silence, eyes blazing with patient thought. A snake waiting on a foolish move by its prey would wait thus, Cotton thought.

Max's eye alighted on a glass bowl of fruit on the table beside his chair. It had been there during the recent interviews but he'd not particularly noticed. Now it leapt into his view, panning slowly into a close-up.

Hesitantly, he reached for an orange, completely perfect and unbruised. All the food in the castle was of that quality. Organic, probably locally sourced. Awena would be so pleased to know.

He turned the orange round in his hand. Its bar code sticker was still attached.

He looked up at Cotton. "Can you spare one of your people to go over to the vicarage in Nether Monkslip right away? I need you to fetch something for me. Let me call Mrs. Hooser first. Keep your fingers crossed she hasn't tossed it out."

Cotton didn't ask. He knew better than to question any request of Max's. All would be revealed in time.

Max, meanwhile, was thinking of Paul's telling the early Christians, "We see through a glass darkly." Certainly, that was exactly what he had been doing with regard to this case. There was the smallest light shining through now, however. He felt a prickling of his skin, as if he had walked into a spider's web.

And Max withdrew further into himself, as was his habit when troubled by a mass of information—apparently contradictory information that, given time, he knew would organize itself into a coherent pattern. A theory was taking shape in his mind, but the actors in this particular play stood in the shadows of the stage.

And one, he thought, might still be waiting in the wings.

Something about finding Lamorna made him think, too, of the way Lady Baynard had been found. Or was it *where* she had been found? These nagging thoughts that broke the surface of his mind quickly became submerged before he could grasp on to them.

Cotton stood watching him, as if he were a telly with the sound turned down.

"What exactly," Max asked, "were the terms of Oscar's will? Short version?"

"Oscar left the bulk of his money to his sister, a bit to his daughter Jocasta, a bit to the twins, the rest to various charities, including one for hedgehogs and one for donkeys. The legacies to his children were nicely calculated to prevent them from trying to challenge the will. Alec inherits the title."

"And Leticia?"

"Leticia left all her money to her children. Even Lamorna got a token amount. Well, token by this family's standards. There was a lot to go round."

"All the money in the world," Max said, "and they still felt their share wasn't enough."

He thought again of that furious little girl at the beach, of her suppressed rage. This would apply to Lamorna but it applied to Lester and Randolph and Gwynyth and even to Milo and Doris, as well, he realized—to all of them. They'd all been controlled, and kept under control, by Oscar's money, and Leticia's, and the promise of at least some of it coming to them one day.

"Let me call Mrs. Hooser now," said Max.

He had a brief conversation with his housekeeper, who wanted to launch into a long story about Luther the cat and Thea the dog (she thought they needed counseling), but Max cut her off.

"Thank you, Mrs. Hooser. Someone from the police will be by as soon as possible today. Have them call me from there, will you? And whatever you do, don't touch it, all right?"

Cotton looked at Max, the light in his pale eyes showing a dawning comprehension.

"You mean . . . ?"

"Yes."

"You can't be serious."

"I'm afraid I am. It's the only explanation that accounts for everything."

"Holy . . . What nerve! To think anyone could think they could get away with that . . . almost did, in fact."

"Imagine how I feel."

"All because of an apple," Cotton wondered, musingly.

"Not the first time it's been at the center of a major downfall."

"Hmm?" Cotton was still thinking through the ramifications and so was listening with only one ear.

"Adam and Eve," said Max.

"Ah. But—there's something more, isn't there? What's on your mind, Max? Tell."

"It's just that I wonder—"

Just then, Milo came walking by the window, snowblower at maximum volume.

"What was that? You wonder what?" asked Cotton.

"I said, 'Why Oscar, why now?'"

"Go on."

Reframing his thinking, Max said: "I am rather wondering at the timing of the death. After all, they were all hanging about the castle for ages, living well. Free room and board, on rather a grand scale. Free to come and go as they pleased, and to treat the place as a hotel. None of them were needy by the standards of the average person. Why did Oscar have to die when he did?"

Cotton looked mystified, as well he might.

"Surely the question is, why did he have to die at all?"

"No," said Max. "That is not the question." Rather annoyingly, he refused to say more. "I have a few questions I'd like to ask of the police doctor. With your permission."

For Max felt a growing unease. The carelessness of Lamorna's death—someone had barely had time to escape detection there.

"They are all clamoring to be let go," Cotton was saying. "And even with Lamorna's murder I'm running out of reasons not to let them go in a few more days. I think Wintermute put a flea in their ears about their rights in this situation."

"Lamorna's murder is problematic in many ways," said Max.

Cotton said, "Motive didn't appear to be a big question, until one excluded Leticia—the obvious person to gain by Oscar's death. It was always possible she was indeed the killer, and struck down in some biblical way for her crime soon after it was committed. Barring that explanation, that it was Leticia who did the killing, it is hard to see money as a motive for killing Oscar. They only had to wait awhile, after all, and so much of his money went to charity."

"Ah, but who knew that?" Max asked.

"No one who will admit to it now. And of course there is not a shred of evidence to connect Leticia with the killing. Which leaves us with revenge. Or blighted love (unlikely) and/or the good old crime reaching into the past, some misdeed from Oscar's youth in finance or sexual frolics, which leaves us with quite an old mess to sort out—a mess that might never *be* sorted out."

"Oh, it will be sorted out," said Max.

"I'm glad you're so confident," said Cotton. "I don't mind saying I'm not."

"There's one more inquiry I'd like you to make."

Cotton picked up the mobile again. This time the call was to headquarters. He relayed Max's request.

"They're on it," he told Max. "I think we already have that information in our files. It's just a matter of someone's searching."

"I need to call Awena," said Max.

Cotton, assuming this was a personal call, grinned widely at him, like the Cheshire Cat.

Max powered up his own mobile. Cotton was amused but not surprised to see he had Awena on speed dial.

She came on the line. In the background Max could hear Celtic music playing in the Goddessspell shop. He could picture her surrounded by amulets and talismans, the air rich with the aroma of herbs and perfumed oils and scented candles. She always smelled of the most exotic blend of everything beautiful in the world.

He asked her, "What was Leticia wearing that day you came to consult over her garden?"

"What was she *wearing*?" Awena repeated. "Max, it was ages ago. Let me think." Finally she said, "She looked like she was in mourning. You know, like someone wearing a beekeeper's costume, circa 1900—with some sort of a beekeeper's veil or perhaps a mosquito veil. It's why she was content to be outside but I was in danger of being stung to pieces and had to leave."

Max thanked her and rang off.

But first he said, blushingly conscious of Cotton's amused eyes on him: "I will see you very soon."

He turned back to his all-ears friend Cotton, who was busy trying without success to smother the smile.

"You will need to search the house and grounds again," Max told him. "This time, they're looking for a beekeeper's outfit. Try the hothouse."

"You've got it."

When Cotton ended this brief conversation, Max said, "On the day Oscar died, we know Milo found the body. Correct?"

Cotton nodded.

"And Milo went to tell Leticia, but he found her body instead."

"Correct," said Cotton.

Max sat for a long moment in thought. He eyed the bowl of fruit. "What I really want to know is, who told Leticia?"

"Hmm?"

"We've been thinking she may have died of shock or remorse over Oscar."

"Yes?"

"But we don't seriously believe she stabbed her brother to death, do we? There was no forensic evidence on her clothes or body to indicate she'd been involved in some maniacal rampage. But if she died of shock . . ."

Cotton was now smiling ear to ear. Max could easily imagine the lightbulb going on over his head as in a cartoon. "Who told her . . . ?"

"Precisely. Who told her Oscar was dead?"

CHAPTER 32

Castling

Max's fine gray eyes met all of theirs in turn. He knew this conversation was not going to be pleasant or easy. He had to plan each move to block in his prey, leaving no way out.

He'd asked Cotton to have them gather together in the library. It was one of Max's usual unorthodox, Poirot-y procedures but Cotton quickly had learned to give him his lead.

"Servants, too?"

"Oh, yes," said Max. "Milo hasn't told us everything yet."

The lack of a rush to flock to the library told of the suspects' uneasiness. It took them half an hour to straggle in. Milo and Doris arrived with trays of strong drink and glasses. It seemed like that sort of occasion.

They were soon strewn about the room, sitting in chairs or leaning against the library shelves: Randolph and Cilla. Lester and Felberta. Lady Jocasta Jones and Simon. Gwyn and the Twyns. The Vladimirovs.

"These were audacious crimes," Max began. "I must say that while I always felt a clever mind was at work, yet still I may have been guilty of underestimating my opponent. There was meticulous planning tied to flexibility in execution of the plan. No rigid thinking here—the 'mind map' allowed for improvisation and covered nearly every conceivable eventuality. There were even dress rehearsals and practices. Nothing was left to chance."

Lester and Felberta exchanged puzzled glances.

"But throughout, too many out-of-the-ordinary things happened that needed to be explained," continued Max. "Things that could only be explained once I stopped peering through the wrong end of the telescope."

Max breathed deeply and said, "Let's start with Oscar's illness. His poisoning. We can't ever be sure but I think the Christmas tree is a clue to what poisoned Oscar. Holly and mistletoe won't kill but they can make a person very ill, especially an elderly one. The point was to make it seem someone was after Oscar."

Jocasta looked around the group uncomfortably, for every head had swiveled toward her: It was "her" tree.

"I wonder which it was?" Max asked. "Holly or mistletoe? But again, the aim was to spread suspicion to the whole household, in case a doctor was brought in and collected samples for analysis. And then there was at least one other attempt on his life: Amanda mentioned some falling masonry that nearly killed him. These little torments were the lead-up to the main event.

"But what really misled investigators was *Leticia's* death."

"My mother's wasn't a natural death, after all? I thought so," said Randolph, as he turned to Amanda, next to him. "I *thought* so! It was too great a coincidence."

"It certainly was, but not in the way you mean." Max went on. "There had been an overinsistence throughout the investigation on the idea of Leticia's dying a natural death, an insistence that had come from the police, from all of those with knowledge and know-how. That very insistence misled me—I was trained to question every clue.

"But sometimes," he went on, "as Freud famously said, a cigar is just a cigar. The woman had died. And it was her death that had provoked the unnatural death of her brother."

The group looked at one another, mystified.

"What on earth are you talking about?" demanded Felberta. She began to fiddle nervously again with her necklace.

"Timing," said Max. "I'm talking about timing. The only reason the police thought Leticia died when she did is because of eyewitnesses who saw her alive, including me. The police doctors would naturally use that as a baseline, a starting point in their calculations. They never questioned it. The deaths were so close together there was no way to tell for certain and *no one questioned it.* Least of all me."

"You know," said Lester, starting to get up from his chair. "I'm a busy man. You'll have to stop talking in riddles or I'll have to leave."

"Sit down," said Cotton, and Sergeant Essex took a step nearer. She had to tilt her head back to stare him down, but Lester sat.

"This was all about the wills of the deceased, Oscar and Leticia," Max continued. "Leticia had some money of her own to dispose of, just not a lot. But if she outlived Oscar, she'd get a significant amount from him. Probably Oscar was fond of her, with that special bond most twins have. After all, they'd lived together for many years.

"The money she inherited from Oscar would transfer to her heirs—her children—at her death. But it is the *timing* of her death and Oscar's that made my train ride with Leticia crucial to the investigation. I had seen her *after* Oscar's death. She had outlived Oscar."

"Yes. So?" This was Gwynyth. "I saw her leave for the train that day myself. So did Milo. I daresay, so did several of us."

Max nodded and said, "There were clouds of witnesses, weren't there? I just kept wishing I'd paid more attention to her on the train. She was such a type, a fossilized scrap of nobility, the sort to be rather a plague to clergymen of all stripes—I'm afraid we tend to avoid the Lady Baynards of the world where possible. They always have perfectly impractical suggestions for how the church—their local church in particular—should be run, although they seldom set foot in church themselves. I tried to dodge her, I'm afraid, but in a tiny compartment there is no escape."

"Don't feel too bad. We've all run screaming from her at times," said Lester.

Max went on, "Then I realized, she *was* a type. A *type*, not a person."

"What do you mean?" asked Jocasta, suspiciously. She'd had more than one critic mention her tendency to play to type.

"I'll get to that in a minute," said Max. He lowered the timbre of his voice until it was a rumble, intimate and soothing. "Let's go back to when Leticia was found dead. *Before* Milo found her dead. Yes, someone else found her, and realized they would have to act fast to kill Oscar, with no more lead-in attempts to kill him and spread suspicion. No more rehearsals. It was time to raise the curtain."

"Before Milo . . . ?" this from Gwynyth.

Max held up one hand to forestall her. "It didn't really matter, of course, if one of the previous attempts on Oscar's life had been successful. It was perhaps by chance the early attempts were not, but there was all the time in the world. Then the day came when it was time to be in earnest."

"I'm not following this," said Alec. He turned to his sister. "Are you?" She nodded, a trifle smugly.

Max, who had been sitting in his usual chair, walked over to the fireplace. Resting one arm on the mantelpiece, he turned back into the room. He was enjoying himself now.

"You slipped up in several places," he said, but he was looking at the hearth rug, not at anyone in the room. "For example: That was not Lady Baynard's phone I heard on the train. She had a mobile that, according to the phone company records, was seldom used. For example, it did not receive a call on the day of her death.

That sort of record can be traced, and I asked DCI Cotton to have someone try to trace it. There was no record."

Max looked up suddenly. Seeing the trap into which she had unwittingly fallen, one of the group visibly shut down. It was one slipup in an otherwise flawless plan, thought Max.

"You called your accomplice from the station so this person would know you were there, that your presence as Leticia was being witnessed by many people, so your accomplice could now safely act to eliminate Oscar. That was why you had your own phone with you, wasn't it? The phone with the ringtone that was wholly unlikely and inappropriate for someone of Leticia's age and background."

Still Max met no one's eyes. Cotton and Essex, on the other hand, scanned each face in the room with an ardent, electrified awareness.

Max continued, "I eventually realized my first question should have been whether Lady Baynard owned a mobile phone in the first place. All of you have said how old-fashioned she was, and how resistant to change. She did own one, as it turns out, but it was not the one I heard. When that mobile phone rang it was quickly shut off. Too quickly, I realized later. Why? Because the song was not what an elderly woman like Leticia would set as her ringtone."

Jocasta said, with evident relief, "Well, don't look at me. Talking to me about high-tech gadgets is like talking to a rabbit about astrophysics. But what difference does it make? She came back from her shopping, went out into the garden, and died. What's her phone got to do with it?"

Max said, "It is true that Leticia was found in the hothouse by Milo. The woman on the train spoke to me of her plants, implying that her gardening was uppermost on her mind, and that she would go straight to the hothouse on returning to the castle. There was a reason for that misdirection.

"But first—there were lies told to DCI Cotton here. Let's clear those up first. For example, Milo claimed never to have met any of the members of this household before coming to work here."

Milo succumbed to the implied accusation without resistance and without evident concern. "Yes, I knew Gwynyth, Lady Footrustle. Gwynyth Lavener, as she was then. We were both part of the staff on a cruise of the Baltics. In my old country, one did not run about spouting the truth about what one knew at the first opportunity. Of course I recognized her here as one of the ship's performers. One would recognize her—she is memorable." Gwynyth visibly preened at this. "I doubt she recognized me. I was meant to be invisible on the ship; there to serve only. Just like here."

"It was foolish of you to lie to the police."

"Do you think so, sir? Where I come from, it is foolish to tell them the truth."

"I do see the problem," Max acknowledged. "The habits learned in youth are hard to break."

Milo nodded, looking to his wife, who gave him an encouraging nod.

"Then there were some misleading statements made about how you all came to be here," said Max. "Those were less serious lies. But for one of you to gin up a fake e-mail—you, Lester—that might have been over the top."

"I did not."

"You were the only one to receive such a message. It is inconceivable that Oscar would single you out for special treatment like that. If anyone got such a message, it would have been Randolph." Lester began reasserting his denial, and Max interrupted him: "Remember, that sort of thing is traceable."

"I didn't want to seem like a party crasher," Lester finally muttered. "That's all."

"For me the question remains," said Max, "of why he invited *any* of you here—especially since it led to his murder. I think Oscar wanted to get a sense of you, to decide once and for all on the disposal of his fortune, to remind himself of who and what you all were. Perhaps you'd changed. He got a sense all right, and soon made an appointment with his solicitor to change his will. I think a few of you would have been out of things soon."

Max added, "There was a further reason Oscar invited you, and this is the real shame of the situation. I do think there was this element: He was lonely. After a lifetime of ignoring all of you, he was lonely."

"I don't know about the rest of you, but he invited me because he was dying to see me," said Jocasta. She fluffed out her petticoats. "I don't know what it is about me; people positively throng about wherever I go in the world."

She gave the group a sunny smile. Felberta aimed a look at her, then turning to Lester said, without bothering to lower her voice, "I really am starting to think madness runs in this family."

They all exchanged glances, perhaps thinking the same thing.

Max cleared his throat and said, "Let's talk about another element I noticed—perhaps was meant to notice. There was a bit of a secret romance going on, wasn't there? Between Randolph and Gwynyth."

Those two exchanged glances. It was Randolph who said, "I fail to see how that's any of your business, even if it were true."

Judging by the look she gave him, it struck Gwynyth as news it was not true.

"Do you? You're experiencing a failure of belief? Very well," said Max. "Let me see if I can explain why it's my business."

He let a pause hang in the air, a pause timed with exquisite precision. It was only Lester, predictably, who began to squirm. There was an appreciable accretion of stiffness in the poses of the rest of them, as they waited, slowly freezing into a tableau.

"We've had large and small lies," said Max. "But through all of them I wondered why the story of Esau and Jacob was so much on my mind. It was on poor Lamorna's mind, too. It was a story of an enormous, cold-blooded deception. And it was a story of twins."

Amanda and Alec exchanged glances. With their special telepathy, they shrugged simultaneously, their expressions reflecting each other's.

"We had two sets of twins in this situation: Oscar and Leticia; Alec and Amanda. I put my fixation down to that. Twins often run in families, so there was nothing strange about it, and I tried to dismiss it from my reasoning as the minor point that it was. But what did factor in here is that Oscar was minutes older than his sister Leticia, just as Alec is a few minutes older than Amanda. And unfair as it may seem, it made Oscar's, and his son Alec's, position as the heir to the Footrustle title and entailed heirlooms unassailable.

"In leaving his 'liquid' fortune, his money, Oscar had a little more leeway in deciding who got what.

"But the *real* point of the tale of the twins Esau and Jacob was not precisely that they were twins, but the trickery used to secure an inheritance. Deception and disguise used to gain an inheritance.

"This type of trickery was what Cilla employed, posing as Lady Baynard."

CHAPTER 33

One Bad Apple

Max, turning to Randolph, said: "Your flirtation with Gwynyth, which you were careful to carry out in my view, was a decoy. The real love interest here is Cilla."

Gwynyth was actually startled out of her chair. She stood as if to flee. Cotton motioned her down.

"Don't be absurd," Cilla said, by contrast with Gwynyth completely unruffled. "I'm engaged to be married. I told you that."

She might not have spoken. Max went on: "Again, this is a story of deception. Of impersonation. I recalled how Cilla had imitated Lamorna as we sat talking after dinner. Cilla is a gifted mimic—as is Amanda, by the way. But someone realized this mimicry could be a clue for the police, her 'showing off' of this gift that played such a large part in the murder plot. Alec happens to have overheard this conversation, right, Alec? A couple arguing: 'Quit showing off' and 'You're overplaying your hand.' Why would anyone make such an issue of it? I think because it could give the whole game away.

"You, Cilla, and Randolph kept your close relationship secret because Cilla would remain unsuspected only if she did not seem to profit, if she was 'only' an assistant. Meanwhile, Randolph played up to Gwynyth, to mislead me and others. You two, Randolph and Cilla, worked out a story in advance, a story that Cilla was going away with her fiancé to a new job with an American photographer. All that checked out with the police. But you, Randolph, planned to join her. In New Mexico, where the chances were no one would connect you with this tragedy, especially if you lived in a remote part of the state, perhaps altered your appearance slightly. You'd be free to spend your money. Perhaps one day, after a few years of lying low, you'd be free to move on, to Europe or wherever you chose to live."

Randolph examined his nails and said casually, without looking up, "And your proof for this is—what again?"

Again, Max might not have heard. "I remember Jocasta's saying at dinner something about the actor Lon Chaney. The 'Man of a Thousand Faces.'"

Jocasta nodded earnestly. They were on to a topic about which she knew a thing or two. "He used makeup techniques that were revolutionary for the time. He was a genius."

"This conversation about Chaney came back to me," said Max, "as I pondered the fact there were two deaths in the family very close together, and why that was significant. It had to be significant but I couldn't put it together. Until I began to think in terms of disguise. If Lon Chaney could become the Phantom of the Opera, how hard would it be for someone skilled with makeup to make herself look older, helped by the recent fashion for ladies' veils?"

Cilla had been staring straight ahead, but she blinked almost imperceptibly on his last word.

"Now I asked myself who could pull off such a charade. Jocasta, the actress, was the obvious choice, but this was a role calling for subtlety, nuance, and fine shading, not the more bombastic style that is Jocasta's specialty."

Jocasta seemed to take this as a compliment, or perhaps was not really listening, preening and fussing as she was with the sparkly bracelet at her wrist. Or perhaps she didn't know what bombastic meant.

"It couldn't have been Lamorna," Max went on. "She was too large a person for the role. Padding out a thin person is possible but shrinking a large one—there are limits. The woman I sat with on the train had a small, cinched-in waist. Felberta was also the wrong build.

"That left Gwynyth and Cilla, Amanda being much too young to be a candidate for the role. Gwynyth was a possibility, although this was a specialized performance. She had been a dancer of sorts, but nothing in her background suggested the ability to act or impersonate."

"'Of sorts'?" Gwynyth interrupted. "What do you mean, 'of sorts'?" Her face hardened, losing its usual ingratiating simper. "I was ruddy good. Ask Milo."

Max said, "And that is when I recalled Cilla was a stylist, who worked doing hair and makeup in places such as Hollywood. Where they specialize in such special effects as aging—making stars look decades older. The way Brad Pitt in *The Curious Case of Benjamin Button* was made up to age backward in time. At dinner it was you, Cilla, who mentioned *Benjamin Button*. It won an Oscar for best makeup. Someone in your field would understand perfectly the reasons why. Possibly the mention of that movie was another of your little slipups that angered Randolph so."

Randolph gave Max a look of twisted scorn. "You're mistaken, Father Brown," he said.

"Not at all am I mistaken," Max said coldly. "Now, Gwynyth could have been made up by Cilla to play the role, a possibility I played with for a while. But the 'why' eluded me—the 'why' of their connection to each other. And again—you must pardon me, Gwynyth—this role would not call to your particular talents. It wasn't until Alec told me of an argument he overheard between a man and woman, and I considered that it might have been Cilla and Randolph quarreling, that the nature of their relationship became clearer. More than 'boss' and 'assistant.' Much more. It was not just a lovers' quarrel, either. The stakes were higher than that.

"The disguise was brilliant and thoroughly professional, Cilla, if you don't mind my saying so," said Max. "For example: Few people remember someone's eye color unless it's a startling color." An image of Awena's unusual violet eye color flashed from his memory. "But I did recall the color I could just glimpse through the veil—a striking blue. Cilla's eyes are a deep brown, and that threw me off. That she was the impersonator, much less that there *was* an impersonator, didn't occur to me as I spoke with her."

Max looked at them singly. "But wouldn't a clever killer use contact lenses? Yes, of course. And what does that tell you?"

It was Amanda who answered. "It tells you that she had lots of time to plan and prepare. There was nothing spur of the moment about what she did."

"Precisely what I thought, too," said Max.

"Nonsense," said Cilla. "A lot of people just like a change of eye color, just for fun."

Max, knowing he was right, didn't stay to argue the point.

"Do you know how to knit?" he suddenly asked her. She hesitated, clearly churning over how best to respond.

"Really, it's a simple question," said Max. "Yes or no. Do you know how to knit?"

"Yes, I do. Of course. So what? Most women know how to knit."

"I don't think that's actually true, you know. Nor do most men necessarily know how to change a tyre."

Doris piped up. "I never learned how to knit. Never tried to learn. Ruddy waste of time when Marks and Sparks has such nice woolens."

321

"The woman I met on the train was knitting some white, fluffy thing," said Max. "A blanket."

Cilla arched an eyebrow and looked pointedly at him. "So? First contact lenses, now knitting. Is this what you call evidence?"

"So, nothing," Max said, still with the same calm yet insistent demeanor. "It's just one more piece in the puzzle. The police found Leticia's knitting in the drawing room. You remembered to replace it. You thought of everything. Nearly."

He went on, Cilla watching him closely now. But he spoke to the group. "The woman I saw on the train wore a hat and scarf. The compartment was cold but really those items were just part of the disguise. Also, Cilla had something on her neck to hide: a butterfly tattoo. And of course she wore a gray wig. It was an impersonation that was not very difficult for an accomplished makeup artist."

"Leticia always looked ten years younger than she was, anyway," said Jocasta. "Have you ever noticed how often that is true of very difficult, selfish people? It's almost as if, having sucked all the life out of everyone around them, they erase years of wear and tear on themselves."

Simon looked at his wife with ill-disguised wonder: The lack of self-awareness was total.

Max was saying, "I talked with one of the experts in disguise at MI5, who is an old friend. She says nothing too dramatic like a complete latex mask would be required to achieve the appearance of an older woman—a ruse with a complete mask that has been attempted in recent years, by the way. Not too long ago a young man boarded a plane with a false ID, wearing a mask of a very elderly man. Only his hands gave him away. In this case, our imposter even thought to wear gloves. But the disguise technology today has improved beyond measure, so I'm told. Here, in this case, maybe a touch of latex was glued on to create wrinkles about the eyes, but mostly some shadowing, and a change in coloring, were all that were needed. Particularly since I had never met the original Leticia. Cilla used a wig, a scarf to cover her neck, and gloves for her hands, as I've said—always the main giveaway, says my expert: the hands. Cilla even pretended to have Leticia's cold, which came in handy—she could obscure her face with a handkerchief if she thought I was looking at her too closely.

"So Cilla, tell us: Precisely what was your job again at Ealing, and Pinewood, and in Hollywood?"

She paused for a long moment before answering. "Hair. Makeup. The same job as it is now. Prepping people to be photographed."

"No. It was a lot more than that. I asked DCI Cotton earlier for a little more detail on your job description. It wasn't just hair and makeup. Drucilla Petrie specialized in the rarified field of special effects."

In a Florentine gesture of operatic surprise, Jocasta threw up her hands and tossed back her head (Janne Endive, *What the F**k Was That?*—a film title that had reviewers competing to guess what other titles had been rejected in its favor). *"Special effects!"* she gasped. It was the insane type of performance perfected in the days of the silent film, thought Simon. One wondered how cretinous the audience in those days had to have been, how starved for diversion—any diversion. He smiled and patted his wife's hand. It was best to keep her calm if possible.

Max waited until the other eruptions of astonishment and outrage died down. He turned to the others one by one as he spoke. "Cilla—Drucilla—was in the makeup department. She was understandably a bit vague when talking with the police about what she did at the studios. But her job did not involve making people look pretty for the camera, as it does now, but aging them or otherwise altering their appearance drastically—attaching horns and snaggleteeth to monsters and so forth. The person I spoke with at MI5 called it the zombie department, because it's where they zombie-fy the characters. It's more lucrative than what she's doing now for Randolph, requiring extraordinary levels of training and expertise, so I wondered why she gave it up. It sounds as if she was pushed rather than jumped—she 'had artistic differences' with several of the directors—and was a bit at loose ends when Randolph took her on. Maybe even then he saw the possibilities—foresaw a day when she might be useful. Who knows? Maybe they planned to put Lady Baynard in the frame for the murder, by having her—or Cilla dressed as her—be seen fleeing the scene. I'd say that's likely but proving that will be the very devil. All we can say for certain is that the best-laid plans and hopes of Randolph and Cilla went awry when Lady Baynard died first, and they had to act quickly—put Cilla into the long-ago prepared costume, and send her out as Lady Baynard, while Randolph stayed behind to do the real dirty work of stabbing his uncle. Stabbing a defenseless old man while he slept, I might add. It really *was* a dirty job, a despicable act.

"You, Cilla, used the train to create an alibi, because despite the eccentricities of the local train schedule, the stationmaster at least always notes the time of departure and arrival. I imagine you even created some sort of commotion, an official complaint about the service, so you'd be remembered.

"So, Lady Baynard was 'alive.' Her distinctive hairstyle and the netted hat and traveling garb made her easy to impersonate. People see what they expect to see. It was your good luck to run into me, but it didn't really matter. You only needed someone reputable and you would have latched on to anyone vaguely fitting that description.

"Leticia had a reputation as a bit of a recluse because she avoided the villagers. However, she entertained lavishly when it was someone she deemed important, Doris told me. Meaning: Someone from London. But she'd feuded with the villagers in the past and as far as they were concerned she kept to herself; no one could have sworn to her exact recent appearance.

"You, Cilla, even talked with me on the train about the hothouse since you knew that was where the body already was, and where it would be found later, once you'd safely returned and gotten out of costume."

The others, one by one, had inched their faces around to look at her, taking in her general size and appearance. Those who knew

Leticia best seemed slowly to be admitting the possibility of what Max was saying: "It is possible for a younger woman to imitate an older one. Impossible for an older woman to imitate a much younger one, especially the walk, the spring in the step. It is easy for a younger woman to imitate an older one who walks with difficulty. I should know—I felt and looked one hundred years old using that crutch.

"But covering all the bases, you used Awena for your dress rehearsal. An habitué of the sound stage and the theater, you wanted a dress rehearsal, didn't you, Cilla? A dry run. If it didn't work, the impersonation could all be passed off as a joke.

"Again, anyone would do for your purposes. But it was Awena who met you on your dry run on the train. You actually invited her to the house—that could have been a step too far, but it came off beautifully, reinforcing the idea in Awena's mind that she had met Lady Baynard of Chedrow Castle. When I compared notes with Awena, our descriptions of the person we met matched. Of course, neither of us had met the real Leticia.

"So Cilla arranged for Awena to visit Leticia on a day Leticia was gone, or perhaps bedridden with one of her ailments, ostensibly so Awena could share her renowned knowledge of plants, particularly medicinal. Why wouldn't Awena believe Lady Baynard had it in mind to plant a special garden of such plants and wanted to take Awena's advice? But your idea was in part to reinforce that the imposter—you, Cilla—were the real Lady Baynard so later descriptions from people like me, from those outside the family, would match more closely. It was a risky ploy, even an unnecessary gilding of the lily, but you were using Awena as a practice witness. Randolph, who is clearly the more cautious of the two of you, may also have been angry with you, Cilla, over this ploy which he saw as unnecessary and risky. And this was a part of the argument Alec later overheard.

"But once you set this in motion, Randolph had to play along to ensure that you weren't caught out. Randolph escorted Awena to the garden where he introduced her to the fake Leticia. Again, this was to establish what 'Leticia' looked like for future use. Cilla dressed as Leticia wore gardening gloves and a veil to blur her face.

"As to alibis: What mattered were alibis for the time of Oscar's murder. Now, Cilla would make sure she was in the clear for that. I'm sure she showed herself *as* herself in Staincross Minster, then slipped back into her Leticia disguise. This explains in part why she was traveling with such a large bag—she had to carry around a change of clothing. But Randolph had no alibi for the time of Oscar's death. That was the risk he had to take—no one else had an alibi for that time, either. So long as he left no incriminating evidence to link him to the crime, the authorities could not legally single him out.

"But you two also gave yourselves some leeway with the time of death. It would be warm and humid in the hothouse, affecting the coroner's estimates. You probably hid her body under a tarp, just in case of anyone's walking by and peering in the window. This had the bonus effect of helping keep her body warm, making her death appear to be more recent, and fudging the time of death for investigators."

"I'm not hearing anything that sounds like proof," said Randolph.

"Ah," said Max. "I'm so glad you asked. Now we arrive. When I was with the fake Leticia, she had a little mishap with her belongings, and the contents of her shopping spilled everywhere. One apple inadvertently ended up in my pocket. Earlier I sent the police to fetch it from the vicarage, and mercifully it was still there and undisturbed. That is to say, the fingerprints on it were undisturbed: It's a good thing for us you were wearing gloves after you first handled it, Cilla."

They all looked at each other, mystified. But two of them, Max noted, had turned a whiter shade of pale.

"You see," said Max, "the imposter did not have time actually to shop, not with all the changes of costume she had to deal with in the ladies' room at the station, and so she carried shopping with her *from the castle and onto the train.*

"Let's trace the sequence of events. The impersonator has gone by taxi to Nether Monkslip, and from there by train to Staincross Minster and back again. Since ostensibly she was shopping, she carried from Staincross Minster an old-fashioned string bag full of a mixture of things from the chemist's and other shops. But she has brought those items with her—stuffed into her pockets as she left the castle, or into that large bag. But the fake Leticia did *not* visit the shop she claimed to me to have visited. She simply did not have time. Not if Cilla had to make a point of showing herself around as Cilla, to establish an alibi."

"You could not possibly know who bought what where," said Cilla, starting to rise. "I'm not going to sit and listen to more of this."

Sergeant Essex stood. "Actually, you know, I think you are."

"Your downfall was an apple," said Max. "And this is why and how: The apple I picked up on the train had a sticker label on it—one of those bar codes. Those numbered codes reveal a date and place of origin of the apple. You can even look it up on the Internet. You, Cilla, had taken fruit from the bowls that Doris set out at the castle—either from breakfast, or from the bowl kept in here." He indicated the glass bowl by the armchair. "The date on this particular label on this particular apple showed it was an apple that had gone on sale a week ago."

"You have got to be kidding me . . ." said Cilla, but her expression was increasingly wary. For the first time, she stole a glance at Randolph.

"The store mentioned by the fake Leticia on the train was Fast Freddie's Market. Now, as it happens, Fast Freddie's had sold out of its apples the day before, and on the morning of the murder had received all new stock. Cilla, where you put your foot in it was by claiming to have gone to Fast Freddie's Market, which was nearest the station. That apple came *not* from Fast Freddie's but from somewhere else. And we can prove it."

Doris piped up: "I would never shop at Fast Freddie's. They sell rotten fruit coated in pesticides." She clearly took umbrage at the very idea. "I only shop for produce at Manfree's. They sell fine, *fresh* produce. Organic. Local grown."

"The apple that fell out of your bag," said Max, "the apple I picked up on the train, was sold by Manfree's."

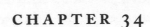

CHAPTER 34

Cliff-hanger

A dead silence seeped into the room. Someone coughed, a gentle cough that reverberated against the vaulted ceiling, echoing back into the quiet room.

It was Lester who finally spoke. "What's all this got to do with Lamorna's being killed, then?"

"What do *you* think?" said Amanda. "Lamorna never could mind her own business. And she didn't have the sense to stay out of something as dangerous as this situation was." She turned to Max. "Am I right?"

"I'm afraid so," said Max. "Lamorna's snooping about had everything to do with her need to control things and people. If she could keep tabs on what was going on, she felt more secure in her little universe. This is true of all of us, but Lamorna was such an outsider, she felt spying and prying were the only way to gain the control she craved.

"Lamorna was killed only in part because she saw Cilla and Randolph going to meet up at the Old Kitchen. She also saw Cilla (in her Leticia disguise) returning from the train journey she shared with me, and going into Cilla's room. Then she overheard quarreling. It was just odd, she thought at first—she was not alarmed. She said something to me about it at dinner. Only later did she connect Cilla with two unusual occurrences, and decide to try a spot of blackmail.

"Here's the part I missed, which was what Lamorna actually saw and heard the day of the two deaths. What she saw was Cilla returning from the train *dressed as Leticia*. Once I knew I was dealing with an imposter, it could only be an imposter—Cilla—going into her own room. And, fearing Lamorna would either recognize her dressed in costume, or would wonder at seeing Leticia entering Cilla's room, Cilla—thinking fast, knowing she'd been spotted— simply closed the door into her room and started a fake quarrel 'with herself,' so Lamorna would think Leticia was still alive. Remember that Cilla is a gifted mimic.

"Lamorna told me what she'd seen and heard—rather, what she *thought* she'd seen and heard. And once again I was half listening, not understanding the import, or that what she saw and heard *was* important, until after Lamorna was killed. Then there was a skirmish among the ladies at the table and I forgot all about it. I imagine Lamorna did, too. Then later than night, Lamorna was killed."

Max said, "There was one further thing, an odd thing: It was as I was standing at the top of the cliff with DCI Cotton this morning that I thought how easy it would have been for someone to dispose of Lamorna that way. And the question then occurred to me: Why was Lamorna not pushed over into the water—which could have been done pretty much at the killer's convenience? The easiest thing in the world would be to lure her out there, and just give her a nicely timed shove. Could it be she was killed in a place where she'd be *guaranteed* to be found so there would be no question about money from her grandmother going to her? Otherwise, why not just push her into the sea to drown? A much easier, much surer method. Quieter, also. But her body *had* to be found. The killers wanted no delays or legal entanglements, which would happen if she simply disappeared."

Max sighed. "It's a sad tale all around. The night she died, she'd been spying on Cilla and Randolph, and had followed them to the Old Kitchen tower with its upstairs bedroom. That's where they met to conduct their affair, and to discuss what to do next. It was private, unlike the castle, which was too full of ways to be seen and overheard, as Alec and Amanda know well. Lamorna followed at least one of them there—Cilla or Randolph—and one of them followed her back. Probably Randolph.

"The note Lamorna was clutching—'D' was signed on the note. Cilla can be short for Drucilla, as well as Priscilla. Or Cecilia. But Drucilla is what it happens to stand for in this case. 'Meet me at the OK at midnight. [Signed] D.' Old Kitchen. It explains how Lamorna knew where to look for you. She found that note, or possibly she even went through the things in your room and found it.

"I think Lamorna then tried some blackmail, not for herself but for some cause she was fond of. It was the way her mind worked. We may yet find proof of that hidden among her effects. She may have written down what she thought, what she saw."

Randolph's mind was clearly racing. "This is absurd!" His expression of contempt exaggerated the aristocratic cragginess of his features.

Max decided to press him. "You've had both good and bad luck. It would normally have been Father Arthnot who dealt with comforting the bereaved here at the castle. My presence here reinforced the success of your plan, of the impersonation. In all sincerity, I kept telling the police I saw Leticia alive."

Randolph had shut down for the moment into a mulish silence. He studied the expensive old carpet with a sudden intensity, as if he'd never seen it before.

"You were counting on 'luck' quite a lot—two aging people, both with weakening constitutions. Statistically speaking, Oscar the male should have gone first. But luck was not on your side then, was it?"

"How could I have known my mother would die?" demanded Randolph. "I couldn't possibly. This is preposterous."

"I asked myself that very question. Whoever did this had to have acted very quickly indeed. It couldn't have been done without some planning and preparation. Some very cold-blooded calculation, in fact. For you, everything rode on Leticia's outliving her brother. You or Cilla found Leticia dead in the hothouse—anyone else would have raised the alarm, not kept her death a secret.

"Randolph, those solicitous daily visits that Simon commented on—your deep concern, your spending as much time as possible in her company—all that was nothing more than to make sure she was still living, wasn't it? The buzzer installed by her bed—at your insistence. Why not a buzzer by Oscar's bed, too, I wondered? *Because when he died didn't matter*—Leticia's inheriting from him was all that mattered.

"Then one morning, your worst fear came to pass. She died first—*before* Lord Footrustle. But, thanks to Cilla, you had prepared for the unlikely eventuality that your mother would die first.

"And you, Cilla, like some modern-day Lady Macbeth, sent Randolph out to kill Lord Footrustle while you donned your disguise to establish 'proof' that Leticia had outlived her brother."

"I did not," said Cilla. Her voice was brittle, its normally smooth cadences crackled with heat. She compressed her lips until they all but disappeared. Suddenly, unwittingly she burst out, "It was his—"

Randolph rounded on her, his look warning her to silence.

"It was his idea?" said Max. "Really? Well, I don't suppose it matters."

He noticed calmly that Randolph was in the grip of strong emotion. Years of concealing his feelings briefly won out, but his face was red, flooded with the effort of suppressing the anger and self-pity. Max could have sworn his eyes were moist—not with tears for his mother or Oscar, of course, but for himself.

Randolph's voice rose to an unattractive bleat.

"It was easy," Randolph said, "because the old man was asleep. He didn't suffer. Neither of them suffered. They *never* suffered. They only made everyone around them suffer."

Ignoring the warning looks from Cilla, he began his tale, and a self-absorbed little tale it was, of his neglect as a child by his mother and Oscar. Max listened closely: He knew the ego of men like Randolph, their weak spot, could never be underestimated. Once given the impression that someone was hanging on their every word, their defenses came down. Listening cost nothing, and it worked—almost without fail, it worked in any tense, high-stakes situation, Max knew. Lester began to stir and Max gave him a look that telegraphed, *Be quiet*. He then leaned in to be sure Randolph knew he had his complete attention.

"His contempt for me was the grain of sand in the oyster shell—it irritated, but it created in me a pearl of excellence, and of resistance to tyranny," Randolph was saying.

Whoa. Max, listening to the grandiosity of the words, wondered if it weren't the signs of a megalomania kept well hidden.

"We quarreled. Oscar and I quarreled. We always seemed to quarrel. And then Oscar 'suggested' I leave as soon as the holidays were over. The nerve. Giving me the bum's rush. As if I weren't as entitled to be here—more entitled—than the rest of them."

In a low, moving voice, the voice of persuasion and encouragement he was often called on to use, Max said: "And then Leticia died."

"Yes. We might not have done it. Gone through with it. But when she died . . ."

"It pushed you over the edge, didn't it?" asked Max. "You could have turned back at any time, even after the attempted poisoning. But when she died, you knew she had died with almost no money of her own. She had to inherit Oscar's money or you would end up with very little."

"If my father hadn't lost it all, been such a loser . . ."

"Let me be sure I'm hearing you correctly," said Max, deciding to pile the flattery on, layer upon layer. "Because I think it was brilliant, the way you thought on your feet here. Your mother died a natural death during the early morning hours. She would often go out to her hothouse, regardless of weather—that was her routine. But her death moved up the planned timeline, so Oscar had to be murdered. And Cilla had to don the disguise you were planning to use as an alibi if needed. That planning for any eventuality really paid off, didn't it?"

Randolph seemed to glory in the attention, the acknowledgement of how clever he'd been.

But Cilla had pulled away from him. It was an imperceptible shift in body language but Max thought that when questioned separately she would let Randolph fend for himself. She seemed to be drawing on her great reserves of will to survive.

"I think, too, Randolph, that you realized dying people are a soft touch. Perhaps over the years you worked on Oscar, persuading him to leave more money to Leticia. The strategy didn't entirely work—he left millions to charity and you couldn't talk him out of that."

"All that money left to good causes," said Randolph bitterly. "Donkeys, for god's sake. I think he had less a fondness for the poor and for animals than a willingness to shaft his family."

"Perhaps there was an element of that," said Max mildly. "I don't think he was the happiest of men, despite his wealth and success.

"But there is another element here, since you've shown yourself to be, shall we say, quick to react, Randolph. I personally wonder how long Lester and his wife had to live if by chance Lester left any of his inheritance to you in his own will. Perhaps Lester could have been persuaded in time to do so."

At this, Lester and Felberta exchanged startled glances, then their heads turned, as if tethered to the same string, to look at Randolph.

"Wait a minute," said Felberta. "You're saying . . ."

"I'm saying if Leticia died first, as it happens she did, she had little money of her own to leave anyone. The bulk of Oscar's money on his later demise would go to charity, with some smaller amounts to his children—Jocasta and the twins." He added to himself but did not say aloud: *And* by extension to Lamorna—Jocasta's natural issue. It was Jocasta's secret and Lamorna's. He was leaving it to Cotton whether any of that information had to come out as part of the case.

"Yes, your mother died first," Max said to Randolph and Lester, "leaving behind for you and her grandchild mere coins in comparison with Oscar's wealth. The situation for you, Randolph, was unbearable. You'd done what you could to persuade Oscar to your way of thinking. I would bet you hated him for refusing to bend entirely to your will. So killing him became almost a pleasure, didn't it?"

Randolph's eyes darted about, glancing off the onlookers, who viewed him with varying degrees of astonishment, distaste, and dislike. Then his eyes turned to Cilla, seeking assurance from his partner. But there was no consolation to be had from that quarter, either, noted Max.

"I wondered a bit why there was an insistence on Alec as a prankster, a bad kid," said Max. "You both, Randolph and Cilla, spoke of him like this. It was very subtly done, but it was there. Were you trying to set him up as a suspect? I think so. He, after all, was the one to gain a title and money from his father's death."

Jocasta suddenly turned on Randolph in a fury: The penny had dropped. "You were trying to cheat me," she said. Taking in the enormity of this, she put down her glass, as if to bring a sober mind to bear on the situation. "To cheat all of us."

Randolph gave his cousin a cool, insolent, yet quizzical stare. How, he seemed to say, did this person come to be here? He merely said, "The older generation owes it to the younger to get out of the way."

Max found that comment especially provocative. It was his own uncle that the man had dispatched without a moment's hesitation. Max drew upon every vestige of self-control that he had stored in his considerable armory, saying merely, "Your uncle was a vigorous and healthy man who may have had ten or even twenty good years left to him. You robbed him of those years.

"Money means different things to different people," Max went on, looking at each of them in turn. "Love, given or withheld. Security. The freedom to pursue the goals one holds most dear. There's nothing wrong with having or wanting money but wanting it too much for the wrong reasons can be a sign of sickness, as it is here.

"But there was this, too: Randolph has a clear sentimental attachment to the castle, and knows a lot of its history. I believe this was part of the motivation. The castle was as much his as Alec's, he reasoned, and it is an irreplaceable bit of history. He wanted to be sure he had the wherewithal to help make decisions as to how it was run in the future. Perhaps to try to influence Alec when and where he could. That wouldn't be possible if he had to grub around making a living from his photography."

"You don't understand what it's like," said Randolph.

"So, tell me."

After a long silence, Randolph said: "They look down their noses at you, the people of our class, if you've only a title and no money." Randolph, staring at Max, who was "robbing" him of all he'd worked so hard to achieve, uttered this almost inaudibly, a guttural rumble of frustration. Cilla maintained her composure. Only the concentrated stillness of her posture revealed her anxiety. Max imagined this was the usual distribution of emotion between the pair.

When Randolph again began to speak, it was with a complete switch in mood. Max wondered for the first time if perhaps he used drugs, and was high or low on something now.

"I was actually with Leticia when she died," he said. His voice was a dull monotone. And then he added with a sort of wooden smile, "She was in the middle of trying to show me some stupid plant or other she was so fond of." Again the note of self-pity crept in. "Fonder than she was of me."

"So," said Max, "your first thought when your mother actually died was of concealing the death—of the inconvenience to you that she had predeceased your uncle."

Even Randolph seemed to realize this was not his finest moment. "If you want to put it like that," he snapped. "This is nothing but trickery and grandstanding. You won't get away with it."

Max thought that was rich, coming from a man with all the personal integrity of a banana republic dictator. He said, with a spurt of anger, "Clearly this eventuality had occurred to you long before, judging by the rapidity with which you swung into action. There was always a chance, with two elderly people so nearly identical in age, that it would be impossible to call which one might go before the other. And that eventuality haunted you, meaning, as it might do, so many millions slipping through your hands. You had thought through this quite often, I'm sure. And when it did actually happen, and you happened to be with her, you didn't hesitate to act. You put in place your plan B. I would imagine you'd dwelled on and brooded over this for many years. Since the twins came along, in fact."

Randolph said, "That creepy old man and his child bride. Oscar's marriage, obscene cliché that it was, changed everything for the rest of us. The arrival of twins changed everything."

"I can see that it would," Max said. There was the odd note of what almost sounded like compassion in his voice, but then he added, with all the force of his personality, "What was it you just said about the old having to make way for the young? By the way, tell me: When did you plan to ditch Cilla? Don't tell me you planned to split this fortune with her."

From Cilla's expression, she was already aware that her partner in murder might prove to be an unreliable partner in life.

"It raises the stakes, murder," said Max to Cilla. "But Randolph was already showing signs that a fortune shared by two was . . . half a fortune. He'd gotten you to do what he wanted, to carry the lion's share of the risk, it could be said. And now perhaps he was reneging? It would be small wonder if you, Cilla, simply lost it, as they say. If you were pushed past all reason. If you told the police everything you knew to save yourself."

Cilla seemed to warm to this sympathetic view of her motives. But she maintained her silence. Draped sullenly over her chair, and with her thin figure in its black dress and ultra-high heels, Cilla was suddenly looking like a spider caught in its own web. She looked tired and drawn beneath the masklike makeup, like a woman waiting on a kidney transplant.

"I would say you had Cilla dead to rights, especially with

those fingerprints," said her fine-weather lover. Randolph stood. "But I have to say her impersonation of my mother was perfect, even to the old-fashioned phrases she used, and to the way she held her head, nose high in the air." He said this apparently unaware he tended to hold his own head in the same way.

And suddenly, Randolph made a lunging grab at Amanda, pulling her to him. Planting one hand under her chin, the other atop her head, he said, "Anyone comes near me, I'll twist her head off her neck." He began dragging the terrified, struggling girl toward the open doorway. Her mother Gwynyth screamed but remained frozen in place. Alec made as if to follow and Randolph made a violent, wrenching gesture to show he intended to carry through on his threat. Max grabbed the boy and held him back.

Amanda began to make a gasping sound as she clawed at Randolph's hands, a sound harsh and loud against the stunned silence of the room. It was the sound of someone choking and it seemed to have nothing to do with Randolph's chokehold on her neck. Her eyes frantically sought out those of her twin, desperate to communicate.

Alec said, quite loudly and clearly, "She has severe asthma, cousin Randolph. *Please* let her go. She's no use to you. *Let her go.* She'll die in minutes without her inhaler." He made a gasping sound himself and repeated, "She's no use to you. She'll only hold you up."

It stopped Randolph, who clearly had no idea what to do— Amanda was indeed useless to him now. She began to kick and thrash about, her mouth wide as she fought for air. The girl's rasping cries were harsh in their ears as Alec made a frantic leap to save his twin, propelling himself across the room at the same moment Max, Cotton, and Essex made a dive for Randolph's knees. His inarticulate grunts of frustration suddenly turned into a howl of anger.

Randolph threw the girl from him. She spun across the room from the force, arms windmilling to catch her balance. Sergeant Essex, catching her, put an arm around her shoulders, noticing that her hysterical, grating breathing had abruptly ceased. Had the girl been faking? Amanda looked up at her with gratitude. Apparently so.

Randolph, meanwhile, had bolted for the door, Max and Cotton in pursuit. Randolph disappeared up the stairs, headed toward the courtyard. Both men saw him as he disappeared under the archway into the garden.

"He must be headed for the cliff path," Max shouted. "There's no other exit from the garden." He turned back to Cotton. "Go the other way. Head him off." And he indicated with one arm a U-turn around the castle, where a steep set of stairs led down to the cliff. It was gated but an agile man could just climb over it.

Max saw the gate from the garden standing open, confirming his hunch. He shot through and caught up with Randolph on the cliff's ledge. He was peering over the edge, gathering his nerve to jump. Randolph looked up at Max's approach; Max tried to outstare him but Randolph looked away, his intent plain. Grabbing him by the collar and pulling him round, Max pulled back a fist and delivered an uppercut to the chin. He thought he'd knocked him out but Randolph struggled to his feet groggily, looked straight at Max, and took a swing. Instinctively Max ducked into a crouch. Randolph lost his balance, and like a tumbler took a dive over Max's back. As Max stood, Randolph lost his footing at the edge and slipped on the loosened dirt and rock, screaming as he barely grasped the ledge with one hand, the other hand flailing uselessly in the air. Suddenly, faced with the certainty of death, Randolph wanted to live.

Max grabbed him by the arm. He felt and heard a sickening crunch as Randolph's arm pulled out of its socket. The screams were deafening.

Max experienced another stomach-turning moment when the combination of his own weight with Randolph's nearly propelled both men over the edge. He looked over the precipice with flayed nerves. Still he held on. His free arm waving as if he were caught in some macabre rodeo act, and his stomach lurching from the view of hell below, Max tried and failed to grab Randolph's other hand. Finally, Max heaved himself backward with all his might, hauling Randolph's dead weight with him. Regaining his center of gravity at last, still Max fell against his weakened ankle at an angle; the shock of the pain further jolted him backward, just saving him from joining Randolph in a headlong plunge onto the rocks below. Max sat hard against the ground with a thump—anything to take the pressure off those shrieking tendons. Still he held on to Randolph's arm.

Randolph let out another piercing scream and then was silent. He'd passed out from the pain.

Better than dead, Max thought. One day you'll thank me. Maybe.

Cotton came running from the opposite direction at a gallop, followed by Essex and a swarm of constables.

The fabled career of Randolph, Viscount Nathersby, was history.

CHAPTER 35

Good King Wenceslas

Randolph and Cilla were dispatched quickly. Cotton and his team gave every appearance of scooping them up and removing them like unwanted parcels, which in fact, Max supposed, is what they were.

As to the rest, they were all sorting themselves out. Some going, some staying. Jocasta and Simon had announced almost immediately that they would leave. Actually, Jocasta had announced it. Simon's stony silence indicated to Max they might not be in harmony on this decision.

Amanda and Alec had convinced their mother they'd been away from civilization too long. They came to the library to wish Max well, Amanda clearly in the bloom of health.

"I see the asthma attack has passed," said Max.

She smiled broadly.

"We thought you were going to be an old stodge and try to convert us," said Alec.

"I gave up forcible baptisms some time ago," said Max with a grin. "It caused too much backlash in the end."

"You're all right," said Amanda.

"I think," Max said, "you'll do well. Just don't think of joining MI5, will you? You'd be brilliant. But there's a cost."

Amanda shook her head determinedly.

"Not me. But I may open my own PI service."

DCI Cotton came back into the room just then. The twins politely shook both men's hands and left to start their packing.

"We were led astray, weren't we?" said Cotton.

"Question authority. Question the evidence of your own eyes. Question everything," said Max. "When will I learn?"

"Actually, I'd say you were quite good at questioning everything. You got us there."

Max shook his head. "But not in time to save Lamorna. We were led deliberately astray by Randolph and Cilla, of course, coupled with the 'evidence' of my own eyes. What we thought we knew to be true was confirmed by the medical evidence—which in a Catch-22, was using my own eyewitness testimony as a baseline. And yet there was nothing medical to contradict what I said. Also we had Awena's descriptions of Leticia—her manner and way of dressing. It all added up, but then as the facts accumulated, I could see it added up to the *wrong number.*

"Oscar left a fortune to Leticia to dispose of as she wished. *Her* will left nearly everything to her children but no one looking into the murder of Oscar was concerned about *her* will; they thought it didn't matter."

"It was a daring impersonation," said Cotton. "But at almost any point, if Cilla had been caught out, she could have passed it off as a joke, an elaborate charade, something done on a dare, perhaps. But no one really takes time to question or really to see things, do they? Particularly in a train station, when they're rushing about anyway."

"Just as Churchill bore a certain resemblance to Queen Victoria in her later years," said Max. "Part his hair in the middle and put a scarf on his head—you'd never know the difference. Again, people see what they expect to see."

"As to Lamorna—can we be quite certain she wasn't killed for her inheritance?"

"That could have been a factor, but I doubt it. I don't think anyone but Jocasta knew, and she wasn't going to tell anyone. I did briefly consider once I knew what their relationship was that she could have killed Lamorna to increase her own share, but no, thank God, that didn't happen. But Oscar's will talks about natural issue—meaning Jocasta's legitimate or illegitimate child, just covering the bases in legalese. Lamorna inherited along with Jocasta, or would have done."

Max reflected on the irony that the despised Lamorna was a Footrustle, even if born on the wrong side of the blanket.

"So Gwynyth was the only one to lose out on the inheritance," said Cotton. "That must sting."

"Don't worry about her," said Max. "She'll live to be one hundred and she's got all she needs, if she'd but realize it. Still, she's a survivor, that one. And I think her children will look out for her. It's almost as if the roles are reversed there. They are already more adult than their mother, and they know it. And I think more forgiving, luckily for her."

"Oscar fooled them all in the end, didn't he? The poor benefited, and the guilty will now be punished. Very Dickensian."

Max nodded. "A bit like Scrooge, Oscar developed a sudden fondness for the poor over a wish to pass along all of his wealth to family, most of whom he held in no high regard. Or maybe like Good King Wenceslas he was a saint at heart, to begin with."

"He actually left five hundred thousand pounds to a local

man named Jake Sloop—I gather he's a local character who collects wood to sell as firewood," said Cotton. "It was a drop in the bucket for Oscar but it will certainly change Sloop's life."

"Nice." Max quoted: "'Ye who now will bless the poor, Shall yourselves find blessing.' In any event the money will be well received by the charities. Too bad he didn't remember St. Edwold's while he was at it."

Cotton stopped in the process of packing up his briefcase to stare at Max.

"You didn't know? Didn't Wintermute say? St. Edwold's is to receive the interest from two hundred thousand pounds, in perpetuity. For the roof fund."

Max stared at him, speechless.

"I don't suppose we ever told Wintermute you were the vicar of St. Edwold's. I just told him your name. It would appear you were a suspect all along, Max. But a minor one."

❄ ❄ ❄

Somehow Max felt that the pair, brother and sister, were watching from above with grim satisfaction. The orthodoxy of his theology may have been on shaky ground, and it wouldn't be for the first time, but it was a feeling he couldn't shake off—a feeling of being watched by very old eyes. The castle seemed to do that to him.

He needed to start packing and was most anxious to get back to the village. Passing through the Great Hall, he ran into Simon, and recalled that there might be unfinished business there.

"You and Jocasta will be returning to the States now, I take it?" said Max.

"Jocasta will. As for me, I am not certain how long I can sit through another seven-hour waxen performance on another low-budget stage set."

Max, who suspected as much, still felt there was a bond in the relationship that was worth saving. "You never had dreams of your own?" he asked.

"Dreams?" Simon repeated, as if he'd forgotten the meaning

of the word. "To tell you the truth, my dream was to marry a rich woman. I guess I peaked early."

"She's richer still, now that we've got the wills sorted."

"I know. And I thought that would solve everything. But now I'm wondering: Is it enough to make a life?"

"It's what you make of it. Besides, being with someone who needs you is a powerful tie. I don't see Jocasta lasting very long without you. You know she drinks too much as it is."

"I know. Don't think I don't know I'm needed."

"But you need a life beyond being her caretaker," said Max. "Don't you?"

"Yes. Just not as an actor. It's unconscionably hard to think of another job where thinking about yourself all day is a key part of the required skill set." He paused and said, "It's incredible. I once considered Jocasta to be a great catch. What kind of person does that make me?"

"To be honest, I think you're wrong to feel that way. She needs you. You need her. So long as it harms no one, what is wrong with that arrangement?" said Max.

"I think it's harming me," said Simon. "I don't like the person I'm becoming. Tell me the truth: Was she a prime suspect for this? I have to admit, I considered it a real possibility." Simon realized he'd gotten so used to covering for his wife he hadn't noticed when his moral compass had shifted completely out of whack.

"They were all suspects," said Max neutrally. He didn't add that the ferocity of the crime also had made him think that Jocasta, coming completely undone over some triviality, was more than capable.

Simon was saying, "I have been thinking I might try to write a screenplay about all this. I know at least some of the right people in Hollywood. Who knows what might happen?"

"I wish you success," said Max. "I think you should know, Jocasta may be looking for a new business manager. You'll need to set things right with her—stay or go. Financially, I mean. I don't think it's automatic she'll want you to stay otherwise."

Max didn't spell out his warning but it was clear Simon took his meaning exactly. So long as Simon took steps to correct his wrongdoing, Max didn't see it as his job to report his misconduct to the U.S. authorities. He was sure Cotton would feel the same.

"Thank you," Simon said quietly.

Jocasta came into the hall just then, trailing olive-green scarves. They all said their good-byes, and Max watched the departure of the newly wealthy Jocasta, escorted by her newly attentive younger husband. He wondered if money could buy you love. Not the real thing, certainly not, but how many people settled happily for a facsimile?

❋ ❋ ❋

There was something Max wanted to do before he left. The money left to St. Edwold's was literally an answer to a prayer, although he'd never have chosen the way it was delivered. God answered prayers in his own way, he'd noticed, without the need for direction from humans.

Max took the path leading to the small stone chapel in the bailey.

He pulled open the wooden door and stepped inside. The old chapel—hadn't Randolph said it was eleventh century?—had been spared much of the mindlessly destructive Cromwellian fervor wreaked on churches the width and breadth of England. Presumably because of its isolation, it appeared untouched by the thugs of that particular chapter of history. Even so, iron bars had been installed on the windows to protect the elegant tracery and glass from vandals.

Six small pews bore the arms of the Footrustles. Max sat in one of them, beneath the barrel roof, and let the hush descend, his handsome face dappled now by a mosaic of light from the stained-glass windows with their pointed arches.

He stared at the altar table and closed his eyes, letting the old sanctity of the place wash over him. He was wearier than he could remember being for some time. It was the weariness of mental exhaustion, the worst kind.

Randolph and Cilla had been faced with a choice, and had taken the decision to kill for gain. They had had many a chance to back out of their scheme, but there seemed to be some sort of "rush" at work—the challenge and thrill of taking a shortcut to riches. Of eliminating threat, in the form of Lamorna. It was risk-taking of a sort Max didn't entirely understand.

But he didn't doubt he'd done the right thing, as he had doubted so often during his MI5 days. Here, at least, it had been clear-cut who the villains were, and that they couldn't be allowed to thrive. He may have saved lives in the future, for would Randolph ever have been content with his share?

Who could say.

It was time to go home.

EPILOGUE

DECEMBER 21

Sing we joyous, all together,
Fa la la, la la la, la la la.
Heedless of the wind and weather,
Fa la la la la, la la la la.

"Fuck whoever invented goddamn tinsel," said Suzanna Winship.

Her brother looked up from where he was knee-and-elbow deep in a snarl of electric wire.

"There's the Christmas spirit that's been so lacking around here," said Bruce. "And fuck whoever first thought of fairy lights, for that matter."

She grinned at him, frustration momentarily forgotten. "Except they might enjoy it. Seriously, if we can put a man on the moon . . ." She gave the tinsel another fierce shake, which, as in some devilish invention from the ancient Orient, knotted it tighter than ever.

Bruce finished the thought for her: "Why can't someone invent Christmas stuff that doesn't tangle itself in the box—the very box where one laid it all out neatly, in perfect working order, one year before?"

"We'll be late for the party," she said. Strands of tinsel like shiny dreadlocks had attached themselves to her hair, making her look like a particularly festive member of a reggae band. "I've still got to do my hair and nails. And the cleaners left a great crease in my dress that will have to be ironed out. And I'm really not sure about those shoes, and—"

Bruce, who knew perfectly well what the fuss was about, or rather, whom the fuss was about, interrupted her. "Don't worry. The villagers like you just the way you are."

"The Monkslippers? Like I care. Bumpkins all."

Bruce said in his most innocent voice, "But I thought you liked the vicar."

"Oh. Well, there's Max, of course," she said dreamily. Her voice sank a few octaves, caressing the name. "And Elka's all right underneath it all. And I suppose Lily . . ." Her voice trailed off. "It's actually Maxen, did you know? I was thinking I'll have to ask him to stop by the house for some . . . libation during the holidays. Libation of a secular nature, of course."

Bruce thought, as he often did, that Suzanna was chasing a hopeless cause in trying to gain Max's attention. It's not that Max didn't notice her—no man could not notice Suzanna—but that he wasn't interested. The vicar found her entirely alarming, in fact. Bruce, having a good idea whom he might be interested in, wisely kept his opinions to himself.

"Thank God he's back," said Suzanna. "Things will return to normal, now Father Max is back."

A freshening wind was attempting to shred snow-laden clouds as they lumbered slowly across the sky. It was not the best day for a party, although the forecasters were calling for a clear night to view the lunar eclipse.

Max had returned home from some business at the church, where he was greeted by the sounds of Luther and Thea in mid-negotiation, and by Mrs. Hooser saying, "You talk to them."

Max, who wondered what on earth could be the matter now, didn't have long to wonder. The cat Luther now had taken to crouching atop an end table, waiting for Thea to walk by, then leaping onto her back. Thea had learned to dislodge him by the simple expedient of walking under the same table and scraping the cat off like a barnacle. This process had been repeated several times, complete with screeching and other sounds of retaliatory scuffle, until Max finally had banished Luther to the kitchen so that he, Max, could work on his sermon. The silence was short-lived—Luther had discovered that a small box of cereal batted at just the right velocity across the kitchen floor made an enthralling rattling noise, like mice scrabbling behind a wall.

Once the lethal Christmas decorations were removed from St. Edwold's the cat would go back to his job of mousing, thought Max. Without delay.

On his desk he found a message from Mrs. Hooser. As it was inked onto one edge of a circular advertising a jewelry sale, which was typical of Mrs. Hooser's usual method of grabbing whatever was to hand to write on, it was a miracle each time she managed to communicate. This missive said, simply, "CALL YOUR BISHOP."

My bishop. Mrs. Hooser's distancing of herself from the situation was interesting. Amazing what meaning three little words could hold if one only knew the key. Clearly the bishop—Max's bishop, not hers (*don't blame me, I never liked the man*)—was agitated about something. It was not the first time. No doubt it was a routine matter, perhaps some notes or advice about the Christmas service. It could wait.

Max had made a bit of a splash since coming to Nether Monkslip. For the most part the bishop managed to put aside any personal jealousies, seeing Max's star qualities as all to the good of the Church. And the money seeming to fall from heaven for the church repairs should have placated the man, thought Max. But human nature, even in bishops, didn't seem to work that way.

The success of the Women's Institute calendar, juxtaposed with the death of the leader of the WI, had brought a certain amount of fame verging on notoriety to the community, but it had been short-lived. The members of the media had moved on to the next great noisy thing. The village's two pubs, the Hidden Fox and the Horseshoe, had enjoyed a brief spurt in revenue from the reporters, who spent so much time in each pub everyone wondered how they found time to pound out their daily quotas of wild speculation and innuendo couched in yappy prose.

A more burgeoning problem in terms of potential notoriety lay inside St. Edwold's Church, in the form of the "miraculous" image that kept reappearing on one of its walls, despite numerous paintings-over. Max considered it little short of a miracle itself that the press had managed to avoid getting a whiff of this phenomenon, although on further reflection he realized few of them probably spent much time in churches.

The bells of St. Edwold's rang out jubilantly, as if announcing a royal birth or a peace treaty, and they reminded him of everything he had to do before setting off to Awena's party. The sun already had begun its headlong plunge from the sky.

His sermon for the Christmas Day services was nearly done but needed some finishing touches. To jump-start his thinking, he pulled out one of the massive tomes left behind by his predecessor Walter Bokeler. He began scanning the pages describing the executions of the martyrs during the Reformation, then quickly replaced the book on the shelf. There was nothing like reading about a fiery death to put one's own problems in perspective, but Max felt overall a modern congregation might enjoy a more uplifting topic.

He also had promised a short article for the *e-Pistles*, the parish e-mail newsletter. He had intended to write something about the issues currently coming up before the God Squad (the Parochial Church Council), but given the inflammatory rhetoric at the last meeting, Max felt overall a safer topic might be better. Something about the coming Christmas holidays and the church decorations. Something dull. Something safe. Reminded by the decorations of the cat's provenance, Max glanced grimly over at Luther, who sat by the hearth cleaning every individual one of his claws in a process that seemed to fill many hours on the cat's activity log—whichever hours were not taken up with terrorizing Thea or covering Max's favorite chair with fur. Luther, noticing Max's regard, gazed back and—Max could have sworn it—smiled.

Some hours later, his dark hair freshly washed and combed, his gray eyes gleaming in anticipation, Max reached for the door knocker of Awena's house, where the party was already in full swing. A holly wreath decorated with pinecones encircled the brass knocker, which represented the face of a Celtic goddess. He was arriving late, as he had stopped on the way to watch the very beginnings of the solar eclipse. And Luther, who seemed to suffer from separation anxiety in addition to his other flaws, had flung himself at Max's knees as Max opened the door to leave. Max had leaned down and scooped the cat in his arms, gently stroking its fur, and saying, "Luther, I'll be back soon. I promise you. But it's time for you to go back to work. Take your mind off all this nonsense."

Awena's house, always a happy mix of eclectic folk art and clean, modern design, shone with extra polish and—yes, it could even be said, with anticipation of gaily dressed guests and holiday talk and laughter. She had hired Maria Delacruz and the Ladies of Perpetual Help to come and scrub the house top to bottom.

The Yuletide party décor was also a mix of the multidenominational, the folkloric, and the traditional. There was both an enormous Christmas tree and a Yule log. And of course mistletoe was everywhere along with evergreen, holly, and ivy curling round the rafters. The house smelled of fir and pine mixed with the intoxicating aromas of baking pies and biscuits. The oak Yule log roared in its merry, cheering way in the hearth.

The tree was decorated with handblown glass balls in swirled colors of blue and green, subtly different in style from the usual Christmas ornaments. They seemed to contain some sort of powder. Suzanna saw Max admiring them and came over to stand at his elbow.

"They're called witchballs," she said, her lips curved in a catlike smile. Light from the tree ornaments danced off her lip gloss.

I am not going to ask, he thought. *I am* not *going to ask.*

"Witchballs," she said loudly, in a clear and melodious voice, "are a tradition dating from the eighteenth century. They generally are hung in windows and often contain a spice like nutmeg—for good luck, you know. They protect against evil by bewitching the beholder with their beauty." She threw a significant, dart-like glance in Awena's direction. It was a glance that could have repelled invading hordes of riders led by Genghis Khan. Awena caught the look and returned a radiant smile. She loved having her house full of guests. She also was sweetly unaware that Suzanna had launched an undeclared war over possession of Max's mind, soul, and—most of all—body.

"Quite *pagan*, I believe," Suzanna added, significantly. Coming from anyone else—someone not wearing, for example, a bright red, low-cut, skintight dress, daringly parted at strategic intervals to display her considerable advantages to full advantage, this statement might not have seemed so irredeemably ludicrous. But Suzanna looked like nothing so much as a walking invitation to a wanton romp under moonlit pagan skies.

Max, busy returning Awena's happy smile, aimed beneficently and generally at her assembled guests, didn't hear. Then Awena caught Max's eye and it was like a bolt of lightning had blazed across the room.

"Of course mistletoe," Suzanna was saying, "is the most pagan thing imaginable. Human sacrifice was *such* a large part of their culture, the pagans. They were probably buried with a stake of holly through the heart, as per Scrooge. It— Oh, hello, Awena. I was just telling Father Max here that mistletoe was used by the Druids." She batted her eyes at Max. "It also was a fertility drug."

"Used for animals. Yes. Lucky it didn't carry them off." Awena wore one of her high-waisted, Greco-Roman style dresses. Tonight it was simple green velvet with a deep V neckline, and it was gathered high on her rib cage to emphasize her bust. She'd bundled her hair at the nape into a hairnet made of finely woven gold wires. Max thought she looked like a marble statue come to life.

"How are you, Max?" she asked him.

"That's why people kiss beneath the mistletoe," Suzanna carried on with pointed emphasis. Awena, she noticed, was looking a little dreamy. Of course, Awena always looked dreamy, like she was just coming out of a hypnotic trance.

"What is interesting," Awena was saying to her, "is that mistletoe plants are male or female."

"Yes," said Suzanna brightly. "*Such* a good idea, I feel. Why should animals have all the fun? I suppose eventually the plants learn to tell each other apart."

"Only the females produce berries. Anyway, let me show you to the food and drinks, Max. I was going to have a bowl of flaming brandy so we could play snapdragon, but overall it seemed wisest to skip some traditions. Snatching raisins out of a burning bowl is probably just asking for trouble." She took Max by the arm to show him into the dining room where the food was on display. "Otherwise, we've got a feast in there. I'm afraid we're running out of eggnog already."

"What would Oprah do?" Suzanna said sarcastically, watching Max being expertly plucked from her clutches. The hell of it was, Awena wasn't even trying. Max looked like he'd follow her across a burning bridge, eggnog or no eggnog.

The villagers, gathered by the tables of food, balancing glasses and plates, turned nearly as one to greet him. It was now he began to get an inkling of what the bishop might want to talk with him about.

"You know you've made the news, don't you?" asked Frank Cuthbert.

"Saw your photo on the telly," several other parishioners told him excitedly. "I didn't know you were involved in that murder over at the castle. Do tell us all about it. Is it true Lord Footrustle was done in with a machete?"

It seemed Fleet Street and BBC television and a hundred or so blogs had picked up the news of his involvement in solving the murder, following up the lead provided by the *Bugle* photographer who had hidden outside the castle gates on Max's arrival.

Suzanna, who had trailed sulkily in behind Max and Awena, watched as they stood side by side, Max parrying and deflecting the questions as best he could, Awena all sparkling eyes and sculpted profile. Her weird ability to project an aura was on full display. She was aglow.

Suzanna, with her radar finely tuned to the station for all matters sexual, watched with growing alarm the emergent Awena/ Max attraction.

This couldn't be. No! But it was. Suzanna was never wrong about these things. A blind woman could see the way he watched Awena move, the way he hung on her every word. The vicar had it bad.

Elka Garth, the Cavalier's miracle worker with butter and flour, had provided the mini-desserts, the sweet biscuits and tarts, the miniscule fairy cakes—each a tiny gem designed to make the consumer believe something so small and light couldn't really count as part of one's daily calorie allotment. Mme. Lucie Cuthbert, proprietress of *La Maison Bleue*, provided excellent yet inexpensive wine and cheese and chocolate; the fairy lights, the colorful decorations, and the scented candles were from Awena's own shop. Elka also had specially made the ginger biscuits called Cornish fairings, which were favorites of Awena's. These were decorated with marzipan peace symbols. And Miss Agnes Pitchford had brought her famous fruitcake, steeped in enough alcohol to destroy half the village.

On the savory side, there were all manner of veggie spreads and hummus dips, and flatbread and oatcakes coated with creamy goat cheese, and minute quiches fresh from the oven. Miniature pasties came from a new shop in town run by young Dorsie Luke called Not Your Mother's Pasties—these were low-fat, whole-wheat vegetarian pasties filled with lentils, potatoes, onions, carrots, and mushrooms. Dorsie had been doing a brisk business in overnight shipping to London celebrities, and had been thinking of expanding to expats in Europe.

"But if I have to freeze them, it won't be the same," Dorsie was now heard to say in response to the compliments she was receiving. "And I just won't compromise the quality." Nether Monkslip was like that in creating perfectionist craftspeople.

There were in addition tiny sandwiches on whole-grain bread, cut into the shapes of the moon and stars and Christmas ornaments. They were filled with goat cheese and herbs and spiced vegetable spreads. No one noticed every offering was vegetarian, and before the night was out every morsel would disappear.

Of course there was a wassail bowl, and endless bottles of wine and ale.

And soon the dancing started.

Awena had rolled up the carpet in the living room for dancing. Good old rock and roll, Max was happy to hear, as "Start Me Up" blared out of the speakers. Happily, they were to be spared "Jingle Bell Rock."

The villagers began to dance, some shuffling shyly onto the dance floor, some enthusiastically bounding in from the sidelines, already at full tilt. Frank in particular exhibited a unique style of dancing, arms and legs flailing, like someone trying to saddle a recalcitrant pony, while Elka Garth looked like she might be trying to start up a power chainsaw. Still, she had a surprisingly natural rhythm, her low center of gravity allowing a graceful swing of her wide hips. Max, who loved to dance, was easily persuaded to join in on the Temptations' "Ain't Too Proud to Beg." At the opening sound of the drum followed by insistent, dinner-bell clanging, Max grabbed the woman nearest him, which happened to be Awena, and twirled her onto the dance floor. She danced with her usual stately grace, as tuned in to the music as she always seemed to be to life. Likely, she made no distinctions. The chords and rhythms of the song seemed to pulse through her, at one with her breathing.

Now Frank, who for the past few minutes had resembled a man boxing a kangaroo, was taking a breather by the drinks table. He turned to Adam, who ran The Onlie Begetter—the local bookshop—and said, "I could never leave this village. The food alone is a siren call."

"Awena knows how to entertain," Adam agreed. "Even the Major is letting his hair down."

They watched the elfin Lily Iverson, owner of a local yarn and textile-design business, dancing with the man they called simply "the Major," who always looked as if the concept of the chain of command continued to rule his life. He danced, finally persuaded by Lily after a few glasses of rum punch, but no matter the tune he appeared to be marching in box step, an interesting interpretation, as Frank pointed out, of the more traditional choreography for "Jumpin' Jack Flash."

"Marching to his own distant drummer," agreed Adam.

"He's positively Kiplingesque," nodded Frank. "The age of the Raj is not forgotten while the Major lives. Still, he and Lily make a handsome couple, don't you think?"

"He's smitten, no question. She's got so many suitors now, though, since the calendar came out."

The Women's Institute charity calendar had created quite a stir in Nether Monkslip and beyond. The calendar photos were in no way indecent, and were in all ways charming. An expert photographer in the village, donating his time and services ("A difficult job, but someone has to do it," he'd remarked repeatedly) had captured each of the women in poses brave and utterly captivating. Max, having purchased a copy from Adam's bookshop, had flipped through the pages until his eye caught on Awena's April photo. The photographer had gone for mystery over humor here, despite the "witchy" props: A cauldron, a broom, the cat Luther in a starring role as familiar. He had captured well the bottomless depths of Awena's searching gaze. It was Awena in a new light, so to speak, and it was bewitching—there was no other word for it. Max, putting the calendar in a desk drawer—it somehow did not amount to suitable décor for a vicarage study—reflected nonetheless that he could hardly wait for April to arrive.

Lily, posed with her spinning wheel, was the surprise hit. She was still fielding offers from the fan mail that had rained in— much of it containing marriage proposals.

The ecstatic villagers continued to pour onto the dance floor until they spilled out of the available space and into the dining room.

It seemed everyone was there, including Mr. Vijay and Prema, who had closed up the restaurant early; Felicity Gates, the potter; church handyman Maurice; and even Mr. Stackpole, the church's dour sexton. He looked like he might actually be enjoying himself: At least he allowed one foot to tap in time to the music, and something not quite a smile had settled on his lips. Tara Raine, a rope of red hair tied up on her head with mistletoe and ivy, pranced by Frank and Adam. She wore a white T-shirt with abstract splashes of vivid colors like a Georgia O'Keeffe painting. She was dancing alone, as were most of the villagers, with a graceful sway that suggested the suppleness promised by the yoga classes she taught. Right now she was a dancing advertisement for the intestine exercise class she had recently started offering, and as a result of which had endured some good-natured joking.

"Fine," she had said. "Laugh all you want. It cures what ails you. Given the diet some of you lot eat, you should all sign up."

Mme. Lucie Cuthbert had aimed a well-directed glance at her husband Frank's girth.

"We're in," said Mme. Cuthbert.

Meanwhile, Suzanna had slithered onto the dance floor. Her dancing bore a close resemblance to a striptease act.

Awena continued with her graceful swimming motion, the porcelain-white hands sluicing the air.

And now the rapturous dancing was coming to an end. The opening chords of a slower tune began.

Awena stood, her feet planted. She swayed to the music, invaded by it, a part of it.

Elka Garth had come to rest by Adam Birch.

"What fun," she said. "I've made a decision tonight—I'm selling the espresso machine to the Coffee Pot people. Let *them* deal with the specialty coffees. I'll stick to what I do best. Life is too short."

"A good plan. I remain loyal to the regular coffee of the Cavalier. It's been the fuel keeping me going for so many years."

Elka asked, not without some trepidation, "How is the book coming along?"

Adam had been creating a masterwork little known to those outside the writing circle that met in The Onlie Begetter, on which circle he'd forced numerous revised copies over the years. He had a batch of query letters out to London agents and publishers, and was puzzled not to have heard anything from them in weeks.

"Of course, they do say that nothing happens during the holiday season. Positively *nothing*. The New York publishing scene is even worse."

"Why? Are they all drunk?" asked Elka innocently.

"No! No, no. Of course not. At least, I don't think so . . . Well, not *all* of them, surely. It's just that, well, nothing . . . gets done." He finished weakly, for in truth this possible explanation for the stoney silence greeting his fifteen-page query letter had not occurred to him, and he was quite willing to seize upon this or any alternate scenario: The grander lanes and avenues of London and New York filled to capacity with tipsy, riotous literary workers, on a monthlong binge. Yes, it was just possible. Adam turned to Elka with a renewed spark of hope in his eyes.

"Dance?" he asked brightly.

"I thought you'd never ask."

Max and Awena were again dancing, Max shielding her with his body to prevent anyone's getting the idea they could cut in. At one moment, Awena threw up her bare left arm, index and middle finger extended, reminding him of a gesture in a Renaissance painting, a Leonardo, perhaps. In the soft light, Max's eye caught the movement like a camera lens, a flash of memory forever preserved. Now her white fingers, as she raised both hands above her head in the candlelight, were splayed like starfish in a dark sea.

Max, a good dancer, unself-conscious and energetic, was also of the moment. The healing ankle, tightly bandaged, and over which he'd received a stern lecture on moderation from Dr. Bruce Winship, barely gave him a twinge. He was too caught up in the dancing to care. His physicality was as much a part of his nature as a panther's.

Awena was thinking what an extraordinarily nice and damnably attractive man Max was, and that perhaps she and Max could manage to spend more time together with no one in the village noticing.

Suzanna, watching from the sidelines, muttered to Mme. Cuthbert, "Just my luck. The biggest hottie in the village—in any village for hundreds of miles round—and he happens to be the vicar." Lucie Cuthbert, who thought that was probably part of the attraction for Suzanna, turned to respond, only to find Suzanna had churned her way onto the dance floor and was determinedly cutting into Max's dance with Awena. Awena was scooped up by Frank before Max could protest.

Miss Pitchford, retired schoolmistress, stood watching from the sidelines, twittering away, although her twitterings usually could not be limited to 140 characters. Max had seen her from the dance floor, waved at her, and privately wondered why she was there. Surely it was all a lot of excitement for a woman who claimed to be in bed with a good book by eight o'clock every night. He was forgetting for the moment her essential Mission Control duties, coordinating various gossip command posts for the village, a role of which he would have been reminded had he noted the keen attention she had been paying to his dance with Awena.

At one point Miss Pitchford had approached him and placed

a lace-mittened hand on his arm, her face avid with interest. "The rot had begun to set into those Footrustles years ago," she said. "And I could have told you who the killer was."

To think, all he'd had to do was ask! He thanked her for her rare acumen and insight, however belated, and pushed on through the throng of thrashing limbs, newly energized by the Stones— this time it was "Honky Tonk Women." One of his favorite songs to dance to. Where was Awena?

Miss Pitchford had closely watched him go. She wore a newly washed and starched lace fichu in honor of the occasion and she gave it a little fluff against her neck. Noah Caraway of Noah's Ark Antiques had pitched up next to her. She had commandeered a place nearest the wassail bowl to be sure of interacting with as many villagers as possible.

She nodded her head significantly in the direction of Max and Awena as they danced. "I saw them, heads together, at the Indian restaurant. I nearly went in to say hello, but far be it from me to play the gooseberry."

Even now she was considering the best method to disseminate this news. The village post office was the easiest and surest method but she didn't want the proprietress stealing her thunder— the woman was *such* a gossip. It was all most vexing.

Miss Pitchford's gooseberry remark was relayed by Noah to a mystified Tara, who later said to Suzanna, "What on earth can she have meant by that?"

"You've never heard the expression? It means if two people want to be alone—and I do mean alone—you're the gooseberry if you try to join them. The third wheel. De trop."

"You really think . . . ?"

"Oh, puh-leeze," said Suzanna. She sighed. There was no use. "When a man is running on hormones, there's no stopping him."

"Do you think? Oh. That would be nice. They'd make such a good couple."

"Let's start calling them Maxena, shall we? Just look at Awena. Larking about like some sort of pagan fertility goddess." Suzanna was drinking brandy and tipped back a good slug of it now. Her eyes, chocolate brown, matched the brandy spark for spark in the firelight. *Of all the far-off villages in all the flipping world, Max Tudor had to walk into mine.*

Max by this point had once again reclaimed Awena's hand. The Seekers were now singing in the background, "I'll Never Find Another You," the female singer effortlessly lilting through the lyrics to the classic folk song. Since it was a difficult song to dance to, he and Awena by unspoken agreement moved over toward the drinks table.

"Randolph actually thought he could fool everyone into thinking Leticia outlived her brother?" she asked him.

"He did fool everyone. Everyone watching the crime shows thinks that time of death can be pinpointed to the minute. We're not there yet, forensically speaking."

"So your seeing 'her' in the train . . ."

"Seeing her imposter, yes. It simply confirmed the rough timeline the coroner had worked out, helping pinpoint the time of her death to an earlier time. The scheme would only have failed to work if they'd tried to pretend she'd been alive, say, half a day longer than she actually was. But let's talk about something else. That's too gloomy a subject for tonight. I must say that after my time spent among the upper crust, it's a welcome relief to reenter real life in Nether Monkslip," said Max.

Awena leaned in and said something, smiling up at him. He laughed uproariously. The villagers, all of whom were catching on by now, nearly toppled one another over, using pointed elbows to dig into their neighbor's ribs. They stood silently, watching the sparks fly. Someone had to say it, and predictably, it was Frank. "No smoke without fire," he said.

A glance passed between Suzanna and Elka, only Elka's tinged with gentle amusement. Suzanna's look, quite different, was easy to read by all but the least perceptive in the room.

Elka was thinking Max was a man to marry: He was every woman's dream of the civilized, thoughtful, and dead-sexy male.

Her thoughts held no shred of jealousy. Instead she looked at Adam and smiled. It was a conspiratorial smile—the sort of smile indulged in by two well-meaning people preparing to play Cupid.

❅ ❅ ❅

It was growing late. With a palpable reluctance the villagers, sated and tipsy, began to depart on their short walks home. It was a weekday night and most of them had jobs to go to, shops to open, or, in the case of Miss Pitchford, news to analyze.

As she was leaving Suzanna could be heard to say, "Looking on the bright side, at least now I can stop wearing this tummy-tamer." Suzanna hated to admit defeat, but with a longing look backward, she saw Max helping Awena collect plates for washing in the kitchen.

It was this kind of thing Max did that set the women of Nether Monkslip scrolling with renewed determination through their Rolodexes, looking for a friend or relative who wouldn't mind being the wife of a devilishly handsome, sexy yet thoughtful vicar in an obscure but picturesque village not far from the English Channel. Many were called but none were chosen. It was *so* frustrating.

"It's *so* frustrating," said Suzanna to her brother. Bruce Winship, without prompting, knew exactly what she was talking about. So did several of the women. One said, "If I thought I'd be in with a chance, I'd dump my old misery-guts of a husband and go after Father Max myself."

"I wonder if he has a brother or cousin," said Suzanna. "Does anybody know?"

Half an hour later Awena and Max stood beneath the thick open beams of the kitchen, doing the dishes. The room with its giant butcher-block table, its fireplace, and a state-of-the-art cooker was homey but modern enough for a celebrity chef.

Max's elbows were deep in soapy water as he looked out the kitchen window. The eclipse of the moon, which had changed it from white to bloodred, had long since passed. Awena glided back and forth between the dining room and the kitchen, bringing in plates and glasses to wash.

They were alone, Awena having refused all other offers of help. Max asked Awena, on her next trip out to the dining room, to play that folk song again, that old Seekers song, which had somehow become stuck in his head. The guitar shortly began the lead-in, and the woman—he seemed to remember her name was Judith Durham—began to sing:

> *There's a new world somewhere, they call the Promised Land.*

Max began humming to the music. Awena brought out a towel and started drying the crystal by hand.

"What?" he said, off her look.

"I asked you, 'Do you think we'll ever recover? From the unpleasantness at the Village Hall? And now, at Chedrow?"

"If no more murders take place. Yes. Tonight's party was the start of healing. Thank you for all the trouble you took; you made them happy."

They worked awhile in silence, letting their eyes rest occasionally on the peaceful scene outside. Snow was melting in patches on Awena's kitchen garden.

He was helping dry the dishes now, using an old terry cloth dish towel that had a pattern of moon and stars on it. They were talking of nothing in particular, as he later recalled. The village, the upcoming play in the Village Hall, the book club. The unseasonable weather and what it meant for their planet. Judith was telling her lover, *"It's a long, long journey, so stay by my side,"* when suddenly Awena looked straight up at him and smiled.

Max did something extraordinary, and for years to come he would wonder what made him do it. He took both her hands, which now happened to be submerged in hot, soapy water, in his. He dried those hands, slowly and carefully, with the dish towel he'd been using.

His gray eyes looked into hers, which seemed to him as clear and everlasting as the sea, and he said, "I don't think I can live without you. I don't see why I'd be expected to." And he held his breath as he waited for her answer.

"You had me at 'let me help you with those dishes,'" Awena said. "But you know there are those who won't understand."

"I'm tempted to say it's no one's business but our own," said Max. "But of course that's not true."

"Your bishop will . . . I think the poor man may explode. I just think it's best we keep it quiet."

"There's no reason anyone should know," said Max. "Not until we're ready to tell them."